M

BY

FRANK N. ANDERSON

Life doesn't offer much besides survival and misery these days...this has put excitement into my bones I have not felt for years.

Tony Teach

This is a work of fiction. Similarities to real people, places, or events are entirely coincidental.

MOMENTUM'S FORCE

First edition. April 10, 2020.

ISBN: 978-1777031602

Written by Frank N. Anderson.

CHAPTER 1

"No Insurance"

July 1979

Several weeks had passed since Larnie had made his surreptitious visit to the jewelry store, when the phone rang.

"Hello?"

"Hi Larnie. It's Graeme. How are you and the family?"

"Fine Graeme. What's the occasion you callin me? I'm...well kinda busy right now."

"Oh sorry to bother you. I can keep it short if you like or call back later, perhaps?"

Larnie was unnerved hearing Graeme's voice on the other end of the line. Graeme's friendly phone manner had a feel of superficial courtesy, and Larnie couldn't recall another time he had phoned his house. His call could only be about the visit he made to Graeme's store. He expected the assistant he dealt with in the store would call him in due course - not the storeowner. He wanted to squeeze any knowledge of his visit to the store into a tiny ball that no one could see.

After they exchanged a few niceties about their families, Graeme transitioned quickly to the reason for his intrusion.

"Larnie, I'm calling about that necklace you brought into my store for an appraisal."

His suspicions about the reason for the call were confirmed – it was about the jewelry. The mention of it caused a stressful restriction in his throat that his secret may get out, freezing his voice momentarily, as his mind raced.

How could he ensure that Graeme didn't tell anyone in the family? He looked into the mirror as if it would provide answers and saw the sweat beads on his forehead, and the grimace of anxiety on his face. Then, the hope of what the necklace may fetch in real dollars rose into his being. He unhitched his breath and kept his voice just above a whisper.

"Oh yeah, that. Of course. I forgot all about it actually. I was just cleanin out some old family jewelry and thought I should get an idea of its worth before I put it away again. I didn't mean to bother you with it. I was thinking your assistant would...um, you know...handle it. It's no big deal."

"No problem. It's just that I had to do some research on this. Quite a bit actually. But now I have an idea of its value and you should come to my store to retrieve it."

"Oh, okay. Would sometime next week work?"

"Not really, my old friend. I don't want it in my store much longer and would appreciate it if you could come tomorrow, or even today, to retrieve it."

"It's really that urgent? I can come next week."

"No, I don't want to wait that long."

"Well, can you tell me what its appraised value is and what about the other jewelry I brought in?"

"Larnie, I can hardly hear you, could you repeat that?"

"kumph."

"Huh?"

"Sorry, just clearly my throat. I was just asking how much you think it's worth and if you looked at the other jewelry I brought in?"

"You brought in other jewelry? I don't know anything about that. I only know about this necklace. What else did you bring in?"

"Oh. Um. Well, I need to check the box...um; maybe I just thought I brought in other..."

"The box?"

"My jewelry box."

"Well, my good friend, I can hardly hear you again. I need you to come in and pick up your necklace."

"Yes. Yes, of course. Well can you tell me the appraised value of the necklace then?"

"rrshquek. cukcuk."

The yowl of the front door opening filled his ears. Mae was home. He could feel the heat of her presence in the house.

"Graeme, I have to go."

"Okay, just come to my store today or tomorrow please. I don't have the right insurance to keep your necklace here."

"click"

Someone had hung up on the party line.

"Okay I will. Bye."

After the abrupt end to the call, Graeme looked down at the necklace in his hand. Its blue diamond flashed at him. If only it belonged to him and not Larnie Teach. When he discovered its value and connection to a lost treasure from the Second World War, his thoughts quickly shifted to the risks of keeping it in the store and the insurance he would need. He took a moment to admire its details again, including the gold pieces circling the diamond. It appeared to draw all the light in the room to its brilliance.

Graeme exhaled the air from his cheeks and carefully laid the necklace into a velvet case. He didn't like the idea of keeping it in the store any longer, but he moved to place it back into the wall safe, when he stopped suddenly. The domino teetering in his mind as to what do next, had fallen.

He looked over at his car keys resting on the counter and reached for them. Larnie's house was a mere ten minutes away. He moved to the door, when the phone rang. Suddenly annoyed at its intrusion, he picked up the receiver with aggression and his voice carried his agitation.

"Hello?!"

"Oh...hi."

"Larnie?"

"Oh, it is *you* Graeme. What time are you open til?"

CHAPTER 2

"No moss"

Two months prior, May 1979

Silence filled the car on the drive home. Before they left, Larnie was purposely chatty about great plays and the enjoyment of watching the game. Eddie gave little verbal response and then went silent. Now the only words spoken came when Larnie's thoughts spilled out in an audible voice. He had listened to his dad have conversations with himself. He would laugh and make fun of it. Now he had picked up the same practice.

Larnie felt neglected when it came to encouragement and support from his alcoholic father and promised himself to be the father to his kids that he wished he had. But the offerings of life - the busyness, the bills, the maintenance of things, the daily routines and his own anxiety – had slowly built walls that he now struggled to deconstruct. His anxiety was a wall that crippled him at times with fear that he may fail to provide for his family - an irony given what he would later discover. His own self-doubt – like a nagging old injury – shadowed him and threatened to sabotage all that was good in his life. He combated it with a predictable life that deliberately shunned change. He still clung to the hope that he made a difference. Hope that he made a positive impact on them, even when he saw little evidence of it. He provided for his family and took them on a vacation to Hathaway Lake ever year. Yet scraping at his heart was a desire for something more.

As his foot pressed harder on the gas, while accelerating out of a corner, he had an ill feeling that hope was not enough. The routine of life had become busy and mundane. Even when he broke the routine and worked harder, it felt he was in cement. No progress. No movements forward. He pressed the break in the turn as he thought of the abrupt turn in his thinking that occurred in his life recently. Yet, he still felt his failure to inspire his children for a different life. Now his biggest fear was in his rear view mirror - as he looked to see Eddie asleep. Had he become his father, as a parent?

His daughter Bev had graduated from high school a year ago and Eddie had one year remaining. He wonders what Bev's plans are for the future, as she doesn't share such things with him nor does she seek him out for advice. For that, she goes to her mom or "Ma" as the kids call Mae.

Eddie's team had just lost the championship game and the winning goal was on his stick in the slot, but he froze. The opportunity was lost and so was the game. Eddie was despondent and quiet afterwards. Larnie tried to encourage him as he talked about the great season of hockey that just concluded. When Eddie responded with, "I suck" and "I don't want to play hockey again", Larnie could hear his own father's voice when he offered the same platitudes: "that's ridiculous, no you don't" and "you can't let one game or one play make you quit something."

A riot of thoughts started their drum in his head. He wanted to do and say the right things to inspire Eddie, yet also push him to be the best he can and to learn his own strengths and weaknesses. How can he do that when the boy can be so uncommunicative, keeping his thoughts and feelings to himself. Then when he does express them, it is often negative, self-depreciating. What is going on in that 16-year-old head of his? Had Eddie inherited his own "self-doubt" gene? The thought looms like a threatening cloud over his life. Larnie shook his head, as if to scatter the negativity from his mind. He lectured his own self-doubt, determined to press on. He has life lessons and he has to find a way to pass on to his children.

Six months had passed since his own outlook on life undertook a transformation. It all started with a conversation at work that set off the unspooling of the tight and constricted view from which he saw his life.

When he was sixteen, he quit school to take a job as a truck driver for Thetis. Many at the time quit school early for good paying jobs. His thoughts of the future was a basic plan followed by many. Get a good paying job, get married, buy a house, have kids and retire with a pension. The job with Thetis appeared to promise all of that. He was a teenager when he started, the same week the company was celebrating its 50th anniversary. He walked out of the high school before he completed grade ten and onto a path with a well-defined and certain future. He didn't think much about the future after that, except for plans to go fishing on the weekends and holidays, or to go to the odd hockey game. He had a general idea from the company pension at what age he would be able to retire. He'd be able to fish more often then. He didn't particularly enjoy his job. He didn't think he was suppose to. Did anyone enjoy their job? Work was work. He was one of the more experienced drivers and he was efficient and good at it. That seemed enough.

His desires were simple. He wanted a better life for his kids than he had and figured he was doing that. "A good father who provides for his family and takes them on camping vacations", was the description given at his 40th birthday party a few years ago. He went to church, found joy in sports and they always did something as a family during the holidays. Thanksgiving, Christmas and New Years were all family time.

He failed to realize that the slow boil approach to his work had permeated most other aspects of his life, which included his relationship with his kids. "Failed." He used that word as he described it to his wife Mae when he told her he felt awoken to a new way of thinking. She disputed his analysis and pointed out the annual camping trips to Hathaway as an example. Perhaps he was a bit too harsh on himself, but he was resolute to make a change.

It was a conversation with Stan Thetis that broke an ostensible spell on his life and changed it's trajectory.

The company owner, Stan "Stringbean" Thetis, treated everyone well. He was fond of saying he didn't need a union in his shop because he treats employees as family. Larnie would often see Stringbean, with his long legs and swimmers build, walking around the warehouse. He'd say hi to the staff and ask them about their families and their vacation plans. Larnie enjoyed the seven weeks' of vacation every year and the benefits largely paid for Bev's braces. His work was stable and he completed most tasks by rote. His life had become a long string of routines.

If there was a particularly long day at work that broke that routine, he'd pause and wonder what his life could have been. What if he had been encouraged to explore his skills and passions? Could he have been a hockey player or a teacher? Would he inspire and change lives if he had a different path? As his mind went down such holes, bitterness would build within his soul. It blackened many of his days. Anxiety. Bitterness. His dad would often be the primary target of the blame. "You're mind never shuts off" his mom would say, before adding, "You think too much." Well, he says in his head, as if conversing with his now deceased mom, this thing called life is much more complicated than I was led to believe. Then he would shut out those voices for a period as he steered back into the groove of his routines.

The day that changed was like most other days. Larnie was at the warehouse loading furniture and appliances into his truck when he saw Stan Thetis walk towards him with a purpose in his step.

His big hand engulfed Larnie's as he shook it.

"Hi Larnie."

"Hello Mr. Thetis."

"Please, call me Stan or Stringbean for that matter. Many people call me by my nickname."

"How are you today?"

"Good sir."

"You have a family at home, right?

"Yes a son and a daughter."

"Of course. It's Bev and Edward?"

"Yes. That's right."

Stringbean smiled at the confirmation.

"Glad to know my memory still works. Your wife, Mae, how's she doing?"

Stringbean's ability to connect with people was legendary. He had captured Larnie's attention and devotion to the company.

"She's good. Thanks for asking."

"That's nice. I hope they all make it to the company picnic this year. We have some great entertainers that I think everyone will enjoy. Larnie, I know our company has gotten quite large, but I consider all of our employees - and you are one of our best - as part of our family."

Stringbean put his finger to Larnie's chest to emphasize his point.

"We simply couldn't make it as a company without devoted people like you, delivering the products to our stores."

"Thank you Mr. Thetis."

"I believe you've been with us since you were a teenager and I hear good things about you and the exemplary customer service you provide. So Larnie, I came to talk to you today as we have an opening coming up in our warehouse and I was wondering if you might be interested?

"Thank you Mr. Thetis. Can I ask what the job is?"

"Of course. It's an entry-level position in the warehouse. As a warehouseman, you would report to a warehouse foreman. Yours would be Keith Oakguard. You'd enjoy working with Keith, all the staff do. It would be more money than you're making now, ninety cents an hour more. You'd have the same benefits you have now. I am not sure what days you'd work."

"Thank you Mr. Thetis. I'm very interested. What should I do next?"

"Well, first let me say, you are a real asset to our company, Larnie. I hope you take this opportunity. We could use the skills and knowledge you have gained with us as a truck driver in the warehouse. You'd be a valuable asset there. I'll have Keith contact you and answer any other questions you may have. Now, before you get back to work, I'm going to shake your hand and you're going to call me something other than Mr. Thetis, okay?"

"Thank you, Stan."

Larnie shook Stan Thetis' hand and with that ended one of the most important conversations in his life.

Prior to that conversation, he didn't think of life beyond being a truck driver for Thetis. That conversation meant more than just a change in jobs. It altered his thought process. It lifted a blind spot in his life and opened up a new view. Someone believed in him enough to consider him "an asset" to the company.

The new job brought an excitement he could feel in his steps when he'd walk into the warehouse. Almost immediately, Larnie felt this is something he could do well. Made for. Why had no one told him about this before or steered him in this direction? Knowing the products and customers from his truck driving, he knew what to order and instinctively what would be the most popular. When a new product came in, like a new sofa or appliance, he would examine it carefully for its workmanship. He developed an intuition of what would sell and to what kind of customers. He realized he was learning as much about himself as he was the products. He took great pride in his work. Gone were the days where he'd "watch the clock" waiting for the day to go quicker. When the whistle would go at 5:00

PM to end the workday, it seemed too soon. His capacity to retain information had increased along with his energy.

With the confidence boost came a view towards life that was less restrictive and reactive. A view that changed the script he was following and made life more like an adventure. His old approach to work and life seemed foreign to him now. Like he'd lived in someone else's body.

Soon after he started in the warehouse, Thetis' expanded its department stores to include groceries. He embraced it with a renewed enthusiasm. Some of his co-workers were skeptical and said the company shouldn't expand in an area they are not known for. He bristled at such comments. The company was strong and well known in the community. Other department stores hadn't moved into groceries because they lacked the forward thinking and innovation of Thetis, he'd say. His thoughts, approach, and how he articulated things had changed. He saw those co-workers as people who only ever wanted the status quo and that just mirrored the "old Larnie" he had shed.

One night after passionate lovemaking, Mae pushed on her elbows and looked down on him lying on the bed.

"What's going on?"

"What do yeah mean?"

"What do I mean? You suddenly have all this energy. You'd often forget things I tell you and lately you remember."

She lifted the sheet covering his chest.

"You have a superman costume under there?"

Their laughter filled the room as she laid her head on his chest.

"All kidding aside, this job has taught me a life lesson I should have figured out years ago. It's about momentum. All of life has momentum to it. You can use it to your advantage, if you choose. You can passively allow whatever wave of momentum catches you to take hold, and hope for the best. A better life awaits for when you choose to watch for the waves that will fuel your passions, and give you energy and purpose. Watch for those waves to come in and catch them."

"This new job has taught that?"

"Mae, this job has brought a new momentum to my life. I know people at work who seem miserable. Misery has its own momentum. I was caught in that myself. The best way to combat misery's grip is to create a positive momentum that continues to grow. The momentum I have now, gives me more energy. More purpose."

As he was replaying that moment with Mae in his head, he glanced in the rear-view mirror to see Eddie's eyes still closed.

How could he impart these things to his son and daughter, so they'd challenge themselves and experience all that they may be capable of? In work, in play, in relationships, in love. In life. Larnie wanted to stop and write down some of the thoughts bouncing in his head as he repeated them in his mind. Life does not mean always taking the easiest path or the road most likely to be devoid of conflict or adversary. A life that is passive, just taking what comes our way isn't the way a person should live. "No moss" he'd tell them.

"Dad?"

"Yes, Eddie."

"Did you say something about moss?"

"Just thinking out loud."

"Oh, okay."

"Hey, let me explain. You should approach life with a no moss attitude."

"Okay. I will."

"You haven't even heard me explain it yet. Moss grows on trees over long periods of time. Trees that don't move and are in one place a long time."

"There are trees that move?"

"Oh funny, smarty pants. Actually, that's a witty response, Eddie. Good for you. But what I'm saying is that your life should have no moss. It's okay to take breaks and relax at times and even necessary, but you should always be learning things in life and not staying still like the trees."

"Okay."

"Make sense to you?"

"Sure. Don't be like a tree."

"Well...yeah. Don't just stay in one place in life like a tree."

The conversation hatched an idea in his head. They always took the family vacation to his favourite fishing spot. Had it become moss? What if he could take them to a place that none of them had been before for a vacation? A place where they could have a shared experience and bring more depth to his relationship with the kids. But how would he pay for such a thing? They pulled in the driveway, as Larnie made a mental list of things he might sell.

CHAPTER 3

The Diary

Practicing with his dad made his shot worse. That was Eddie's assessment. His dad kept telling him "you are getting better with every shot, Eddie." Eddie's stick had just made connection with the puck, after missing it entirely three times in row. He was certain he'd miss the next one and his dad would be silent. Silent. Until he finally caught the puck on his stick again.

"Dad, hockey season's over. Do I have to do this now?"

Eddie tried to summon the courage to say that he was old enough to make his own decisions and he was done with hockey, but his dad responded before he could push the words out.

"Practice can't end just because the season's over, Eddie. Breaks are important, but a break for many months without any practice is not good. That can dull your skills and make you rusty."

Eddie stared at his dad with a look of confusion before he surrendered his head to gravity's force and looked at the small nicks on the edges of the puck.

"Okay, Eddie, look up, please. I get it. Maybe you do need a break from hockey right now."

With that and another lecture from his dad, Eddie took a break from hockey. It would be the last discussion they'd have about his hockey. Eddie hoped that would also be the case with his classmates as he headed out the door to walk to school the next day.

It was the last day of the school year. The bell rang, signally the beginning of classes, as he shut his locker. He wasn't often late, but he'd join several others in their tardiness as the asperity of the teacher's response belied her powerless to do anything on the last day. His true hope was to survive the day without any mention of *the* game. Chuck was the one he dreaded the most hearing about "the shot", or rather non-shot, which cost them the championship. His best friend Gabe would tell him that Chuck needs to grow up, but Eddie still felt the sting of his taunts, even if not as sharply as when they first started a few years earlier. He told himself, "I don't need to be told I am the loser who blew the game, I already know that."

Keith was the first one Eddie saw as he walked through the doors. Quiet Keith would not likely say much, even if he was their best defenceman.

"Hey Eddie. My dad said it was a good game last night, even though we lost."

"Yeah."

Eddie wondered if Keith's dad said it would have been great had he not fanned on that shot.

During recess, Eddie stayed in the classroom and chatted with the teacher, Ms. Steale. He asked her what other sports or arts might be offered the next year. She mentioned soccer, theatre, and that he should talk to the gym teacher. He asked about her plans for the summer as he looked around to see who else remained in the classroom. He was content to have eaten up almost half the recess – a time delay before he would face others who may comment on "the game".

He saw him as soon as he left the classroom.

"Hey Teach!"

Whenever Chuck referred to Eddie by his last name, his abs would tighten in preparation for the blow to come. Chuck delivered.

"Teach, you should change your last name to Miss."

He walked in the opposite direction, but Chuck followed.

"Hey Teach, remember our bet? You owe me two dollars. You said your team would win and well, we all know what happened. Don't run away from me."

Eddie wouldn't have bet Chuck anything except that he goaded him, saying that his team was made of losers. Eddie was with his small group of friends when Chuck added that he bet him two dollars on the game. "Sure," was all Eddie said. He regretted it immediately. Now Chuck was going to hunt him down for it.

Chuck grabbed Eddie by the elbow and catapulted himself in front of his shaken prey. "Well Teach, where is it? My two bucks. Give it to me now." Eddie started to reach into his pockets when Ms. Steale came into view and Chuck quickly cowered.

"Chuck, what are doing? Leave him alone. You can't just grab someone like that. Now get on your way."

As Chuck left without a word, he gave Eddie one final stare and Eddie's eyes hit the floor.

"You okay Eddie?"

"I'm fine."

"Don't let him bully you like that, okay?"

"Okay."

Eddie knew that she meant well, but Ms. Steale would just make things more miserable for the next encounter he'd have with Chuck.

"Hey, don't pay any attention to him; he's a jerk that acts like a child and everyone knows it."

"Thanks Gabe." The pain in Eddie's gut subsided at the voice of his best friend. He wished he had Gabe's confidence and smarts.

"Hey, a bunch of us are getting together for lunch, to celebrate the end of the school year. We're meeting outside the yellow building. See you then."

Gabe lifted Eddie's spirts, as did the prospects of lunch with trusted friends.

Classes ended early, giving them an extended lunch break. There were fourteen of them crowded into the small café, a block from the school. Eddie looked at the faces of his friends, many that he had known most of his life. He wondered if they would still be friends when they finished high school in a year's time. Raj, Pete and Gabe had played soccer, hockey and video games with him on many weekends. Nadia, Yvonne and Mina were some of the girls they would hang out with and invite to movies and roller skating events. Cheryl and Carl would join them too as would Angelo, Kathy, Connie, Keith and Ty. They were all there. They had grown up together and had many shared experiences. Some dated each other, off and on. Eddie's shyness would pulse at any such opportunity. Gabe had once told him that Mina was interested in him and then Gabe set up a double date. It was Gabe, Connie, Mina and him. He sat beside Mina in a darkened theatre, and they went for a walk alone afterwards. But his timidity won out and nothing happened.

The café was bursting with teenage voices in a crescendo of laughter, dramatic gestures and whispers of gossip. The chatter included what teachers they liked, the ones they didn't and the ones they made fun of. A few others came in and joined them. Mickey, Lisa and Cindy were not part of their regular clique of friends, but jumped into the conversations. They talked about their plans for the summer. Many had plans to be out of their small town of Ranvon for most of the summer. Others, like Eddie, were hoping to get a summer job.

"So Dr. Big Bones, what are you up to this summer?"

Connie's question to Gabe signaled to everyone that they were no longer a couple and it was the catalyst for everyone sharing their nicknames. For several it was just a shortened version of the full name. Mickey was Mick, Connie Con, Kathy Kath. Cindy kept the momentum of the discussion going as she shared her nickname at home as Loq.

"Ty, why do some call you Oz?"

"When we first moved here, someone called me Aussie because of my accent and it got shorten to Oz and then just stuck. But what the hell does Lock stand for?"

"It's L-O-Q, not like something you lock. My mom says I'm loquacious and my sister shortened that to Loq."

There was a pause in the group until Mina finally asked the question.

"What does loquacious mean?"

"Talkative."

Cindy flashed a wide smile at Eddie's quick response.

"Wow, Dr. Big Bones is suppose to be the brainiac here, how'd you know that word Eddie?"

"My mom has used it sarcastically with my dad."

Nadia offered "Nad" as the only nickname she has had. Eddie joined the secret smiles of the guys around the table who knew many called her "Bo" after the movie "10" with Bo Derek. While she didn't have the cornrows in her hair, she had the defined cheekbones, the blue eyes, the Cleopatra nose and hourglass figure that had many of the boys fantasizing about when they saw the movie.

The bills came and many shared hugs, as the realization that the end of the school year had arrived and the summer was upon them. Eddie stood to the side and took it in. He forgot about the hockey game the previous night and no one mentioned it. Nadia gave him a quick hug as did Mina before they left, wishing him a good summer.

The last one to say goodbye was Cindy. His pulse raced as she waited for him and then she reached out and embraced him in a hug that lingered long enough for her to whisper in his ear.

“If we're both staying around town this summer, we should hang out.”

Then as she turned to walk away, she added: “You can call me if you like. My number's in the phone book under Jeffery Wade, my dad’s name.”

Eddie felt awkward around girls and just didn’t know what to say. He'd never had a girl directly express interest in him before, and he wondered if that's what just happened?

Did she really expect him to call her? Cindy was a beautiful brunette with long wavy hair and deep brown eyes that lit up when she smiled. Eyes that looked directly at him as she stood just an inch shorter than his small five foot six inch frame. Now he wished he'd said something in response. Maybe they could have made plans right then.

Eddie looked up Cindy's phone number that night, but didn't call her. A few days later, he saw her at the local 7-11. Her smile captivated him as she waved, but then she left holding hands with a guy he didn't recognize.

His summer quickly became full of lazy days and evenings of hanging out with friends and playing video games. He got a job working evenings at a local burger joint and most days he would sleep in, sometimes close to noon – a routine interrupted by the occasional lecture from his mom.

Lying in bed in the morning, he would let his mind wander, and invent ways to suppress the boredom. Video games and hanging out at the 7-11 had lost its appeal. His birthday just over a week away and he wondered what his parents had bought for him. His mom always planned some surprise. Lying in bed, wiping sleep from his eyes, he began to devise ways to find out what the surprise might be.

"Eddie. Eddie! You still in bed?"

"Yeah, why?"

"It's almost 11:30 in the morning. You shouldn't sleep the day away."

Klock! Klock! Klock! Klock! He could hear her heels hitting the hardwood steps as her voice grew nearer.

"I'll get up, Ma."

"Now, Eddie."

"Soooon, Ma. In a few minutes."

"Are you being sarcastic with me? You sleep away half the day when you sleep in this late. Your father may think it's okay, but I think it's making you lethargic."

"Lethargic?"

"Tired, lazy, stupid and low on energy."

His mom liked to introduce new words to their conversations. She said it would help him grow his vocabulary and help him "in school and in life". If Eddie didn't ask her the meaning of a new word, she would volunteer it. Eddie's dad didn't know all the words she'd use either. Sometimes his dad would roll his eyes when she used a word he didn't know. Occasionally he would hear his dad mumble, "It doesn't mean that."

His mom failed to complete high school but "self-educated" herself. Eddie knew his mom set the tempo in the house. She set the regulations of the family, enforced them and would reprimand his dad when he didn't comply.

"So, what are your plans today, Eddie?"

"I dunno, thought I'd hang out with some friends."

"Friends, eh? Like maybe Cindy?"

His mom's voice hit a high exciting pitch when she said "Cindy". Eddie's heart leaped.

"Cindy?"

"Someone named Cindy phoned for you while you were sleeping in."

His chest tightened and things in the room started to move as he felt a burn in his stomach.

"Eddie?"

"Okay."

"Okay, what? Is she a friend of yours?"

"She's just a girl from school, Ma."

"Oh, so you don't want the phone number she left?"

"Sure, okay."

"Oh, don't be so bashful Eddie. That means shy. Of course, you want her number. If she comes over to visit, she is not allowed, *under – any - circumstances*, to be in your room alone with you and door closed. Okay?"

"Okay."

"Eddie, has your father talked to you about sex?"

Eddie wished his mom wouldn't be so blunt and direct.

"Huh?"

"Okay, I'll take that as a no. I'll talk to your father and make sure he does. Right now, I'm going out to meet with some of my friends. I'll be back in a couple of hours. If you decide to go to a friend's house, leave a note as to where so I can call and confirm, okay?"

"Okay."

"And it has to be someone I know and have met. I am sure Cindy is nice, but I don't want you going to her house until I've met her. Okay?"

"Ma, it's okay."

"Say yes that you agree, Eddie."

Eddie visualized his mom in a striped shirt outside his door. Like the referee at one of his hockey games, where his disagreements outweighed the agreements, though he'd comply with them regardless.

"Yes, Ma."

With that, she opened his door, blew him a kiss and put a piece of paper on top of his dresser. As she closed the door, she shouted over her shoulder,

"Okay Eddie, there's milk in the fridge so you can get yourself some cereal or make yourself a sandwich. I love you."

"Thanks Ma, love you too."

A few minutes later, the "click" of the front door meant that she'd left the house. He was now alone. It was something he had looked forward to the moment she said she was going out. Now his plans were disrupted by thoughts of Cindy as he reached for the dresser to get her number. He held it in his hand and tried to memorize it. Shaking his head, as if clearing the thoughts from his mind, he stuffed the paper in his jeans' pocket as he reached down to put them on.

Having friends over was his plan, but he didn't want to be distracted from his first mission of the day: to spy on his parents' bedroom. He had been thinking about it for the last week or so. It's not something he had done before. He's not even sure what all would be in their bedroom, but the determination to find his birthday surprise had heightened his curiosity and added audacity to his courage.

He also saw his dad sneaking something into their bedroom the other day. He seemed very secretive about it and acted like some intruder as he checked the surroundings several times before he came into the house with whatever it was. He knows his dad didn't see him. Whatever his dad had in the bag though wasn't very big. While Eddie had his hopes on a new bike for his birthday, the size of the box his dad brought in put a dent in that.

Eddie's presence in his parents' bedroom only happened when he was invited. Even that was a rare occurrence. It was an unwritten rule of the house that their bedroom was "off limits" – a statement made with the always closed door. Just down the hall from his room, Eddie didn't have to go far and he kept the lights on the hallway off, adding further stealth to his mission. Feeling he was entering some mysterious place, he opened the door to their room.

The outside light protruding through the curtains illuminated the room enough for what he had planned. The large bed, flanked by oak bedside tables, was neatly made. To the left of the door was the six-drawer dresser his dad had told him was his grandma's. Eddie was familiar with these things, having seen them the few times he had been in the room and so when his eyes caught the closet door ajar, it was like a window to a new discovery.

One of his mom's dresses hung from the top of the closet door. As Eddie pulled on the door, his mom's dress fell on top on him, and he jumped to wiggle free from it. He could smell her perfume on the dress, like the smell of the peeled mandarin oranges they enjoyed at Christmas. It now laid in a clump on the floor when he reached down and, with his thumb and index finger, he picked it up and plopped it on the bed.

As soon as Eddie entered the closet, he realized just how much more room there was in theirs, than his. Big enough for his bed, he thought. As his eyes adjusted to the lesser light, he scanned its contents and he saw the box his dad had snuck into their bedroom - sitting on the top shelf and well out of reach.

He looked around, to see if there was anything he could stand on. After sliding clothes and their hangers to the side, he spotted a bigger box in the corner that looked like it could serve as a stool. He reached down to pull the box out and something fell off the top of it, plunging it deeper into the corner. Not wanting to disturb anything, he reached behind to retrieve what fell and felt a glossy magazine. He stepped back into the light in the room as he clutched it in his hand.

The black and white picture of a striking blond with her big smile and arm in the air under the heading "PLAYBOY. Entertainment For Men" would never fall out of his memory. He flipped it open to the centerfold and there was the same blond beauty naked. Eddie's emotions were a mixture of excitement and confusion. He never imagined his dad with a Playboy Magazine.

He turned back to the cover and couldn't find a date anywhere but the price was listed as "50 cents". Must be old, he thought.

He left the magazine on the bed, returned to the closet and pulled out the box. Thick black felt covered the lid of the box: "DAD'S STUFF".

Eddie opened the box to find several more Playboy magazines. "Is this dad's secret stash?" he wondered. Dates on the magazines were from the 1950s and 60s.

Under the magazines, were war medals, a thimble, old black and white postcards of ships and buildings that looked like castles, and some old spoons with hard glass like handles that were scattered in with the postcards. While he carefully removed each item from the box and placed it on the floor beside him, Eddie could see old black and white pictures in the box and on top of them a small black notebook. He picked it up as his curiosity heightened. He carefully untied the cloth string around the notebook, pausing as his mind took a picture - everything had to be as he found them when he'd leave.

He opened the first page and the words in the centre were framed by a yellow tinge of age at the corners. The words in black handwriting:

DIARY AND THOUGHTS OF
TONY TEACH V 2

Eddie froze. Grandpa kept a diary? When his grandpa died a year ago, there wasn't much talk about his life. His dad would lament that Grandpa led a hard life. The service they had was mostly at the grave where they buried him next to his grandma. It was a confusing time. People seemed sad but also happy at times. He didn't know much about his grandpa and when his dad did talk about him, it came with sadness or anger.

The sound of the door "click", followed by the squeal of its hinges was like a loud church bell.

Eddie stuffed the postcards, the medals, the spoons and the thimble back into the box. He laid the Playboy magazines on top, except for the one he found on top of the box. He then frantically stuffed the box back into the corner of the closet and placed the one Playboy on top of the box. He ruffled the clothes on hangers to make sure they were concealing any disturbance. As he exited the closet and reached to close its door, he looked down and saw the diary on the floor. Frantically he picked it up and stuffed it into his pants. He closed the closet door as quietly as he could and walked gingerly to the door.

As soon as he exited the bedroom, he could hear her voice as she ascended the stairs.

"Eddie. Eddie. You home? I hope you are not still in bed."

As the light in the hallway hit his eyes, Eddie moved to meet her on the stairs. Holding his heavy breathing, he quickened his pace down the hall as he heard the "Klock! Klock! Klock! picking up volume. At the top of the stairs, their eyes met.

"Oh there you are", as she reached out and gave Eddie a hug, he maneuvered to ensure the diary in his pants was concealed.

Escaping the hug, the smell of oranges filled his nostrils. She looked intently into his eyes.

"Hey, you in a hurry to go somewhere?"

"No Ma, just hungry and going to get something to eat."

"Okay, where've you been?"

"Um, here?"

"Of course you're here, I can see that! Eddie, your pupils look dilated. What have you been up too?"

"Oh, um, just in my room, getting up."

Her hand moved the hair now falling over his eyes as her stare pierced his gaze.

"What've you been up to Eddie?"

"Nothin. Just getting up."

"Oh, alright. You going to the kitchen now?"

"Yes Ma."

"Well next time, flick the light on in your room first and let your eyes adjust. I thought you were getting together with your friends?"

"Yeah, I'm going to call them. I thought you were going to be out for a while?"

"I forgot something in our bedroom that I need. I'm going out again."

She hugged him again.

The smell of oranges awakened his senses.

"Ma, can you make me something to eat?"

"Like what honey? You can get something for yourself. There's lunch meat in the fridge or you could have cereal."

"I would like some eggs but can't make them like you do."

"Oh dear, you can make your own eggs."

Eddie's eyes dropped in a desperate plea for sympathy, as he lobbied for her to follow him to the kitchen.

"Oh, okay. Look, I'll make you some eggs. But first, I need to get something from the bedroom. I'll meet you in the kitchen in a minute."

With that, he could only hope that somehow she wouldn't notice anything in her bedroom as he made his way downstairs. Once in the kitchen, he poured some cheerios, filled the top of the bowl with milk and stuffed the diary inside the cheerios box.

"Honey, you don't want any eggs?"

Eddie didn't even see her come into the kitchen when he looked up to her serious and quizzical look.

"I was hungry and didn't want to wait."

"Okay. You sure?"

"Yeah, I'm fine Ma. I'm going to phone some of my friends when I'm done eating."

"Okay then, I'm heading back out and will be back in a couple of hours."

With that, his mom reached over and grabbed the cheerios box.

"I was going have more of those."

"It's okay, Eddie. I'm just getting a handful. "

Then giving into his sad eyes, she handed the box back to him and instead scooped up the loose pulverized oats that had fallen from Eddie's bowl. She hugged him again and turned to leave.

His shoulders slumped to their relaxed posture as she turned her back to him.

Then, with her mouth full of the donut shaped oats, she turned back,

"Say, did your dad come home while I was gone?"

"No."

"Oh, you sure he didn't while you were in bed? Maybe he slipped into our bedroom and you didn't notice."

"No I don't think so."

"Okay then. I'll have to ask him. See you later honey."

CHAPTER 4

The Jewelry Box

Though it was a Saturday morning and Larnie's day off, he was up early. He enjoyed the early mornings when he would sit in quiet contemplation and gather his thoughts for the day before the sound of Mae's alarm would break the silence in the house. This particular morning had his thoughts focussed on one thing.

Larnie had a secret that he hid from the family, including Mae. The secret filled him with excitement but also brought, its friend, stress in tow. The brewing coffee fumes awoke his senses as he stood in the kitchen. The voice inside him released his thoughts in a whisper over the aroma that filled him. "Why can't this excitement separate itself from the stress I feel as well? As one starts to crowd out the other, the other comes back with renewed force."

Planning a family vacation, especially one they have never had before, was exciting, exhilarating and gave a jolt to his energy as he thought about it. Even as the thoughts of it infused him with happiness, the added stress and worry would start to pull on the rope of that happiness and unspool it. The costs, the planning involved, all the potential things that could go wrong and the choices to make gnawed away at his initial enthusiasm. It's just a vacation, he'd tell himself. Mae would say they couldn't afford it. If he let the secret out and it didn't happen, it would add to the pile of failures that gave fuel to the anxious person he worked hard to keep at bay.

He was determined to make it a vacation beyond anything they had even dreamed of. The pictures from the vacations camping in tents and visiting relatives could sing anthems of the stories they tell. But he wanted this one to be the mountain peak of experience. His thoughts would drift to places that are exotic and exciting. Somewhere they only had knowledge of from magazines or television.

Somewhere mysterious and mystical. Magical even. Perhaps Disneyland in California? It opened when he was a teenager; the same age that Eddie was now. He had never been to California, let alone Disneyland. Or maybe they could all fly to New York. Watching New Year's Eve, in New York on TV, was an annual tradition. Was Africa too crazy of an idea, he wondered. The wildlife from Africa filled picture frames at their house and the family all loved the movie Born Free and are excited to see the sequel: Living Free. He had tried to gather more information at the library, but it lacked the details he wanted. The maps and travel books helped, but details about costs were not easy to ascertain. He was sure the travel agent in town could help, but one of their neighbours works there.

His mind churned with different ways to save money for the trip. Mae didn't know about the recently created vacation allowance the company had set up for long-term employees like himself. He kept the money in a shoebox in their closet. The savings was meager and building at too slow of a pace. Bev was already out of high school and Eddie had a year to go; the trip had to happen in the next year. He needed more funds if they were to go to one of the places that filled his dreams. He had stashed more money away by taking some of the grocery money without notice; but it was going to take too long to save and he needed more money.

One cost saving option Larnie thought of was to drive to the destination. But driving eliminated places like New York and certainly Africa or even Mexico seemed just too far away. If he were reading the maps he saw at the library right, it would take at least three days of driving to get to Mexico. Would their station wagon even make it that far? What if he borrowed his cousin Chad's van?

California and Disneyland were drivable, at least that is what he heard from two ladies he overheard talking about it at the grocery store several months ago. Their conversation at the checkout played in his head with such clarity it is as if it was happening in front of him again.

She looked to be in her 30s as she stood behind him at the checkout. Her strawberry blond hair done up in a bun that rested at the top and kept her curls from springing as evidenced from the fuzz all around it. Signs of previous acne in her cheeks gave an edge and ruggedness to her natural beauty. Her green eyes caught his glance and she smiled at him before returning to the book she was reading while waiting in line. He caught a glimpse of the book that was splashed with "Disneyland" in multiple colours across the cover.

The interruption in her reading was abrupt and loud from another, that had joined the line.

"Eva, how are you? Is that Disneyland you're reading about?"

"Hey Maryla. Of course it is, Earl and I are planning our trip and I want to be as prepared as possible."

"Do you have the flights booked already?"

"Well we've decided against flying. It's very expensive. So we're going to drive and are leaving in just two weeks."

"Drive? Really? Isn't that going to take days to get there and what about the cost of gas?"

"We researched it and we can actually drive there in just over a day if we switch off the driving between the two of us. We're also thinking of taking our time and seeing some of the countryside. It certainly is drivable and the cost of gas would not be nearly as bad as the cost of flights. The last estimate we got from the travel agent on flights was $1300 for all of us."

"$1300! Really? It'd take us years to save that much."

"It's too much. I don't know how anyone affords to fly."

"Well there is no way that we afford a trip like that with the kids. I am happy for you though and can't wait to hear all about it afterwards."

"It wouldn't be possible for us either if we didn't have the inheritance money we received from Earl's mom."

"Sir. Sir. Will you need a hand out with your groceries?" Larnie hadn't noticed half his groceries had already been bagged. He always watched the prices they typed into the register as he had caught errors before. The voices of the two ladies behind him faded into the background as he turned his mind to the cash register.

Thinking about that conversation again, excited him about the possibility of Disneyland and perhaps the drive there. He also read that one could take the train. Those costs of flying may be out of his reach. He certainly didn't have inheritance money to rely on. The thought leached into an idea. They do have some old jewelry that has been handed down from previous generations. Perhaps it has some value? They hardly held any sentimental value to him, that was for sure. No one would miss that jewelry if it were to disappear.

He sat at the kitchen table the next morning and the steam from his cup fogged his glasses as he thought of the excitement Disneyland would bring to the family, when the sound of the alarm clock jumped the air in his throat. It was time to put his plan in action.

As he could hear Mae coming down the stairs, his mind was on the jewelry box and the potential treasures it held, and he immediately turned to head up to their bedroom, so that he would pass her on the steps. In his haste, he didn't regulate his pace before Mae saw him.

"What are you rushing to Larnie? Something important? You're starting to sweat."

"Oh, um yeah...just...just forgot something in our room. Nothing important, just have things to do today and don't want to waste time."

"Like what things? I thought today you were going to get together with cousin Chad?"

"Yes....yes, just have to go to the store first. The hardware store. I think there is a leak in the sink upstairs. I...um...need to check the size of the pipes there and see where it is coming from."

"Really? Shouldn't you turn the water off first?"

He leaned over and kissed her. "If I turn the water off, I won't be able to tell if there is a leak or not. Nothing for you to be worried about."

"You looked frazzled. Is something up?"

"Of course not dear, you think too much about everything." He slowed his pace to a casual gait as he climbed the stairs, hoping Mae didn't suspect anything besides what he told her.

Then he tripped and fell up the stairs. He would always fall up the stairs, never down.

"You okay?"

"I'm fine. Just lost my footing."

"Hope you don't think we have to fix the stairs now too."

He thought he heard her mumble "clumsy fool", as her voice trailed off into the distance. He swallowed his words, as his nostrils flared.

When he made it to the bedroom his pace quickened and he immediately opened the closet door and glanced at the top shelf where the shoe box was resting. It contained the money and information he gathered on potential vacation destinations. While he was certain Mae wouldn't ventured to the top shelf of the closet, he felt comfort knowing that the box was undisturbed where he left.

With that knowledge, he smiled to himself and reached for the drawer where the jewelry box was. It was buried under old lingerie of Mae's. He paused and remarked to himself that she didn't wear any of these things anymore. He removed the lingerie from the drawer, revealing the old wooden jewelry box and took it to the bed.

Deciding to take the whole box with him, he quickly scoured the room for something to put it into when he saw a discarded brown bag in the garbage by the bed. "Perfect" his heart sang.

He put the lingerie back into the drawer and then paused at the red lacy one. He took it out and placed it on her side of the bed. Maybe she will notice he is no stumbling fool now, he thought. He tucked the brown bag and its contents under his arm and headed down the stairs, with a spring in his steps.

Mae was in the kitchen when he arrived downstairs and he shouted a goodbye and I love you as he opened the door.

~~~~~~

As soon as he entered the store, his old friend Graeme saw him.

"Well, how're you Larnie and what brings you into my fine store?"

This is the reason he often thought of escaping this small town, for a larger city. While it can be comforting, even romantic, to be in a town where so many people know your name, sometimes you just want to do your business without all eyes on you. Sometimes he just wants to close the curtains, without others gossiping about what is going on behind them.

His heart raced as he took air into his lungs, lecturing to himself that he had no reason to be on edge. He was doing nothing wrong. He smiled at Graeme and was about to respond when Graeme was distracted by another customer. A woman with a smile and a sparkle in her eyes, as she lent her beauty to the scene, had waved him over.

Larnie looked around and saw a clerk and made eye contact with her as she moved in his direction.

"May I help you sir?"

Meagan, was typed on her name tag. Perfect. Someone he doesn't know. Someone who won't ask too many questions. He then launched into the speech he had rehearsed on the way over.
~~~~~~

"Yes, thank you. I have some old jewelry from my family history. It isn't much really and I was just cleaning out some old things and came across it. I was actually going to just store it somewhere. But then I told myself, "Larnie, maybe you should see if any of it has any value". So I thought I'd bring it here to see if you can help."

"For sure, let's see what you have."

He saw out of the corner of his eye that Graeme had disappeared into the back, and he smiled at the clerk.

"Thank you Meagan. If it's just a bunch of junk, just let me know. I wasn't sure if it was worth the bother, but this jewelry store was on the way to my cousin's anyway."

He reached into the brown bag and pulled out the wooden box.

"That certainly looks old. I think my dad has an old wooden box like that."

"That's nice. Meagan, I'm in a bit of a hurry, so could we make this fairly quick?"

"Sure, let's see what you have and I'll label each piece separately."

"That's fine, thanks."

"Sir, there are..., well, quite a few pieces in here. Are you sure you want me to catalogue everything and have them evaluated? Perhaps you have some that are a priority?"

"Oh, sorry. Of course." Larnie reached for the box and his eyes widened when Meagan pulled it back.

"Oh, sorry sir, I haven't looked at them all, I just wonder if there are some pieces you don't need appraised?"

Looking in the box, he gasped as panic hit him in the chest. Taking a deep breath, he apologized for any confusion and then took out a watch that looked gold and a set of earrings that he hoped would be diamonds, and another set that looked like pears. He also took out two necklaces, one that had some real weight to it he thought, though its finish was quite dull, it had a fairly large gem in the middle. Then after a long pause, he put them back in the box and pushed it back in Meagan's direction.

"How about if you take what appears to have value and leave the things in the box that you think will have little to no value? I...I just don't know. There's a necklace in there that seems heavier than the other and so I'd like to get that one appraised for sure."

"For sure...can you give me your name, so I can put them on the labels?"

Larnie's eyes were focused on the back of the store as he watched to see any signs of Graeme.

"Sir?"

"Yes?"

"Your name for the labels."

"Sorry, Larnie Teach." As soon as he finished his response, he was wishing he had used a synonym, but all that came to mind in that brief second was Dick Tracey.

Meagan gave a simple nod and wrote down his name. She then took each piece and placed them in separate plastic bags, each of which she labelled with Larnie's name.

Meagan performed her work in silence as Larnie watched, with his eyes darting back and forth towards the back of the store. His nerves were on high alert.

"Sorry, Meagan, I don't mean to be rude, but I'm in a bit of rush, perhaps you could just take out what you think is of value and I'll leave you to label them?"

"Of course Mr. Teach." With that, Meagan removed all the pieces Larnie had at first taken out of the box plus a few others. She clipped the box shut with the remaining jewelry inside and handed it back to Larnie.

"Oh, okay. Thanks." With that, Larnie put the box back in the brown paper bag.

"Will you call me once the jewelry has been appraised?"

"Of course Mr. Teach. I don't know how long that will be. Is there a time you need this by?"

"Not really. Whatever is reasonable. Thanks Meagan. I appreciate this. I need to go now."

CHAPTER 5
The Girlfriend

Journal #3. June 12, 1936. I can't tell Elizabeth that I lost the job at the fish plant today. Six months ago when I was laid off from the cement plant, the fear in her eyes frightened me and then she stopped eating for several days "so the kids could eat". I felt like a failure. The riots in the street added to the fear that dominates our lives. They finally hired me at the fish plant when I slept outside the gate for two days and when I got home to tell Liz, the blanket of fear lost its grip. I can't tell her the news that I've now been laid off from the fish plant. I have to find work. But where? Some guys camp out at the mine, hoping for work. I will try that tomorrow.

"Hey, why'd you close it?"

"Cindy, it's my grandfathers and it's kind of depressing."

"I think it's interesting, I want to hear more."

"After I've read more of it myself."

"Oh, I see. So your new girlfriend isn't important enough read it with you?"

"Girlfriend?"

"You don't want me to be your girlfriend?"

"Um, well, of course."

Eddie wasn't sure what to make of Cindy. When he phoned her, she insisted on coming over immediately and when she arrived, she hugged him and kissed him on the cheek. The excitement coloured his face immediately. She wanted to see his room right away and he was certain she detected his nervousness with that suggestion. He thought his grandfather's journal would provide a good distraction and keep them in the living room. He enjoyed her closeness as they read it together but then realized he had no idea what his grandfather hadn't written, and what family secrets it may reveal.

Cindy, in an assertive gesture, brushed her wavy hair to the side.

"Okay, what do ya want to do then? You obviously don't want me to see your room."

"Um, it's not that, it's just that my mom..."

"Oh, mommy's boy, eh? She wouldn't want you to have a girl in your bedroom? Silly, I just want to see it. We haven't even kissed yet."

"It's pretty boring. My room, I mean."

"Well show it to me, so I can decide."

"Ok. It's upstairs."

As Eddie got up, Cindy grabbed his hand and she led the way up the stairs. As they approached his room, while still holding her hand, Eddie sprung himself in front of her, as he reached for the door. He would be the one to open the door.

"Well, you room certainly looks more tidy than mine. You always make your bed, or does your mom?"

"No, I do."

"So, what is with the Farrah Fawcett picture?"

"I dunno. I like the show."

"You probably like her in a swim suit."

Eddie felt the blood rushing to his face as he looked away for something else to draw the attention to.

"I have a comic collection. Would you like to see?"

"Shuure."

Eddie pulled the binder with his comics from the closet, while his grandpa's journal remained in the tight grip of his fingers.

"So, what're the trophies on your shelves for?"

"Hockey trophies. Get at least one at the end of every year."

"What about this one with the bow and arrow?" Cindy had pulled the trophy down as she examined it.

"Oh, that one. I entered a competition at summer camp once and won that."

"Summer camp?"

"Yeah, every summer I go to camp for a week. It's called Camp Sunshine. My sister's there now."

Cindy put the trophy back and pointed to another one.

"What about that trophy with the pen? It's for first place for something?"

"It was for a short story I wrote a couple of years ago."

"Really, can I read it?"

"Maybe later, Cindy. How about we take my comics downstairs to look at them?"

"Oh, can't have your girlfriend in your bedroom, eh?" Cindy leaned into Eddie, whose arms were full, and kissed him on the lips gently.

"It's okay, Eddie. We can go. I won't kiss and tell." Cindy giggled.

Eddie wanted to feel her lips on his again, but the conflict he felt of her being in his room was too great. He didn't want them caught there if his mom suddenly came back, and so he started to head towards the door.

"Okay, I guess we are leaving now? You should probably put that journal of your grandfather's away somewhere safe first?"

"Oh yeah, good idea," Eddie responded as he turned around, rested the comics on the bed and lifted the mattress just enough to shove the journal between it and the box spring.

"That journal is highly secretive, eh?"

"Well, I just don't want anyone else finding it."

"So, your parents don't know about it?"

"I don't know. They don't know I have it."

"Eddie, you are a man of secrets! I like that. So, how'd you get the journal then?"

"I found it in my parents' bedroom closet. We should get going."

"Wait!" Cindy said rather forcefully as she placed her hand flat on Eddie's chest. "You were in your parents' closet? What else is in there?"

"It's a long story, can we go?"

"I want to see what's in your parents' closest."

"Out of the question."

"Oh, you are cute when you get assertive."

Eddie took her hand and led her into the hall.

Cindy stopped Eddie's momentum pulling on his arm. "Can we just peek in your parents' room?"

Eddie heard a distinctive "click".

"Sssh, I think someone just came home."

"Hello, anyone home?"

Eddie looked at Cindy and whispered, "it's Dad."

"Is that as bad as if it was your mom?"

"Sssh. Maybe you should hide?"

"I don't think that's a good idea."

"Hello, anyone home?"

His dad's voice increased in volume.

"Yeah Dad, I am."

"Oh, okay. Anyone else here?"

"I've a friend visiting." Eddie looked right into Cindy's deep chestnut brown eyes as a signal to be quiet.

"So, Mom isn't home?"

His dad's clear voice put him at least at the top of the stairs. Eddie stood frozen in the hallway, he let his hand drop out of Cindy's.

"No she isn't."

"Do you know when she left? Oh, hi."

His dad quickly shuffled his hands and slipped a brown bag behind his back, as he stiffened in front of them.

"Hi Mr. Teach. I'm Cindy. I know Eddie from school. He was just going to show me his comic collection."

"Oh, I see. Okay. Um, Eddie?" His dad's stare seemed to go right into Eddie's being and he felt as if the hallway was starting to spin.

"Yeah?"

"Do you? I mean, do you know when Mom left?"

Eddie paused as he looked briefly into Cindy's eyes, trying to nudge his sluggish thoughts.

"Eddie?"

"She left about an hour ago."

"Okay, do you know where she was going?"

"She said to see her friends."

"Oh. Did she say when she'd be back?"

"She said a few hours."

"Okay. I just have some things to get from our bedroom. Make sure you put your comics away when you are done. You don't want Mom finding them downstairs."

"Of course."

With that, Larnie moved past them and headed towards his bedroom. As he passed, Cindy gently pushed Eddie to move towards the stairs.

Once his dad was clearly out of sight, Eddie reached for Cindy's hand as he took the lead.

"Let's go into the kitchen, that way we should be able to hear him when he comes down the stairs."

"Okay. Wow, you are really nervous about what he might say?"

"Um. Yaaaa", Eddie looked at her quizzically as if she missed something obvious.

"More what he says to my mom. She would not be happy knowing we were up there."

"Okay. But I thought your dad looked distracted with something and not really interested in what *we* are doing?"

"You think so?"

"I don't know your dad, but he didn't really look right at us and his questions were about your mom. I thought it was a little weird actually."

"Hmmm...maybe you are right. You okay if I hold your hand like this?"

"Oh you're so cute, being polite and all. Of course."

Cindy unlocked her thumbs from his hands and used them to trace each of Eddie's fingers that were locked in with hers as she looked directly into his eyes.

"So, what do you want to do now? I mean, you don't really want to just look at comics, do you?"

Eddie knew that could be an invitation for a kiss, but he had never initiated a kiss with a girl before and his nerves froze him from making a move.

"Um. I dunno. My dad's just upstairs, you know."

Cindy moved her other arm around Eddie's waist and then started trailing his back with her index finger as her lips were now a few inches from his. The invitation had become an urging bid. Eddie responded with an infinitesimal tilt of his head – it was all the encouragement she needed as she pulled him in tight for a long kiss. A kiss unlike anything Eddie had experienced. The pause afterwards was measured in milliseconds as Eddie took the initiative. Everything else in his life was muted in the moment, but Cindy kept alert as she abruptly stopped and looked him.

"Did you hear that?"

"Hear what?"

"I'm sure I heard a voice. You parents' bedroom is above the kitchen and it sounds like someone is talking in there."

"Really? I can't hear anything."

"Ssssh. There it is again. You hear that?"

"No, did it sound like a whisper?"

"Yes! That's it. Someone else is in the house."

"Oh, no I don't think so. It's probably my dad talking to himself."

"Huh? He does that?"

"Yeah, sometimes when I am in the car with him, I'll shut my eyes and he thinks I'm asleep and I will hear him talking to himself."

"Your dad's really weird."

"No...not really. He's actually not bad. He just gets distracted in his thoughts I think. My mom tells him to stop day dreaming all the time."

"Really? What's your mom like?"

"My mom's great. She can be quite serious at times and I can't always understand what she means. But she cooks great meals and keeps my dad straight on things. How about your parents?"

"Well I love my mom. She is awesome. In some ways, I want to be like her. But it's very hard."

"What do you mean?"

"Well...when she walks, her left foot drags a bit. She uses her right hand to write, to eat with, to turn a doorknob, to turn on a faucet, to pour coffee and to drink. Things like that. Even putting on a jacket, she uses mostly her right arm and it just isn't normal."

"Really, why is that?"

"I just don't want you to be freaked out when you meet her. If she turns her head to the right, you will see a scar just below her neck. It's from a car accident she had when she was 19. She was engaged to be married to this guy and they were driving and hit by a semi. Her fiancé died from it, but she survived. Barely, I guess. She spent nine months in the hospital in recovery. She told me they had to cut her open and push her windpipe to the side so they could work on her spine. Anyway, she survived but has these restrictions. But she never makes any excuses for anything. I can tell when she is in pain, but she just goes about her life.

"Wow, she does sound amazin."

"Yeah, she has told me many times that she feels lucky, that life is a gift and we should live it to the fullest."

"I'd like to meet her."

"You will my Eddie, but I have to warn you that she kinda freaks out when I bring a boyfriend home. At least she did with Ryan."

"Ryan?"

"Yeah, you know that guy in grade 12 I was with at the end of school. It didn't last long but when my mom met him, she was asking him all kinds of questions about his plans for life and stuff, like I am going to marry him or something. She might be the same with you."

"Really? I just finished grade 11, I don't really know what I want to do with my life."

Cindy squeezed his hand as a show of solidarity and comfort.

"It's okay. I'll deflect her questions. She got married when she was young and she just acts sometimes like she wants her girls to do the same. Have someone that will look after us."

"I thought you said she is a positive person encouraging you to live life?"

"She is. It's just sometimes I think she has lived a sheltered life, and so she wants us to live out "our dreams", but also wants us to be comfortable. That's how Meagan puts it anyway."

"Meagan?"

"Yeah, my older sister. My mom treats her the same way. Meagan wouldn't tell her about her last boyfriend. But my mom has not had an easy life and still is a positive person. She likes to sing and talk to people."

Cindy leaned in and kissed him again. He felt his body escape into the moment as if he was somewhere else. As soon as their lips unlocked, Cindy naturally kept the conversation going.

"So what about *your* sister, where is she?"

"Bev is volunteering as a counsellor at camp sunshine for the summer. She'll back just before the Labour Day weekend. You have a brother too, right?"

"Yeah, Tommy and he's a good kid. I'm going to have to protect him though when he gets to high school."

"Why?"

"He can be a bit nerdy, is short for his age and not very athletic. But he's a smart kid. I'll be there if anyone tries to mess with him."

"I don't think anyone will want to mess with you."

Cindy, in a mocking fashion lightly punched him in the stomach and laughed again.

"You see, I had someone look after me when I was younger, cause I've an older a sister too."

"Meagan? I don't think I've met her. Does she go to our school?"

"No, and you probably haven't met her. She's 21 and out of school."

"Does she live with you?"

"Yeah, she is at the house, though we'll see how much longer. She's working at a jewelry store. But she wants to leave town. She doesn't really get along with my dad and she talks about going to school elsewhere."

"Where'd she go?"

"I dunno. Vancouver or Toronto maybe. One day she wants to be a jeweller and then a nurse or an airline stewardess. It seems to change every week."

"She sounds interesting. Would you miss her?"

"Of course, I would. She's my sister. Wouldn't you miss Bev if she left the house?"

"Oh, of course. How about your dad, what's he like?"

"Oh, he's an ass."

"Oh. Sorry. What makes you say that?"

Cindy pulled Eddie in close again and tilted her head towards his, “I don’t want to talk about him. I want to kiss my new boyfriend.”

As Eddie was learning the fun of using his tongue in a long kiss, Cindy’s ears perked and she quickly pulled away.

CHAPTER 6
The Teeth

As Larnie stepped into his bedroom, the walls seemed to crowd close. Should he have thought this through more? He had just handed over family jewelry, some of which could be family heirlooms, without much thought or attention, to a young woman he had not met before. While they should be safe in Graeme's store, in his haste he took no stock of what he left or even what he took to the store. The very thought made his body feel detached from his surroundings. Could he have carelessly handed over jewelry from Mae's family?

He paused to regulate his heavy breathing before he put the jewelry box down and opened it to examine what remained. He peered into the box and spotted a small leather pouch he hadn't notice before. Is this Mae's too? He lifted it out, untied the leather strings that held it closed and dumped the contents on the dresser. His breath suspended in his throat as his eyes widened at the sight. "Someone' teeth?" Larnie asked out loud, as if expecting an answer to the discovery. They look to have gold in them too. Teeth! Like actually adult teeth, he told himself. "Gawd, no wonder the clerk asked me if I wanted to leave everything or not", he whispered to himself. Where did those teeth come from? Do they have real gold? Whose teeth are they? Does Mae know about them? The dialogue in his head continued, as he swiftly put the teeth back into the pouch and buried it in the jewelry box under the other items – as if burying it would keep it out of his mind.

When he finally refocused on the scene in his bedroom, a new panic struck his bones. Mae had left a dress of hers on the bed, along with a note. Does she know something is up?

As he moved towards the bed, he saw in the corner of his eye the open closet door. He picked up the note, shook his head upon reading it, and then stuffed it into his pocket. He wished Mae wouldn't write him notes like that, but at least it isn't about the jewelry box, as he feared.

The dress on the bed and the open closet door meant she was in the bedroom after he left, and perhaps looking for something. As he looked into the closet, his eyes glanced upwards to confirm that the shoebox remained undisturbed. Larnie shook his head and lectured himself that his paranoid mind was sabotaging his thinking again.

He opened the dresser drawer to return the jewelry box when the shine off the silk of red lingerie hit his eyes. Mae had returned the lingerie he left out for her. Larnie's shoulders sagged and he felt weak as the drum started beating in his head again. The voice in his head, spoke in a whisper into the room. "Did she notice the jewelry box was missing when she opened the drawer?" She would be furious and he would receive her fury in passive aggressive actions. Silence, dirty dishes, an unmade bed. Things telling him he needs to fess up to something. The last time he experienced this was when he sold their old rocking chair without telling her. It had been put in the garage and so he thought why not get some money for it? He didn't know she planned to "refurbish it". It took him almost two weeks to find that out. Two weeks of a lot of silence, a messy house and no sex.

He began to stew as he chewed on the thoughts of what Mae put him through for that rocking chair.

Then, he thinks, maybe he's wrong. Maybe she would be sad, thinking he has taken some of her family heirlooms or maybe worried that they are lost? But what about the teeth? There is a story behind them for sure and she must know it. Maybe she will fear that he has found out something he is not supposed to know? What is she not telling him? Are there other secrets she is keeping from him?

Larnie then slammed the drawer shut, as if the force would shut out any problems that may come with it.

He abruptly left the room, hoping to leave his thoughts with it. As he was walking down the hallway, Mae's note jumped into his head. While he didn't appreciate her lecturing note, it is something he had put off and had made plans for previously, even picking something up for it. He turned around and headed back to their bedroom.

With a mission to retrieve what he needed and to then get out of there, he opened the closet door, moved some clothes on the left and looked down. His eyes caught the box of his dad's stuff, including that playboy on top. His male instincts overruled other thoughts and he picked up the magazine and started flipping the pages, past Marilyn Monroe's captivating smile on the cover, to her naked breasts.

"Not now", his whisper filled the closet as he put the magazine back on top of the box.

He then looked to the right of the closet where he had stashed it, picked it up without allowing any further distractions, and left the room. As he reached the bottom of the stairs, he could hear Eddie and his friend, what was her name?

He made his way into the kitchen as Eddie and his new friend just exited a kiss. Larnie stopped abruptly, as the scene threw a smirk on his face and took him back to his first kiss when he was a teenager.

"Oh, hi Mr. Teach. Didn't see you there."

"It's okay, I...I just got here."

"Hi Dad. Um...we're just talking" Eddie knew the response was weird as he stopped himself from asking why his dad was smiling.

"Eddie...I need to talk to you."

"Oh, okay. Can it wait? Cindy and I were just going to look at my comics."

"Um, well. No...no, it can't. Your mom left me a note."

"A note? About what?"

"We should talk in private, Eddie."

"It's okay, I should go anyway."

"No, you can wait here Cindy. Is that okay, Dad?"

"Um, sure. Why don't we go into the living room?"

"I'm going to go, Eddie. We can plan another time with your comics."

Before Eddie could respond, Cindy was up and heading to the door.

"Okay, bye. I'll call you later."

As the door closed, Larnie looked at Eddie and just stared as his mind churned with what to say.

"Dad?"

"Yes, yes. Sorry. Let's sit down in the living room."

Eddie moved to the living room and immediately sat in the loveseat, leaving the couch for his dad.

"Did Mom talk to you today?"

"Um, yeah before she went out."

"Oh, what'd she talk to you about?"

"I dunno. Stuff. Like what I want to eat."

"Of course. Did she say anything about something in our bedroom?"

"Your bedroom? Um, no. I don't know anything about your bedroom."

"Okay. I'm probably confusing you here. So, I've been putting off talking to you about something and am wondering if Mom had said something."

"Oh, about what?"

"Well, you know...the birds and the bees."

"You mean sex? Yeah, Mom asked if you had talked to me about sex."

"She really put it that way?"

As Eddie was nodding his head, Larnie reached into the bag he brought from his bedroom and handed a book to Eddie.

"I bought this for you some time ago. I know the title says "Almost 13" and you are like 16 now, but I looked it over and it explains everything in there for you."

"Okay. Thanks."

"You will read it, right?"

"Of course."

"Okay and one other thing. Don't tell your mom I gave you a book on it, okay? "

"Should I hide the book?"

"Um. Yeah, I think that would be a good idea."

CHAPTER 7
Meagan

The minute the customer came in with his box of jewelry, Meagan saw her opportunity. On several occasions, she had hatched the plan in her head, rehearsing it and playing it on rewind in her mind. It had been almost two years, beginning when they moved to Ranvon, that she had been contemplating her options.

In the last month, she decided on her course of action. But with each potential customer, she either would acquiesce to her nerves or, her boss, Graeme Montgomery, would be close enough to conceivably see everything. Was this just her constant paranoia creating the chasm between her plans and her actions? The paranoia that could easily morph into terror in her heart and hold her back, as it had before. It also gave wings to the suspicions she had that led to the discovery. Sometimes she wished she could erase it from her memory. Pretend it didn't exist.

She had never met the customer in front of her before and Mr. Montgomery was in the back of the store. The jewelry box he brought in presented the right opportunity and right place. "Now or never", she told herself.

Then the opportunity was about to be lost when the customer reached for his jewelry box back. Meagan had replayed that scene in her head several times in the last few hours of her shift. She hoped she hadn't raised suspicions when she held the box back for that brief second. She was focussed on not missing the opportunity and it crushed her common sense in the moment.

Thankfully, the customer seemed distracted as he was repetitively looking towards the back of the store. His distraction gave her the window she was hoping for, and she was positive he didn't see her slip the leather pouch with the teeth and note into the jewelry box.

She made sure to clip the box shut before handing it back to him so that he would leave the store before making the discovery.

Now she just needed to get through the rest of her shift without raising any suspicions.

"Brrrring! Brrring!"

The ring of the phone echoed in the store and throughout Meagan's body, sending shock waves through her, before the adrenaline raced through her veins and sparked her into action.

"I'll get it, Mr. Montgomery!"

"Hello, Danoon Jewelers."

"Click."

Her chest heaved at the sudden dial tone on the line. Teens had been making prank calls in the area; perhaps that is what it was? Meagan just could not bear it if it was *that* customer on the other end of the line. What would she say? What was his name, again? She was so distracted by her thoughts; she couldn't even remember the customer's name. If the customer made the discovery before her shift was over, everything she had planned could come crashing in on her. That phone call made her wish she had made the move sooner and had this over with already.

When her dad announced two years ago that they were moving from their small town to "a bigger centre of Ranvon", she could have made the change then and just refused to move with them. She was 19 after all. But she didn't have the money in savings or the confidence she could manage it on her own, and certainly didn't want to stay in that small town. Regardless, her dad would not give any financial support for her to be on her own unless she was "doing something meaningful" with her life. Whatever that was. So she moved with them and the job at the jewelry store had been lucrative enough that she was close to making her move.

It was the night she graduated from high school when she discovered the teeth with the note inside. Her dad had used her grad as a reason to celebrate and get drunk. While it made him unpredictable, it also meant his memory the next day could be distorted and easily manipulated.

After the grad party, Meagan went out with friends for a couple of hours and then stopped at home to ask her parents if she could spend the rest of the night out. As soon as she walked in the house, she knew her dad was sloshed as she could hear him on the couch. She imagined him there in a tee shirt and undergarments. It would embarrass and annoy her that he somehow thought it was acceptable at night to sit in his undergarments on the couch and eat, drink and smoke. She made a passing remark of disgust about it once and he dismissed it as "it's my house and I will wear whatever I want."

Before making her presence known, she could hear him yelling at an imaginary person in the living room and she assumed her mom had retreated to the kitchen.

Meagan's first instinct was to leave, but she couldn't do that to her mom and she could only get to her mom by passing through the living room first. She took a deep breath and decided that maybe she could take advantage of the situation. Her dad spotted her as soon as she stepped into the living room.

"Meg, how're you sweetheart! Come here! I'm so proud of you."

"Um, thanks Dad, but I just need to talk to Mom. Oh, hey....Dad?"

"Yes, sweetie? Come here; give your old man a hug."

"Dad, I...I'm going out with friends to celebrate. Nothing serious. I won't drink or anything...but we'll probably go to a restaurant later. Could I possibly get a little bit of money?"

"Sure, sure!" She watched her dad reach into his imaginary pockets.

"Shit, I left my wallet upstairs. Meg, could ya go get it for me? It...let me think...it'd be in my pants on the floor."

Well that was new one. Being asked to go upstairs and fetch his wallet.

"Sure. I'll say hi to Mom, first."

"Thanks honey."

Meagan's hands burled up into fists at the sound of her father calling her honey and sweetie. After a quick hello to her mom in the kitchen, she quickly made her way to her parents' bedroom.

As soon as she entered the room, she saw his pants on the floor and her first thought was to limit her stay in that room to as short as possible. Then as she was leaving, she spotted the jewelry boxes on the dresser. Feeling a wind of courage, she stopped as she wondered if she might find something to wear for the evening. The first box was clearly her mom's and most of it very old or at least something an old person would wear, she thought. The other jewelry box looked rougher. Perhaps her dad's? The latch on it wouldn't open. It was locked. Her curiosity and now suspicious nature spiked. She went back to her dad's pants, where she retrieved his keys.

After trying a few keys, she found the one that worked and unlatched the box. An old watch that looked like gold caught her attention and she reached in to claim it. As she pulled the watch towards her, a small leather pouch had caught on the watch's latch. Her attention shifted to the leather pouch and its potential contents. She placed the watch back into the box and sat on the edge of the bed, as she worked to untie the knot of the leather strings of the pouch. It had been tied tight and took considerable effort to untie it. Finally, with the task completed, she turned the pouch upside down to empty its contents on the bed. What landed on the bed caused Meagan to silence her own gasp, as she put her hand to her mouth. Teeth. Someone's teeth?

Her initial shock was replaced by the intermingling of questions that almost overwhelmed her. Who's? Why? Is the person alive or dead? Then it occurred to her that the pouch may not have emptied entirely, and she put her fingers inside and pulled out the piece of paper that flooded her mind with more questions. The discovery would later springboard her to research the origins of the teeth, while it raged within her as to what to do with what she found. It would ultimately lead to her placing the pouch, with the teeth and the note, into the hands of a stranger – Larnie Teach. It was with the hope that it would eventually liberate her from the secret she bottled up inside. The details on the small note inside the leather pouch are seared in her memory:

WG
JB
LM
PF
Teddy?

The research she embarked on confirmed inklings she had in the past. There is a criminal in the family who should be in jail. She buried those thoughts many times until they made the move out to Ranvon. Capitalizing on the activities of the family move, she took the pouch with the teeth and had been hiding them since. Until this shift.

Working for a jeweller, though a cranky and unpredictable individual, had given her an idea of what she wanted to do with her life. Each piece of jewelry that came in she viewed with the wonderment of its origins and what more she could make it into. Thoughts of crafting jewelry would often occupy her mind. Her mom was hopeful that she would marry and become "a housewife". She would roll her eyes every time her mom would mention it.

Meagan looked up at the clock. 4:54. Six minutes left in her shift and one more important task to complete. Moving towards the back of the store, she saw Mr. Montgomery working away setting some ring in place.

"Sorry to disturb you sir, but it's 5 to 5. Should I lock up in 5 minutes?"

"Oh, yes. Thanks Meagan. Let me get your pay and then you can lock up and leave by the side door."

"Thank you Mr. Montgomery."

Meagan always received her pay in cash and as she counted the money to verify it was all there, a mischievous grin crossed her face. This day was going even better than planned.

She stopped at the counter on her way to the door and opened up the drawer that had all the intake items from the last two days.

"Meagan, when you lock the door, don't forget to turn the sign to show we are closed."

Mr. Montgomery's voice caused a leap in her throat and Meagan quickly grabbed several items from the drawer, without looking at them, put them in her purse and then quickly made her way to the door so that her boss could hear her shoes clacking on the tile floor as she left.

CHAPTER 8
TNT

"Hey Eddie. Big news at our place today."

"What's that? Don't tell me you're moving, cause I'll just hang up."

"Oh you're so cute the way you worry about things that are not going to happen. Meagan quit her job at the jewelry store."

"Oh?"

"Yeah, and my dad freaked. But then the real big news is that she's leaving in the morning and has already bought a bus ticket for Vancouver. My mom started to cry when she told them."

"Really? What's she goin to do in Vancouver?"

"Work. Go to school. I dunno really. She has a place to stay for while anyway."

"Where?"

"Well we have a Great Uncle and Aunt in Vancouver. They're from my mom's side. Meagan phoned them to see if she could stay for a while. She didn't even tell our parents and my dad wanted to phone Uncle Jim right away but Mom stopped him. Now the three of them are out at a café to talk about it."

"The three of them?"

"My dad, my mom and Meagan. Eddie, were you not tracking what I was saying? I think my parents are hoping to talk her out of it, but Meagan didn't even want to go out with them. I think the tears in my mom's...."

"Cindy, you there?"

"Sorry, yes. I just....I just."

"You okay?" Eddie was certain he could hear her sob, but he didn't want to assume anything with Cindy.

"Of course I'm not, you dimwit. My sister is moving out and leaving me all alone here. She didn't even tell me about this..."

Her words gave way to sobs and Eddie retreated to silence rather than say something that could upset her more.

"You there Eddie?"

"Yes...of course."

"Sorry to dump on you. It's just that I'm so confused with what's happening and then seeing my mom cry like that....My mom's been through a lot already and Meagan leaving could crush her. And what about me? Leaving me alone here with everything to look after."

"I know its hard Cindy, but why do you feel alone? Your parents will still be there and your brother."

"Oh, you just don't understand my family. Your family's so perfect, even if your dad talks to himself."

"I'm sorry Cindy. My family isn't perfect."

"It is compared to mine. My dad's an ass and now I'll have to take care of more around here. Oh gawd, I feel sick thinking about it. My mom tries really hard, but she's in pain and so Megs and I try to help her out where we can. Things like getting the groceries for her and putting them away, some of the cooking and laundry and making lunches. Now it'll all be on me. Tommy's going to need help in school and I won't have Megs here to talk to and sort things out. I was hoping we could do things together like go to parties and stuff. She was so excited the other day when I told her about you and now she won't even meet you."

"I am sure she will stay in contact."

"Oh sure, but she is going to be six hours away Eddie. The calls will be long distance and my parents will probably only let me talk to her after six o'clock when it's cheaper. I wish she would stay here. Actually I wish I had a family like yours."

"Why? My family isn't that great."

"It's way better than mine. You take holidays together and your place just seems more real."

"Um...okay. I don't think it's quite as great as you make it sound. Do you want to come over here now? Or I could ride my bike to your place?"

"Oh that's sweet, but I can't right now. I'm just going to wait here until they get back and then go for a walk with Megs. I don't know when they will be back, but I want to be ready and I don't think it would work if you were here. Sorry."

"Okay. Does Meagan have enough money to move like that or are your parents helping?"

"My parents? That's a laugh. No chance. Maybe my mom will slip her some money, but she must have enough from what she made at the jewelry store. That's what she said when my mom asked the same question. My mom..."

"I'm sorry Cindy. I didn't mean to upset you."

"That's okay. Actually it's nice to talk to you about it."

"That's a big decision your sister is making. My dad tells me to think about decisions we make, cause they can set off a momentum of other decisions that determine a lot in our lives. He says a lot of people don't think much of their decisions or they let others make them for them."

"That's kinda deep, Eddie. You're really close to your dad."

"I dunno. He drives me crazy sometimes."

"But you talk about him, at least to me you do."

"Oh yeah. I guess I do. Is that weird?"

"Well, none of my friends talk about their parents much, except to complain. But I don't think it's weird. Actually I'm jealous. I wish my dad was someone I could admire."

"What about your mom? You talk about how much you admire her."

"She's so sweet and I don't know how she manages to see such positive outlooks in life with the pain she's in and having to deal with my father all the time. I wouldn't share too much about what's happening in my life with her though and I guess Meagan feels the same way. My mom's great and all but, she can be quite restrictive in how she sees life. She wants us all to get married and have kids and white picket fences - like we're playing out some perfect movie."

"Oh. Is that so....um...well...you think Meagan leaving has come as a surprise to them then? You told me she was thinking about it."

"Oh totally. Can we talk about something else now? I don't want to talk about this right now."

"Sure, like what?"

"I don't know. I think it's your turn Eddie. What do you want to talk about?"

"Well..."

"Not comics again please and definitely not school! The other day my mom asked me if I was excited about going back to school. Can you imagine? Who gets excited about going back to school? Except to maybe see friends again, of course. But sitting in a classroom listening to Ms. Norclift lecture with her squeaky irritating voice while watching the clock until the next break? Pulleeease! Or watching Mr. North favour the kids who suck up to him all the time. Gives them grades they don't deserve or the easy assignments. Personally, I think he's disgusting. I saw him picking his nose one time in class. Yuk! No Eddie, I can't take it. School talk right now is out of bounds, agreed?"

Eddie had discovered that if he paused long enough, Cindy would keep talking and thus afford his thoughts time to chew over how to respond. He was going to suggest some of the changes there will be for the school year and what classes they may have together, but he quickly ditched such thoughts to the side.

"Agreed, of course. No school talk. I don't want to talk about it either. School sucks. So, would you be interested in more from my grandpa's journal?"

"Really? You still have it, eh? You're not worried that your dad will see that it's missing?"

"Actually, I'm not sure he knows it exists. It was just one thing in my grandpa's old box and it doesn't look like it had been touched for a while, until I found it."

"Well then, my Eddie, you must share some more with me. I thought what we read together was very interesting. Something about a time in the 1930s and your grandpa lost his job and was worried how your grandma would react?"

"Yes, that's right. Well, he did find another job. Maybe I'll read that part to you?"

"Stop asking and just read it."

"Okay. Here is one entry.

"Sept 23, 1936. Landing the job at the Mail and Empire newspaper was like a great gift, and just in time. I am forever in debt to my friend Larnie Toth for getting me this job. When Larnie called and told me that his cousin needed someone who can research and write and that he thought about me right away, it felt like I was in this impossible dream where a job I didn't even apply for was given to me.

I had to write a short story about something real first, but that was easy. They didn't even advertise the job. If they had, guys would have lined up and fought over it. So many people out of work and desperate these days. While I am excited about it, I feel like a thief taking the job without anyone else having a chance. I have to make good on this. This one could be my real opportunity.

Now I have to come up with a story to tell Liz, as she thinks I am still working at the fish plant and just that the work has been a bit spo-

radic. Now at least I don't have to pretend to be at work, but what do I say to her? The headline I just wrote for the paper: When Will the Dust Bowl End? Is coming out tomorrow and I am going to be paid for it then. I am excited to tell her about it. I'd have to give her a reason for spending money on a newspaper anyway. I hope she is proud of me. It doesn't pay much, but it's work and work I like. Work that could be my future - our future together.

When I interviewed the two farmers about the drought that is killing their crops, they seemed to know more about the weather than anyone I've ever met. That story could give people hope and I am part of it. Life doesn't offer much besides survival and misery these days. Besides my love for Liz, this has put excitement into my bones I have not felt for years. Liz has to see and experience that same excitement with me, without knowing about my deception. Maybe I could tell her it was "TNT" that combined again. She rolls her eyes anytime I mention the moniker my mom came up for Larnie and me. The first time I told her it was for Toth and Teach, she laughed. To hear her laugh right now would be a great gift."

"Hey! Did you stop? Why stop reading, I want to hear more."

"Cind, I still need to read more of it myself. But what do you think of that part?"

"It's incredible. It's like a letter from the past. Your grandpa worked as a newspaper reporter?

"Yeah, it seems like. I know after world war two he worked for a publishing house, but I thought he was just a driver or something. At least that's what I remember. Anything else you notice from it?"

"I am not sure. I thought you told me your dad described your grandpa as difficult and that he had a hard life? Sure doesn't sound like it from what you read."

"Yeah, I know. It's like I'm discovering a grandpa I didn't know. I think it was the war that changed his life for the worse. It sounds like he had dreams and plans for his future and maybe the war just took that from him and crushed it within him."

"There you go with that deep thinking again. Could you read that passage over? I think there was things in there I don't understand."

Eddie read the passage out again to Cindy, this time at a slower pace and after a pause of being forever in debt to his friend Larnie Toth.

"Wait, Larnie. Is that your dad's name?"

"Yes! I didn't know if you knew that?"

"Well it's such an unusual name so I guess I remembered it from when I heard it. Do you think your dad was named after your grandpa's friend?"

"I dunno. Makes sense. Like you said, an unusual name."

"You should ask your dad. That's really cool."

"I can't ask him. He doesn't know I have this diary, remember?"

"Right. Of course. Well then, don't tell him. Just ask him why he thinks his parents gave him that name?"

"Smart. That's what I'll do."

"See, aren't you glad you read that to me? You should read me more. I bet I can help with other things you find in there. I'm pretty smart you know."

"Yeah, I probably will. So, anything else from what I read from my grandpa?"

"Well I find it interesting that he lied to your grandma so she wouldn't worry. Kind of like to protect her, I guess. But I bet you she found out anyway."

"That's what my dad says, that you shouldn't lie and the other person will find out eventually."

"I dunno, is that always true? So what about the dust bowl? What is a dust bowl, anyway?"

"From his diary, it had something to do with farmers. My grandpa wrote an article on it. I sure wish I could get a copy of it."

"We could check the library. They keep some old stuff in there. If they don't have it, maybe they'll at least have something on what a dust bowl is."

"They do. It's called archives. Not sure if they would have a newspaper article from Ontario and that far back though."

"Archives? How do you know that word?"

"My mom. She throws different words at me all the time, some of them stick. She spends a lot of time in the library, so when we go, we should make sure she's not there."

"Eddie, I see that they have just pulled into the driveway. Meagan doesn't look too happy. I should go."

"Okay. Chat later? Let me know how it goes with Meagan."

"For sure and thanks for the chat. I knew you'd make a good boyfriend. I could see it in your eyes. Bye."

Eddie heard the click before he could offer his own goodbye. Cindy could tear at his nerves and leave him panicked about saying the wrong thing, but she also gave him things to think about with his grandpa.

CHAPTER 9
The Journalist

July 1979

Larnie hadn't forgotten about the jewelry he took into Graeme's store over two months ago, but it had recessed into the background as he assumed the value of the heirlooms were not worth the stress of departing with them.

Instead, he had focused on saving money by other means and recently stumbled into the possibility of additional income from writing stories for the local newspaper. It was like a found gem when he overheard two war veterans at the coffee shop talking about a plane that went down in 1943 in the area and was still lying in its "resting spot" in the rain forest. He was nearly late for dinner that day as he quizzed his two new friends about the plane. With curiosity fueling him, he researched the subject more and discovered the plane could indeed be seen by following an old goat trail in the woods. He then wrote a story about it and sent it to the local newspaper for consideration.

His thoughts about the value of the jewelry were pushed deeper down the moment the editor of the paper phoned and offered Larnie $35 for the story; then asked him if he would be interested in writing other "human interest" stories for "remuneration". As he thought about additional stories to research and write about, concealing the extra income from Mae occupied space in his thoughts as well. It's a deception he was not accustom to, but he wanted the vacation he planned to be memorable and keeping it a surprise was part of that.

But then the call from Graeme unnerved him, unearthed the image of the jewelry box and its contents, and placed it in front of him. He could no longer focus on anything else. He told Graeme that he would see him the next day. He was too anxious to wait that long.

Why would Graeme insist he take back the jewelry and what about the comment that he doesn't have the insurance to keep it in his store? Could it be worth so much he can't get insurance or maybe he only has insurance for so many items?

Larnie watched Mae's legs disappear on the steps up to their room and seized the opportunity to use the phone in the kitchen.

"Hello?"

"Larnie?"

"Oh, it is *you* Graeme. What time are you open til?"

"I close at 5, so in about 7 minutes."

"Oh, I see."

"Were you thinking...you might come in tonight, instead?"

"I don't think there is time, unfortunately."

"I can wait for you, what time could you get here?"

"Maybe a half hour? Say 5:30?"

"Great, I'll wait for you then."

"Graeme, that necklace you mentioned, can you tell me if you had it appraised?"

"Let's talk about it when you get here, my friend."

"For sure. Bye."

"Who was that on the phone Hun?"

"Oh hi Mae. Didn't see you there."

"Well I just heard you say goodbye to someone, who was it?"

"Oh, it was Lance from work. I need to go in to help set up something for tomorrow. I won't be long."

"On a Friday night? Well, I was just going out myself to meet with Elizabeth. I'm hoping she'll have something for the new quilt I've started and I can borrow some pasta from her for dinner. If you're going out, could you pick up some carrots and tomatoes to go with it?"

"For sure Hun."

CHAPTER 10

The Kishaimoto Treasure

As Larnie approached the jewelry store, the only light visible was coming from the very back and he was thankful that his visit with Graeme would be in private. He paused at the door and took a deep breath. He reached for the handle, as the feeling of walking into something momentous stirred up emotions.

The door moved less than an inch forward before it was pulled back by the deadbolt, which protested with a "thunk". The noise gave way to the image of Graeme coming from the back. Larnie wiped his face with his sleeve as Graeme reached the door, turned the deadbolt and greeted him.

"Hi there my friend. Sorry, I locked it; I didn't want any other customers coming in before you arrived. Shall we go to the back of the store?"

"Sure, I'll follow you."

Graeme started towards the back, with Larnie following and his voice echoed off the walls as Larnie picked up his pace to match Graeme's brisk gait.

"Is it warm out there?"

"A little."

"You're sweating pretty good." Graeme lowered his voice and motioned for Larnie to walk beside him as he strained to hear.

"The piece is in my safe. It was quite the adventure for me to determine its origins and value. It's like unlocking real life mysteries and what you have there is quite rare. I am glad you're finally here. I tell you, I've been waiting to talk about this necklace. With the blue diamond and gold in it, the even colour and translucency in the other parts of the necklace..." Graeme's voice trailed off into a dreamlike whisper, before he pronounced: "it is a rare piece indeed! He turned his head towards Larnie and met his eyes as he asked, "do you know where you got it from?"

"Not really. It was...well its part of a collection of family jewelry. It has real gold?"

"Oh, yeah, no doubt about that. Something very rare too."

"Really, what's it worth?"

"I'll get into that in a bit, let's take a look at it and I'll explain what I discovered."

The two of them arrived at the back of the store and Graeme promptly removed a picture from the wall exposing a previously concealed safe.

"I guess it's safe for you to know where this is hidden. We may find a few secrets we have to keep to each other."

With that, Graeme opened the safe, put on white gloves, reached in and pulled out a velvet case.

"I put your piece in this case to protect it. You brought it in loose with nothing to protect it." Graeme's head shook disapprovingly.

"It was fairly tarnished and so I cleaned it and you may not recognize it right away."

When Graeme opened the case, Larnie could hardly recall the necklace. He remembered the significance of its weight compared to the other jewelry. Was this stunning necklace he looked at now really his? The diamond and gold certainly stood out. Was it truly authentic?

"Now that it's clean, I can guess what you thinking. It's striking, but is it real or fake? Is that a real diamond? Is that real gold? All questions I asked myself. Well, my friend", Graeme rested his hand on Larnie's shoulder to emphasize his sincerity, "let me assure you the answer to those questions is...yes." Then pausing, seemly for effect, he added, "without a doubt."

Graeme then traced his fingers over the necklace as if stroking it to purr and he stopped at the glistening diamond.

"That there is a blue diamond. What we know in the business as a type IIb diamond. Extremely rare. This one has a very intense deep blue greyish color, which makes it that much more rare and valuable. One of the rarest kinds of diamonds known in the world. I actually had only seen something like this in pictures, before this."

Larnie stood with a feeling of bewilderment in what he was hearing as his mind started to process what this meant. Graeme looked at him, taking in his expression before Larnie finally met his eyes and then Graeme nodded and continued.

"Now some blue diamonds are only blue because someone has colored them as such. Those so-called blue diamonds are not authentic and obviously not worth nearly as much. I can explain to you the process I went through to verify that this diamond is an authentic blue diamond. But before I get to that, there are a couple of other features of this necklace."

Graeme moved his fingers past the diamond and over one of four little square chunks of gold, which circled the diamond like a tribe saluting to its beauty.

"Wait, is that a symbol on the gold or something? Looks like a cat or something?"

"Ah, you noticed, my friend. That may be a tiger, I don't know for sure. Maybe not, but that symbol, gives an indication of the mint the gold came from. That brings me to the next discovery. We will need a magnifying glass for this one."

Graeme placed the necklace back into the velvet case and laid it in the open safe before walking across the room to a desk where he retrieved a hand held magnifier. Larnie stood still as Graeme moved about, feeling as if he was just playing a part in some movie and not sure what would happen next.

Graeme returned to the safe, took out the necklace and turned it over. Hovering the magnifying glass over the backside of one of the gold chunks, he found what he was looking for.

"You see that there?"

Larnie was startled by the excitement in his friend's voice as he moved in for a closer look.

"It's very small...some sort of writing. What does it say?"

"Well, I've studied this and took pictures of it. I sent it off to someone I know in the jewelry business. While some of the symbols are faded and less clear, you see those there?

"Looks Chinese?"

"Close. It's Japanese and those are the symbols for: AK in English."

"Oh, okay. What does that mean?"

"I believe it's from the Second World War. There was a Japanese general during the war whose name was Akitsugu Kishaimoto. He was notoriously known for his brutality. His nickname was the "Tiger of Malaya". There is a story, legend of sorts I guess, that Kishaimoto had a stash of gold bricks and jewelry. The Kishaimoto treasure and where some of it may be found is the stuff of legends."

"So you think this is from that?"

"I'm not sure. An educated guess from my research. You'd probably have to send it off to a museum to determine its origin for sure. Do you know someone from the Second World War?"

"Well, my dad."

"Is he alive?"

"Died last year."

"I see. Your mom alive?"

"No. She died years ago."

"Oh, I'm sorry, my friend. Just thought they might be able to shed some light on this. Something to fill in the missing puzzle pieces, if you know what I mean."

"I do. They don't speak from the grave."

"I don't mean to pry, but was your dad a prisoner of war to the Japanese during world war two?"

"My dad didn't talk much about the war."

Larnie was pleased with his quick answer. He wasn't sure where Graeme was going with his questions but his senses were telling him to be cautious in what he shared. His dad didn't talk about the war and so that was a very true statement. But he also knows that his dad was dispatched to the pacific and survived a capture by the Japanese. The clarity of a conversation with his mom years ago rushed to the front of his thoughts. He had asked his mom about a German friend of his dad's and if the war impacted their friendship at all and his mom responded that his dad's experience in the war was with the Japanese, not the Germans. It was from that conversation that he learnt his dad fought in the pacific and was captured. He obviously survived, but the details for Larnie are sketchy at best. His mom wouldn't talk about it after that. He tried bringing it up in on a few occasions with his dad, but it was clear it wasn't something to talk about. Then again, it's not like he and his dad talked much about anything. Now this necklace may have come from him?

"Ah I see. Well, it may be that my research on this is on the wrong track, but it is certainly intriguing, no?"

"Yeah...Yeah. For sure Graeme. But what does this mean for the value of the necklace?"

"I'm not entirely sure. If it *is* from the Second World War and the Kishaimoto treasure, it could be quite the discovery. That would increase its value significantly, without a doubt."

"Hmmm. So, what do you think the necklace is worth?"

"I can break it down for you if you like, but with the gold and blue diamond and then the potential history of it, I would say half a million dollars or more."

Graeme's words hit Larnie with a force that tore him from where he was. The disbelief in what he just heard blunted other thoughts and his tongue dried up as he struggled to speak.

Graeme grabbed Larnie and with a sense of urgency led him to a chair nearby.

"I'm sorry, I'll get you a glass of water. I should have anticipated the shock it might bring to hear that this could make you a very rich man."

The two men sat in silence, holding glasses of water, as Graeme watched and waited on Larnie.

"Sorry, what did you say it's worth?"

"Well, the actual value is hard to determine with the potential historical significance, but I would appraise it to be worth at least a half a million dollars."

"I make twenty thousand a year." Larnie mumbled to himself.

Graeme simply nodded in response before asking if he should continue. While Larnie sat in the chair sipping water, Graeme explained to him the process he followed in determining the necklace's value. He started with holding up the diamond in the light to demonstrate how the light bends through it, revealing an intense and sparkling blue colour - a clear indication of its authenticity. If the light was to shine a straight line through it, it's not a diamond. Graeme then brought out a hand held ultra violet light and turned off the rest of the lights for the effect. When the light hit the diamond, a swirl of deep blue and purple colors in the diamond popped out. Graeme turned and saw Larnie was able to focus on the diamond as he told him how the blue in the diamond is caused by carbon transfused with nitrogen within the diamond and that it is very rare. "Very rare indeed" he emphasized. He restated this was the first real blue diamond he has seen. Graeme then reached over and turned on the light, giving a moment for their eyes to adjust.

"The blue diamond caught my attention almost the moment I saw it. I was in some disbelief before I looked it as we just did. But when I started to look at the rest of the necklace, I found the blue diamond may not be the most intriguing feature."

Graeme let the weight of the diamond drop through his fingers until the necklace stopped at his waiting thumb on one of the gold pieces. Rolling the gold piece between his thumb and index finger, he revealed his belief of its origins. He spoke as if telling a tale around a campfire.

He believes the gold came from bigger pieces that were likely melted into molds made specific for the necklace. He mused about the possibility of there being other necklaces similar to this one, maybe even identical. "Kishaimoto's Gold from the Kishaimoto Treasure." It was a statement he made twice, as some sort of proclamation. Graeme talked about Kishaimoto as a mystical person who was a Japanese General during the Second World War and who horded treasurers, mostly gold, that the Japanese had plundered from Korea, Malaysia and Indonesia. The story included bricks of gold worth billions that were stored in prisoner of war camps, tunnels, caves and other underground structures - some of which were dynamited near the end of the war in order to bury the treasure. What has happened to all the gold and treasure is an unsolved mystery.

He explained that some think the Americans were able to retrieve most of the treasure in a secret operation and have since hidden it in various foreign banks around the world. Others believe it is still hidden somewhere, some think most of it was buried at sea when ships, carrying the loot, were sunk during the war, while others that the stories are largely exaggerated and are just legend and myth making. There is no question of some known facts, emphasized Graeme. Kishaimoto, a known brutal Japanese General, was in charge of prisoners at war camps during world war two. He had treasure, including gold, that he accumulated during the war. The necklace fits the kind of treasure he would have had and the gold appears to have his initials and symbol on it. He was executed for war crimes and died without disclosing anything about the treasure.

"I've been wondering." Graeme paused as he looked at Larnie and was sure he had his attention, "how it is that such a piece could find its way into your jewelry box? I believe it must be from a family member of yours who was likely captured by the Japanese in the war. It must be quite the tale in itself of how the necklace came into their possession and how they brought it back from the war."

"Thank you Graeme. What you've told me is, well...it's incredible. I'm not sure what to say. It sounds like this necklace has far more to it than I ever imagined. The worth of it...is staggering and hard for me to comprehend, in all honestly. I'm not sure what to do here. Perhaps you can keep the necklace in your safe while I sort out things?"

Graeme, shaking his head while Larnie was speaking, was quick in his response.

"Absolutely not. You have to understand that a jewelry store can be a target for thieves. I've been broken into twice since I opened and then there was that young assistant of mine that I am pretty sure was ripping me off. I have insurance, but not to cover your necklace. Honestly, I think it would be safer back in your wooden jewelry box."

"How could that be? Anyone could break into my house."

"Have they before? That necklace has sat inside in that jewelry box of yours for how many years? Look Larnie, I'm not going to say anything to anyone, unless you want me to help you sell it?"

"Sell it? I don't know about that. That would bring a mountain of attention and change to our lives. I just want a holiday with my family, not to disrupt everything. I guess I'll just take it home."

With that, Larnie frantically looked at his watch and bolted from the chair.

"My goodness. Mae will wonder what happened to me. I better get going."

"Okay, but before you go, you mentioned earlier that you brought in other pieces of jewelry?"

"Oh yes, nothing significant...at least I don't think so."

"Ah, I was afraid you were going to say that. See I had an assistant who used to work here."

"Used to?"

"Yes, in fact she quit right after her shift the day you came in. Well, I don't know how to say this, but I'm fairly certain she took whatever other jewelry you brought in. I have reason to believe that isn't the only time she took jewelry from a customer."

"Okay, where's she now?"

"I believe she's somewhere in Vancouver. I phoned her house and chatted with her mom, whom I've met, and that's what she told me. I feel sorry for her mom. That poor woman struggles to walk properly from an accident from her youth. I didn't have the heart to tell her that I think her daughter's a thief. But it's your jewelry, so if *you* want me to call the police?"

"The police? Oh, no, that wouldn't be necessary. It was just a bunch of old trinkets anyway. I had only identified the necklace in particular to be appraised because of its unusual weight."

"Alright then, I'll put the necklace in a bag for you. I do have a bill for the appraisal of it."

"Of course. Could I get you the money for that later? I just don't have the cash on me right now. I wasn't expecting this."

"For sure my friend. I know you are good for it."

Larnie stood still as he continued to process what he had learnt. Are there things about his dad that he doesn't know? Should he investigate that further? While he certainly didn't want the police involved and then having to explain to Mae why he brought in their jewelry box, he wished he had paid more attention to what the assistant took from him that day. What was her name?

"Graeme, that assistant of yours...that quit, what was her name?"

"Meagan. I should have suspected things sooner Larnie. I trusted her and often left her alone out front. I should have paid more attention to the large purse she brought in every day. On the day you were here, I saw her with this leather pouch that she pulled out of her purse and thought it was odd. Now I wonder if she put something in it. Anyway, she's gone now and I moved on. Thanks for your understanding."

"Um yeah, Meagan...what did the...oh it's okay. I should go."

"Okay...but, Larnie, I have decided not to pursue things with Meagan because of her mom. If you decide you want to do that you need to tell me, okay?"

"Oh for sure. Don't worry, I won't be doing that."

Graeme put the necklace in the velvet case and that in a brown paper bag as Larnie had requested. He stood for several minutes after he left the store. He was glad not to have the potential liability in his store any longer but the mysteries behind the necklace, and what he discovered, kept him awake some nights. The unanswered questions had urged him to explore its history. Questions still lingered in his head as it left his store. How did Larnie come into possession of it? One does not simply purchase something like that or have it made; it had to belong to someone powerful at one time. Is that person Kishaimoto and how did it leave his ownership? As the questions were still fresh in his mind, he saw Larnie sitting in his car just outside the store. He ran out and made eye contact as he approached the vehicle. Larnie rolled down the window as he saw him coming.

"Hey, just a thought I had. Was he an America by chance?"

"Who?"

"Your father."

"Oh. Yeah, he was born in the States but lived most of his life in Canada. Why?"

"Oh, just that I read that more Americans spent time in the pacific during the war. The Japanese captured soldiers there. Might mean nothing."

"Okay. Hey, wait, Graeme?"

"Yes."

"You said the assistant...Meagan. She had a leather pouch?"

"Yes, just something I saw her with. Why?"

"Can you describe it?"

"I didn't really get a good look at it. It looked kind of worn and old and was tied with leather strings I believe. Why?"

"Oh just that I...I saw something similar, that's all."

Larnie reached out of his window and squeezed Graeme's hand in a warm show of appreciation as he thanked him. As he put the vehicle into first gear to drive off, striking images and questions flashed in his mind. The necklace with the gold and blue diamond. His dad in a Japanese POW camp and somehow escaping with the necklace? Is there another explanation? Meagan and the other jewelry? Is that leather pouch and teeth hers? Trying to quiet the confusing images and questions in his head, Larnie kept his foot on the break as the vehicle idled and he sat with his eyes closed and took a deep breath. What does his dad's American citizenship have to do with all this? Feeling sweat on his brow, he just sat there, breathing and begging his nerves to calm down when his most urgent matter flashed before him. Mae would be in the kitchen working on dinner. He opened his eyes as the new found urgency found its way into his right foot, while his mind switched to rehearsing what he would say when he got home.

When Larnie pulled into the driveway, he was relieved that Mae wasn't at the door waiting for him. He tucked the brown bag into the sleeve of his jacket and briskly marched up the steps to the door and as he reached for the handle, the door opened.

"So there you are. Your dinner's cold. Where've you been?"

"Oh sorry hun. I lost track of time. We were sorting out an order at work and with the sales coming for the Labour Day weekend; I wanted to get it right."

"Ah. Well I phoned your work looking for you."

"You did?"

Larnie could hear his own voice stutter as he responded. He wasn't used to lying and his nerves were betraying him with Mae's response. He could feel her eyes on him, as she squinted, studying him, seeing through him. Her pause was long and deliberate and Larnie could feel the bag tucked in his sleeve. He started to wiggle it free, to pull it out and braced himself to tell the whole story and then Mae responded.

"Yeah and it just rang and rang. No one picks up the phone at your work?"

"Oh yeah, sorry hun. I heard the phone ring and didn't think it could be you. We were just...just trying to not be disturbed, you know. I wanted to get home sooner."

Mae shook her head as he spun his tale.

"You heard the phone ring and didn't answer it? Maybe that place needs a woman to look after things."

Mae then kissed him, and turned back to the kitchen as she shouted over her shoulder.

"I assume you forgot the carrots and tomatoes I asked for, but never mind, I'll reheat your food for you, foolish man."

"Okay, thanks hun. I'm just going upstairs to refresh for dinner then."

"Your dinner that is. Eddie and I've already eaten."

Larnie closed the door of their bedroom behind him and locked it. If Mae came up, he'd come up with an excuse for the lock - that would be easier than explaining the necklace. He stood at the foot of the bed and pulled his arms out of the sleeves of his jacket. The brown paper bag plunged free, landing on the bed. He took out of the velvet case, opened it and looked at his now prized possession. He quickly got lost in his thoughts. How could he have missed the beauty spilling out of that necklace? The size of the diamond and the gold framing it in a circle? Could that thing really be worth a half a million dollars?

He caught his own reflection in the mirror behind him, which snapped him back to the moment and quickened him into action. He had to move fast to avoid any further suspicions. He moved to the closet, moved the clothes on the left side, reached down and pulled out the box. The playboy magazine on top fell off the box and Larnie caught it with his fingers. He opened the lid and placed the magazine inside, closed the lid and pushed the box back into the corner. He then stood up and looked up at the bag on the top shelf. Think fast he told himself. He then moved the clothes back on the left side and pulled the hanged clothes on the right, to give access to the right side of the closet floor. He knelt down and pulled out the box. His bold felt writing on the top stood strong: Dad's Stuff Box 2. He couldn't recall even looking at the stuff inside when he labelled it. Carefully removing tape he had fastened the lid to the box with, he popped the lid off. On top were magazines, which he took out and placed on the floor beside him. He then put the necklace into the box, covered it with the magazines, closed the lid, resealed the tape and slid it back into the corner of the closet.

Larnie changed his shirt and made his way to the kitchen where Mae greeted him with a kiss.

"I warmed your dinner up in the oven and it's on the table for you. You throw your dirty shirt in the laundry?"

"Of course dear."

"What did you do with your jacket?"

"My jacket?"

"Yeah, I didn't know it was cool enough out for a jacket, but you had it on when you went up-stairs."

CHAPTER 11

Meagan Come Home

Meagan didn't expect to be at Uncle Jim and Aunty Marg's for longer than a couple of weeks. But now that two months had passed, she had established a routine and discovered that they afforded her the kind of freedom she craved when she lived in Ranvon.

She wasn't sure she could have escaped the moorings of her parents' place without the support from her Uncle and Aunt. Anxiety danced through her body while she endured two hours at the coffee shop where her parents told her, as a matter of fact, that the choice wasn't hers to move out. Her mom told her she just needed to meet a "nice young man" and then "settle down" and then her dad demanded to see the bus ticket she bought. Her mom's tears and claims she was abandoning them and her father calling her "cruel" to leave when her mom needed her - almost sucked out all her resolve. She kept her tears inside through it all, but the weight of the pressure was almost too much when they got home and she crumpled the bus ticket into her hand with plans to lobby it at her father's head before retreating for a long walk.

But then her dad quickened his pace as they entered their house with a straight line to the phone where he feverishly dialed Uncle Jim. That call gave new wings to her hopes for an independent life. She could only hear her father's side of the conversation, but that was enough. When her dad said, "Jim, she isn't ready for the independence you want to give her", she knew the conversation was leaning in her favour. Then when her dad almost screamed into the phone, "don't call me a dimwit!", she struggled to keep the laugh to herself as she clutched the bus ticket and slipped it back into her pocket. She had never enjoyed her father's rapid rising rage before – but she did in that moment. When he slammed the phone down on the receiver, she took sanctuary outside on a walk with Cindy, knowing her departure was just hours away. The jewelry she brought with her was easily sold in one of the many shops in Vancouver and, along with the money she saved, it bought her time.

She was glad to part with the jewelry she took from Mr. Montgomery's store as its presence in her belongings made her feel dirty and on edge. She justified the weekly heist she made as her only means of a breakout from the prison she felt at home. It is not the kind of person she is or wants to be, she'd tell herself. Initially she was horrified to discover how much she took on her last shift that belonged to Larnie Teach, which she'd lifted out of the drawer recklessly and in haste, though she made sure to leave the heavier piece that he had specifically identified. Larnie Teach. She will remember that name now. He was the person she had entrusted with the teeth. Somehow she thought if a stranger were to have possession of them, her family wouldn't be ripped apart by the discovery and she would escape blame. But she had heard nothing. She had asked Cindy several times if there is any news in town since she left with nothing more than the "usual boring stuff" coming back in response.

Larnie Teach's jewelry didn't fetch much and now that two months had passed, she assumed none of it caught anyone's attention – including the teeth. Perhaps the teeth were just thrown out when discovered? She shrugged her shoulders thinking about it. It is just as well. At this point, she didn't want anything to do with her family except for her phone chats with Cindy, concerns about Tommy, and the occasional conversation with her mom. She felt compassion for her mom, but had tired of hearing what she should do with her life.

She was so grateful to land at her Uncle and Aunt's. Their support for her meant she didn't have to answer the first help wanted signs at one of the various fast food outlets. Aunt Marg told her she should set a schedule every day to look for work but to be patient for something she would enjoy. The strategy paid off and two and half weeks after she arrived she landed the job at the Unique Things Jewelry and Art store. Aunt Marg also encouraged her to look at options for college, perhaps next year.

She missed her sis Cindy and looked forward to their phone chats in evenings when she could get the privacy to call. She could always tell from Cindy's voice when the call was no longer for their ears only.

Her Uncle and Aunt's place was small but she had her own room and they actually had a yard, unlike many of the newer houses in the neighbourhood where the house took up all the real estate. The only things they insisted on were that she keep the room clean, she tell them if she was going to be "home" for dinner and she help with some of the general cleaning, which she enjoyed anyway. Uncle Jim, at age 79, still enjoyed his gardening. Once she grasped the relaxation for the mind that it provided, she found pleasure in helping him dig, weed, clip and plant, as she would admire the handiwork and pride he took maintaining the yard.

Meagan was looking out from her window at the garden with such contented thoughts when she heard the loud ring of the phone from the living room. Aunt Marg kept the ringer on the phone "extra loud so she could hear it if she was outside", but its volume startled Meagan almost every time. She noted that Aunt Marg kept many things loud and was careful to keep eye contact in any conversation. The phone stopped ringing and within seconds she heard her Aunt's voice, also vociferous, "Meagan, Cindy's on the phone."

Aunt Marg handed her the phone with her customary parting words, "I'll leave and give you some privacy."

"Hi Cindy. So nice to hear from you...you alone?"

"At the moment. Mom's outside and so I'll watch to see when she comes in."

"So how're things? How's Mom and Tommy?"

"Things are okay. Tommy's good. We went to the lake a couple of days ago and Tommy swam all the way across it. Dad said he looks to be a better swimmer than me."

"Of course, just what you need, comparisons. Is Tommy playing football this year."

"Yeah, Dad finally let him do that and even bought him some equipment, but Tommy told me it's kind of embarrassing because not all the equipment fits. It seems Dad bought him used equipment without too much consideration to Tommy's size. But he played a couple of games and Mom went to watch him and I was there for one game."

"Wow, seems my little brother's growing up. What position does he play?"

"I dunno what position, he runs down the field to catch the ball. He tries hard, but he looks a little awkward out there with oversized equipment. I heard one of the parents telling Mom that she has some shoulder pads that will probably fit Tommy better... But I miss you Megs. It just doesn't feel as secure around here."

"Secure?"

"Well, you know, we would talk and I could tell you what's actually going and stuff and now I keep a lot of it inside. Sometimes I feel like it's about to explode inside me."

"I'm sorry Cindy. I couldn't stay any longer or I think I was going to get physically sick or kill someone. I still feel bad not telling you my plans beforehand, but that particular week was kind of crazy and things happened quickly. Plus, I was terrified that Dad or Mom would find out and then grill you and I didn't want to put you in that spot."

"I know. We talked about this, but you've never told me what happened that week that triggered things so quickly."

"Hey, I will. I promise. Just not yet. So, we're talking now, what's going on that you've been bottling up inside?"

"Well Dad's had more than a few of his outbursts. Mostly over petty stuff like when we had no sugar for his coffee the other day. He is so unpredictable I don't want to have friends over in case he humiliates me in front of them. You know how it is, I ask to go to a friend's place and Mom says, "Have them come over here." There is so much in this house that is never talked about. The other day Dad came home, the car had a new dent in the door, and so it's hard to even open it now. Nothing said. So much treated like it's just normal, but I don't think it is anymore."

"I know exactly how you feel. It's so different here. Uncle Jim and Aunt Marg treat me like an adult with my own decisions. Aunt Marg will tell me what they have planned for dinner and then say, "If you'd like something else, feel free to make whatever you want." She tells me they just eat simple and they like simple, but their lives are, I dunno, so much richer I guess."

"You goin to just stay there then?"

"I dunno. For now. They told me that I should pay rent after the first two months and so I have started paying now. It's still a lot cheaper than I could find on my own. It's comfortable here, easy to get to my work by bus and they're such fun and easygoing people to live with, even if they are so old."

"Sounds like you have a great life there."

"Oh, don't be too down sis, your time will come. Once you're finished high school, you and I will make a plan for you to get out on your own, okay?"

"You think so? Would give me a lot to look forward to."

"For sure. What about Mom, how's she?

"That's the other thing. Mom's been acting a bit weird lately. Kinda feels like something's up."

"Really? What do you mean weird?"

"I dunno. She's suddenly paying more attention to what we're doing and asking me all kinds of questions about my plans after high school. She has asked about you too."

"Really?! Like what?"

"Well she says you don't say much to her and she wanted to know if you were happy and what your plans might be and if you have a boyfriend yet. Those kind of things."

"Good grief. She just wants me to get married and find someone to look after me."

"Yeah and she's been very friendly with Eddie when he comes over, asking him questions like what his plans are and commenting how "nice of a young man" he is."

"Geez, I can see her doing that. It's a reason I wouldn't tell her about any of my boyfriends. How are things with Eddie?"

"Great actually. He's so nice, maybe too nice for me sometimes I think. His family's great too. Remember the diary of his grandfather's he found?"

"Yeah, of course. He let you read more of it?"

"He reads it to me. He doesn't let me actually hold the diary. Usually he reads it over the phone and I have to ask him to read it again. The stories are amazing, Megs."

"Like what?"

"You remember I told you that his grandfather had been laid off from his job but didn't want to tell his wife as it would worry her?"

"It was during the great depression, right?"

"Yes, that's right. Megs, it sure sounds like they didn't have much to eat during that time and most of the food was pretty basic...just breads and soup and stuff. Anyway, his grandfather gets a job as a reporter for a newspaper. He says it doesn't pay much and they continue to struggle with money and having enough food. But he loves the job. He writes great stories about what's happening in the world around them."

"Really, like what kinds of stories?"

"He wrote one about dust bowls. That made Eddie and I wonder what he was talking about and so we researched it at the library. We couldn't find the article his grandpa wrote, but we learnt that the dust bowls were the droughts. They didn't have much rain and it really affected the farmers, as their crops couldn't grow during the dust bowls. Anyway, his grandfather wrote a story on when the dust bowls might end. He wrote it to encourage everyone that they wouldn't last forever and once the farmers got some relief from the dust bowls, so would everyone else. His grandfather writes about the excitement he feels in bringing these stories to people and he interviews the farmers and weathermen for his story. Then there's another story he wrote about people being laid off from a cannery. He wrote about the impact it'd have on families and people moving away to find work."

"Sounds fascinating. What a treasure for Eddie to have that diary."

"Yeah, it is. We also discovered something really cool. The guy who got his grandfather the job at the newspaper was a close friend of his. Here's the cool part - his name was Larnie."

"Larnie? Really? That...that's quite an unusual name."

"Yeah, we found out it's Hungarian. Anyway, Eddie's father's name is Larnie. And so....we figure his grandfather named Eddie's father after his close friend that got him the job at the newspaper."

"You there Megs? Did you hear what I said?"

"Oh yes. Of course. Cindy, what is Eddie's last name?"

"Teach. Eddie Teach. Why?"

"Oh...um, it's nothin. Just wonderin."

"Oh, Megs, Mom's in the house now."

"Okay, maybe I should go."

"She saw me and has her hand up to her ear like she would be talking on the phone. I think she wants to talk to you."

As her mom approached, her pace was slow as she lugged her leg with a pronounced drag across the floor.

"Hold on a sec Megs, she's coming."

As her mom reached for the phone, Cindy watched her turn her head to look to the right, exposing the scar just below her neck. The sight of it reminded her about the scar that crawls across her mom's neck and to the edges of her collarbone. Her mom told her the length of the incision was necessary for the surgeon to push her windpipe to the side, giving access to her spinal cord in the back when they did the operation when she was 19. The sight of it caused Cindy to reach for her own neck and feel down to the spot where her mom has her scar, as if she should have one too.

"Cindy, can you give us some privacy, please?"

Cindy didn't move. What could be so private that she couldn't hear it? Knowing her father wasn't in the house to order her otherwise, she just looked at her mom.

"Oh okay. Hold on Megs. Your sister is giving me the Eeyore look. Alright, you both probably should hear this at the same time anyway. Cindy, I didn't want to tell you anything until I had a chance to talk to Meagan."

"What's up Mom?"

The concern in Meagan's voice caused a swell in Cindy's eyes. Her mom suddenly looked old to her. The grey hairs staking their claim in the roots of her head, the brown spot on her cheek and wrinkles around her eyes.

"Okay, here goes. You girls know that I've told you for many years that life is like a gift and I have been fortunate to walk all these years without a wheel chair. Walking's becoming more challenging though and I've noticed some things getting worse lately..."

"Oh Mom..."

As if needing energy to continue, she grabbed Cindy's hand and squeezed.

"It's...it's okay girls. I just...well lately it's been more of a struggle. A struggle with my speech at times and my walk and I don't know, I seem to forget some things. So I went to see the doctor the other day."

"Mom..."

"Cindy, my baby, you're always so sensitive. Getting all emotional before you even hear all the news. Well, I don't have all the news yet. The doctor told me that I may have Parkinson's disease and so they are going to send me for some tests."

"What's Parkinson's disease, Mom?"

"Cindy, did you hear Meagan's question?" Cindy nodded as her lip quivered.

"Well, it's a disease that attacks the central nervous system, he said. It causes things like shaking, slow movements, problems with walking and it can affect the brain and cause memory loss. I'm going for more tests though."

"Mom, who've you told this to? I don't think Uncle Jim or Aunt Marg know."

"Of course they don't Megs. Just your father and now the two of you. But Megs, I wanted to tell you because I need to ask you to do something for me."

"Sure Mom. What ever you want."

"I want you to come home."

Cindy was always used to her older sister coming to her defense, but this time it was her turn as she quickly filled the silence that followed her mom's request.

"Mom, we don't know everything yet. I can give you more help around here."

"Oh, thanks honey, I know you will. But I also need your sister here. What do you say Megs?"

"I don't know Mom. I'm working here at a good job. Aunt Marg and Uncle Jim..."

"Sweetie, those things can wait. You could get a job here. I need you here, can't you understand that?"

"Mom, like Cindy said, we don't know everything yet. Can we at least wait and see before I make any decisions to pack up my life."

"Pack up your life? Megs, you've only been there for a couple of months. Your life is here and I need you here. Please tell me you'll come home."

Meagan sat down as the room started to spin and she wished this were one call that Aunt Marg didn't give her privacy for. She wanted to do the right thing, but felt the life she had created was stable and fulfilling. If she went back to Ranvon, the glue of that life would lose its hold.

"Mom, I just can't right now."

"Meagan, sweetie, you know I wouldn't ask if it wasn't important. I don't know if my life is worth living with the disease and I need you here for support."

Cindy jumped in, she wanted Meagan to know she had her back. If Meagan came back, her fate in the future could be the same.

"But Mom, we don't even know if you have that disease yet."

"It's okay, Cindy. Mom says she needs me, I'll come home."

"Oh, that's so good to hear that Megs. You've made your mom's old heart glad. Let me know when you can get a bus ride back. Your dad and I will pay you back for the bus ticket."

Meagan suddenly felt like a zombie took hold of her body, draining her of all feelings. It's something she had often felt in the past. Acquiescing to what her parents wanted or needed and wrapping up her own desires tightly into the recess of her being. Feeling exhausted, she ended the conversation.

"Okay. Will do. I should go. Bye."

Immediately after the call Meagan felt overwhelmed and tired as she tried to sort out all the clutter the call stuffed into her brain and emotions. Instead, she got up to get her coat. A walk and some fresh air was her go-to survival medicine in these situations.

"Just heading out for a walk, Aunt Marg."

"Okay, Megs. You here for dinner? I've a basic cheese and tuna casserole ready to go."

"For sure and sounds great. I'll be back in a half hour or so."

The walking always helped her process and compartmentalize things in her head. She was just thinking of the potential complications of Eddie's dad being Larnie Teach when her mom dumped the news on her. How was it she agreed to go home? She isn't a selfish person, but why is she so accommodating? It is the right thing to do, she tells herself. Her mom is sick and needs her, how do you argue with that?

Meagan spent the rest of the walk visualizing the conversation with her boss at the store. He had just hired her and now she had to quit because her mom was sick. She would be packing up all her stuff again. She wondered how she could avoid Mr. Montgomery and Eddie's father when she returned to her life in Ranvon. Cindy would be glad to see her for sure. The joy of pride pounced on her, as she thought of her sister sticking up for her like that. Not sure she was that brave at 17. Then she stopped walking as she thought of her father and how she'd handle him. All the thoughts bouncing in her head had her crying as she made the final loop back to her Aunt and Uncle's place. On the steps of their house, she took a moment to regulate her breathing and wipe her face before she opened the door and stepped into the living room where Aunt Marg was sitting.

"You okay Megs?"

"Yeah, I'm okay."

"You look like you've been through an emotional shower. Something you want to talk about?"

"Aunt Marg, I don't want to bother you guys with this. You have been so good to me, but it looks like I have to go back home."

"What? Why? What's happening?"

Standing in the living room, Meagan filled her in about the phone call. When she was done, she felt almost as exhausted as she did after the call and she deposited herself onto the loveseat in the room and just stared into the empty space.

"Well dear, you are an adult and you'll have to decide for yourself what you're going to do. But I think you should stay here. Your mom will manage. You have a life here and it's selfish of your mom to expect you to pick up your life to help her."

"Selfish? You really think my mom's being selfish?"

"Absolutely! She's only thinking of herself. She isn't thinking of you at all."

"I didn't think of it that way."

"Meagan you are a grown woman, but the lens you're seeing this through is filtered by your mom. You need to look through the lens without her filter and what this will mean for *your* life. Not just this decision, but also the impact of this decision on decisions you make later. Decisions like where you want to live, what kind of work you want to do, and what kinds of friends you want. You want to go school, right? Are there school options in Ranvon?"

"If I move back it'd only be temporary Aunt Marg."

"Sweetie, I know your mom and she will extend that temporary as long as she can. Listen dear, your family is important to you and I understand that. You can still have your family as an important part of your circle and stay here."

"My circle?"

"All the people that are important to you are in your circle. You're at an age where your circle should be expanding. Well, that could be true of anyone at any age, I suppose. My point is, your family's always going to be a major part of your circle and you staying here now, doesn't change that."

"Thanks Aunt Marg. I wish you were on the call with her tonight. I didn't see this coming."

"Well, regardless, don't make a decision tonight. Sleep on it. I put the casserole in, let's have some."

"Thanks. I told my mom I was going to come home and so I can't imagine phoning her back to say I'm not."

"Well then I'll phone her and maybe your dad too."

"Oh, I didn't see you there Uncle Jim."

"Sorry, I don't mean to ease drop, but I think it's crazy for you to go back there and if you want I will phone your parents and tell them that."

"Now...now Jim. Meagan needs to make this decision herself and deal with it herself. I don't think either you or I should be phoning them."

"I would enjoy having the conversation with that dimwit."

"Jim, that's Meagan's father you are talking about. Your Uncle wants to help anyway he can, as do I," Marg paused as she gave Jim a hard stare, "but I think if you decide to stay here, you're the one that needs to communicate that to your parents."

Meagan pushed herself off the loveseat to give her Aunt a hug.

"Thank you so much. I love you guys."

"Meagan, as your Uncle I want to say that you need to stay here. Don't shake your head at me Marg. I'm not saying it isn't Meagan's decision."

He looked at Meagan as her swollen eyes started to moist again.

"It's your decision and we'll respect and support you in whatever you decide. But I have to say, we've seen your confidence grow each day you've been here. When you arrived, you looked confused and honestly frightened like an animal in a set of headlights. Each day since you've been moving the needle off that. I think you've been discovering new things about yourself and are finding new excitement and joy in that. Wouldn't you agree?"

"Absolutely Uncle Jim and you guys have made a huge difference in my life."

"Okay, before everyone gets too mushy, let's eat, I don't want the casserole going cold and I'm hungry."

"I'm too Aunt Marg. I'll set the table for us."

As Meagan made her way to the kitchen, she forced a smile to conceal just how insecure and scared she felt. The excitement of being with her aunt and uncle in the big city had provided an illusory mask, which she often displayed in overt bravado, to how scared she was of failing and ending up on the streets or unable to support herself. The call to go back to Ranvon offered security, safety and the familiar. Feelings that sought to overpower her fears in the big city, despite the support and assurances from her aunt and uncle. Her "excuse" for giving up her dreams - and the uncertainty and potential heartache they offer - was wrapped in the warm blanket of needing to be there for her ill mom. She knew in her soul that was a cop out and had other longer-term ramifications, but the secure comfort that Ranvon offered was an attractive invitation.

As they sat down to eat, Meagan's appetite was failing to follow the cover up of her emotions.

"Meagan, you haven't touched your food. I know it's not my cooking. You want to talk more about this?"

Chapter 12
Library Date

Eddie's pulse went for a sprint, as did his feet when the phone rang. Somehow, he knew when Cindy would phone. No one else was home and he grabbed his grandpa's diary, with the bookmark on the latest piece he was anxious to share with her.

"Eddie, I have some...well news that's a bit depressing and exciting, I guess."

"Oh...oh..kay."

"Well, do you want to hear it?"

Stretching the phone cord to its capacity, he moved to the couch and pushed the diary under his thigh as he sunk his body into the cushion.

"Of course, Cindy."

"So, it sounds like my sis is coming home."

"Oh, Meagan's coming home? That must be surprising, but depressing too?"

"That's not depressing. Well not really. See my mom's sick and she told Meagan that she needs to come home to look after her. I love my mom and I'm worried about her Eddie, but my mom has been sick for a while and sometimes it's just a bit rougher. I think she's using this to get Meagan to come home."

"You're not happy Meagan's coming home? I thought you missed her?"

"Oh Eddie. See you have this perfect little family that talks to each other and you just don't understand what it's like for me. My family doesn't talk about things or to each other properly, except for Megs and me of course. We can talk on the phone, but I don't want her to give up her dreams to come back here. My dad would make her life miserable and my mom's so needy right now she would hardly have a life."

"Okay. I wish I was as close to my sister as you are with Meagan. So your mom's sick?"

"Yeah, you know you've seen her. She just seems worse and is now saying she might have Parkinson's disease or something. When she first said it I was emotional and all and I'm worried about her, but now I think it's just a big manipulative thing to get Megs to come home."

"Parkinson's disease? What's that? Sounds serious."

"Oh yeah, sure...it might be. But she can't be asking Megs to give up her life like that for her. What will happen to me when I leave home?"

Eddie could hear the raw emotion in Cindy's voice as if her lips were quivering and he could see her. He suspected it from the moment she called and his anxiety spiked with her emotion.

"You okay Cindy?"

"Yeah, just the thought of Megs having to come home is upsetting. Can we.....can we talk about something else now please?"

Eddie reached his fidgeting fingers down to feel the diary under his leg as he pushed out the words that he hoped would be the right ones.

"Um sure, but I dunno maybe you should call Meagan?"

"Eddie you just don't get it! You don't understand my family. I have to go now. Bye."

The sudden dial tone left him bewildered and confused. Did Cindy just break up with him or just hang up? Should he call her back right away or give her space? What would he say if he did call her? He knows he doesn't understand her family but she doesn't understand his either and why does that matter anyway?

Cindy knew Eddie was right about her calling Meagan, but she already called once and no one answered and she doesn't know what to say to her. Meagan had always been there for her, to give her advice and help her with anything. If she tells Meagan she should stay in Vancouver, will her sister think she doesn't want her to come home or care? She looks at the clock and sees its only 5:30 and a half hour before the magical 6 o'clock.

Still trying to shift her emotions, Cindy grabs the phone as if it is a weapon against her feelings and dials.

"Eddie, I asked you if we could talk about something else because I needed a distraction. I don't need you to tell me what to do with my sister."

"Okay. I'm sorry....hey, glad you phoned back."

"Really?"

"Yeah, I just wasn't sure what it meant when you hung up."

"I didn't hang! Well, not really anyway. I just said goodbye."

"Okay."

"So, maybe you could read me more of your grandpa's journal?"

"Oh sure. Give me a sec."

The phone hung, swinging from its perch as Eddie leapt towards the couch to retrieve the diary. While no one else was home, relief filled his being when he found the diary where he had forgot it, wedged into the cushion.

"Hey, I'm back. I'll just turn to the page I marked. You sure you want to hear this now?"

"Yes. Please, I'm waiting. I thought maybe you had hung up on me for a second there."

"Oh no, no. I was just...just had to go get the diary. So, here we go. My grandpa writes about how my grandma receives the news about his job at the newspaper."

"Sept 27, 1936. When I showed Margaret the newspaper article, I thought she'd be excited for me. Her response, "how much did they pay

you for that?" let the air out of my enthusiasm. She followed it up with the calculated statement, "I hope you are good enough at it to keep this job and feed us with it." I knew then I had to come clean about my job search and the layoff at the fish plant. It was TNT again, I said as I explained Larnie's part in landing the job for me. There was no eye roll in response. No laughter. She just stood there as if to say, "You better offer something better than that." My disappointment and self-pity was absorbed by the look on Margaret's face and the reality of our situation. Hope was fading with dwindling food supplies and use of blankets for warmth. The lurk of cold weather on the horizon is a reality we can't avoid. Then a baby and toddler consuming ever more of our resources, time and the reservoir of available love in these trying time; had it become too much?

The crows' feet making deeper tracks around her eyes and the sternness in her cheekbones had pushed off the mask my wife was holding tight to. I thought I was sparing her heartache by not saying anything about the layoff at the fish plant, but clearly, she knew all along. I could feel the struggle she had to keep the tears at bay. She had been holding the sad knowledge about my job situation and with nowhere to deposit some of that emotion, the pressure just built.

I wanted to tell her how invigorating the job at the paper is. The interactions with the others at the paper, the hunting down the story and the writing - all breathing new life into my bones. I want her to feel this dream of mine taking shape. The dream of being a writer one day and with the journalism and my diary writings, I could write a book and become an author. Instead, I just reached out to comfort her, but she pushed me back. "I need to know Tony, will this job last?", she asked.

Unable to hold her gaze any longer, I looked past it to the plaster that is peeling off the wall at the entrance of the kitchen and the shedding carpet that is losing its grip to the floor in the corner. The walls of our small two bedroom house appeared closer than ever, as I caste my eyes towards the ceiling when I see dark stains. I can't tell Margaret that it may be mold, but then maybe she knows already and I am the one in denial. I wish the enthusiasm I brought with me when I stepped through the front door were as contagious as the gloom that is felt all around us.

When I caught her eyes again, her gaze had not left me as she channeled her emotion into a stern look, waiting for my response. I promised to bring home enough to keep us a float and then I mumbled that things will get better – my soft lobby that hope might still have a chance. It was enough to release the flood of tears from her as we shared a moment of tenderness together. I wanted to just hold that moment and stay there. Wait out the storm, however long it may be. But then as I looked over her shoulder, the reality of our hungry bodies couldn't be ignored.

I told her I had money from the paper for food and I left to pick up the much-needed groceries. As I stepped out the door, the fresh air bit into my cheeks and allowed my mind to depart our very real situation and transport me into the dreamscape of writing my next story. A story of how the banks are squeezing the farmers and the unemployed and could leave some homeless. Hope I am not among them. "

"So what do you think of that part Cindy?"

"Eddie, it sounds awful and...I don't know, kind of wonderful too. Your grandpa I mean. He seems like he was such a...I don't know, real and alive. He also writes so good it's like I can feel what he is saying. I wish I could write like that. Do you know if he ever wrote a book like he talks about?"

"I don't know, um, well, I don't think so. No one has ever mentioned it anyway. I didn't even know he wrote for a newspaper until I started reading his diary. Maybe we could go to the library again and see if we can find anything? I mean, would you go to the library with me?"

"Of course. You've never had a girlfriend before, have you? I want to do things with you and you just asked me out to the library! Ha-haha...oh Eddie, I don't think anyone has ever asked me out for a date to the library."

Eddie could feel the heat rushing into his cheeks as Cindy was talking. Everyone knows he hasn't had a girlfriend before, don't they? Are all girlfriends like this?

"You still there?"

"Yes...yes of course. Just listening to you Cind. Hey, if we go to the library, maybe we can also see if we can find more on what it was like to live in the 30s?"

"Yeah for sure. That's incredibly sad the way your grandfather describes it, without much food or heat and people out of work. I can't imagine. So is your father one of the babies he mentions?"

"Yeah, he must be. My dad has an older sister, so I assume he would be the baby that my grandpa mentions there. I just..."

"What is it?"

"I just knew nothing like this about my grandpa and that he was a writer and such."

"Oh. You going to tell your dad about the diary then?"

"No way. Not a chance. He would drill me about where I got it and I couldn't look at my mom if she knew I was in their closet."

"Of course. Your secret's with me Eddie. I won't tell anyone about the diary."

"Thanks Cind. You promise? It's important to me."

"Promise. Okay, I need to go. Can we talk tomorrow about our library date? huha"

"For sure Cind. I like your laugh. My parents should be home soon, but maybe we can get together tonight?"

"Yes, I was waiting for you to ask that."

"Sure. So you're going to phone Meagan first?"

"Don't talk to me about my sister Eddie."

"Oh, sorry."

"It's okay, just not now. Okay? I should go. Bye."

Eddie heard the dial tone before he could return her goodbye. Standing looking at the phone as if it represented his girlfriend, his desire to embrace it in a hug contrasted the energy boiling inside to toss it at the wall.

CHAPTER 13
Write a Letter

Meagan hit the snooze on her alarm, wishing for a few more hours sleep from a restless night. The discussion during dinner bounced from her future plans to what her life would be if she decided to return to Ranvon. Her Aunt Marg reinforced several times that it was her decision and she reminded her Uncle of that, but their gentle persuasion was as heavy as a coat at the first signs of winter. As warm and comforting too, as Meagan took security in knowing she wouldn't brave the decision alone if she stayed in Vancouver.

As she stood in the shower with the warm water cascading down, her thoughts were not on the day ahead and the time left to catch her bus for work as her routine dictated. Instead, she was back to when she laid awake late during the night with her eyes open thinking about her life in Ranvon. She didn't want what her mom desired; for her to marry a local and grow old in that town. Ranvon isn't as small as the resort town they had moved from a few years earlier, but she had seen the faces of living in a small town many times. A town where everything is familiar and hardly anything new. The new movie showing in the one cinema in town would create the wonderment and excitement it hardly ever justified, except that it announced something novel had arrived. A town where far too many people know far too much of what you did in your daily life and what they didn't know they filled in the gossip corners in town – in the cafés, the hairdressers, the movie theatre, the jewelry store and wherever else people would congregate. A town where there were one or two principle occupations – the mill, or the mine and everyone else fed off that. A town where a stranger walks into a café and in the span of several minutes gets a steady glance that is just short of an uncomfortable stare from all the "regulars". The thoughts of it made her feel claustrophobic, as she shut off the water and reached for the towel, as if she could dry off the feelings of dread.

The crowdedness of the bus, with its noise of chatter, squeaky wheels and announcement of the stops from the driver brought the relief Meagan sought from her thoughts; as she people watched and absorbed the sounds and smells of the commuters. At first, she didn't hear the man sitting kitty corner to her.

"Excuse me miss, I guess you can't help me then?"

"Oh, I'm sorry. I didn't hear you, what did you say?"

"Well, I was just wondering if you might have a pen, as the ink is no longer flowing from mine."

She reached into her purse and rummaged around until the pen at the bottom pricked her finger. As she pulled it out, she glanced over at him. His shoulder length waving dirty blond hair that threatened to cover his eyes was highlighted by his reserved smile.

"Here you go. I'd like it back though; can you tell me how far you're going?"

"I'm stopping just past Fraser street, you?"

"Main. So not far from you."

"Well that works well then. I can finish my letter by that time I think."

"Your letter?"

"Yes, sorry. I'm writing a letter to my mom. She's back in Ontario and I want to let her know what it's like here and that I plan to stay a while."

"Oh, is she expecting you to go home soon?"

He reached out his hand.

"Sorry, my name is Cleve."

"Ah, nice to meet you Cleve...Meagan." Meagan pointed her finger to her chest as she said her name.

"Nice to meet you Meagan. My parents haven't said they expect me to come back home, I just didn't put a timeframe on it. But, they're my parents, you know. When I came here I just got the sense that they figured I would stay in Ontario and become a fisherman like my dad."

"Oh, and you don't want to be a fisherman?"

"Oh I dunno. I quite like fishing actually, among other things. But I'm enjoying it here and making a bit of a life here, you know."

Cleve twirled the pen between his fingers as their conversation continued. Cleve had arrived in Vancouver about six months before Meagan and was renting a one-bedroom basement suite and working as a cook at an Italian pizzeria. He grew up close to Lake Ontario where his dad worked as a fisherman. When he told his parents he wanted to explore and move out to British Columbia, his dad was quick to point out that BC had fishing opportunities that are "world class". He thinks they are disappointed that he's working as a cook at a restaurant and anytime he talks to them, his dad asks him about the fishing. He is looking into one of the community colleges and their culinary arts program - he often still fishes on his days off.

"Culinary arts? So you want to be a cook?"

"Well a chef actually. I dunno, maybe. If I'm not going to be a full time fisherman, I have to find something I enjoy. I don't want to work just above minimum wage all my life, you know. How about you. Meagan?"

Meagan thought she had escaped the "what are you going to do with your life?" questions, but Cleve's question had a different texture to it. He looked to be close to her age and in a similar situation and his questions felt more born from genuine curiosity than a worried expression.

"Well I enjoy working with jewelry and am looking into that more. I am also checking out colleges, just to get some ideas. My parents want me to just get married and settle down, so I haven't had much encouragement or direction."

As soon as the words escaped from her thoughts, Meagan wished she could collect them back and stuff them away. Why did she just say that to this good-looking stranger?

"Hey, so you talk to your parents on the phone or just write them letters?"

"Oh, sometimes. But just after 6 pm. When it's cheaper, you know."

"Me too."

"Ah, well Meagan, hope your search goes well. My stop is next, so here's your pen back."

"Oh sorry, you didn't even get to write your letter."

"That's okay. I'll do it on the bus tomorrow. Maybe I'll see you here again sometime?"

"Oh yes. Yes, this is my usual..." Meagan stopped mid sentence as Cleve stood up and reached out his hand and said goodbye.

She watched him leave as she felt a stab to her chest for her little white lie. She was running late this particular morning and this was not her regular route. She ran several blocks to catch this bus line instead, as she realized she could be late for work if she had to wait for another bus. As she watched Cleve leave, she took note of his height. Definitely taller than her five foot seven frame, probably close to six feet and with a slim body but stocky legs. The dirty blond mullet with the curls at the end made its way past his shoulder blades, resting about a third of the way down his back.

As she got up for her stop, the thought hit her like a sudden shot of light in a room. She should do what Cleve is doing. Write her mom a letter.

CHAPTER 14

Secrets in the Closet

Eddie and Cindy's "date" at the library plunged them into stories from the great depression. They discovered articles and journals from the '30s that took them on a voyage into a past they knew little about.

While neither of them could comprehend what thirty percent unemployment or the drop in domestic product or lower wages really meant, it was the stories of what living was like then that absorbed several hours of their day in the library. They found the best stories in old newspaper articles. They read how soup, beans and noodles were usually the main meal and if there was meat, it might have been horse meat. A family didn't even think of buying clothes, existing clothes were sewed and patched and when outgrown were traded with friends for other used clothes that had been patched. Families typically lived in small houses and many took in extra boarders who would sleep in the living room or even the kitchen. Heat was a luxury and only turned on if the clothing hanging to dry started to freeze. They read how many simply didn't have heat and would just huddle together by a potbelly stove.

They followed the stories of protests and hunger marches in the streets. Christmas, for those that worked was a day off, but it was a day off without pay and thus hardly celebrated. They read about one girl who was in grade school at the time and her parents sent her to live with others so they could feed themselves. She was sent to live in a house where several other children were also exiled from their families out of necessity. It was a three-bedroom house with twelve children living in it. Cindy read that story twice imagining what would have happened in their family with her mom's restrictions. She read another story about a family where the father had died and the mother and her eight children were placed on the side-walk with their possessions, when they lost their house because they couldn't pay the mortgage. She read how the community came to the family's aid and housed the kids and the mother in various places, but they were no longer together as a family.

While the riveting stories about the great depression captivated them, Eddie left the library discouraged, as the hunt for his grandpa's writings bared no fruit. "Not a single morsel", Eddie said as they sat at the table in his kitchen and he recounted their futile efforts to find anything at all on his grandpa's writings.

"Your grandpa didn't live here, Eddie. If we want to find newspaper articles he wrote, we probably should go to a library in Ontario where he wrote them."

"Yeah, that's not going to happen."

"Oh don't be such a sourpuss, look at what we discovered about the great depression and how it fits with your grandpa's diary."

"A sourpuss?"

"Yeah that's what my mom calls someone when they are too negative and miss the positive things. Well, at least she used to say that. Lately she's the sourpuss...hey I have an idea."

Eddie looked at Cindy with suspicion. Her ideas often would trumpet that trouble was on its way.

"Oookay."

"Oh don't be so skeptical. It's a good idea. You want more information about your grandpa, right? Well, the diary you've been reading says it's volume two, right""

"Well, that's what we think it might mean."

"Of course that's what it means. That means he wrote other diaries."

"I realize that's possible, but..."

"But what? What we need to do is look in that box you told me about. There has to be more in there."

"Oh Cindy, I just can't..."

"Can't? Of course you can sourpuss."

"Please, Cindy, don't use that word around my mom. If you do, she'll use it. Probably look it up and lecture me on what it means."

"On what means?"

"Oh hi Mrs. Teach."

Eddie could feel his mom's hand on his shoulder as he stiffened with thoughts of how long she had been listening in.

"Sounds like you two are having an interesting discussion. Relax your shoulders Eddie. That's not good for your back. Something you didn't want me to hear?"

Eddie held his breath any time Cindy started to talk to one of his parents. He didn't trust her filter even if he could benefit from her quick-on-her-feet responses.

"Just a word that my mom uses sometimes Ms. Teach."

"Well, what's the word?"

"Oh, it's nothing really."

Mae Teach had many passive aggressive tricks in her repertoire. It was her patient stare in a conversation that she employed on Cindy. Like she was in combat with her and would just will her to speak.

"Well...it's a word she uses if she thinks I am grumpy or too negative and she tells me not to be a sourpuss."

"Sourpuss, eh? That's a good word. I'll have to look that one up. Your mom's a very pleasant person, so sad about her health and that accident many years ago."

"You know my mom?"

"Yes, Eddie might have told you, I like to meet the parents of his close friends. So, I contacted her and we had tea the other day. I'm so sorry that she struggles with her health like that. She certainly has some fascinating stories from her youth."

"Yeah she does. You meet my dad then?"

"No I haven't had the pleasure yet."

"You should and let me know if it's a pleasure."

"Oh...well I guess I will. Your mom has stories from her youth that could make an entertaining movie, that's for sure."

"I don't think my mom would want a movie of her life, that's for sure."

Mae Teach looked at her son, wondering how it was that he found such a feisty girlfriend.

"Cindy, do your parents ever meet the parents of your friends?"

"It depends on the friend. Hey Mrs. Teach, do you know where Mr. Teach got his first name Larnie from?"

Eddie watched his mom spar with his girlfriend with some delight until Cindy jabbed back with that question. He resisted too long of a stare at her so his mom wouldn't see it, but Cindy's cheeky smile showed she caught the intense glance he threw at her. His mom picked up the exchange too.

"Well that's a bit of an unusual question for a young lady to ask."

"I just ask because it's an unusual name, that's all. No big deal."

"Okay. It was the name of an old friend of Eddie's grandpa. He died in World War Two. Um, the friend that is. Eddie, has your dad told you this?"

"No. He hasn't told me where his name came from."

"Okay...so, there. Now you know. You should ask your dad about it sometime."

Eddie noticed his mom's voice hit a less certain tone and he sensed her uncomfortableness in the conversation. She confirmed it when she abruptly changed the subject.

"So, school starts again in a couple of weeks. You two excited about it?"

"Mom, I don't think teenagers get excited about school too much."

"Well, I am excited to see my friends, Mrs. Teach."

"Eddie, you won't be able to sleep in any more. Your sister will be home in a few days and your dad has planned our annual camping trip on the Labour Day long weekend."

Eddie didn't feel the excited anticipation for the annual trip up to Hathaway Lake as he had in past years. He just wanted to stay home. Then he could spend more time with Cindy.

"Cindy, does your family camp?"

"Not really. We've just camped a couple of times with my aunt and uncle."

"Well anyway, I'm heading out to my friend's across the street. We have some material patterns to go through for our quilts. Eddie, what are you up to this afternoon?"

"We're just going to hang out Mom. Gabe and some friends are playing video games later at his house and I might go there, just waiting for him to call me."

"Oh, okay. You know the rules with just the two of you here."

With that, Mae looked at Cindy with a slight nod. Something that said more than a friendly gesture of goodbye, but a pantomime that told her who was in charge in this house.

As soon as the door clicked shut behind his mom, Cindy's strapped down thoughts sprung out.

"Okay, we have to do it now!"

"Do what?"

"What we talked about! We need to go into your parents' bedroom and see what else is in that box."

"What *we* talked about?"

"Oh don't be such a wus Eddie! Not sure your mom will find that word in her dictionary. Come on let's go."

She stood up from her chair and grabbed his hand. He didn't resist. His tendency, to let the flow of her energy carry him, took over. The pace Cindy set as they made their way up the stairs was brisk enough that Eddie could hear himself breathing. He finally stopped her at the door to his parents' bedroom.

"Really? Are you really going to chicken out now and say we can't go in there? We couldn't find what you hoped for at that library. The things you want to know are behind that door."

"We don't know that for sure."

Cindy put her hand on the door handle and turned it.

"Well there's only one way to find out."

Eddie stopped her again once they were inside.

"Okay we'll do this. But let me go in the closet and leave it to me to move things and get the box out. I know where things are in there. You can keep your ears awake, in case someone comes home."

"Ears awake?"

"You know what I mean."

Eddie took a deep breath as he moved toward the closet. He glanced back at Cindy, lifted his index finger to his puckered lips and then opened the bi-fold doors.

The closet appeared more spacious than he remembered. He cast his eyes to the top shelf and confirmed the bag he had seen before was still there. His curiosity of its contents couldn't be satisfied at that moment, certainly not with Cindy's knowing eyes on him. Eddie then moved the hanging clothes on the left side of the closet to give better access to the corner. He knelt down, looked up at Cindy and held up his left hand as a stop sign, before reaching in for the box. He first felt the top of it where he expected the playboy magazine, it wasn't there. His breathing stopped as he gently pulled the box out. He exhaled slowly, keeping his sense of panic below the surface. Opening the lid, the naked glossy picture of Marylyn Monroe stared up at him. He was certain he had left the magazine on top of the box as he had found it. "Someone's been in here", he whispered to himself as he closed the lid again.

"You say something, Eddie?"

"Sssh."

"Bring it out and up to the bed, let's have a look."

"Give me sec, and let's be quiet, okay?"

With the box now halfway out of the closet, Eddie reached up and swung the clothes on the hangers back to the left. His fretfulness pushed him into an unintended rush and a couple of the clothes let go of their hangers and fell to the floor.

"Just leave them, we have to put the box back when we are done anyway. Let's look at what's in it."

Eddie looked up at the now disheveled organization of the closet and paused. He then decided to follow his girlfriend's order, and brought the box over to the bed, where she was sitting, fidgeting and waiting.

He firmly placed his hand on the lid of the box as soon as it landed on the bed.

"Look, these are my grandpa's belongings and I need to put them back in the box the same way we found them. So I want to be the only one to touch the things in it, okay?"

"Oh alright then, but can we get on with it?"

Eddie had been inspired by the focused determination that Cindy would show, but he also knew she could rush ahead, "like a bull in a china shop" his mom would say. He witnessed it in the Library when he would be reading one newspaper article, while she was hunting down more information on something she discovered. That part of her personality was also on display when she was in kitchen with his mom and when she insisted they rush to his parents' bedroom afterwards. He knew he had to muster what was in him to wrestle some control of the situation.

Before prying the lid off the box, Eddie turned to her again.

"I know what some of the things are in here and...there are some girly magazines."

"What, like playboys? Worried I'll think your grandpa was a dirty old man? Relax Eddie, let's get on with it and get it opened to see if there's another diary."

Eddie lifted the lid and placed it on the bed. He immediately took out the playboys on top and placed them face down beside the lid. Cindy rolled her eyes in demonstration of her impatience.

"A lot of this stuff I remember from last time, so I'll just take those things out and keep them in the same order."

Eddie could feel Cindy's weight leave the bed before he had time to react.

"Hey, you see that? There's another box on the other side of the closet."

"Cindy, please!"

Eddie's desperate cry was enough to stop her from picking up the second box. She had recklessly pushed the hanging clothes to the other side and several took to the floor. Cindy's action exposed the right side of the closet and its corner, where the second box rested.

"I wasn't going to pick it up. Just relax Eddie. I'll leave that for you to do. You're so sensitive about me touching any of your grandpa's stuff. We should look at this box first though, since you've already been through most of that one."

Eddie moved quickly to the closet but paused to survey the scene. Cindy's impulsive actions had disturbed any image he had left of what the closet looked like before.

The box labelled "Dad's Stuff Box 2" wasn't as deep in the corner of the closet as the box on the left side. When Eddie put it on the bed beside the first box, he held his gaze at it, while he studied the writing and the tape down the sides of the lid. He waved off protests from Cindy to simply open it.

"I'm fairly certain that writing on the top is my dad's. This tape is a problem. I don't know how to open it without disturbing things. I need to put it back as we found it."

Eddie grabbed Cindy's hand as she reached for the box. As he held her hand, he saw the same thing she had spotted. The translucent tape on one end was curled and frayed on its ends. Perhaps from age or a previous intruder into the box? Either way, it gave access as Eddie meticulously rolled up the tape from the bottom, carefully avoiding striping any of the cardboard from the box. Once his fingers were comfortably clear under the tape, he pulled it up with a steady and cautious movement. He then carried out the same procedure with two other pieces of tape and was confident he could remove the lid enough to access the contents. The lid now dangled over the side of the box, as tape from one side kept it attached.

Eddie lifted out the black and white "Time" magazines as his eyes widened with curiosity of his find.

"What's that?"

Cindy's eyes focused on the velvet case that lay under the magazines and she reached in to snag it. Eddie's sharp reflexes caught her hand before she could grab it like a prize. He gave her a stare and then pulled out the velvet case. As they both sat on the bed, he opened the case. The necklace captured their stares and held them in silence for several seconds.

"That's...that's not what I expected to find."

"It's beautiful Eddie. Would this be your grandpa's?"

"I've never seen this before, I don't..."

"Hello! Anyone home?!

"Who's that?"

Eddie looked at Cindy with fear in his eyes as he motioned with his index finger to his lips and whispered in her ear.

"It's Bev. She must be home early. We need to get all this shit back in the closet quickly and quietly."

His use of a four letter word silenced her - she had never heard him talk like that before. Knowing he needed help in case Bev came up stairs, Eddie motioned for Cindy to restore the hanging clothes to their former configuration while he packed things back into the boxes and placed them back in their place of residence in the corners of the closet. As they exited his parents' bedroom, Eddie turned around to face Cindy. They were close enough for a passionate kiss, when he whispered.

"Maybe you should hide in my bedroom?"

"Eddie, I'm not hiding from your sister."

"Eddie, is that you up there?"

He shifted to move quickly down the stairs to avoid any chance of meeting Bev on the stairway. With Cindy close on this heals, Bev greeted him at the landing.

"There you are. How's my little brother? Oh, hi. Cindy?"

Bev acknowledged Cindy with a nod of her head.

"Hi Bev. How are you?"

"Great. Sooo...you are here?"

"Yes. I'm...well, your cute brother here is now my boyfriend."

Bev gave Eddie a look that had him expecting a finger wagging next.

"So, you two know each other?"

"Oh, yes. I'm friends with Meagan, Cindy's sister. I've been at their house a couple of times. So, yes, we've met."

Eddie's gaze shifted to Cindy as he mimicked his sister's look at him.

"Well, yes, of course. So...perhaps I should get going. Sounds like you two should catch up on your summers."

"No...no don't leave because of me. Actually, Eddie where's Mom?"

"Oh, she's out at Mrs. Michaels across the street. Working on quilts."

"Great, cause I need to talk to her."

Eddie's fearful look at Bev triggered their sibling solidarity.

"Oh hey. Don't worry I won't say anything about you being upstairs with Cindy."

"Thanks sis."

Bev smiled with a slight nod and wink to Cindy.

"The reason I came home early was to get my pictures from the camp developed before the family camping trip and I need Mom's help. So, if Mom's at the neighbours, I think I'll go over there now."

With that, Bev left the two of them standing there.

"Well that's great. Let's go back up and see what's in those boxes."

"Cindy, no. I...not now. She might come back right away and my mom could come home with her."

Eddie held strong against Cindy's pout and campaign to return to the bedroom. Besides the risk he felt, the second box and the necklace they saw took him by surprise. If he was to get another opportunity to see what his grandpa left from the past, he wanted to do that where he could mentally process it and filter what he would disclose to his overly curious girlfriend.

Eddie ultimately succeeded in keeping Cindy downstairs when he changed the subject by asking how she knows his sister and why she hadn't told him before? Cindy brushed it off as uneventful. She casually remarked that she thinks their two sisters met at a local swimming pool or "something" and she had visited their house a couple of times. Her blasé explanation with little inflection in her voice was a departure from the edge and animated manner that Eddie had come to anticipate from her.

As Eddie was about to explore more, the phone rang and it was his friend Gabe inviting him over to play video games with other friends. As he hung up Cindy kissed him goodbye with a promise to see him the next day.

After an afternoon of video games at Gabe's house, Eddie arrived home in time for dinner. Over the soup and biscuits, Bev told the family about her summer volunteering at camp. Later that evening as he was heading to bed, Bev stopped him in the hallway.

"Hey bud. I want to hear about your summer too. I'm sure we will have lots of time at Hathaway, but maybe we could take some time in the next few days?"

"Sure."

"So, I didn't know you had a girlfriend. I just want to say I'm happy for you and don't worry I won't say anything about you being upstairs with her."

"Thanks. You know Cindy?"

"I thought you might ask that. Remember last year when I was doing a research project at school about physiotherapy?"

Bev took Eddie's imperceptible nod as a sign to continue.

"Well, anyway, it was part of the career week where we had to do a story on something we may be interested in and I picked physiotherapy. I went to see a physiotherapist to understand what they do. The therapist there was helping a client at the time who turned out to be Meagan's ...well and Cindy's, mom. We got to talking about her challenges and then Meagan came to pick her up from that appointment. So then Meagan and I started chatting and we became friends. I haven't seen her all summer of course and am hoping to go to the jewelry store where she works and say hi."

"She won't be there, she quit."

"Really? How do you know?"

"Cindy told me. She moved to Vancouver but she's moving back because their mom's sick."

His bedside table light illuminated just enough brightness that he could read before going to sleep. His mom insisted it be part of his routine to read in bed each night. His memories still include her reading to him before he insisted he could read himself. As he headed to bed, recited in his head are the habits of her words, "reading expands your mind and if you read a bit each day, you'll be surprised how many books you will read each year."

Before climbing between the sheets, Eddie pulled out the two things he kept between the mattress and the box spring and slid them under his pillow. Lying in bed, he reached under his pillow and pulled the magazine into the light. He had read some of the stories in it, which certainly increased his vocabulary. Not what he could "charm" his mom with he tells himself with a smirk. Flipping through the naked pictures had him wondering how old his grandpa was when he bought the magazines. As his thoughts drifted back to his grandpa, he reached under the pillow for the diary. The last place he left off was marked by the presence of the piece of paper with Cindy's name and phone number.

"Oct 15, 1933. This is the 12th year I have woken up on October 15th thinking about her. I know Mom will be too and I will have to phone her later. I wish I could afford to take her out to dinner and have our visit over good food, but maybe a phone call is better. I will call later this afternoon after Mom has had the morning to herself without someone reminding her. A morning she will take off from work. She will pray and list things she is thankful for. She will read her list to me when we talk.

My Aunt Anna will phone her too. Mom will ignore her calls until the afternoon, and Mom will tell me about that too. It has become out ritual. Grousing about Aunt Anna is part of the ritual. Aunt Anna of all people should know better, I will tell her, and that will start the discussion about Annabella. My sister. Born on Oct 15, 1905. A "new century baby" my mom would say. I will stop Mom from going down the hole of "if onlys'. If only we didn't move to Windsor from Traverse City. From one country to another. If only my father hadn't been one of those who died in the Great War. It just seems so random the people who died and suffered from the war. If only she had not stopped for gas before getting to her sisters, then Annabella wouldn't have had the opportunity to run away. If only she knew what city Annabella was in then she could...It's usually on the third or fourth if only that I would stop her and read from her thankful list that I had copied down. We would talk about what the rest of the week holds and when the winter will take its grip on us. It's all part of the ritual. A time for breathing, a time for thankfulness, a time for mourning infused with regretful emotions, a time to reminisce and a time to put one foot in front of the other and continue our quest to bring meaning to our lives."

Eddie reached over and turned off the light as the diary laid on top of him. The darkness brought a stillness and quiet the light could not attain. In that stillness, he worked to unspool the details from his grandpa's diary. His Aunt Annabella visits them every Christmas. His grandpa is dead but she is alive. What unspoken stories and family mysteries are alive with her?

CHAPTER 15

Haunts from the Past

Her chest heaved from the sprint to the bus, and she paused on the steps to catch her breath and scan the faces for Cleve, who'd saved a seat for her. Their friendship hadn't developed into anything romantic, but he had invited her to go fishing with him on the weekend. They both had the same three days off and that was just four days away.

He asked her opinion on the letter he wrote to his mom. His letter was warm and detailed his daily routine, including the bus rides to work with "his new friend". He even provided a brief description of her as having "long brown hair with curls and soft green/grey eyes that squint with a smile" and then he added that she is a "thoughtful and curious soul who is also new to the city". He expanded on details of his work and in his salutations, he included a statement that "BC is home now". Meagan read his letter and made mental notes of changes to make to the third version of her own letter. She would not be mentioning her "new friend", that she was certain of. Feeling an obligate reciprocity, she promised to share her letter to her mom with him. That commitment made Cleve part of the audience she was writing for, which included her dad and Cindy. She looked at Cleve, studying him, as the words "thoughtful and curious" were swirling in her ears. Perhaps she should add something about him to the version of the letter she'd show only to him.

Meagan's journey home after work afforded the time to organize her thoughts, as she would wait another half hour to be on the same bus as Cleve. During her shift, a customer who looked strikingly like Larnie Teach had startled her. Now as she waited for the bus, she tried to focus on the letter to her mom, but the seared image of the teeth and the knowledge that it was Eddie's dad whom she left them with, crowded out everything else.

When she arrived home, after a cursory hello to her Aunt, who was working on dinner in the kitchen, Meagan headed straight to her bedroom, on a mission to solve the riddle in her head.

As soon as she walked in the room, her eyes focused on the suitcase that stood just off the corner of the room beside the bedside table. A glance at the bedside table, where the third version of her letter sat, stole her thoughts for a moment as she murmured to herself to finish it "tonight". She returned her attention to the suitcase where she left the envelope. Throwing the suitcase on the bed, she opened it and from the zippered storage space inside, retrieved the envelope with the newspaper story. Her evidence of the origins of the teeth.

After she discovered the teeth, she hid them with other personal things. She hid them well enough that *she* had to search to find them; which happened two months before their families move to Ranvon.

Meagan had watched her mom struggle to pack up a box in anticipation of the move. Alone in the house one day, she decided, as a gift to her mom, to pack up some of the belongings from their storage area. It was there that she found the clipped article from the Coastal Advocate. The article was dated September 13, 1956. Its heading: HUMAN REMAINS FOUND. The article says they found human remains at a site where a barn had burnt down. The barn, which was likely in "a state of disrepair" before being destroyed by fire, had burnt down eight years previously. The fire was attributed to mischievous teenagers in the area. However, this new discovery had a "curious and potentially criminal nature" to it. The body found had its teeth removed. Without the teeth, "the authorities couldn't identify the body with dental records but it is believed to have been a male in his 40's". The remains had signs of fire damage, indicating the person may have died in the fire. The article ends with a line asking anyone who may know of a person who went missing eight years previously, around the time of the barn fire, to contact the police. The address of where the barn was located and the phone number to the police were included at the end of the article.

Reading the article again brought back the familiar churn of bile in her stomach that hit her when she found the clipped newspaper article in her parents' belonging. Her ill feelings quickly gave way to the disgust and ire she held towards her father. Clearly, he had clipped the article because he had the teeth the police were looking for. The teeth that she found. The teeth she slipped to Larnie Teach.

Meagan then pulled out the piece of paper where she had copied down the names from the tiny paper that was inside the leather pouch with those teeth.

WG. JB. LM. PF. Teddy? She suspected the first initials to be from the guy who died in the fire; whose teeth she had. There was a homeless person in town during that time that some speculated was the dead person, but his name was unknown. The second initials on the paper she knows are her dads. She heard stories from her uncle about her dad's fascination with fire when he was younger. "A pyromaniac" her aunt called him. She had to look the term up in the dictionary. One story was that they had to shut the school down for a week when he and a friend nearly burnt it to the ground. The story, that her aunt asserts gets additions to each time it's told, was that they climbed the fire escape to the roof top where they had a campfire. When it created a hole in the roof, they rappelled into the classroom with rope and found the math test sheets that had been handed in and burnt them. "Gunterson, the math teacher, wasn't very popular with the boys and so adding that to the story made your dad a hero to some", Aunt Marg told her.

Another story was about a local barn that was burnt down and the "suspects were teens" and she was told that her dad would have been the first suspect to come to mind. "Must be the same barn in the article," she surmised. Fits with the timeframe the newspaper article gives, as that is the time when her dad would have been in his "troubled youth" as her Uncle put it. Then there are the burn marks her dad has on his arm, supposedly from an incident that he claims he got from saving his friend Packer's life. A story she has heard many times over the years. Packer must be PF on the list. That burn mark must have been his "souvenir" from the barn he burnt down and she guessed Packer was there to help. Since her discovery, she would think about the tale her dad spun every time she saw the burn marks on his arm. "LM" fits for a dentist she knew in town and "Teddy" must be another friend of her dads.

The gears churned in her head as she thought through the rationale she had created for handing those teeth to a stranger. She didn't want to go to the police. But if someone else were to make the discovery, then when the police arrested her dad, there would be sympathy for the whole family and people would rush in the spirit of love to help. The government may step in to help too. The police could check dental records and the truth would be revealed without her having to be part of it all. She was turning the plan over in her mind again when the sudden knock on the door jerked her off the bed.

"Hi sweetie. Dinner will be ready in about five minutes. I hope stew and biscuits are okay?"

"Oh...yes, yes, thanks Aunt Marg. That sounds wonderful. I'll be down in a few minutes."

Taking a deep breath to calm her suddenly frayed nerves, Meagan's thoughts were full of doubts as her mind brimmed with questions. What if Larnie Teach doesn't do anything with the teeth and maybe just throws them away? Perhaps she should have put the newspaper article in with them? If her plan somehow works, will her father be arrested without a disturbance? Will her mom, brother and sister really be looked after and are they safe?

During dinner, purposeful pauses and thoughtful looks told her that her aunt and uncle had decided to leave the topic of her moving back to Ranvon as hers. The respect they showed for her own decisions was a new and liberating experience that she was still adjusting to appreciate the freedom it brought. The room filled with effortless conversations as they talked about Uncle Jim's plans for the garden and Meagan's new friend Cleve, which led to a story from Aunt Marg about a boyfriend she had before she met her uncle that was full of mishaps and humour. Aunt Marg ended the story with a wink to Meagan as she said, "Remember there are lots of fish in the sea," and then she patted Uncle Jim's hand as she added, "And I'm glad I found the one right for me."

She retreated to her room after dinner, determined to finish the letter to her mom. It was on the fourth version before she read it again and was satisfied it was ready to send. She wrote it out again to give herself a copy and while she had planned to show it to Cleve first, she felt a sudden urgency to mail it as if the ink might lift off the paper if she didn't. She put it in an envelope and before time could liquefy her courage, sealed it, put a stamp on it, and went for a walk to drop it in the mailbox at the end of their street.

She returned to the house and as soon as she opened the door, she heard her Aunt on the phone.

"Oh, here she is. Meagan, your mom's on the phone." Her aunt trotted out of the room as soon as Meagan had the phone.

"Hi Mom."

"Hi sweetie. I was just phoning to see if you have booked your bus ticket yet?"

"No, I haven't Mom. I...well I have to talk to work about my plans and..."

"Oh, you haven't told your work yet? You better do that Meagan. I'm sure they will understand. You can't put it off, it would just make it awkward. As I've always told you, don't procrastinate. Delaying things doesn't make it easier, quite the opposite honey. You have to bite the bullet so to speak. Promise me you will talk to them tomorrow?"

"Mom I'm not..."

"You're not?"

"I'm not going to....talk to them tomorrow. I have to talk to the manager Charlie and he's away. It'll have to wait 'til next week."

"Oh, okay. Next week is fine, I guess. Just don't delay it longer. You'll feel better once you tell them your plans."

"Yes, I know."

"Anyway, I wanted to let you know we found out we can pre pay your bus ticket from here. That way you can just pick it up at the bus depot in Vancouver. We just need to know the date and time."

"That's convenient."

"So you let me know the date once you have that figured and we will plan to pick you up at the bus depot too."

"Yeah Mom...I'll keep you informed. So...I'm going away on a trip tomorrow. With some friends...girl friends from work and we're going camping near Capilano. We'll be gone 'til next Tuesday. It should be fun."

"Well good for you Meagan. I was at the Capilano suspension bridge many years ago. It's very beautiful there."

"How are you doing Mom?"

"I'm okay. Better knowing you're coming home. It's a struggle some days. This disease is pretty awful. It's sapping my energy and walking is painful."

"So the doctor confirmed that you have Parkinson's?"

"Not officially yet, no. But I'm sure that is what it is. Cindy's here and she wants to talk to you, so I should go. Let's chat when you get back so we can get that bus ticket booked for you."

"Okay, bye Mom."

"Hey."

"Hi Cindy. Nice to hear your voice. You able to talk?"

"Maybe better later. Just wanted to say hi."

"Oh, Mom's still there, eh?"

"Yes."

"Okay, why don't you call me later? Or maybe tomorrow?"

"That would be better. Tomorrow."

"Six o'clock?"

"Yes."

"Okay, let's chat then sis. Don't let Mom know we're going to chat, she thinks I'm going to be away on a camping trip. I'm going away camping, but not tomorrow."

"For sure. That should work."

"Okay, love you sis."

"Love you too. Bye."

CHAPTER 16

The Other Larnie

The handwriting on the envelope was unmistakable. The only other time she had received a letter from her daughter was when her daughter was in high school and had gone on a field trip for a week. She thinks all the kids wrote their moms on that trip. Why would she write now and not just call? Trudy stuffed the letter into the pocket of her housecoat and carried the rest of the mail to its abode on the kitchen counter. Jeff would open the bills when he gets home and comment on the size of the electrical bill. She hoped he would not comment about her living in a housecoat like he did the previous day.

Lately Trudy felt disconnected from her spirit, her personality and her previous inspirations. She used to start her day with tea and think about the latest quilting project as she savoured the hot lemony taste in her mouth. Not every quilt won a prize at the local fair like her last one, but she expected each would as she constructed her own creative designs. She would write a piece of poetry to go with each quilt. Around the house, she'd make a list of the chores to do with a sense of determination. She was part of a network of friends who would go for walks, have lunches together and play games of cribbage, canasta or whist.

Memories of the person she was before are detached from her being now. It's as if she lived in a different body and a different life when she would wake up in anticipation as to what the day may hold and how she may make a difference in the lives of those around her. The meaning to her life was losing its grip and she sensed that the letter from Meagan, whatever it said, would likely add to the despair. Or maybe she wouldn't care - indifference was becoming easier to live with.

When she woke up on this morning her muscles felt stiff and she couldn't balance right coming down the stairs. The doctor told her it could be signs of Parkinson's disease and she was certain she could feel the disease moving in her body and making a home in it. With Cindy out at her boyfriends and Tommy with his cousin, she was alone in the house. The quiet and loneliness was a comforting fog that blocked her view of the day's activities and responsibilities.

She approached the cupboard and the excuses that were always there was what she reached for. She didn't have the energy for a walk that would be painful anyway. Her award winning quilt hung over the arm of the couch beside a basket of yarn. It is as if someone else created it and all she sees now are piles of yarn and needles stuck in the start of a pattern. She just didn't feel like phoning her friends to hear their cheery voices that were so opposite to how she was feeling and she was certain she couldn't concentrate to play a game. If she ate at all, it would be mechanically; the food had no taste. She could stay in her pajamas because no one really cared what she looked like anyway and she didn't plan to go out or have anyone over.

Gathering up the excuses she had filled her mind with, Trudy retreated to the living room and her familiar place on the couch. The soft cushions offered the perfect landing spot to deposit her body for the day.

The palm of her right hand dripped from sweat as she held tight to the envelope in her pocket. She pulled it out and started flipping it between her fingers as if the movement would affect the contents to her favour. Suddenly she stopped and just stared at it. She closed her eyes and turned the envelope over to open it. Her index finger had lifted the seal from the corner, when the sharp ring from the phone startled her to her feet. She went to the wall where it hung and stopped as it rang several times. She could just ignore it. But what if it were Meagan, Cindy, or Jeff? If she didn't answer and it was Jeff, he might come home to check on her. With that thought, her hand swiftly picked up the receiver and moved it to her ear.

"Hello."

"Hi. Is this Trudy Wade?"

"Yes. Who is this?"

"Oh, hi...I am actually looking for Meagan. I took something into the jewelry store that she worked at and just wanted to ask her a question about it."

"Well she doesn't work there anymore."

"I know. I just had a couple of questions I think she could help me with."

"Sorry, who is this?"

"Oh, sorry Trudy. My name is Larnie Teach. It is just that I took something into the jeweler that is...well interesting and I think she might help me with it."

"Well she doesn't live here now...well not at the moment anyway as she is....sorry, why don't I take down your number and I can pass it on for her to call you?"

"That would be wonderful. Thank you."

"I think she is still away on a camping trip, but I'll pass it on." Judy wondered if Meagan would phone her after her camping trip, or perhaps she'd phone this stranger instead if she had the number.

"That'll be fine, thanks."

Larnie left his number and hung up. Larnie was not used to acting on some impulse but his call to Trudy Wade was fueled by a sudden desire for answers. Answers about the other jewelry he took into the store, the necklace and those teeth. Possible explanations ricocheted like a pinball in his brain before flashing like a light as it settled on the second box of his dad's stuff. Perhaps he could find answers in there?

When Larnie pulled the box out of the right side of the closet, he had a sense that he was unearthing a treasure of his own. Regret was pulling at the strings of his emotions, as he wondered why he didn't take more time to look over his dad's stuff. When his dad died they shared some family stories at the funeral, but the only mention of his service in world war two was about lost years and that they didn't talk about those years, it was as if they were missing from his dad's life. Why didn't they talk about his time in the war?

He began by removing items from the box and depositing them on the bed. Knowing Mae was out for at least an hour gave him the time to carry out the exercise with patience.

He knew the necklace was in its case, under the Time magazines and so lifted it out and placed it on the bed with the magazines, while chasing from his mind thoughts of taking it out of its case. Two medals he lifted from the box he had seen before but didn't pay much attention to, until now. The gold star shaped medals both had a smaller silver star in the middle. Turning one medal over on the backside revealed the raised text: ***For Gallantry in Action.*** And beside that, engraved, his dad's name: ***Anthony Teach.*** Repeating the same action with the second medal confirmed they are identical with the same raised text and engravings on the backs.

Vague memories that presented themselves as dreams precipitously gripped him as if he had no control over their sudden presence in his mind. Memories of his mom explaining that his dad had won "silver stars" in the war and had saved the lives of many. Larnie gave his head a shake, as if it would jar loose more details and clarity to those memories. He felt the weight of the medals as he studied their details, as if the stories they held would come to life. What had he missed about his dad? Was he a war hero? What happened that decorated his father with these medals? Images of his dad and what he must have seen and experienced flooded his mind. His dad's quiet demeanour framed by deep grey eyes that looked at you but also through you, always gave him the sense that his dad knew more about what was happening than was ever expressed. On the exceptional occasion when those eyes would sparkle, with the deepening of the grooves around them and the sign of dimples in his cheeks, Larnie would feel the joy radiate from his dad. His mind transported him back to one such rare occasion when his dad had finished reading a short story Larnie had written and had won a prize with in a competition. His mom often told him that his dad was proud of him, as she filled the gap between the few times his dad expressed that.

Why was he missing so many pieces of the puzzle of his dad's life? He knows his dear friend Larnie, whom he was named after, died in the war. How did he die though? Why wasn't his dad killed if he was with him? "Larnie?" he whispered the name as if it was foreign to him and someone would answer. The room filled with silence in response.

Larnie felt the pressure in his eyes before the salty drop reached his cheek. The desire to be able to speak to his dad or someone about him threatened to consume him as the weight of the medals resting in his hands took on a heaviness. It had been over a year since his death and the mourning he'd done in private had returned with a new level of intensity. He placed the medals on the bed as if they were brittle and needing further preservation before he got up and made his way to the bathroom.

Returning from the bathroom, he wasn't sure how much time had passed, but felt a renewed sense of urgency to see what else was in the box that sat waiting on the bed. As he approached the bedside, he peered over the box's edge and spotted a black bound book sticking out from a piece of cloth. Like reaching for something with his name on it on Christmas morning, Larnie immediately pulled the book out and held it in his hands as he sat on the bed. Furrows on its frayed edges saluted to its age and journey. "What passage has this book taken?" Larnie spoke to himself out loud as he read the words on the cover.

Thoughts of TONY TEACH V. 4

The first entry in the diary was dated June 23, 1940. Larnie would have been 7 years old and the time marked a period prior to his dad's sojourn into world war two. The entry is about their improving financial situation as his dad worked as a reporter for the local newspaper. The words jump off the page at Larnie as he sensed his dad's excitement in the story he was working on for the paper. A story about the prominence of the local fishermen in the community and their importance to the economy. He began to read of the trials and tribulations of a local fisherman, when he remembered his own quest to unearth a story. The story of the necklace. Flipping through the pages of diary, he read an entry when his dad was heading off to the "Pacific with Larnie to fight in the war with the Japanese." It is at the last entry in the diary where the pieces of the puzzle in his head tumble into place.

"I want to document what happened but the feeling of numbness provides calmer waters in my soul. A numbness allows me to believe that somehow many of those things didn't happen and are just part of recurring nightmares. My dear friend Larnie pulls me back to write. I didn't even know where we were when they compacted us like cattle in the railcar coming out of the camp in the Philippines. We were not permitted to make any sounds and we had to remain standing the entire trip for several hours. My mind escaped reality for much of the trip and I saw Larnie standing beside me in the boxcar, talking to my sister. I was kept alive with those images and the thin string left in my will to live for my family back home.

I would have died like my friend if I stayed in that camp though, where his body vanished. When Larnie was caught with the Japanese coins, I thought we were both dead. Somehow, the coins I had hid went undetected. They made him sit naked in the boiling sun without cover or food for three days. My soul was tortured every time I looked and saw mosquitos feasting on his switching body that was baked and cracked from the sun's heat. I saw him collapse on the third day. They removed his body and that was the last I saw of my friend. The friend who shared memories with me that only the two of us experienced together. The friend who encouraged, motivated me, and called me brother. He gave so much meaning to my life.

At the next camp, I took that damn necklace from the commander's office as a defiant act in solidarity to my friend. Keeping it buried close to my bed gave me a peculiar sense of solidarity with my fallen friend as well as retribution and defiant hope each night. It was reckless but I needed something to keep the bank of my willpower from emptying. When the war ended, the food and water that dropped from planes brought relief and celebration I had not felt before. I hid the necklace in amongst the food I took with me on the helicopter that flew us out of that awful place. I am lucky to be alive. Not sure how it is, I am alive. At least part of me is. My heart pumps, my eyes see, my legs still work and my mind still processes things, even if painfully.

Larnie should be alive today and raising his family like, I am. If only I hadn't led him to take those coins. If we hadn't gone to the Pacific together. My friend, my brother, is dead because of my choices. I don't want this war to be what defines my life, but now my greatest fear is that it has. My pen was silenced for a while by the thoughts of Larnie and the war. Its voice now is fleeting in my thoughts. My focus, when I can focus, has to be on providing for my three children, so they can have a better life and hopefully a better world. A world without wars."

Larnie felt his dad's quiet contemplation as he took in his own stillness on the edge of the bed. He sat there and stared at the last written words in the diary. Words that were written 39 years previously. Was that the last time his dad wrote anything?

The alarm clock on the bedside table caught his peripheral vision and told him his time was running short. Mae would be home soon. It sparked him into action as he held the diary tight and he put everything else back into the box before returning it to its place in the closet.

Once downstairs, he proceeded straight to the garage and his tool box where it would join other items concealed in the false bottom. As he placed the diary in the bottom of the box, the last page caught his ring finger and his eyes brightened at the presence of his dad's writing. When Larnie finished reading about his dad's thoughts of hope for a world without wars, he thought he had reached the end. The next two pages were blank and the parting thoughts that he read had the feel of a final salutations from his dad. Now he spotted writing on the last page of the book and quickly reached in to grab the diary as if rescuing it from a fire. While there were several blank pages before it, there was writing on the last three pages and Larnie read them in haste as if they were water to a parched throat. His mind swirled in disbelief of their contents. He finished it and his emotions seemed suspended outside of himself, as if waiting for permission to be released from the numbness he felt. If his dad's pen hadn't fallen silent from the war itself, this probably spiked the final nail in it. He hoped that he missed something. That he read it wrong. That perhaps his dad was speaking about someone else. He read it again with anxious despair and when he finished, his emotions splashed out as he slammed the diary down into the bottom of the tool box, closed and locked it and turned to make his way back into the house.

By the time Larnie got to the kitchen he was on the hunt for something to take the edge off the embers he felt inside.

The head of the beer had just lost its foam when the sound from the front door announced her presence.

"Hi! I am home."

"Hi hun. I am in the kitchen. Just boiled some water if you'd like some tea?"

Mae walked over, kissed her husband and took the cup of tea from his hand. Leaning against the counter and using the spoon to push the tea bag down, she decided to broach the subject that had been on her mind all day.

"So, I was reading the newspaper at the hair dressers and there is a story that Thetis may be in financial trouble?"

"It's in the news? I didn't see that."

"So, how come you didn't mention this to me?"

"Oh hun, I don't want to worry you unnecessarily. The sales were down in the last quarter and the new warehouse being built is over budget apparently."

"Should we be worried?"

"No I don't think so."

"You don't *think* so?"

"Sorry, I should have worded that differently. Economic cycles come and go in retail Mae; That's what this is. I am more concerned that Stringbean is in the hospital and the talk around the warehouse is his son is kind of looking after things."

"Oh dear. In the hospital? I hope it's not serious?"

"I don't know. It's a lot of hush hush and rumours at work right now. But surely they can't leave some 28 year old to run the company."

"Oh that doesn't sound good. Is the company going to survive?"

Larnie walked over and rubbed Mae's shoulders, as if to relieve her tension and concern.

"I think that is a very dire outlook. The company has been around for over 70 years. Companies that old don't go under. There are challenging times with new competition, but no one is talking about the company being at risk. There is talk about selling their credit department though."

"The credit department? I guess that would help to bring in money if it is sold?"

"Oh sure, but its basically easy money for the company to make. Interests on the credit that isn't paid. Selling it would be a short term gain for a long term loss."

"That doesn't sound good."

Larnie dug his fingers deeper into her shoulders as he massaged them.

"Hun, I am sure it will be fine. All companies go through good times and bad."

"Yeah, but that newspaper report made it sound serious. What would we do if you lost your job Larnie?"

"Mae, I am not going to lose my job. Even if that ever happened, I am sure there would be lots of notice and time for me to find something else."

"Like what? Is the writing you are doing for the newspaper paying you anything?"

The conversation was venturing into territory Larnie didn't want to enter into and yet he wanted to avoid it ending with the uncertainty she was feeling. The company may be going through a rough patch and Stan Thetis' illness is a lot graver than he had let Mae know. Larnie was avoiding asking himself the same questions that his wife had hung in the room. He was particularly worried if they sold the credit department. He couldn't imagine them doing that unless they were short of funds. Maybe it was just the foolish thinking of Stringbean's son. Larnie didn't realize he was holding his breath as he was chewing on Mae's last question.

Mae reached over her shoulder to touch Larnie's hand.

"Larnie, your fingers are digging too deep into my shoulders, let up a bit, eh. You seem tense. You sure you're not worried about the company?"

"Oh hun, it's retail. It has its ups and downs. This isn't the first time the company has had to scale things back a bit. I'm sure it's temporary."

“Scale things back? You mean the credit department or something else?”

The voice inside Larnie’s head lectured him on his choice of words. The conversation reminded him of trying to tame a large fish on his line as it takes off for another run. Like letting the fish go for a run, Larnie shifted his fingers to a softer touch on Mae’s shoulders.

“Hun, you don’t need to worry about things. I am not losing my job and the company will be okay. I am one of the senior workers at the warehouse. They need me and we are busy. This is like watching a storm come in and you would stand by the window and say “quite the storm coming in” but we all know it will be temporary. This is no different. It will be temporary.”

Mae reached for the newspaper on the counter and flipped to the article as Larnie was speaking.

“Well, the article in the newspaper here makes it sound like a lot more than a temporary storm. It says, "The climate is changing in retail and Thetis has to adjust to survive." That sounds serious."

Larnie bristled at the words she read and lashed out with emotion in his voice.

"That newspaper is sensationalizing it. Sure, any business has to adjust with the times and some times, they have to tear some things apart to build something better. You can't make an omelette without cracking some eggs."

"Cracking eggs? What eggs are they cracking Larnie? Is that referring to the credit department they are selling?"

"Oh hun. You are getting all concerned for nothing. It will be fine. Don't let some newspaper article change your mood, okay?"

"Oh, okay. I hope you are right.”

"I am hun. Trust me. I am going to head upstairs to wash up and change my socks that got dirty when I was in the garage early."

"Okay. Thanks sweetheart."

As soon as Larnie stepped into their bedroom, he dropped his suddenly tired body into the bed and placed his face into the soft duvet to muffle his cries of anguish as the tears broke through.

~~~~~~

Trudy lingered with the envelope in her hand as she thought of the sudden phone call. Why would Larnie Teach be phoning her about Meagan? Meagan left so quickly a couple of months ago; there must be something she hasn't told her. Trudy found her emotions to be simultaneously concern and anger towards Meagan. She slid open the envelope, pulled out the letter and grimaced as she laid it on her lap and read it.

"Dear Mom:

I am writing you as I think it is easier for me to communicate what I am feeling and experiencing in a letter than over the phone. I am really enjoying Vancouver. The big city has given me new friends and opened up my mind and aspirations for my future.

I ride the bus to work every day and I just love the sounds and smells of the city. I enjoyed my growing up years and the time in Ranvon. I will be forever grateful for those years. You know I have talked a lot about living somewhere other than a small town and Vancouver seems to really fit for me.

I help Aunty Marg and Uncle Jim around the house and even do some of the cooking. You taught me well Mom and I am thankful you showed me how to cook. I am also starting to pay rent for my stay here.

I am in the city and almost 22 and I think of you at that age and the life you had before I came along. I realize that you had that terrible accident and the long recovery before you were 20. That must have been very hard, Mom, as it changed a lot in your life. I also think of you as a young lady at my age – it would have been 1953? I
~~~~~~

know the world was changing then. I wonder what possibilities you thought could be for your life at that time.

The world is changing even more now and I really see that in the city. Certainly, more so than in a small town like Ranvon. Things are changing in Ranvon too I know, but it seems at a slower pace. It is truly exciting here. Mom, a lot of women my age are going to university or college or making plans to travel. Remember how you often told me that I could do and be anything I put my mind and determination behind? I have thought a lot about that lately and the way you've encouraged me.

I don't know what all my plans are yet, and I have a lot of things to figure out for sure. I've looked at college and even university. Perhaps in the culinary arts or social work or something working with jewelry. I'm not sure yet, but I've discovered I really enjoy working with my hands and creating things. I also enjoy working with people. I want you to be proud of me, Mom.

Mom I am so worried about you and your health. I wish I could do something to make it all better for you. It has even made me think of going into nursing, though I don't really like hospitals.

My life is here in Vancouver now as I explore what the future is for me. I can't do that in Ranvon. I can't get my mind to think of how all the possibilities would work for me in Ranvon.

I hope you understand that just like when you were my age, you had so many possibilities in front of you to discover what you wanted do. The possibilities today are even greater, Mom.

I will come to visit when I get a block of time off and of course will remain in regular contact by phone. I think that is the best way I can support you now and not disrupt the momentum of my life here now in Vancouver.

Mom, you are a hero of mine in so many ways and are a big part of who I am today. I wouldn't be on this exciting adventure if it wasn't for you. Thank you for understanding and respecting my decision.

Love you always,

Meagan."

CHAPTER 17
Let's Go Fishing

"Meagan, Cindy is on the phone for you."

"Cindy." Meagan pushed the air out of her cheeks as she sat alone in her room and repeated her sister's name. She gulped in more air as if she had just come up from a deep dive under water. Seconds before, her mind kept her at the campsite and the deep sense of satisfaction she felt, even as her tired bones clutch to the softness of the mattress. When she first got back, she expended what little energy she had to separate the items from the camping trip into things to put away and items to wash, which now laid in two piles in the room. She then collapsed on the bed and felt her tired bones release into the inviting mattress. When she heard the phone ring from downstairs the sound captured her breath and held it as her mind raced to the letter she sent to her mom. She had hoped to remain in the avoidance stage with her mom for at least a while longer. Her aunt's voice announcing it was Cindy on the phone allowed her to come up for air.

"Aunty, could you ask her if it is possible for her to phone back in say 20 minutes?"

Meagan could hear the message being relayed to Cindy as she hoped the wait wouldn't disturb their chance to speak with privacy. She needed time to collect her thoughts and extract her fatigued body from the comfort of the bed. She was eager to talk to Cindy and it awaked her bones to move as she realized they would be able to do that before she talked to her mom. She was restless to hear from Cindy what their mom's reaction was to the letter. But that was trumped by the anticipated delight she could feel building inside to tell someone about her experiences on the camping trip and what she'd learnt about herself and life. It certainly crystalized her decision to stay away from Ranvon.

The notion of a camping trip was planted when Cleve asked her if she would be interested. "A fishing and camping trip", he had said. One day of fishing became four days and three nights. She immediately said yes and told him that she had gone on fishing trips as a kid with her uncle, but would be "a little rusty on the fine art of it." Later that night she starting visualizing the camping with just the two of them. Would there be romance as well? She wondered if she should be so forward as to ask him what his expectations may be. Would he misinterpret that the wrong way and not realize she wanted romance included in the "package" for the trip. She giggled to herself thinking about it. Maybe she would just go with the flow and see what happens? But they would have to talk about taking one tent or two and that could be a statement in itself. She decided she would suggest one tent, "no need to carry more" she would say. It would come without a promise but a possibility. Meagan's thoughts bounced from anticipation to angst as she thought of the trip.

When they met on the bus the next day, Cleve mentioned bringing a guy friend of his and suggested that maybe she would want to bring a friend as well? At least he mentioned it before she blurted out her one tent idea. This development confused her. Was he interested in her or just wanted a few days away with friends that included her? She doesn't even remember how she responded to Cleve's question, as she felt stunned by his suggestion. It didn't fit with everything her mind was imagining the night before. She knows she told him she'd see if she could find a friend who would want to join them. She was relieved that Cleve told her this just before he got off the bus for work. It eliminated the possibility of their remaining time being filled with questions or worse yet - silence. Perhaps that is why he waited to tell her?

As soon as she got to work, Meagan's determination kicked in as her mind shifted gears to finding someone else to come on the camping trip with her. She didn't want further awkwardness by camping with Cleve and a friend of his that she didn't even know. She needed to equal the playing field.

Being new to the city, she couldn't think of who to invite and so on her break she mentioned it to her coworkers – a collection of guys and gals her age whom she had no idea would be interested in camping. When Amanda and then Keith quickly jumped on the idea and piqued the interests of others at work, it swiftly morphed into something that was quite the departure from her initial thoughts of a quiet getaway with Cleve. The next day on the bus, still navigating these new social relationships with caution, she told Cleve, in an apologetic tone, that "probably half a dozen" people at her work would go. Cleve's reaction startled her as his pupils dilated and his voice gave a squeak of excitement when he responded, "sounds like fun!"

The trip didn't bring the romance she had first hoped for. Not for her anyway. Instead of one tent, there were four. Instead of just Cleve and herself, there were eight of them. Four guys and four girls. Cleve invited his friend Pete, a couple, Nora and Rory, and another friend Amelia. Meagan's invite to her coworkers initially received a lot of interest, but in the end, it was the initial two, Amanda and Keith, who came on the trip. They took five tents, which Cleve said would be close to the maximum for two campsites at Trophy Lake Park.

When Cleve told her who he had joining them, she was relieved to hear it was a total of five as that would make it an even number with herself and her two coworkers. In all her thoughts about the trip, she hadn't spent much time thinking about what tent to take, as she assumed her Aunt and Uncle would have one. The only camping trips she took as a kid was the few times she was with them. It turned out they no longer had any tents as her Aunt said, "can't imagine I'd do well sleeping on the ground these days" but she quickly pointed out that they still had camping gear, including a stove, pots, dishes and tarps. Uncle Jim overheard the conversation and jumped in with a trill in his voice as he offered to lend his fishing rod and to give her some lessons on casting with it in the yard. Meagan instantly caught the contagion of Uncle Jim's enthusiasm and they were soon out in the yard casting with various weights and lures. She watched her uncle and how smoothly the line left his rod, seemingly, with no effort and making her wish she could do something, anything, so well and with such grace and expertise. After about an hour, she was able to cast well enough that she was confident she wouldn't make a fool of herself on the trip - now she just needed to resolve the matter of a tent.

Meagan scouted out a few stores for a tent as she debated how much to spend versus comfort. The next day at work, she vocalized some of that debate to Amanda. While Meagan was hoping Amanda might have a tent, she hadn't reached the comfort of asking such a question directly and was relieved when Amanda said she had a two person tent and suggested they share it. She quickly embraced the offer as she mentally checked off the last thing on her list for the trip.

The details of the trip had fallen into place. Meagan and Amanda travelled to the campsite in Keith's car where they met Cleve and his friends. Cleve and Pete shared a tent and so did Nora and Rory while Amelia and Keith had their own tents.

The first day of the trip set the pace for the weekend. Cleve didn't hide his immediate attraction to Amanda when he quizzed about her fishing experience and then quickly offered to show her "how it's done" while promising "you will catch you first fish." Meagan took out her uncle's fishing rode and gear and immediately realized she was the only girl that brought any fishing gear. She quelled the nerves in her voice and looked at the rod in her hands as she proclaimed, "Oh my uncle's fishing rod, I hope I can remember how to cast this thing." She intended the statement to dispel the awkwardness, but didn't realize that Pete was standing nearby and took it as an invitation.

"Well I can cast a line with the best of them, so how about I give you some pointers?"

Pete's obvious interest in her spiked her confidence and comfort in the group. She and Pete went off together and enjoyed most of the day fishing, splashed with moments of flirting. It started with Pete standing behind her and placing his hands over hers on the fishing rod as he showed her how to cast. At first, Meagan forced a clumsy effort so that Pete would continue with his hands on instructions. They actually caught a couple of fish and Meagan was considering what to make of Pete. She felt a spark, even though they seemed to avoid any depth or potential vulnerability in their conversations. They started walking back towards the campsite, as her mind rifled through what she was feeling for Pete or if it was just that she enjoyed the attention. As they approached the campsite, they saw the silhouette of a couple in a deep embrace. The image appeared to encourage Pete, as he reached to grab Meagan's hand. She kept her fingers intertwined with Pete's until they reached the campsite.

"Hi guys. Where are the rest?"

"Oh hi Meagan. Pete. Not sure. Amanda and I just got back here ourselves."

"Hey Cleve, want to give me a hand cleaning the fish Meagan and I caught?"

As Pete and Cleve were cleaning the fish, the other four arrived back at the campsite with more fish and Keith took charge to start a fire. The events of the day with her and Pete quickly faded around the campfire as she watched Pete and Cleve drink beer after beer. They seemed intent on getting drunk. A familiar scene that she had witnessed before with her dad. As she observed the faces of the others, she caught Nora's eye and they shared the same look. A look of dismay and disappointment. That was the kindling for a friendship that would change the trajectory of Meagan's life.

She learnt several things about herself on the weekend trip, including the need to be self aware of her feelings for a guy before rushing into anything. The real revelation from the weekend though was her new found love for the outdoors and the beauty, solitude and nurturing that it provided. She arrived at the campsite, carrying a weight of anxiety as to what would happen on the weekend, and discovered that camping and the outdoors had the effect of calming her spirit. Her connection with Nora opened up possibilities she wonders if she would have missed otherwise. Nora talked about overnight hiking trips and kayaking and camping and other trips with boating, fishing, swimming and cliff diving. It was like opening a new book of ideas that leapt to life from the pages and tilled her tamped down imagination.

As Meagan was thinking about how to explain this all to Cindy, the phone rang and this time she sprung herself off the bed as she rushed to get downstairs.

"Here she is, Cindy."

Marg nodded to Meagan as she handed her the receiver and left the room.

"Hey Cind. Sorry I didn't take the call earlier. I was unpacking a few things from the weekend and wow, sis, what-a-weekend-it-was. I've been wanting to tell you more about it."

"Oh okay. You sound excited about it. I don't have much time though without Mom listening in. She's in the kitchen right now and doesn't know I'm on the phone with you."

"Of course. How is Mom?"

"She's acting weird. She stays in her housecoat all day and doesn't talk much anymore. She doesn't cook much either, except for real simple stuff like grilled cheese. I'm doing a lot of the cooking."

"Oh Cind. I'm sorry. Hey, did Mom get my letter?"

"Your letter?"

"Yeah, I wrote her a letter. She should have it by now."

"She hasn't said anything about it. What does the letter say?"

"Really? She hasn't said anything about it?"

"Not to me anyway. What does it say?"

"Oh its just about my life here and my plans."

"Well, she hasn't said anything. She doesn't say much of anything about anything these days. She's even stopped talking about you coming home."

"Oh, that's interesting."

"So *are* you coming home? I wish you were here but I know you have a life there too."

"Cind, I'm staying in Vancouver. I'm not coming back to Ranvon to live. I'm sorry."

"Oh that's okay. I am glad for you. I thought it was really unfair for Mom to expect you to come back here."

"Ah, thanks Cindy. That means a lot to me."

"So when are you going to tell Mom though?"

"I did. It's in the letter."

"Oh. You sure she got it?"

"Well, I don't know for sure, but she should have it by now. Do you think you could find out?"

"I'm not sure how, but I'll try."

"Thanks Cind."

"So, your camping trip was good? Did you spend time with Cleve?"

"Oh the trip was truly incredible. Cleve and I are not going to happen though, that's for sure."

"Oh that's too bad. I thought maybe I could meet your boyfriend sometime and you could meet Eddie."

"It's okay Cindy. I'm sure I will meet Eddie Teach sometime." Meagan said with a definitive, almost inevitable tone.

"I think I hear Mom coming, so I should go. Love you sis."

"Love you too. Bye."

CHAPTER 18
Show and Tell

The floorboards creaked in protest as he rambled into the kitchen, saw her facing the counter chopping up vegetables, and moved to wrap his arms around her waist before he kissed the back of her neck. They had made love that morning and Mae immediately showered afterwards and headed downstairs to work on breakfast. Larnie always approached the next conversation after sex with an element of caution.

Their routine had developed to where Mae would initiate the next conversation with some sort of chatter about someone else and so Larnie was content to put off the next conversation as long as possible. It had developed into a tradition of theirs that started on their honeymoon. After they first made love as a married couple, Mae quickly shifted the conversation about Larnie's cousin Chad and why he hadn't found someone to marry yet. He had never gotten along with Chad, as he felt bullied by him when they were younger and Mae knew that. Yet, she filled the void with a conversation about Chad. It was like she needed to create an immediate distraction.

Like their finances, his parents' crusty relationship, and his dad's time in the Second World War, sex was something that was off limits for discussion. Communication on those matters was usually in a passive aggressive manner or second hand way. Larnie was determined to change that one time after they made love. So he made a comment, with as flirtatious voice as he could muster, about how much he enjoyed it when she moved on top of him and moaned with pleasure. Mae starred at him, not blinking, for several seconds. The look of disapproval was the same she would use on the kids, with a sharp edge of sternness. The quickly developed wrinkles that formed at the top of her brow were for him to interpret. It was if he had blasphemed the pope. He then looked away and changed the subject to something happening at work.

Meanwhile any gossip about the neighbours, friends or their friends' kids and family members was fair game and often embraced with enthusiasm. He found that kind of chatter generally distasteful and at times wished they hadn't inherited the culture from their parents of remaining silent on some important life matters. This particular morning, his dad's diary and his dad's time in the war was on his mind and he wanted to talk about it and was thinking of ways to bring it up without revealing he had found his dad's diary. Mae's voice jumped into his thoughts.

"Did you hear that Cindy's mom has Parkinson's disease?"

"Cindy?"

"You know, the girl Eddie hangs out with. I hope you enforce our rule about his bedroom?"

"Of course, dear."

"Good. Anyway, I feel sorry for Cindy. She's just a teenager and burdened with her mom's restrictions."

"How do know this about her mom?"

"Because we had a visit. I figured I should meet the woman who is the mother of the girl that is dating our son. They are dating it seems. I caught them smooching in the kitchen one day."

"Oh okay. Is she a nice person?"

"Trudy Blackstock? Yes, she is. In fact, when I went to her house I immediately recognized her from one of my community quilting get-togethers. She's been out a few times and her quilt won a prize at the fair last year."

"Her name is Trudy Blackstock?"

"Yes of course. You sound like you just discovered who shot JFK. Have you met her?"

"Oh ah. No....no. Just, ah....I didn't realize she was Cindy's mom. Does she have other children?"

"Yes, an older daughter who has moved to Vancouver. Meagan I believe it is. Trudy hopes she'll come home to help her out. I think that's a crazy idea, asking your child to put their lives on hold for you."

Larnie tossed thoughts of Meagan from his mind as he kissed her neck again and felt the warmth of her smile in response.

"Well, what do you think?"

"Yes, yes I agree hun. Children need to learn their own independence and not be hamstringed by their parent's worries and concerns."

Larnie said it with conviction, knowing they were almost always on the same page when it came to parenting, even if he was more liberal in his approach than her.

Almost a minute went by, as their embrace pleasantly filled the space before Mae patted his hands, signalling the end of the hug. She then moved to attend to the breakfast on the stove.

"So how well do you know Trudy?"

"Why? You seem quite curious about her?"

"Oh, no not really. As you say, her daughter is dating our son."

"Well, when I was there, we chatting about her life growing up and her interests in quilting."

"Interesting lady? I recall Cindy saying they moved here from a small town on the island."

"Yeah, that's right. She walks with a limp that she got from a horrific accident when she was younger."

"That sounds sad. What kind of accident?"

"A car accident in her home town, Port McInerey. She told me that she was 19 and the time and her boyfriend was the one driving."

"Sounds awful."

"Oh dear it is so very sad. She told me the story but it was a long time ago and she said the hardest part was the mental struggle afterwards. She actually believes that God had punished her for things she did when she was in high school. Can you believe that?"

"Really? What does she think she's being punished for?"

Larnie was sitting down now as Mae dished out a ham and vegetable omelette with toast.

"No, we didn't get into that. She had major surgery after the accident and they had to go into her spine or something that is why she has a limp. Sounds like she has had the limp her entire adult life. Crazy that she would think God would punish her like that."

Mae continued to chatter during breakfast about some of the other ladies she quilts with and the latest gossip. Larnie contributed the odd nod and "hmm" to the conversation as he ate and his mind drifted to Trudy Blackstock and the possibility that she would know about the teeth that Meagan slipped him. Thoughts of bringing up his dad's time in the war were pushed to their familiar residence, deeper into his being.

"So, just a few days before our annual trip to Hathaway Lake. The kids seemed excited?"

"Oh they are. I heard Bev talking that it could be last time she sees that sign in the fork in the road - "Hathaway, thataway."

"Last time? Why."

"Honey, she's 21 and making plans for her life. We are fortunate she has the time now to come on the trip with us. Eddie won't be far behind."

Mae's response turned his thoughts to the family vacation he was planning. That necklace really threw a wrench in his plans. He was hoping it would help pay for a vacation to a different location than some mountain fishing trip with a goofy sign. Now the necklace felt like an intruder that could disturb their lives beyond recognition if he sold it. Even if he attempted to sell it, the questions it could raise. The diary provided potential insightful revelations but those also included some explosive family history that was kept under wraps...the thought itself had sweat beading on his forehead.

"Well, I am going to head to the library to do some research for my next article for the newspaper."

Larnie got up and kissed Mae goodbye as his thoughts turned back to researching what he could find out about Trudy Blackstock and the teeth.

As he stepped outside the door, his neighbour Henry saw him and waved him over. Larnie wanted to just avoid him entirely. Henry collected a lot of things that littered his yard and he usually wanted to sell or borrow something from him. Then referring to himself as the "Double H" just added to the annoyance scale.

"Hey neighbour. Haven't seen you in while."

"Yeah, I've been busy Henry, how are you?"

"Fine. Fine. I see you wrote an article for the newspaper. Some new job?"

"Oh no, that's just a hobby. Kind of like your collection of stuff."

Larnie tried to hide his distain for the look of Henry's yard as he motioned to it in his response.

"Ah, yes. We all have our hobbies. Say, I just wanted to let you know that I didn't mean to listen in on your conversation with the jeweler the other day. I am sure you heard my line click when I hung up. I didn't hear anything, really."

Larnie felt a jolt at Henry's revelation and the hair on his arms started to rise to attention.

"Okay, thanks for letting me know, Henry. You...um...you haven't shared this with anyone else have you?"

"Oh no. Don't worry, I won't say a word. My lips are sealed about that necklace."

"Necklace?"

"Oh yeah...well I didn't hear much just something about a valuable necklace. But I won't say anything to anyone."

Larnie moved closer to Henry as he lowered his voice.

"It's very important to me Henry that no one else knows about it." Larnie then casted his eyes towards his own house to emphasize the point. "I mean no one."

"Got it. So, did he tell you what it's worth?"

"Huh?"

"The necklace? He tell you what it's worth?"

"Listen Henry...it...it's not worth that much actually. It's the sentimental value."

"Oh, I thought the jeweler said it was quite valuable."

"I think you heard wrong there. It is worth a bit of money for sure, but not life altering or anything. I wish you'd just forget about it actually."

Henry pinched his fingers together and moved them across his closed mouth as he whispered, now into Larnie's ear.

"The Double H's lips are sealed."

Larnie left the yard stuffed with thoughts that slammed into each other. He took deep breaths to relieve the pressure as he sat in the car. "Refocus" he told himself between breaths and when he finally stepped off the break and on to the gas, he was thinking of an accident from nearly 30 years ago involving two teenagers in the small town of Port McInerey.

He spent a couple of hours at the library browsing through old newspapers stored on microfiche when he passed the title of an article from the national press: Teenager dies and another in critical condition following a horrific accident in small town BC. The date is July 16, 1950.

The details in the article quickly confirmed his findings:

"The families of two teenagers, both 19, have been altered forever. Peter Fairclough was driving with his fiancé Trudy Wade when the 1944 Volvo Wallpaper veered off the road and ricocheted off a telephone pole, which changed the cars trajectory and set it on a nose dive down an embankment. The car settled just a few feet from the river. That likely saved Trudy Wade's life. While she remains in critical condition in the hospital, Vancouver General Hospital reports she is expected to survive the crash. Ms. Wade was flown immediately to the Vancouver hospital after the accident. Her fiancé, Peter Fairclough died before rescue officials could arrive on the scene.

Jill Bryd, also 19 and a close friend of Trudy Wade, was first on the scene, as she was in a car following the couple. Distraught for her friend, Ms. Bryd described the scene as "something out of horror movie". Clearly worried for her friend, whom she said had a difficult time in high school before she met the love of her life in Peter Fairclough. Ms. Bryd was unable to travel with her friend to the hospital, but was waiting for updates from the family. She started to cry uncontrollably when the reporter told her that Ms. Wade is expected to live. Her voiced cracked as her lips quivered through her sobs, "Thank you. Thank you. Thank God. The funeral service for Peter Fairclough has not been determined yet and the family has requested that they been left alone to grieve."

Larnie figured he now knows more about the accident from Trudy's youth than probably most of her friends in this town. But it doesn't solve the mystery of the teeth. He re-read the words from her old friend Jill Bryd that Trudy had a difficult time in high school. She told Mae that she felt that God caused the accident to punish her for something from high school.

The library kept phone books from around the province and it wasn't difficult for him to find one for McInerey. No Jill Bryd listed though. A Noel Bryd was listed. Larnie went to the library phone and dialed the number.

"Hello, Noel Bryd here."

"Oh. Hi Noel. Is Jill there?"

"Jill? Sorry you must have the wrong number."

"Oh, there is no Jill Bryd there? I'm old high school friend and am trying to locate her."

"Oh, I see. You must mean my sister then. She moved away years ago. Last name isn't Bryd anymore either, it's Eiken."

"Oh I see. Can you tell me where she lives?"

"She lives in Watermet. Has for years. Would you like her number?"

"Sure. Thanks."

Larnie copied down her number as his thoughts churned about Watermet, which wasn't too far from where they would be camping during the coming weekend. He put the phone number in his pocket and reached for the Watermet phone book where he found her address.

He massaged his forehead as he contemplated what to do with the information. The story says Jill was a close friend of Trudy's but that was a long time ago and she may know nothing about the origin of the teeth. It is the mystery of the teeth, not the unearthing of an old accident, which he was on a quest to solve. They may have no connection to each other. The connection he has is Trudy Blackstock. Perhaps Trudy doesn't even know about the teeth? Larnie stopped massaging his forehead at the thought and reached for his keys.

There was no car in their driveway and he didn't know if that meant she was away or perhaps at home by herself. He walked up to the door, took a deep breath and knocked. He always preferred knocking to ringing the bell. Seemed less intrusive. As the seconds went by without an answer, he watched the curtain covered front window for any signs of movement or shadows. He knocked again. Nothing. Talking a deep breath, he turned to leave when the door opened.

"Hello. May I help you?"

Her arms wrapped a housecoat tightly to her body. Her hair looked like it had been freshly brushed, though unwashed and did little to hide an overall dishevelled look. The housecoat showed its use with frayed strings hanging from its sleeves. The screen door provided a barrier between them.

"Oh, hi Mrs. Blackstock?"

"Yes. That's me. Who are you?"

"I'm Larnie Teach. We chatted on the phone briefly the other day. It was about your daughter Meagan and some jewelry?"

"Yes, but as I told you. Meagan isn't here."

"I know you explained. I have something I want to show you though. Could I come in?"

"Something to show *me*? My husband's not home. You can show right here."

"Oh sorry, please don't take that the wrong way. It's just that I have an artifact with me that I wonder if you might know something about. I would prefer to sit down and show you it?"

Trudy's eyes moved around as she was looking him over and Larnie got the uneasy feeling he was being checked out.

"Do I know you from somewhere?"

He hoped to limit the discussion to the teeth, but he had anticipated this may come up and was ready.

"Well, as a matter of fact, you may. You see I just discovered recently myself that your daughter Cindy is dating my son Eddie. My wife Mae met you recently."

Larnie watched Trudy become a bit shorter as her posture relaxed with his response and her arms loosened their grip around her body.

"Oh yes. Mae Teach. Nice woman. Okay, just give me a minute." The door slammed abruptly and Larnie stood there not sure if this was a good sign or not. The seconds turned into minutes and time seemed to take a longer route. The pressure on his feet seemed to increase by the second as he shifted from foot to foot until finally the door opened. She had put on a pair of pants, a tee shirt, some pink lipstick and smiled as she opened the door.

"You want to have a seat on the couch? I put the kettle on for some tea if you'd like."

"That sounds wonderful. Thank you."

Larnie sat on the couch, and looked up at an oil painting of mist coming off the ocean. The picture had a familiar look to it. The varied ripples in the ocean waves came into a curved shoreline. In the right corner of the picture were several boats of various kinds, tied to a marina. They appeared to be standing still to brace for the mist that was drifting in from the sea. A lone crane stood strong in the water just off the shore.

"You like that picture? That's from my hometown."

Trudy brought the tea on a tray, put it on the coffee table, and began pouring.

"Cream and sugar?"

"Just a little bit of cream and two lumps of sugar if you don't mind. You mind if I call you Trudy?"

"Of course not."

"Where is that picture drawn from?"

"That is Port McInerey. Well from a long time ago anyway. In better times."

"In better times?"

"How I remembered it as a kid I guess. Some things from that place I'd just as soon forget."

"Oh yes. I'm sorry, Mae told me about the accident you had when you were younger. You seem to be doing well now though?"

"Me? Oh, some days."

They sipped their tea and talked about life in Ranvon. Larnie learnt that Trudy and her husband Jeff moved to Ranvon, when Jeff transferred with the logging company he works for. She talked about

Ranvon, the quilts she had made and the prize she won at the fair. She showed Larnie the quilt, taking the time to explain the meaning of the details she had included with the poem she wrote about it. She didn't mention Port McInerey again until he asked. She said she grew up and got married there but they moved away for several years and only moved back "for Jeff's work". She said she has some good childhood memories "from the place" but no real connection to it anymore. Larnie mentioned the annual trip to Hathaway they had coming up, which seemed to give Trudy energy. She showed genuine interested in hearing about it and said she wished they had a tradition like that with their kids. Their conversation flowed delightfully and Larnie found her to be a very pleasant woman who could carry a conversation and showed sincere interest in what he had to say. He started to imagine them getting the two families together. Trudy collected the dishes from their tea and stood up.

"Larnie, this has been a very pleasant surprise for me. I don't know if you noticed when I answered the door, I wasn't really expecting to do much today. I haven't been feeling well and your wife may have told you that I have Parkinson's disease."

"She did and I am so sorry to hear that Trudy."

"It's okay. I haven't been getting out much or had any social interaction lately, so you coming here today has been really good for me. Thank you.

"Yes, it has been good and thank you Trudy. I should get going."

"For sure, just let me get these things in the kitchen before saying goodbye."

As Trudy left to take the dirty dishes to the kitchen, Larnie felt the pouch with the teeth in it in his pocket and wondered if he should just forget about the whole thing. What does it matter some person's old set of teeth anyway? Perhaps he should just throw them out on his way home. He got up to gather his jacket, when Trudy re-entered the living room.

"Larnie, before you leave, you mentioned an artifact to show me?"

"Oh, that. It's nothing really."

"Oh, I thought that was your purpose for coming here?"

Still standing between the couch and the door, he reached into his pocket and felt the leather pouch with the teeth in it.

"Is it in your pocket?"

"Yes. You probably know nothing about this though."

Larnie took the pouch out of his pocket and Trudy gasped as she saw it.

"Oh. You know what this is?"

"My husband..."

"Your husband?"

"I don't know what that is."

Larnie pulled out a handkerchief and moved to the coffee table where he placed it down as he untied the leather strings keeping the pouch shut.

"Perhaps you should see the contents then."

As the teeth fell out of the pouch and on to the handkerchief, Trudy clasped her hand to her mouth to muffle the shriek in her voice.

"You know about these then?"

"Where did you...how is..."

Larnie watched her struggle for words as the woman who had transformed from a dishevelled looking hospital patient into a friendly attractive neighbour, now had the look of a scared child.

"You should give those to me."

"Give them to you? I thought you said you didn't know anything about them?"

"Of course. They...they....they are just hideous. I want to throw them out."

Larnie gingerly picked up the handkerchief with the teeth on it and slid them back into the pouch.

"I think I will keep these for now."

"What are you going to...."

"Going to do? Does it matter if you don't know where they came from? Perhaps you want to tell me something more?"

"I think it's time for you to leave Mr. Teach."

CHAPTER 19

Your Grandpa was a POW

"So we have an hour before you leave?"

"Yeah, about that. My parents are out getting the last items for our trip and will be back in an hour."

Cindy's back was to him as she looked up at the Farah Fawcett poster on the wall.

"I wish I was going on the trip with you."

He could hear the melancholy in her voice.

"You okay? You sounded upset on the phone earlier."

She turned and faced him and stretched out to grab hold of his hand.

"You are going away and I don't want to trouble you with my problems."

"What is it? Your mom?"

She nodded as she held back the tears. He let her pause fill the space.

"Eddie, I don't understand what's happening. I go from being worried about her to angry."

"It's all emotion, just expressed in different ways, I guess. Wish I could help."

He reached out and pulled her into his arms.

"Remember I told you that Meagan wrote her a letter about staying Vancouver?"

"Of course. Your mom get the letter?"

"Well that's the thing. She hasn't talk to Meagan since. Meagan phoned once asking for her even and she made some lame excuse for not coming to the phone. I started searching for the letter. I checked their bedroom dresser and her purse, couldn't find it, and was thinking that maybe she didn't get it. Like it got lost in the mail or something. But then I saw her put her hand in her housecoat pocket the next day as if she was reaching for something. The next morning when I got a chance to check it - there it was in that pocket. It is like she's punishing Meagan with silence now."

"That's terrible. How's Meagan doing?"

"I'm worried. She's starting to crack. Last time I talked to her, she mentioned she might just come back to Ranvon and then Mom would have to talk to her. My mom meanwhile is hardly talking to anyone. She just mopes around the house, mostly in her housecoat. My dad is frustrated and his anger makes the whole house feels tense."

"Oh Cindy. What do you think is going on with your mom?"

"Well she's sick but she's also a different person suddenly. She used to be so out going and chatty. She could strike up a conversation with any one. At the grocery store, with the neighbours, with my teachers. Oh gawd..."

Cindy dug her face into Eddie's chest as her shoulders heaved from the emotion. He trailed his fingers up her back and massaged the back of her neck. The silence was pierced by the quiet, muffled blubs of her tears. Several minutes passed before Cindy broke away and took leave to the bathroom. When she returned, she was clearly ready to talk again.

"You are so sweet Eddie, thank you. I am just not sure what to do about my mom."

"So she isn't talking at all?"

"Well, not much. Pass the salt. Your laundry is upstairs. That kind of thing. She will ask me to do things like make dinner and the other day she asked what your dad does for a living. Like that's bizarre. How would I know?"

"She asked about my dad?"

"Just like I said, that's all."

Cindy took to staring at the Farah Facet poster again.

"Okay, I want to talk about something else now. I need to. Eddie, we are in your bedroom. Like it is some normal thing to do. Don't you think your parents will freak out if find out?"

He was always astonished how Cindy would abruptly change the subject, like a defence mechanism against vulnerability.

"Oh, of course they will. You know my mom. But we have Bev. She is downstairs, keeping a watch out for us."

"Really? Your sister's so cool."

"You okay?"

"No I am not Eddie. But I don't want to talk about that anymore with the little bit of time we have left before you leave. You have made such a difference for me this summer. You have made this summer as one to remember – the summer of '79. Next summer we will be finished high school, but I'll always remember this summer with you."

Cindy then dropped herself into the bed and raised her arms.

"Come here and kiss me, my sweet boyfriend."

They had been in his bedroom several times and Eddie was still jumpy about it. He promised Bev they wouldn't have sex while she was keeping watch downstairs. He hadn't had sex. It was deeply ingrained in him that sex was the exclusive domain of married couples.

She watched him hesitate with exasperation in her voice.

"Look silly, I just want to kiss you, okay. I am not going to rip your clothes off. Unless you want me to, of course? Now come join me on the...oooh, now that's more like it...."

As they kissed, she grabbed his hand and moved it to her breasts, which he hungrily accepted. He was able to pull her shirt down far enough to expose her breast and look into her chestnut eyes full of desire as he cupped the left one in his hand.

Then Bev's voice broke in.

"They are just pulling into the driveway. You better get downstairs."

It was nearly four and half hours later, when they pulled into their campsite with their tent trailer and car overstuffed with camping and fishing gear, clothes, two large coolers and food. After they set up the tent trailer, Eddie expected his dad to head out fishing right away. It was part of the routine on the first day. He would get out on the lake as soon as he could and usually come back with something that would form part of their dinner that night. During dinner he would comment how much he needed to get out on the lake, "just his fishing gear and boat" and that it was good for his "soul." Last year, Bev was behind him when he said it and she lip-synced his words with such precision, their mom couldn't hold her laugh. Their dad laughed with them, though a confused look consumed his face. Several times on that trip Bev would mimic the scene over again with Eddie as they entertained themselves reliving how clueless their dad was in that moment. But this time his dad broke from the tradition.

"Well Eddie, I am heading out on the boat. How about you come with me?"

Mae looked at Larnie as if he had forgotten something.

"You don't want to be alone for the first time out on the water, hun?"

Larnie looked right at Eddie as he responded.

"I can carve out time for that later if I want. I really would like if my son joined me."

The request had turned into an expectation.

"For sure, Dad."

~~~~~~

With the line in the water, Larnie dropped the anchor as the wind carried his voice.

"I've had a lot of success in this spot. We can get another line out as soon as the anchor holds."

"I can get the other line ready Dad."
~~~~~~

Larnie looked over his shoulder back at Eddie.

"Hey, thanks for coming out here with me." He let out the remaining rope to give them some slack and turned back to the centre of the boat.

"There, we're anchored. Say, I have been thinking about a few things lately and wanted to share some of that with you."

"Okay."

"I want to tell you some things about your grandfather. My dad."

Larnie picked the fishing rod out of its holder and pulled on it to give it some action, and then held it out towards Eddie.

"You want to try your hand at this?"

"For sure. Maybe I'll catch the first fish this year."

Larnie gave a warm smile in response.

"I think in the past I have been unfair in what I've said to you about your grandpa. You might think I am just saw him as a grumpy old man who was difficult to get along with."

Larnie looked over at Eddie as he completed a cast and the sound of the weights on his line plumped into the water.

"Not always. Grandpa had a caring side to him too."

"Hmmm. Well, I am glad to hear you say that, I had hoped you picked that up about him. Probably not from me, I am afraid. You see lately, he has been on my mind. The story I wrote for the newspaper about the impacts war has had on families was inspired by him. We just passed the anniversary of his death."

"Dad, I read a couple of your stories. You are good it. You should do more writing."

Larnie looked at Eddie as if he hadn't seen him for a while and was taking a good look at the changes. He was not expecting this kind of interaction with him. How much had he underestimated his son's maturity? The line squealed as Larnie was about to express that to him.

"Oh, looks like you got one. Just let him run out the line a bit."

"Yeah, I know Dad."

"Of course you do son."

Eddie played the fish for about 15 minutes before bringing it close to the boat where Larnie snagged it in the net.

"Well, well. There you go Eddie! Looks like close to 5 lbs I'd say. Good size for a rainbow trout. In fact I am not sure I have pulled one that size out of here for a few years."

Eddie spoke through a wide smile as the enthusiasm gave his voice an unexpected falsetto pitch.

"Wow. He's a beauty. We have to get a picture before we cut it up."

"For sure! With you holding the fish. Now you can tell your mom and sister that it is good for *your* soul."

Eddie looked at his dad with the sudden realization that he was the one duped in the joke. He laughed as he spat out the words.

"I will, Dad. I will."

They continued to fish over the next couple of hours and Larnie caught a smaller rainbow and a small fresh water kokanee that he threw back. Their conversation flowed from Larnie's dad to Eddie's plans after high school and to the importance of the annual trip together.

"So, I didn't get to finish what I wanted to say about your grandpa. I have done some research recently on the Second World War and...well, it was terrible the things your grandpa went through. The things he would have seen, that no person should have to endure."

Eddie watched his dad closely as his voice started to crack.

"Dad. I know. I know Grandpa was in the war. I have read one of Grandpa's..."

Larnie put his hand on Eddie's shoulder as he continued to gather his thoughts.

"Eddie, thanks for that, but please let me finish. You see, your grandpa was actually a prisoner of war. A P-O-W. To the Japanese. He fought in the Pacific Ocean. He...."

Eddie was about to speak to fill in the gap as his dad worked to keep his emotions tied down, but his dad held up his hand as a sign that he wanted to continue first.

"Your grandpa saw his best friend, Larnie Toth, killed during the war. Larnie. The name he gave me, after that friend of his. Your grandpa was in the same P-O-W camp with him and watched him being tortured and killed by the commander of that camp. Then when he came back from the war, so much had changed in the world and with his family. I think the drinking and silence and certainly the anger I so often saw from him was all a product of that."

"Dad. Grandpa was a good man. He...'

"I am so pleased to hear you say that, Eddie. Look, I think it's important for you to understand that...well, that the war stole so much from my dad and from our family really."

Larnie went on about how his dad had etched out a career as a journalist before the war and how he was known for his positive outlook in life and someone people sought out and enjoyed being with. Then came the war and he never recovered from it and all the changes that came with it. As Eddie listened, he started to wonder where his dad found all this information, since he had not heard it before. Maybe there was another diary? He wanted to ask.

"Dad, did Grandpa keep things from the war?"

Larnie looked at him as he asked the question and then immediately looked away.

"Hey, why don't you bring in that line and let's check the bait on it."

As Eddie was reeling in the line, his dad's response came concisely and without the gratuitous comments early.

"He has a couple of medals. Silver Stars for honor. I will show them to you when we get home. I think most people didn't want to keep much of anything that reminded them of the war."

"What about his writings? You mentioned he was working as a journalist before the war?"

"I don't think so. I am researching to see if I can find any of the articles he may have written."

"Dad, I..."

"Yes."

Eddie wanted to tell him about the articles he knows his grandpa wrote from the diary, but he still feared the fallout from being in their bedroom and going through the closest.

"I am glad you told me, Dad. Thanks for bringing me fishing."

They both had to adjust their balance as they hugged while the boat swayed and threatened to cast them into the water. Then laughter flooded their hearts as they sat down to steady the movement.

"Well, we should get in, I think. We need to get that picture of you with the fish while there is daylight and your mom will need time to cook it up for supper."

As they walked into the camp, Eddie was holding up the fish he caught.

"Wow! That's a big fish you have there! You catch that or your dad?"

"He caught it Mae. First one today."

"So you have more?"

"Yep, a couple more in this cooler."

"Sounds like you two had a great time."

"We sure Mom. Just the fishing gear, the boat and us. Good for the soul."

Bev was the first to laugh at Eddie's response and it set off a series of giggles amongst them for most of the night as they talked about the fish and the experiences of past trips together.

The next day Larnie tried to convince Bev to join him in the boat, but fishing was just not her thing, she would tell him.

"You have always called these our fishing trips Dad, but I always considered it the camping trip."

Bev then invited him to join her for a walk around the lake. In the past, he would have seen the suggestion as just cutting into his fishing time. He'd always been able to get Bev to join him in the boat, even when it was clearly just to appease him. She usually just watched and would only handle the rod occasionally when he insisted. He had assumed that if he persisted, she'd grow to enjoy it. She wasn't going to play that game this year and he watched with pride as she stood her ground.

"Bev, I am glad you are so much your own person. I am sorry if in the past I made you feel obligated to fish with me. Let's go for that walk."

"It's okay Dad. I made my choices. I was glad to spend the time with you in the boat each year, I just don't want to this year. Walks and hikes are how I like to enjoy nature."

As they made their way around the lake, Bev would point out the names of some of the wild plants and birds. She said she grew to appreciate the woods at summer camp. She pointed at a tree.

"That's a larch tree. In eastern Canada, they have a similar species they call a tamarack. Do you know that the larch trees are coniferous but act like the deciduous trees? They shed their needles every fall. Their needles turn into beautiful yellow and reds and fall to the ground. The tree without it's needles is just a naked, bare stick, until the next spring."

"You seem to have a quite the passion for this. Are you thinking of working in the forests in your future?"

"Maybe. There are a number of schools that have programs in forestry, natural resource management or wildlife and park management."

"So you have looked into this? Anything in Ranvon?"

"Ranvon? Umm, yeah, I don't think so Dad. It's not the first thing I want to do anyway. I want to travel for a year or so. Maybe go to England."

"England? That's a very long ways away."

"It sure is. I want to explore and see a different part of the world. A different culture. It's September now and so it's too late for me to register for a fall semester for school, anyway."

"How would you pay for it and support yourself? It has to be expensive to fly to England."

"Oh, I am planning to swim to England."

Bev punched him in the arm as the sarcasm rolled off her tongue.

"Actually, my plan is to get a job in Ranvon when we get back and save for it. And then I'll get a job when I get over there to support myself."

"Oh boy."

"You mean, oh girl?"

Bev chuckled at her own response as she pointed to a bench overlooking the lake for them to rest.

"I guess I just didn't anticipate you moving away so far. It kind of affects a plan I have."

"Oh, really? What's that?"

"Well, I haven't told anyone this, not even your mother. I want it to be a surprise. You promise to keep it a secret?"

"Of course, Dad. What is it?"

"I have been thinking about these annual trips up here. They have been a great tradition for sure. But I want us to experience something different together. So I have been saving some money to take us all on a vacation somewhere nice."

"It's nice here, Dad. What do you have in mind?"

"Hey look, you see that fish jump over there?"

"Yeah, looks like a good size too. Make you wish you were out there with your rod?"

"I'll get my time to fish. I am glad to be here with you. So, what do I have in mind? Well, I am not sure yet. I have looked into Disneyland."

"Wow. Really? That would be exciting."

"You think so?"

"Oh for sure. But it sounds expensive, you sure you could afford it?"

"I don't know yet."

"I guess the writing for the paper probably helps, but how is Thetis?"

"Stringbean? Doesn't sound too good actually. The chatter at work is that it may be terminal."

"Oh that doesn't sound good for the owner, but what about the company? I read they are in some financial troubles?"

"It's retail and there are some challenges. Things ebb and flow. Stringbean's son is running things. He seems smart and efficient, even if he is humourless."

"Oh, so you think they will be okay? I've been a bit worried about that for you and Mom."

"They'll be fine Bev. The company has been around for over 70 years. Companies that old don't go under."

They continued along their walk, soaking in the activities of various birds, squirrels, rabbits and frogs. Larnie mused aloud about his ideas for a family vacation and the memories it could bring. He also expressed the challenge in saving the necessary money and even mentioned taking some old jewelry in for cash, but he stayed clear of anything specific. When Bev asked if he got much for any of the jewelry, he responded it that it turned out nothing was worth selling. Bev responded that Disneyland may be a good dream, but they would be just as thrilled taking a train to Ottawa or maybe Seattle and spending time there.

"A train ride?" he responded.

"You make it sound like an amusement park ride. I am talking about a passenger train. We'd get to see some of the places as the train went by and we could play cards on the train or whatever. I have looked into how the trains work in Europe from one country to another. It's a popular way to travel between the countries in Europe, from what I've read."

Bev's thoughts lifted Larnie's spirits as it breathed fresh life into the possibility of making a family vacation real. He had daydreamed about it so often but he feared it would never be an experience outside of his dreams.

"Thanks Bev. That gives me more to think about. But what about you? If you take off to Europe, then you won't be available to come with us?"

"Dad, I would love to come on a family vacation like that. It would be about timing. I'm not leaving for Europe right away. I have to save and get a work visa and figure it out. It probably won't be until next year."

"So you don't think you'll be leaving until next year then?"

"I don't know for sure. I don't think I want to get there during the winter, so maybe next spring if I can get things together."

Larnie stopped and gave her hug.

"Thanks for this. You've really given me something to think about. Remember to keep it a secret though, right?"

"Of course."

They decided to turn around, instead of continuing around the entire lake. As they headed back, Larnie brought up his dad in the discussion, as he had with Eddie. It seemed the bank of his emotions had been largely drawn down with Eddie the day previously, as he only had one near break down when he told her about his dad's friend Larnie. Bev was silent as he spoke; he hoped she caught all that he said, as he walked behind her and felt he was speaking to her back. They stopped at the same lookout they had previously seen the fish jump. As soon as they sat down, Larnie could see the redness in Bev's cheeks. He reached out and touched her arm.

"You okay honey?"

"Dad, I didn't know those things about Grandpa. You know I was always closer to Grandma and she was like a hero to me. Now I wish I had spent more time with Grandpa."

"Oh Bev. That isn't why I told you those things. I don't want you to feel regret. I just want..."

"I know. To understand. And I do understand, much better now. Makes me want to know more about him. Did he leave much that I could look at?"

"No, not too much. There are a couple of silver star medals for honor that he received."

"Really? I want to see those!"

"For sure. I'll show you when we get home."

"I wonder if Aunt Annabella would know more?"

Larnie hadn't expected his aunt's name to come up and the air leaped in his throat in response. Could his dad's sister possibly know about the necklace?

"I think I'll phone her when we get home.""

"That sounds like a good idea. Not sure how much she would remember these days, though."

As the finished their walk, Bev's enthusiasm for Europe spilled out in stories she had heard from a friend she met at camp who had spent a year living in England. They stepped into the shadow of the tent trailer and she turned to face him.

"Dad, I just want to say thank you. You've always encouraged me. You've told me many times that I should dream big and reach to make my dreams reality. So when I think about Europe, those words you preached to me many times play in my head. That and your mantra that life is about momentum and keep my momentum going in a positive direction. I believe I am doing that. I hope I can make you proud."

"Bev, you *have* made me proud. Thanks for those kind words. One thing I set out to do today was to encourage you and instead you have done that for me."

"Do you think when we get back we could go and visit Grandpa's gravesite?"

"That's a great idea. He's buried beside your grandma, so we would be visiting them both."

They made smores over the fire that night as Bev told them all more about England and what it could be like to work and live there as a foreigner. She was clearly motivated and determined to make it happen. Larnie wasn't thrilled about the idea, as she would be living far away, but as he watched her eyes light up in the flicker of the fire light, he made a commitment to himself to encourage her and help in anyway to make it happen.

The next day came with a new focus at the forefront of his mind. Prior to leaving for their trip, he had told Mae that he needed to go into nearby Watermet to gather information on a story for the newspaper. Mae didn't ask him any details, figuring she'd read about it in the newspaper one day and he was thankful that he didn't have to elaborate or make something up. It was their last day of camping and he had already arranged to leave after breakfast.

~~~~~~

He sat at Jill Eiken's kitchen table having tea as if they were two old friends. When he contacted her to set up the meeting, he told her he was a reporter working on some human interest stories. The tale he spun was that he was working on a piece about what high school was like in the small towns of BC during the 1940s and 50s. He said his
~~~~~~

research led him to McInerey High School. He got her name from the school there and just happened to be on vacation in the Watermet area.

They had grown up in the same era, with Jill being just two years older. They talked about the Beetle's craze and Elvis Presley. Jill's voice beamed with enthusiasm when she talked about King Cole and Dinah Shore and "then later" as she put it, for Johnny Cash.

"Did you know that Elvis Presley, Johnny Cash and Carl Perkins were all first signed to the same record label? A real small one called Sun Records."

Larnie made a real connection with her as she showed off her music and rock trivia and took him back to his own high school days as they traded stories.

Finally, he navigated the discussion towards Trudy.

"So, I had a brief discussion with someone from your high school."

"Really? You don't say?" Jill sharply enunciated each word, showing a keen interest.

"Yeah, Trudy Blackstock. Well I guess it was Trudy Wade when she was in high school. Were you friends?"

"Trudy? When we were high school we were best friends actually. We hung out all the time. What did she have to say?"

"Not much actually. She didn't really want to talk about her high school years, it seems."

"Well I can't blame her there."

"Really? I thought you enjoyed your high school years?"

"Oh I did and I think Trudy did too. She just had a real difficult time with one teacher who was a real pig and asshole to her. Poor girl. Oh, I am sorry, that just slipped out. Excuse my French."

Larnie raised his right eyebrow at the word. Jill didn't strike him as someone who'd throw cuss words around.

"Oh. Sorry to hear that. What was his name?"

"Um I don't remember exactly. A Brunson or maybe it was Grunson or DUNCson. Anyway, he wasn't there our last year of high school and it was a long time ago."

"Ah doesn't sound like he was too popular?"

"Oh he was with some people and he had his pets. He was...well, I shouldn't talk about it anymore. Like I said, it was a long time ago."

"Understood. So, have you and Trudy kept in touch?"

"Unfortunately not. She was in a terrible accident after high school, her fiancé died from it, and she spent months in the hospital. It was terrible. We stayed close for a couple of years after that and then she married that fire starter Jeff and I moved away not long after that. Haven't been in touch since."

"I see. Not a fan of her husband Jeff?"

"At the time no. He was in our high school and a grade ahead. He had a bad reputation as a troublemaker that liked to start fires. Almost burnt the school down once. Anyway, I don't know them now."

They chatted more about her high school years and the barn that had burnt down. Jill got up to clear the empty teacups.

"So, anything else you want to know about my high school years?"

"As a matter fact I do. We talked a lot about music. What was your favourite song in high school?"

"Well this may sound corny now, but I just loved Dinah Shore's Buttons and Bows. After high school, it was Johnny Cash's Ring of Fire. I had the 45 and would just play that constantly. How about you?"

"Probably seems sounds slow now, but I enjoyed Perry Como's Chi Babe."

As Larnie was leaving, he looked at his watch and was surprised that over 2 hours had gone by.

"Jill thanks for the pleasant visit and information. You have been most helpful on a number of fronts and my article has new life, thanks to you."

"My pleasure. Good luck with that article. I'd love to see the finished product."

"Thanks."

Larnie had just step outside, when he heard her voice again.

"Hey Larnie."

He turned around as he heard her question.

"Before you go, do you happen to have Trudy's phone number?"

"Oh, sorry not on me no."

"Well, maybe I can look her up. What town does she live in now?"

"Ah yes. That would be Ranvon."

CHAPTER 20
Trudy

He walked into the school with a posture and air of confidence that got the notice of the first teacher in sight:

"Look who has made it to the top of the heap. The big grade twelve year. You look like you've grown over the summer too, Eddie."

He felt it to. At the end of the school year he wasn't sure how he'd fit in. He quit hockey and had no real plans for the summer. Now he had a girlfriend who was popular – lifting his social status. He was in the highest grade and one of the taller ones. His stride had a coolness and purpose and people seemed to notice. He walked by Chuck and it was Eddie who initiated this time asking Chuck how his summer was. Chuck only mustered a "good" as the surprise interaction hit his face.

The first day back was only a half day and he spent the afternoon with Cindy as they hung out with friends. Eddie wanted to tell her about his dad's insights into his grandpa. He was sizzling with anticipation on how she would react or what she would say. Would she guess that his dad had discovered another of his grandpa's diaries? Should he tell his dad that he has a diary of his grandpa's?

He hung out with a group that congregated together as they filled the air with chatter comparing tan lines, their summers and what classes they had together. Gossip about the new teachers and relationships formed over the summer mixed with critiques of the latest fashions and hair designs all add to the hum of voices. Cindy and Gabe were there, as was Pete, Nadia, Carl, Keith, Ty, Connie, Angelo, Mickey and Mina. As it got close to three o'clock, Cindy kissed him and told him she was heading home as she promised her mom to be home early to help around the house. "My mom is on some crusade to clean the house from "top to bottom" she says." Eddie smiled as Cindy mimicked her mom.

"Okay, phone you later?"

"For sure Eddie."

When he tried calling her that night, the line was either busy or just rang.

The next day, he kept the diary close so that she would see it in his hands. They had social studies together before the lunch break, when they would get some time alone. He sat on the bench by the pond, their spot, and clutched the diary as he watched the minutes tick away. When nearly half the lunch hour had disappeared, he got up to leave when he saw Cindy at a brisk pace marching towards him. Without any acknowledgment of the time or the diary, she was live with energy and news to share.

"So, guess who my mom talked to last night?"

"Meagan?"

"I am so glad Mom finally phoned her. Meagan was so stressed last time we chatted and I truly thought she might get on a bus and come back here."

The remaining time was consumed by the rapid-fire details Cindy gave of the call with Meagan and her mom. Her mom asked Meagan about her life and her plans with a renewed eagerness. Cindy had not seen this energy in her mom since the news of the Parkinson's disease. Her mom acknowledged the letter Meagan sent her, seemingly without a care to its details. She overheard her telling Meagan it was "absolutely the right decision" to stay in Vancouver and that she is "so proud" of her for being so assertive about it. "A young woman needs to be assertive in this world" she told Meagan. Cindy could barely get the words out as she spoke with excitement and passion in her voice. "It was like my old mom returned, but like on her best day." They appeared to run out of time before Cindy ran out of breath. The last thing she said to him before returning to class dashed his hopes of sharing more about his grandpa that day.

"I have to leave right after school to get home. My mom made me promise to do that today. I guess she wants me home right away. Let's chat tonight on the phone?"

Eddie nodded in response and he drew her in for a kiss.

"Oooh...my boyfriend's assertive side is out."

He smirked in response as they parted to their separate classes.

Eddie saw Gabe at his first class in the afternoon and they made plans to play some soccer after school as Gabe was already putting together a group to join them.

As he was heading out on the soccer field, he saw Cindy wave and blow a kiss his way. That brought some teasing from a few.

"Ah Eddie. Isn't that cute. Eddie and Cindy sittin in a tree..."

He just rolled his eyes, as he voiced aloud that perhaps some of them would be more comfortable with the grade eights. He turned up field, hiding his grin as he basted in the new attention he was drawing.

As soon as Cindy opened the door, she could feel the quietness.

"Mom? Mom?"

She made her way to the kitchen where she expected her mom to be waiting. Her shoulders sank at the sight of the empty room. She spotted the envelope, propped upright, as at attention and waiting for her, on the table. In her mom's own distinctive calligraphy style was Cindy's name on the cover.

She opened the letter inside as if touching something that may be too hot to bear.

"Dear Cindy (and Meagan and Tommy):

Please share this letter with Meagan and Tommy. Please do that before showing it to your father. You don't have to show it to your father if you don't want to."

Cindy read the first sentence and assumed their father would just keep the letter if he saw it.

"I am so proud of each of you. Cindy, you know how to reach for what you want and then you have the determination and dedication to achieve anything you put your mind to. You're outgoing and assertive style will serve you well in the future.

Meagan, I know you are contemplating different directions in your life and I know you will be successful in whatever you choose. You also make decisions after careful consideration of different options. You know how to plan and strategize and I am so impressed that you have gone out on your own and are making your own life. Don't lose sight of that. Please don't think I was just trying to get you married. I know you thought that and it's not true. Choose carefully who your lifelong mate will be – all of you. Tommy, you are still fairly young, but already have shown great character in caring for others and sticking to your commitments, like you did with football last year. I know your sisters too will always be there to support you.

I want all of you to know how much I love you. You all have been such a source of joy and fulfillment for me. You are the stars in my life and I know you each will be that to many people throughout your life.

I have tried to live a good life and be a good mother and wife. I haven't always been perfect, I know. I am sorry for the times I was overly grumpy and difficult. You deserve better than that. All of you do.

I have been in a lot of pain lately and I am afraid I took it out on all three of you in various ways. I know I have been a burden to you all. I hope you will forget how I have acted in the last several months.

I am sorry that I wasn't as forthcoming about somethings from ~~*before* your dad and I married~~ the past. I should have been, perhaps. But I tried to shield you in all honesty. Whatever people tell you about that, please understand that I wanted the best for you and I don't want you negatively impacted by something that had nothing to do with you. No matter what people say, you know that your father and I have been caring and loving people. We are well known for our thoughtfulness and love for our family and community.

I hope that you will always remember me as your loving mother who cared and loved you deeply. As I have told you all in the past, don't be afraid to spread your wings. You might be surprised at the heights you can reach.

Love you all forever,

Your Mom. "

"Mom! Mom!!" Cindy was frantic as she dropped the letter and ran up the stairs. When she got to her parents bedroom, her shouts had been become desperate screams, only muffled by the tears running down her cheeks. She lunged at her parents closed door, turning the handle, only to have her momentum abruptly stopped.

"Mom, unlock the door. Mom! Please Mom, please, open the door!"

Cindy pounded on the door as she pleaded for it to open when she heard the front door close and she turned and raced down the stairs.

"Tommy! Tommy! Something's happening to Mom. Just stay in the living room, please. I am going to call Dad!"

Tommy stood at the door as shock splashed his face on hearing his sister yell at him. He then let out loud sobs of emotion.

"Hi, it's...it's Cindy Blackstock. I need to talk to my dad Jeff Blackstock. It's urgent."

"Okay, just calm down miss. You sound like you are out of breath."

"Just hurry please; I need to talk to him now!"

She could hear her dad's name being called over the intercom as she glanced into the living room and saw Tommy, his face swollen from tears, coming towards her.

"What's happening?"

Cindy reached out and touched his wet cheek with her thumb.

"Tommy. I am sorry I yelled. Please just sit in the living room. I'm going to talk to Dad and will figure this out, okay?"

Tommy nodded with his head down and went back to the living room.

"Hello, Jeff Blackstock here."

"Dad, it's Cindy. Mom is...I...I don't know."

"Calm down Cindy. What is Mom doing?"

"She's in your bedroom...I am pretty sure she is. The door is locked and she isn't answering!"

"Isn't answering? Did you knock?"

"Dad! I knocked! I screamed!. She...she wrote a letter."

"A letter?...Hold on Cindy. I am coming home. Don't do anything. I'll be there quick."

When Jeff Blackstock rushed into the house, he saw the panic on Cindy's face as she ran into his arms.

"Dad, I don't know what to do."

"Both of you stay down here. Don't move. I will come and get you." Jeff had rehearsed in his head what he would do on the drive to the house and he wanted his kids to stay downstairs while he found out what waited him in their bedroom.

He rushed up the stairs taking them three at a time and ran into their door with his shoulder first. The impact of his force and weight was no match for the hinges as he staggered into the room trying to catch his balance.

Trudy laid on the bed motionless. He called her name and rushed to her side. Holding her hand, he felt the side of her neck and her cold skin pulled the heat from his fingers as he looked down at her closed eyes and pale face.

"Cindy call 911 and ask for an ambulance!"

Jeff could hear Cindy calling the ambulance and they must have told her to stay on the line as he didn't hear her hang up.

"You're doing a great job Cindy. You and Tommy just stay down there and look out for the ambulance!" He shouted over his shoulder as he laid beside the bed with Trudy.

When the paramedics arrived, they immediately went upstairs in the direction Cindy pointed. Jeff sat back and watched them check his wife's pulse and perform CPR. He started to sob uncontrollably and one of the paramedics led him into another room. Meagan's old room.

"But my kids."

"Sir. We have someone with them, but if you would like to go downstairs?"

"What's happening?"

"Sir. I am so sorry. We are trying to revive her, but we have phoned the coroner. I know this is hard to take all in right now, but I don't want you to be too alarmed when the police come, too. It's just part of the normal procedure."

Jeff's mind couldn't grab or hold what he was being told and the mention of the police sprung him into action.

"I need to be with my kids."

He raced downstairs where he saw them with one of the paramedics. The sirens had caused a stir in the neighbourhood and a couple of the neighbours were there as well.

Jeff ran over and engulfed them in his arms.

"What's happening Dad?"

"Oh Tommy. Your mom..."

Jeff looked over at Cindy as he told himself to be strong for them. He swallowed and pushed the emotions down.

"A doctor is coming to the house and they said the police too."

"The police! Why the police?"

"It's just the normal procedure, Cindy."

"Is Mom going to die?"

"Oh Tommy....I don't know." The emotions erupted within him, as they did with Cindy and Tommy.

When the coroner arrived, Jeff told his kids it was the doctor and he could tell by her face that Cindy knew why he was there. Within a few minutes, the coroner asked to speak to Jeff in private and told him his wife had passed away. He was told the death appeared to have been from heart failure due to the consumption of a large quantity of sleeping pills.

Jeff didn't want to tell his children that their mother had taken her own life, but then he remembered Cindy saying there was a letter. He approached Cindy and whispered in her ear.

"Cindy, you mentioned a letter?"

She just nodded and pointed towards the kitchen. Jeff found the letter on the floor beside the kitchen table and he ducked into the bathroom to read it by himself. After reading it, he looked to the ceiling and whispered as if speaking out to her.

"Oh Trudy. What brought this up now? We could have solved this together. You should have talked to me." He then stuffed the letter into his pocket and came out of the washroom. Cindy caught his eyes immediately as she rushed towards him.

"Dad, what did the doctor say?" Jeff looked over at Tommy and motioned for him to join them and he took them into the kitchen where he told them their mother "had gone to heaven". A paramedic nearby asked him if he needed anything and he just asked to be given a few minutes. Jeff didn't want to leave them, but he knew that Trudy's body was still upstairs and the police were coming and so he led them out of the kitchen. As they were leaving Cindy turned to him, her voice was quiet.

"Dad, you get the letter?" Jeff nodded.

"We have to show it to Tommy and Meagan. Mom asked for that."

"I know honey. Just not now, okay? I...I want us to talk all together about what happened, okay." Cindy nodded in response.

The police had arrived, and after checking that the neighbours were caring for his kids, Jeff sought them out. He wanted to shield the police from his kids. There was a male and female officer and the three of them went into a separate room. The officers expressed their condolences and said they were there as part of the normal process "in situations like this". They offered to arrange for grief counsellors if the family wished. Jeff thanked them. Jeff told them about his other daughter Meagan and that his kids don't know what led to his wife's death, but he was pretty sure Cindy had figured it out. They asked if she left a letter and he nodded and produced it from his pocket. He first resisted when they took the letter, but then handed it to them with the promise that it would be returned.

When they left the room, the female officer turned to him and suggested the family find somewhere else to stay for the night, as they probably wouldn't want to stay in the house. At the suggestion, their neighbours, the Lenzs, offered to have them stay at their house. Jeff thanked them but that he thought it would be better if they were just together as a family. The female police officer offered to make arrangements for them to stay in a hotel for the night and Jeff simply responded "please."

"Dad. Who is going to phone Meagan? She needs to know."

"I was thinking the same. How about we go to the phone together and I'll call her."

Jeff phoned Meagan with Cindy and Tommy hanging on to each side of him. Jeff took a deep breath and pushed his emotions as far down as he could, but they rushed up into his throat as soon as he told her the news. Meagan was silent for several minutes as he heard her sobs, then Marg, and Jim's voices as they came to the phone to comfort her. Meagan's voice was quiet, broken and almost inaudible.

"Dad, what happened? How'd she die?"

"We don't know honey. The coroner was here and I'll talk to him later." Jeff knew it was inevitable that she would find out, but it wasn't going to be over the phone.

"But...she...she seemed fine and so happy when I talked to her the other night. Oh gawd...."

Meagan broke down again as Cindy reached to take the phone from her dad.

"I want to talk to her."

Both Cindy and Tommy took turns on the phone, as their conversations were through sobs and a repeated refrain of "why?", "how?", "what do we do now without her?"

When Jeff got back on the phone, it was Jim on the other end.

"Jeff. This is just awful. Marg is consoling Meagan right now, but we'll drive her to Ranvon tomorrow. We might even leave tonight after we talk to her and sort things out."

Jeff could hear Jim's voice crack through the phone and so he kept is short telling him that he really appreciated that and he left the phone number of the hotel they would be at.

~~~~~~

As they arrived at the hotel, there was a message from Jim that they were going to leave very soon and would likely arrive late. The hotel clerk also confirmed that another room had been booked for Jim and Marg.

Meanwhile, Eddie sat at home doodling in the margins of his homework as he thought of Cindy. He expected she would phone him and when she didn't, he called and the line was busy. He tried again a couple of hours later and it just rang and rang. He shook his head in protest to the ringing phone as he wondered about his "moody" girlfriend.

Jim, Marg and Meagan arrived just after midnight and Meagan ran to the open arms of her sister. As they all sat up late, Jeff watched Meagan and Cindy in a corner by themselves and he realized he was not going to keep things from Meagan and decided to talked to the two of them alone. Jim, devastated over the loss of his sister, went for a walk with Marg while the three of them "borrowed" their room.

"Cindy, I think you might know what took your mom's life today." Cindy nodded in response and Jeff then told Meagan about the contents of the letter, which he promised to show her when it was returned to them. Meagan keeled over as if she had taken a blow to her abdomen.

"I was scared of that. I must of pushed her over the edge....I should have come home."
~~~~~~

Both Jeff and Cindy responded with an immediate "No! Don't think that way." Cindy told her it had nothing to do with her and Jeff quickly jumped in with his response.

"Your sister is right; it had nothing to do with your decision Meagan. It was...it was other things. Your mom was in a lot of pain."

He then looked at them both and grabbed a hand from each of them.

"Neither of you should feel any blame in this. This had nothing to do with you."

"But I read her letter and she said she felt she was a burden to us. We must have made her feel that way."

"Cindy. Meagan. Please know it wasn't due to anything you did. Your mom was in a lot of pain and life had become very difficult for her. Look, when a tragedy strikes it often brings guilt to the people close to it. The people who care. It shows how much you care. I suppose it can be part of our way of trying to answer the question why? We all want to know why this happened and how we might have prevented it. It is okay to ask those questions, but you can't carry the burden of blaming yourself. Your mom knew how much you cared and she would never have blamed you for anything in her life. You truly can't blame yourself in anyway. If it wasn't for you, your mom would not have experienced the kind of joy you brought to her life."

Cindy looked at her dad as a different person. She had never heard him talk like this before. Cindy was the first one to reach out and wrap her arms around him, as Meagan joined in the tight huddle. They spoke almost in unison.

"Thank you Dad. I love you."

Jeff's emotions overcame him in waves as his body heaved in the embrace and he wished that he could believe those words for himself.

Eddie arrived at the school early the next day and waited outside the front doors, until the warning bell rang. Later the locker room talk was that something happened to Cindy's mom and a couple of people mentioned seeing an ambulance in front of their house. A few asked him if he knew anything and he just shook his head in response. During his last class, where he stared at Cindy's empty seat, the teacher approached him and told him that Cindy's mom had passed away. He walked home after school and stopped at her house but there was no car in the driveway and no one was home.

Larnie was ten minutes to the end of his shift when the foreman approached him to tell him that two police officers were in the office asking for him. His mind raced and brimmed with fretful questions. Was it about the necklace? The teeth maybe? Could Eddie be in trouble?

The male officer spoke first.

"Sorry to bother you at work Mr. Teach. We thought this would be easier than disturbing you at home."

"Sure. What's this all about?"

The female officer could see the apprehension in his eyes as she spoke.

"Mr. Teach."

"It's Larnie. You can call me Larnie."

"For sure. Larnie we are here as part of our normal process to follow up on something and we are just hoping you might assist us with some information."

Her tone and the mention of information relaxed his posture.

"Okay. I'll do what I can."

The male officer took his turn to speak next.

"Well, we understand that you went to visit Trudy Blackstock the other day and we are wondering how she was?"

Trudy's name stiffened his posture and Larnie felt the air holding in his throat as he blew in out in a response that he knew exhibited his anxiousness.

"How she was? Not sure what you mean."

"Was she happy or sad or maybe something else? Was there anything about her appearance that stood out?"

"Oh. Okay. Well when I first got there, she was in her housecoat and that was odd, I thought. But then she changed and we had a good visit, I'd say she was mostly happy."

"Mostly?"

"Well, best I could tell."

"Can you tell us why you went to visit her?"

"Oh..um...well...I...her daughter and my son are dating. I was just stopping by to say hi and get to know her a bit more as our kids are dating."

"So did you know her before?"

"No I just met her. Sorry, why are you asking me these questions?"

It was clearly up to the female officer to answer this one as she jumped in right away and suggested he have a seat.

"Mr. Teach. Larnie. We regret to inform you that Trudy Blackstock died last night. "

"Oh my God, no! What happened?"

"Well, its why we are here but it is confidential, so we ask that you not share it. The coroner's report suggests that she took her own life."

Larnie gasped, his eyes widened and he just sat there shaking his head in bewilderment.

The male officer closed off things.

"We are sorry to bring you this news. We are just following up to see if you might be able to shed any light on things as you visited her recently. Thank you for taking the time. We apologize to have disturbed your evening."

CHAPTER 21
The Drifter

He took the day off work to make the trip to Port McInerey. Curiosity and a sense of justice were the motivating forces to unearth the story of the teeth. The visit from the police changed that and now guilt and determination propelled his research.

The newspaper reported the death but said nothing about its cause, just that it was sudden. Larnie asked Eddie if he had heard anything and Eddie responded that Cindy wouldn't talk about it and that she wasn't talking to him much in general as she said she needed time. It was clear that Eddie didn't know the cause of Trudy's death. But Larnie knew. Someone had told the police that he had visited Trudy. If that someone wasn't from their family, the family must know he was there. Would the family know why? His mind tortured him with the potential answers. Would Trudy Blackstock be alive still if he hadn't shown her those teeth? It was a question he sought to toss from his thoughts and wished he could just throw the teeth away as if the whole matter could be discarded with them. But the question gnawed at his insides and he decided to channel his energy towards solving the mystery of the teeth. Maybe it would help or maybe it would cause more damage. The results would matter. Sleep deprived nights fueled his desire to solve the riddle of the teeth. Finding the answer was now critical to his own well-being.

Larnie wasn't sure if the information he gleaned from Jill about the high school was even related to the teeth, but figured he had to start somewhere. So he went to the high school and with the help of the librarian, he was able to retrieve old high school yearbooks. He found the teacher that Jill referred to. Wayne Gunterson. Must be him, he figured. Math teacher and he wasn't in the yearbook the next year - it all matched with what Jill told him. Looking at the black and white pictures of the much younger Jill Byrd and Trudy Wade took him back to his own high school years and when girls starting growing their hair long and wavy and wearing makeup. As he flipped through the pages, he wished he could transport back to his youth. The freedom they were feeling then, on the dawn of the rock in roll age, came back to him in pictures from the yearbook. Images of 78 record album covers, the A&W drive in restaurants and of the "candy strike", he had forgotten about until he saw the images of kids protesting the increase in chocolate bars from 5 cents to 8 cents.

He came upon the picture of Peter Fairclough. The name and picture were now familiar to him. Trudy's fiancé who had died in the car crash, probably within a year of that picture he figured. Then a picture of Jeff Blackstone a year ahead with the blonde spiked hair and glaring blue eyes. His look declared rebel.

He looked at the pictures and names of the teachers, in hopes of finding one that still worked there and when he asked the librarian, he hit success.

Ethel Peters was now in her mid 60s and when she arrived in Port McInerey, she planned to stay for "a couple of year's maybe". She laughed telling the story. She fell in love, got married, and raised her kids in the small BC town. Now her kids were leaving before her, she said. Her friendly smile and soft comforting voice must have made her a popular teacher over the years, he figured. He told her about Trudy's death and that he was writing an article on her. She remembered Trudy only vaguely and mentioned a couple of other kids from her class back then before realizing it wasn't Trudy. Larnie then mentioned Trudy's car accident after she graduated and her eyes lit up.

"Oh of course. Poor thing. And her fiancé Peter who died. Many people in this town still remember that accident." Larnie wondered how Trudy could escape the reminders living in that small town.

He asked her about Wayne Gunterson and her response was with an immediate dark tone.

"He was only with us for a few years. Thank goodness. I heard he was a good teacher but far too friendly with some of the girls in his class."

When Larnie asked what she meant by that, she said he'd spend too much time with some of his students after class and always the girls. Larnie probed and asked if there was ever any complaints and she just said not that she knew of.

"But he was only in the school for a few years?"

"Yes. He came from Ontario I think. Like a lot of teachers who come from elsewhere, he would leave town during the summer and one year he just didn't return."

"Oh, teachers do that?"

"Well, not like he did. I remember I had to double up some of my classes at the beginning of the year because they just figured he was coming back and he didn't return."

Larnie asked her about the story of the barn that burnt down and the body found there.

"Well, that one is a legend in this town. If you go by there now, you'd see a barn was built to replace it many years later, but many people consider the area haunted."

"Haunted? By anyone in particular?"

"For most it is a drifter. When the body was found years later, it was missing the teeth and so they couldn't identify it by the police records."

"Yes, I read that."

"Oh. Okay, then you know. So you know about the drifter too?"

"The drifter?"

Ethel leaned forward like she was about to tell a story to her class and was seeking their complete attention as her voice took on a softer tone.

"So the story is that around that time a drifter came into town. He was homeless and he would sleep in people's garages and sometimes in a field or a tree fort. Some claimed they were missing food and heard noises at night. He only had a few teeth and so the talk was it was always "soft" food he would steal. The few teeth he had were black and with his unkempt hair, smell and ragged clothes, he looked like a menace. It was said that he carried a large knife with him to chop up his food in little pieces and it was reported that he was seen doing that down by the river. Some of the town folks said they felt unsafe with him in the town. No one knew his name and few would talk to him. Everyone just called him the drifter. School children would see him and call out to him "hey drifter". Some of the town folks wanted the police to escort him out of town. Like capturing a stray animal and relocating it elsewhere. A town hall meeting was called about it and the drifter disappeared that night and was not heard from again. While they didn't see him around town, some folks still reported missing food from their gardens and one person claimed an extra chair was found to have been moved into their dining room. There was the odd report of someone seeing the drifter, but then he would disappear like a ghost before it could be verified. Then many months later, a barn in town caught ablaze and it was burnt to the ground. When they were cleaning up the site years later, the bones of human remains were found where the barn once stood. No one had used the barn for many years and the town folks believe the drifter started living there where he died. His ghost now haunts the place."

"Okay that sounds like quite the story."

"It's a story told every Halloween in this town. About five years ago, the newspaper wrote an article on the 25th anniversary of when the barn burnt down and the drifter went missing. The story of the drifter had always been around, but after that article, it became a Halloween hit with kids dressing up as the drifter and people decorating their place like a barn with hay and everything and tombstones with "drifter" on it outside their house."

As she spoke, Larnie thought back to the pirate outfit Eddie insisted on wearing every Halloween when he was younger.

"Really? Is any of it true?"

"The drifter? Oh there was a homeless person back then that people called the drifter and I think the police figure it was his body found there, but certainly things have been added to the story over the years."

Larnie took down Ethel's information and asked if he could contact her again if he had more questions. He then went over to the small newspaper in town that ran an edition twice a week. He easily found the article from five years previous that Ethel had told him about. The story had many of the same details Ethel described. It spoke of a man believed to be in his mid forties who "drifted" into town and lived off what he could steal. The story had a few quotes from residents twenty-five years previously and one jumped out at him.

"17 year old Jeffery Blackstock said, "He really creeps me out and he scares the younger kids. They should lock him up or force him out of town."

The story ended suggesting that the police also investigated a murder in Vancouver with the possibility that the body was brought up to Port McInerey and buried in the barn that was set on fire to hide the evidence. At odds with that theory, the article went on to say, was that the barn fire had been attributed to reckless youth in the area. Other fires around town in the year prior, including one at the school that shut down the school for a couple of months, were started by local youth.

Larnie also located the local story on the horrific accident that Trudy and Peter were in and he had them make a copy for him.

His last stop before leaving town was the location of the barn. The "new barn" was now almost twenty years old. He walked behind it where a steady flowing creek rambled by. To the left of the barn sat a much older and smaller building that he deduced was the pump house. Somehow, it survived despite its proximity to the barn that was destroyed in a gulf of flames.

~~~~~~

Meagan was jarred by the news that Larnie Teach had visited her mom the week prior to her death. It galvanized her resolve to read her mom's letter. Cindy and she had pestered their dad about it and he just kept saying that the police would get it back to them. The time was ticking away as she was going home to Vancouver in a day and so she decided to take matters in her own hands and went to the police herself for the letter. They delivered it to the house within hours.

When the letter arrived, she retreated to a room by herself. She could feel the heat rising in her as she read it. Cindy had told her the general contents, but not the statement about the past. She read it again, including the piece that had been crossed out: "I am sorry that I wasn't as forthcoming about somethings from ~~*before* your dad and I married~~ the past." The image of the teeth pushed itself to the forefront of her mind. She almost said her thoughts out loud: Mom was tormented from protecting our father. The image of her father as a stricken, loving and soft hearted dad from the past week was quickly replaced by the distant, harsh, cold-hearted, mysterious person she had seen him as over the last few years.

The door opened and their eyes met.

"You read the letter?"

Meagan nodded in response.

"What do you think?"

"Let's go for a walk, Cind, I need to get some air."

As they walked, Meagan asked Cindy what she thought their mom's mention of the past was about? Cindy shrugged her shoulders and said she had asked their dad that same question. Meagan stood
~~~~~~

still and, in a voice more desperate than she intended, she asked what his response was.

"He just said that everyone has things from their past they regret and it is best to leave the past in the past."

"Sounds like our father. Doesn't answer the question."

"I know what you mean. Does he really think we are just little kids and can't handle it?"

"Or maybe he's hiding something."

The words slipped out before Meagan could catch them. She didn't want Cindy knowing about the teeth. At least not yet.

"What do you mean? Is there something you know Meagan?"

"No, no. I just think he was avoiding letting me read the letter. Hey, did you know that Larnie Teach visited Mom the week before her death?"

"Eddie's father? Why would he..."

"Cindy, listen to me. You can't say anything to Eddie. Promise me."

"Okay. Why?"

"I want some time to figure out a few things. I don't know why he visited Mom, but Ms. Lenz said she saw Mom upset after he left."

"I'm confused. You think Dad is hiding something and Eddie's dad visited Mom and upset her?"

"I don't know. It's just a feeling that Dad isn't telling us something. I am going to look into it. Please just leave it to me?"

"Okay, but you are heading back to Vancouver, how you going to do that."

"I don't know yet. I might phone Mr. Teach. I'll figure something out."

"You'd phone Eddie's dad?"

"Yeah. I've met him actually. He came into the jewelry store where I used to work and we chatted, so I wouldn't be a complete stranger. Please Cindy, promise me that you won't say anything to

Eddie or Tommy or anyone else about this? I really need you to trust me on this."

"Okay."

"I'll be back here again in a few weeks anyway to help clean up things in the house as Dad says he is putting it up for sale. We can chat more about this then?"

"Alright. Dad figures if we move to a different place in town it will give us a fresh start, so there's a lot to do here."

From that discussion, Cindy made a decision herself and when she went to school the next day, she had lunch with Eddie. Her eyes wouldn't meet his. She was sorting out things, she said, about her mom and her life. She looked past his shoulder as she delivered the blow.

"I think it's best we go our separate ways".

Eddie's words came out like a moan.

"Are you breaking up with me?"

Cindy just nodded in response, squeezed her body to his just so briefly, got up, and walked away. Within seconds, she turned around and saw him there with his grandfather's diary in his hand and the look of bewildered sadness on his face.

"You are a great guy Eddie. This isn't about you."

Meagan flopped herself on her own bed, while her mind was still process everything that had happened. She'd be back at work in the morning and hadn't even started to think about it. Her body felt the fatigue of spent emotion and clung to the bed as a life preserver. Her mind wouldn't rest though and she was up within ten minutes.

She went to her drawer and pulled out the article on the barn fire. She read again the story from all those years ago and the body found with the missing teeth. If only she could redo the decision to give those teeth to a stranger who ended up being Larnie Teach? She now saw that with the teeth in her possession, she had the control of who knew about them and she had given that away. As her mind churned at the possibilities of who may know about the teeth, she made her way down stairs and with a sense of urgency, she reached for the phone.

"Hello?"

Her breath caught at the greeting from the female voice.

"Hello."

"Oh, hello. I am looking for Larnie Teach."

"Oh, he's not here. Who is this?"

"Oh okay. My name's Meagan. Could I leave him a message to phone me back?"

"Sure. What's this about?"

"He's writing a story for the newspaper and I have some information for him."

"Okay, give me your number."

Chapter 22
Dissecting The List

The small restaurant in Gastown provided a quiet corner for their meeting. If she needed to release her emotions afterwards, the streets of downtown Vancouver and the ocean nearby offered places of shelter from the rest of her life.

She arrived early, trying to remember what he looked like as she consumed copious amounts of water to abate the nervous energy.

"Meagan?"

"Hi Mr. Teach. I wasn't sure if I would recognize you either."

Larnie sat down and apologized that it took him a couple of weeks to meet. He needed to get the two days off for the trip and finish a project he was working on. When they had chatted on the phone, the call was brief and started with Meagan asking him if he still had the teeth. Before she could suggest it, he asked to meet her.

"Mr. Teach, I..."

"Please Meagan, you can call me Larnie."

She wasn't accustomed yet to calling people that were her parents' age by their first name, except for those she worked with.

"Okay. I'm just go to ask you, did you show those teeth to anyone else besides my mom?"

"I've been retched with guilt about that Meagan. I wish I hadn't done that, but no I have not shown them to anyone else."

Meagan wasn't sure if her face physically softened in response to his answer, but she felt the release of tension. She took a drink of her water as her emotions threatened to consume her.

"You don't need to feel bad. I am just glad that no one else knows about them, so thank you. I assume you brought them with you?"

"I did."

Larnie pulled it out and placed it on the table. Meagan precipitately pushed herself back into the seat at the sight of the leather pouch."

"Can I ask you a question?"

Before she could respond, the waitress came to their table and asked if they were ready to order. They both ordered a drink and Meagan ordered some nachos. The hunger that had been pushed away by her nerves made its presence known.

"You wanted to ask me a question?"

"You don't have to answer it, if you don't want to."

Meagan nodded in response as she felt the tension returning.

"Do you know where the teeth came from?"

When Meagan responded with a slow short nod and blink of her eyes, Larnie took it that he wasn't going to get any more information with that question.

"Can I share with you what I have found out about them?"

Meagan took another sip of water as she nodded again.

Larnie reached for the leather pouch and Meagan covered her mouth to muffle the gasp she let out.

"It's okay. I won't take out the teeth. Just the piece of paper inside."

"I made a copy of it, so I know what it says."

"I see. I think we should look at the original, if you don't mind."

Meagan reached into her purse and pulled out a piece of paper where she had written the initials and laid it on the table beside the matching initials on the original.

WG

JB

LM

PF

Teddy?

"Do you know who WG is?" Meagan shook her head in response.

"Well I am not completely certain either, but I believe those initials belong to a Wayne Gunterson."

"Who?"

"He was a school teacher in Port McInerey for a few years when your parents were in high school."

"Why would that be relevant?"

Larnie began to tell her the legend of the drifter, when she stopped him mid sentence. "I know the story, I lived there. Our parents bared us from dressing up as the drifter on Halloween."

Larnie was watching Meagan closely now for her reaction.

"I believe that story is just a mythical legend. A story that grows and gets added to every year. Wayne Gunterson's last year at the high school was the same year the barn burnt down. He was expected to return to the school the next year and he just didn't show up."

Meagan had leaned in closer to him as he spoke.

"So you think he is the dead man in the barn?"

Larnie nodded in response.

"If you look at the list, you see that there is a space after his initials. One logical theory would be that's because those initials represent the person who died. Who ever made the list seems to have put that space there for a reason."

Meagan nodded in agreement.

The waitress brought them their drinks and food and it provided a temporary lift of the heaviness of the discussion. Larnie asked her if she enjoyed living in Vancouver and she opened up about how different it was from a small town. She talked about some of her plans and asked him about the writing he was doing for the paper in Ranvon. He shared the details of one of his stories and told her he had another one in mind he hoped to share with her. It piqued her interest as he looked down at the list again.

"Wish to proceed with the initials on the list?"

Part of Meagan wanted to say no and just walk out with the teeth. She got what she came for and wasn't sure she wanted to talk about her dad's long kept secret.

"Hey, I know you may be hesitant and I understand that, but I may have information you don't."

Meagan nodded as she braced herself for the next question.

"Okay. The initials JB. Do you know who that is?"

Meagan continued with her response of nodding to his questions, but with this one tears came to her eyes and Larnie could see it on her face, as if he could read her mind.

"You are thinking Jeff Blackstock, you father?"

She held her mouth to keep her emotions from erupting as her nod became pronounced, as if with no doubt.

"Meagan, I don't think that refers to your father."

Meagan leaned in as she kept her hand covering her mouth.

"I believe those initials are for Jill Bryd. She went to the same high school as your parents and was a close friend of your mom's. Her name is now Jill Eiken and she lives in Watermet."

"But...but I don't understand."

"I think this is a list of the person who died and the people that know about it. I don't know who LM is unfortunately."

Larnie watched Meagan, keeping his voice slow and even.

"You think you know?"

"A dentist. There was a dentist in town named Larry Maas. Someone had to remove the teeth."

"Hmmm. That is an interesting theory. I'm not sure though. The others on the list were all younger at the time. The school had a teacher named Lauren McIver but she looked to be in her 50s or 60s from the picture in the yearbook and I don't think that fits either."

"There were no students at the school with LM initials then?"

"Not that I found. LM remains a mystery to me."

He casted his eyes back down at the paper on the table.

"The next initials are PF. Peter Fairclough was your mom's fiancé who died in the car crash."

"What? What does all this mean?"

"Please just stay with me on this and I'll get to that, okay?"

He had rehearsed this in his mind on the way over and he wanted to be sure to check with Meagan before proceeding each step of the way. He had learnt in his short time as a journalist that he couldn't rush things and it was critical to establish trust. That was a reason why he hadn't brought up the jewelry she took and he wasn't sure yet if he would. He took a deep breath himself as he thought of what he was going to reveal to the young lady across from him.

"Lastly, we have Teddy with a question mark. I don't know what the question mark means. Perhaps who ever made the list wasn't sure if Teddy knew about it or not?"

Meagan nodded as the thought reflected hers.

"I don't know who Teddy is, but I know that Peter Fairclough had a close friend named Teddy. In their high school yearbook, there are a couple of pictures that show Peter together with a Theodore Radcliffe. I think that could be Teddy."

"Mr. Teach, I am totally confused now. I don't know what any of this means. I thought..."

"Meagan, since your mom's death I have felt so bad about showing her those teeth. I am afraid it made her upset and I didn't intend to cause her any harm."

This time Meagan stopped him.

"You didn't do anything to cause my mom's death Mr. Teach. My mom was very ill and since her death we have discovered that she went to the doctor's the week prior and he told her, she likely only had a few weeks to live. She kept it from all of us, including my dad. My dad talked to the doctor and I went and saw him myself to be certain. The doctor also told me that my mom was in a lot of pain and was refusing to take more of the pain medicine as it made her "dopy and stupid", she'd say. She complained it sapped her energy and her life. Your visit with the teeth may have triggered more feelings that piled things on, but I believe my mom had already made her decision. So you see, my mom takes her life and I blame myself and my sister feels guilty.

Meagan paused as she gulped air into her lungs.

"My dad thinks it's his fault and you are retched with guilt from it. I think suicides cause those things to the people around them, but in the end, my mom lived a good life most of the time. She had heartaches and physical pain that she couldn't overcome and that is what took her life."

Time froze as he absorbed her words. His mind was taking him back to watching Trudy cope with her illness.

"Mr. Teach?"

"Oh, sorry. Thanks. Those are wise and thoughtful words by a young lady. I know from my brief time with your mom that she was quite a determined person."

"I'm still processing all this." Meagan's eyes moved down to the initials on the list, her voice projecting a sudden eagerness.

"I still can't understand what this all means."

Larnie reached over and flipped the original paper over.

"When you copied down the list, did you copy what is on the other side?"

Meagan shook her head as she looked down at the drawing on the other side.

"Just looks like a kid drew something. I figured the list was made from a torn piece of paper and the other side was meaningless. I don't how you make meaning of a couple of squiggly lines and boxes." Meagan squinted at the drawing that was quite faint and faded.

"Yes, I thought that at first, too. Have you been where that old barn was?"

"Of course. Any kid in that town has been down there."

"I went there to check it out myself. There's a small creek that runs behind it. I think those squiggly lines could be for that creek."

Meagan looked at the drawing again as if seeing it from a new angle.

"So, you think that square in front of it was the barn?"

"Yes."

"That small rectangle on the left, what's that?"

"There is old pump house building there."

Larnie looked at Meagan as he could see the realization splashed a surprised look on her face.

"There is one other thing. It isn't easy to see at first, but there's a small dot between the creek and the barn."

"There is!" Their voices had largely straddled between a whisper and normal conversational tones and when Meagan's suddenly spiked a decibel higher, it got the stares of a few customers nearby.

"So, it's just a theory, but I think that dot represents the body. Perhaps the body was initially buried behind the barn and then moved inside when the barn was burnt?"

Meagan just stared at the paper and Larnie took that as a signal to continue.

"I would say this drawing on the back verifies that the piece of paper and the teeth are related to the body that was in that barn that burnt down."

Meagan reached for her water and took a drink and then sat back and took a gulp of air. She told him she needed to use the ladies' room and left Larnie there with the papers and the teeth.

He felt the beads of sweat on his forehead as he told himself the easy part was over and he needed to keep calm and his wits about him for what was ahead. He paid the bill and waited for Meagan to return, as each second seemed to take a long pause. He was putting on his jacket as she came back to the booth.

"You are leaving?"

"No. I paid the bill and I think we should go for a walk and get some air."

"I'm okay talking here."

"Meagan, I think it's best if we talk about the rest of this without anyone around. We could walk down by the ocean if you like?"

Meagan grabbed her sweater and Larnie took that as agreement as he gathered up the pieces of paper and the leather pouch.

They decided to head towards the seawall and Stanley Park.

"Coming here today, I thought you might bring up the jewelry you brought into the store that day. I want you to understand that I was kind of in a tight spot and did some foolish things. I am sorry I took your jewelry."

"It okay, you left the one piece that's worth something."

"The necklace? I remember it being quite heavy and having gold in it."

"You noticed that?"

"Of course and I figured it would be missed. Is it worth much?"

"Oh yeah. Quite a lot as it turns out." He wished he'd quelled the high pitch that touched his voice in that response.

"What about the other jewelry, worth anything?"

"I think I got about $20 for all of it. I am sorry, Mr. Teach. I shouldn't have sold it. I can tell you where I sold it to and pay you back if you like?"

"Meagan, you can just forget it. It's not a big deal. Thanks for letting me know."

The sound of the seagulls announced their arrival to the seawall. Larnie pointed to a bench nearby and suggested they have a seat.

"I just love the sounds and smells of the ocean. The seagulls and the crashing waves I find calm my spirit and bring such peace."

Larnie watched Meagan with her eyes closed and he was glad for the serenity of their surroundings, given what he was about to share with her.

"Meagan, I need to tell you some of my discoveries with the teeth."

She opened her eyes and looked at him from her peripheral vision. She then took a glance around to ensure that no one was within hearing distance.

"Okay, I am ready. What's your theory?"

"As we went through in the restaurant, those teeth I believe came from Wayne Gunterson. A teacher at your parents' high school. It was his body burnt in the barn fire. There are a few more things I have learnt that I haven't shared with you yet."

Meagan closed her eyes again as the wind had picked up and was providing a cool breeze and kept her hair in a wavy flow behind her shoulders.

"Wayne Gunterson was from a small town in Ontario and he didn't return to that town that summer and hasn't been heard from by anyone since. He was single with not much family but I was able to talk to his step brother who confirmed this."

"Okay. I got it. Wayne was the dead guy. By who killed him then and covered it up with a fire?"

"I don't know for certain who killed him or who set the fire. I have more information that, with some assumptions, may lead a person to a conclusion on that."

Meagan opened her eyes and stared at him from the side.

"Wayne Gunterson was known to be inappropriate towards some of his female students. I heard this from a teacher who is still there today. That teacher was really only confirming information I gathered from talking to Jill Byrd. Jill was known as your mom's best friend when they were growing up and throughout high school. Meagan, I did not show or talk to Jill about the teeth. If she knows anything about the teeth at all, it would not have come from me."

Meagan remained silent as Larnie continued.

"Jill Byrd and I talked mostly about music and what it was like to grow up during that era after the Second World War. We didn't talk a lot about your mom, but what she told me is something you need to know. When I brought up the name of Wayne Gunterson, she told me that he was inappropriate towards your mom and then what she told me was something I think she regretted immediately. It just came out as something that had been pent up, begging to be released I would say."

Larnie turned to face Meagan.

"What Jill Bryd told me, she also said she has told no one else and didn't planned to. She clearly regretted disclosing it to me."

He took Meagan's intense stare as permission to continue.

"Jill told me that Wayne Gunterson had raped your mom."

"No! No! Are you sure?"

Larnie nodded as Meagan's emotions hit her like a tsunami, with each wave growing in intensity from the one previously. Larnie sat there saying he was sorry and he touched her on the shoulder as a motion of comfort, but he was lost as to what to do. Meagan then got up from the bench and started to walk further down the seawall before she broke out in a sprint.

Larnie sat on the bench with the leather pouch in his hand and uncertain as to what to do or what would happen. He decided to wait on the bench for her, if she came back. He decided he would wait until night would fall if need be. Maybe until sunrise.

An hour went by. Then another. The crashing waves ushered in nightfall as the sun disappeared over the horizon.

He looked up from the light on his watch, when he saw her silhouette making its way towards him. Her hair was wet as if she had gotten out of a shower and her cheeks red from the salty tears that were still flowing as she approached and sat down beside him.

"So, did my dad kill this teacher because of what he did to my mom?"

"Meagan, I don't know all those answers. Your dad and mom were not dating then and apparently didn't know each other very well. You mom's boyfriend at the time was Peter Fairclough and his initials are on the list."

"So it was him?"

"That's one potential for sure. There are a couple of other things for you to know. As I mentioned, I didn't probe at all about the teeth with Jill Byrd. She may have more information. I tracked down Theodore Radcliffe and he told me that he was good friends with Peter Fairclough. He gave me a confused look when I mentioned the teacher Wayne Gunterson and then said he didn't remember him. I have talked to several individuals when writing a story for the newspaper and Teddy Radcliffe's confused look appeared to be an act. I think he well remembers Gunterson and when I asked him about the barn fire he was swift in his response that it was a drifter that died in the barn."

"Why are you telling me all this?"

"This is the end of the road for me on this. I found out what I needed to. I brought the teeth to return to you and I won't speak a word to anyone about any of this. If you want to talk to Jill Bryd or Teddy Radcliffe, I will give you their contact information. Of course there's another person who likely knows something about all this that I haven't talked to and nor will I."

"My father."

"I leave that all up to you to do with whatever you want." Larnie held out the leather pouch and Meagan shook her head.

"I don't want to touch those or see them again."

Larnie nodded towards the ocean. "Shall I toss them in there?"

"Please."

Larnie got up, opened the leather pouch and held it over the seawall. After the teeth had plopped into the crashing waves below, he threw the pouch with the paper and the initials on it as far as he could. Then he reached into his pocket as he walked back towards her. While her emotions were still close to the surface, Meagan's tears had subsided, as if the well had gone dry.

"Now I understand why my mom always wanted to move away from McInerey and was so excited when my dad got the transfer to Ranvon. I complained at the time about why they would disrupt our lives like that."

Larnie pulled out a piece of paper and sat back down on the bench.

"Meagan, your mom was an exceptional individual, who was known to find something positive out of any situation. She was raised by a single mom. Her dad was killed in World War Two when she was an infant. She showed great determination in her life. You may not know this, but she was selected as valedictorian for her grad class. For a woman at the time, that would have been rare and she declined it. Apparently, she thought another person was more worthy. She overcame that horrific car accident and completed schooling later for nursing, though she didn't practice much due to her disability. She wrote poetry too and some of it was published in the Coast Advocate, a newspaper in Port McInerey. One of her poems won third prize in a provincial competition put on by a Vancouver newspaper."

"Where did you learn all this?"

"I investigated it for an article. Meagan, I have written an article about your mom. It is in draft form and I would like you to look at and approve it so we can print in the newspaper in Ranvon.

Meagan took the article and as she absorbed the words about her mom, it restarted the pump that brought more tears, as the well went deeper.

"Thank you for this Mr. Teach. There are things in there I didn't know. Can I look at it again, when my head isn't so muddled and get back to you?"

"For sure, that's your copy. I would like to print it soon, so if you could phone me by next week that would great."

Meagan nodded and Larnie was about to get up to say goodbye, when he could see something was on her mind as she continued to look down at the article.

"Mr. Teach, you didn't mention anything in the article about the teacher or...or anything about how she died?"

"Somethings are best left unsaid. I think saying your mom was a survivor who overcame challenges and thrived covers it."

"Thank you for that."

"You okay getting home? I could drive you or arrange a ride for you if you like?"

"Thanks but I am okay. I am going to stay a little while longer and let the ocean speak to me."

Larnie said his goodbye and left, feeling relief himself. The weight of the teeth had shifted at times since he discovered them. The load they added each day had lifted and it had added a spring to his step as he headed back.

~~~~~~

Just over a week had passed and Meagan had kept tight lipped about the details of the revelations she learnt from Larnie Teach, until this moment. Sitting in Jill Eiken's living room, she spoke about it for the
~~~~~~

first time. She had already learnt a lot about her mom's years as a youth and Jill had pulled out the few black and white photos she had from that time.

"Mrs. Eiken, it has been good to talk to someone who knew my mom when she was growing up. I came here in large part because I spent time talking to Larnie Teach. This is really difficult but I...I. I'm sorry, give me a minute."

Jill handed her a tissue.

"It's okay dear. When Larnie Teach came to visit me, I let something slip that happened to your mom in high school with a teacher. Is that what you want to talk about?"

Meagan nodded as she blew her nose.

Jill told her that at first her mom enjoyed the extra attention from Wayne Gunterson and had no idea how dangerous it was. She said her mom was like that, where she would just trust people and jump in with both feet on anything that interested her. The rape happened when he used false pretenses to lure her to an old barn by a creek.

Meagan was keeping her emotions pinned down as she looked at Jill and took in every word.

"There is some history with that barn that happened later."

"I know."

Jill took Meagan's abrupt response as a statement that she need not expand any further unless she was invited to do so.

"Meagan, your mom was a survivor and such an inspiration. She went on to be voted the valedictorian for our grad class the next year."

"I know, but why did she reject it?"

"That bastard." Jill saw the quizzical look on Meagan's face from her response.

"Wayne Gunterson I mean. For crazy reasons she thought that whole thing made her unworthy for such an honour. That asshole robbed her of that. Oh, sorry, I don't usually swear like that."

"It's okay Mrs. Eiken. Did my mom ever tell anyone besides you?"

"Not that I know of. She might have told Peter."

"Thank you for sharing this with me."

They didn't talk about the fire or the teeth.

Meagan left Jill Eiken's and headed to Ranvon.

When Larnie got back home, he had to work extra hours to make up for the time that he was away. The events from the trip to Vancouver had become a submerged memory, consumed by the commitments of his daily life. The memory lifted quickly with her phone call.

"Hello Mr. Teach. It's Meagan."

She told him that she was in Ranvon for a few days and that she had a few suggestions about his article. They agreed to meet the next day. His voice softened as he asked her how she was doing and she said "Very good, actually" and told him that his meeting with her had changed her perceptive on life. Then she added, "But ask me again tomorrow. I am sitting down with my dad tonight to talk about things."

They met the next day at the back of a park. Meagan suggested it. She handed him her notes on the article. She added a direct quote from herself, "When I think of all the things my mom had to overcome in her life, some terrible and frightening, and yet she still approached life as an adventure with a determination and a positive attitude. I never heard her blame someone else for anything in her life. It is scary for me lose her when I am only in my 20s, but she will always be with me and the love and inspirations she gave me are mine forever to cherish." There was a quote from Cindy too, "You are my hero, Mom" and Tommy, "I miss you every day, Mom."

"Very nice Meagan. No quote from your dad?"

"He is still too upset and processing things. He really appreciates the article though."

"Do you mind if I add in something like your dad is mourning your mom as the family supports each other through this time?"

"That sounds wonderful. Thank you."

"It should run in the paper this week. How did it go with your dad, if you don't mind me asking?"

She responded that it went as best as she could expect. Her dad was shocked she knew about the rape and said that her mom didn't want anyone to know. She told him she thinks it's important that she and her siblings know and that it would help with their healing. She also told him about her meeting with Jill Eiken. Then she walked closer to him as she whispered,

"Mr. Teach, I didn't talk to Mrs. Eiken or my dad about the teeth or the fire. I haven't said anything to anyone about it. This is the last time I hope that I ever mention it. Some things in the past are best to be left in the past."

"You're a wise young lady."

When Larnie got home, he retreated to the desk in their room where he immediately completed the article on Trudy Blackstock. He would submit it to the paper the next day. As he sat at his desk with the article in a file folder, he looked out the window at a steller jay that had just landed on the branch of a tree nearby. He smiled at the sight and closed the folder, as if he was closing a chapter in his life as well.

He then went to the closet and pulled out the velvet case and his dad's diary and, as if expecting an answer, he said to the empty room, "What do I do with these things, now?"

CHAPTER 23

Winds of Change

Mina grabbed Eddie's hand and pulled him with her as they made their way towards the music. They jumped on the dance floor to the beat of drums as Billy Joel asked them "What's the matter with the clothes I'm wearing? Can't you tell that your tie's too wide? Maybe I should buy some old tab collar?"

They were pressed to the edge of the dance floor and several of their friends jived to the beat with them; as the sand in the hourglass of their high school years was on its final grains. When "Funky Town" immediately followed, Eddie started to sweat as Mina picked up the pace and more joined in.

After Funky Town, many exited the dance floor with the pause in the music, but he followed her lead as they stood waiting for the next song. When the soft piano sound began, Mina turned to him, wrapped her arms around his neck and looked into his eyes as she lip-synced Dennis DeYoung's voice,

"Babe, I'm leavin'. I must be on my way. The time is drawwwwin neeearr. The train is going, see it in your eyes..."

When she rested her head on his shoulder and they swayed to the music, he could see Cindy in the arms of Mickey Rudakavik. A part of him wanted to switch partners with Mickey while the devil on his shoulder would remind him how poorly she treated him over the last year.

Eddie thought that she would reach out to him for support when her mom died and then when his dad wrote the article about her mom, he thought for sure after that. But the opposite happened. He was left confused and hurt and when he saw their house was for sale, he feared they were moving out of town. He asked her after class one day if they were moving and her response was a sharp edged dagger thrown at him.

"Of course Edward. My mom died in that house."

Her sometimes-strident attitude had reached a peak in his mind with that response and he avoided her for several weeks afterwards. His confusion, anger and dismay over the situation affected his mood and he would deposit those emotions on the soccer pitch with his friends and at home. He also watched Cindy hanging out with a different crowd of friends at school and she was clearly hung over one morning when they had a class together. He tried talking to her then too and she responded with "I'm sorry I am not good enough for the perfect little Eddie Teach." Her response baffled him and when he got home, he made a beeline for his room, but his mom stopped him in his tracks.

"Hey, before you retreat up there, can you tell me what's going on? Who has taken your sunshine there, mister thundercloud?"

Eddie didn't really want to talk about it, but his mom had a persistent way of drawing things out of him. When he told her about the group of friends that Cindy hung out with, she raised her eyebrow and referred to it as a "disturbing pernicious influence". He had no idea what that meant and didn't want the explanation if he asked. She then reached out with her hand and physically lifted his chin.

"Eddie, you just need to forget about her. I know it's sad that she lost her mom and she seems to be struggling to deal with it, but she won't let you in. Forget about her. Stop expending your thoughts on her, you have to look after yourself. This may not be the last girl you have to get over in your life and the quicker you do it, the better you will be."

When he asked Bev about it that night she told him "Mom is right, you should forget about her."

Eddie wouldn't succeed with that, as he would often wonder how she was doing. But then her sharp tongue, that he felt somehow was saved just for him, would come out. Just before the Christmas break she had missed several classes and her hair looked tousled on the days she was there. In a voice of concern, he asked her how she was doing and she just said, "What do you think?" Later that day he overheard her saying to a friend, "some people never have to deal with problems in their lives. They are sheltered by the people around them." He was certain she said it just loud enough for him to hear. The interaction jarred and jaded him and he just avoided her the rest of the school year after that. Towards the end of the year, he saw that her and Mickey appeared to have become a couple, which motived him to find a date for their prom. Mina surprised him with her immediate response of "yes" that she said with a broad smile.

Just two days after his grad, he was packing the last of his clothes for the long awaited family vacation that his dad announced on previous Christmas morning. The snow was falling outside and his dad got up to make an announcement. He always had some surprise at Christmas for the family. One time it was a New Year's Eve visit from their Aunt Annabella that everyone already knew about, but pretended to be surprised anyway. Another year he came down dressed as a Star Wars Storm Trooper with a new Star Wars game, that they were all to play in costume that year. Then there was the year he surprised them with a new kitten and it was evident it was a surprise to their mom, too. So Eddie approached these surprises with curiosity as much as anything but it was clear as soon as he said he was going to make an announcement that Bev was in on it, from the look they shared.

"I've been planning this surprise for sometime now and have been saving for it. I know we all have enjoyed going to Hathaway every year, but with Bev's plans to go to Europe this next year, it doesn't sound like she will be able to make it. Soooo, I want us all to go on an adventure we have not done before."

The brochures of the space needle and other sites around Seattle, gave the impression they were going to a glamorous location. They had never been anywhere outside of Canada and he was excited at just the thought of venturing to the United States.

And now the day had arrived. Eddie had never been on a train before and he the excitement was coursing through his veins.

As they boarded the train, Larnie took in the joy on the faces of his family. The smile that made its way across his face was no longer just something he was smothering his worry with.

There were times he thought his plans for the trip would come apart, stitch by stitch. While he had the money saved, the financial viability of Thetis was a topic around town as each month went by. After they sold their credit department, they sold the grocery department and then started a wholesale change of their product line. When Stringbean died early in the New Year, everyone came to work with a sense of pending dread on their faces. Then within a few weeks, there were rumours of them cutting some of the employees' vacation time and even cancelling vacations that had already been booked. He couldn't get straight answers. Larnie was always proud that they didn't have a union at Thetis and didn't need one, since Stringbean treated them like family and gave them a fair deal. Now he was wishing otherwise, particularly as he thought of his company pension that he had built up over twenty-five years. The company had contributed most of the funds to the pension and he was relying on it for his future. The workers no longer seemed to have a voice within the company and he no longer enjoy going to work.

He didn't want to be part of the group that dreaded the place and vocalized it each day and he combatted that with a false façade he'd put on. Instead of his positive exterior becoming infectious, as he had hoped, he was accused of being unrealistic and "naïve". The façade showed signs of wear as his fuse became shorter with each agitation and he feared his reputation of "being calm in a storm" was being lost. His internal turmoil was spilling out at home and it had suppressed his appetite, evidenced by the belt he now needed for his pants.

One Saturday, he got up determined to end his worry about the financial future, retrieved the velvet case from his closet, and went to see Graeme at Danoon Jewelry. As soon as he arrived, he saw the for sale sign on the store's window. Graeme told him that he was selling the business and retiring. Larnie thought he was a little young to be retiring, but Graeme dismissed that with "I've done well on my investments". He was going to retire and move back to Australia, "well at least for the half a year that is summer over there." When Larnie pulled the velvet case out of the bag, Graeme jumped on it right away: "So you want to sell it now?" Larnie was startled at first by his enthusiasm, and wonder if Graeme saw a commission potential. He just wanted to know his options, he told him. Graeme gave him the contact information for a couple of museums that might be interested and two collectors he knew of, including one in Australia that he "knows quite well." He offered to help broker a deal to ensure a fair price. Larnie put the paper with the information into his wallet and turned to leave, when Graeme said something he took as a warning. It was an exchange he remembers well.

"You should know my friend, anyone that you try and sell that to are likely to ask a lot of questions, including its origin. That's because of its potential historical value, and they would want to verify that it is not hot."

"Hot?"

"Stolen. A lot of jewelry and art work gets stolen and honest dealers won't touch anything they think is."

"So I might not be able to sell it?"

"Oh you can sell it, alright. It is about to who and how much. Just saying, it would be of great help if you could verify the origins of it. "

"I see. Thanks."

"So how did it come into your possession??"

"I'm still not sure the answer to that."

Larnie thought it was best to keep the little information he had to himself. He recoiled at the thought of revealing what he knows to someone and then leaving it to them to fill in the rest of the puzzle. But he was there to see if he could sell it.

"Hey, anyone on that list that may not ask as many questions?"

"Yeah, the one in Australia might not. I could talk to him if you like?"

"Thanks for the information, I need time to think about it."

He left the store feeling less certain about selling it than he ever. The more details he gathered about his dad's life, the more he wanted to protect it. His Aunt Annabella visited them for the New Year's celebration, at Bev's insistence, and she gave them insights as to what his dad was like before and after the war. Later, in private, she told him that she had something "of your dad's that you may be interested in." and she gave him another diary. This one labelled v 3. It includes stories from his dad's writing, and his strong relationship with his friend Larnie. Vivid details of his grandma's joy when Annabella returned to their lives take up a few pages in the diary. He figured that is why she had kept the diary and gave it to him in private. He kept these things to himself. He wanted to fill in the entire puzzle, or at least most of it and then decide what to do. He had searched through his dad's stuff over and over looking for other diaries without success, but somehow believed they existed somewhere.

Then there was the explosive particulars in the diaries themselves. The dairy labelled v 4 contained details about the necklace that he didn't want to be known. His mind remained conflicted about selling it even if he resolved those matters. Does he really want their life disturbed with the kind of money and attention it could bring? Then there was final pages of the v 4 diary that revealed what his dad faced when he came home from the war and he was definitely not prepared to talk to anyone about that.

As he was preparing for their trip, his conversation with his neighbour Henry Harris brought a rising wave of panic up his throat, and so he went to the bank with designs to put the necklace in a safety security box. But when he looked into it, he didn't want the extra expense and secrecy that came with it. He checked his closest again, opened the box of his dad's stuff, and saw the velvet case under the stack of time magazines and reminded himself that it had been safe in that box for many years.

Larnie did find an escape and joy in his writing for the local newspaper. It didn't pay well enough to replace his income at Thetis, though he wondered if he could expand on his writing so it could.

The real escape that had kept his spirits up though was this trip. Bev was leaving for Europe, Eddie had graduated from high school, the place he had worked most of his adult life brought little joy anymore. It felt like the ground beneath him was shifting and whatever it settled to, he was determined it would not rob him of this vacation. And now they were off.

The almost five-hour train ride hugged the coastline on its way to Seattle and provided them with stunning views of the ocean and mountains. When Bev spotted Orcas swimming nearby, her excitement carried throughout the train as passengers rushed to the windows. The conductor pointed out many features to them along the way. Tunnels, sailboats, racoons, bald eagles, herons, enormous cedar and spruce trees and the peeling arbutus all gave them a sense they were on an adventure.

When they arrived in Seattle, at two thirty in the afternoon, they stepped outside and the humidity hit them as grey and white flakes were falling. Larnie was beaming with delight.

"Wow! I didn't expect this! IN- credible!"

Eddie brushed his hand over his head to feel the gritty fine flakes that had dotted his hair.

"What is it?"

"It's the ash from Mount Saint Helens."

"But Mom, didn't that blow like over a month ago?" Bev asked in astonishment as she held out her arm to collect some of it.

"It's amazing to be here at this time and witness this. Remember the day the volcano blew?"

"Dad, everyone our age will always remember that. The night before, one of my friends who lives on a farm said the cows were all spooked and they thought something was up. It has been the most talked about thing since."

Larnie mentally put on his list to find out more about the volcano, as he hailed a cab to take them to their hotel.

Eddie had only stayed in a few motels when his hockey team would play in a tournament in another town. He had never stayed in such a fancy place as the "Roosevelt Hotel". The hotel's red neon sign became part of the first pictures they took after leaving the train station. After checking into their rooms, Eddie had a mischievous smile as he discovered the pop machine outside their room would accept Canadian quarters.

With their fannypacks, cameras, maps, tour guide brochures and Larnie's socks with sandals footwear, they embraced the tourist role with enthusiasm as they headed out of the hotel for the first of seven days in Seattle.

Their first destination was a walk to the space needle, a site they had watched on TV each New Year's eve. The aquarium, the zoo and a harbour tour in the evening filled their day and they arrived back at the hotel as they felt the first of two earthquakes they experienced while there – "tremors from the volcano" they were told at the hotel.

Mount Saint Helens dominated the news and the chatter in restaurants and coffee shops. They took in an information session hosted by the hotel and were instructed in what to do in an earthquake and were shown some of the first pictures of the volcano's eruption. Larnie watched the expressions on the faces of his family, knowing that this shared experience together would rest in his heart the rest of his life.

Parks, museums, the zoo, a trip to see Mount Rainer and another for Snoqualmie Falls had filled their days and on their last day they toured a world war two museum just outside of Seattle. As they approached an exhibit titled "Over the Beach: The World War II Pacific Theatre", Bev asked, "Grandpa fought in the Pacific right?" Before Larnie could respond, Eddie, whose eyes were transfixed on the details of the exhibited, stated, "Yep, that was where he was." Larnie looked over at Eddie, taking pleasure in the knowledge that their discussion at Hathaway was still fresh in his mind. The exhibit included many artifacts from the war, including letters, photographs of officers and other memorabilia. There were prayer notes from soldiers, medals, and a "girl guide first aid kit" that Bev pointed out. Various booklets including one on "Waretime Suggestions on Rationing" were in the exhibit along with a Japanese 1933 7.7 mm machine gun and ammunition. Some of the larger pieces included a military motorcycle. Near the back was a section on "POW's in Japanese concentration camps." Eddie was the first to arrive at that section as the others quickly joined him. A sudden silence took over the four of them as they looked at a drawing made of a bunkhouse in a concentration camp and a black and white picture of the skin and bone bodies of POWs in the camp. The smiles on the POWs contrasted their beaten, malnourished bodies as the caption below told the readers the picture was taken on the day they were rescued. Bev broke the silence, "it looks like some of the pictures from starving people in third world countries, but worse." Then Eddie pointed to a diary entry from a soldier at a camp, as he read allowed its words:

"The daily routine in general was like this: I would be awakened at 5 or 6. Not always sure of the time. Like my other mates, I would have had to fight off the bed bugs that had kept me awake most of the night. Sometimes it was lice that was on my bed and I could not clean it all off as I was too weak. I would roll up my mat and wait for breakfast. Breakfast would be a cup of starch, no sugar, no milk, nothing but a cup of starch. Then I would have to line up and be accounted for in my group. Sometimes, they would check the bunks if not everyone was there. Some men would die during the night. Then we would march to our destination, which was usually an area that had been damaged and needed to be fixed. Building fences, digging holes, working in a garden. Those kinds of things. It was very hot of course and we all had practically no clothes left. No shoes, no socks, no shirts. We were out from early in the morning until late at night and thankful if we were not beaten that day by our captors."

"Is that the kind of camp Grandpa would have been in?"

"I suppose so Eddie. He didn't talk about it, but he was a POW in a Japanese concentration camp."

"Actually he was in at least two different camps. That is what Aunt Annabella told me. She said he didn't talk about it much, but told her he was in one camp where a good friend of his died and then he was transported in a cattle car or something to another camp that was worse."

"When did she tell you that Bev?"

Bev looked at her dad as if he asked a dumb question that he knows the answer to.

"When she was with us at New Year's. She said the war really changed her brother and he was never the same afterwards."

"It impacted all of us as a result."

Eddie's follow up words to his sister rang like a bell in Larnie's head as he thought again of his dad's dairy and the impacts on his life. He then pulled both of them together in a hug.

"You two have grown up so much and are wise beyond your ages. I know your grandpa would be very proud of you. What you both said is very true and I can't tell you how deeply it touches my heart to know that you have that understanding. Your grandpa was a hero and he was part of what has made our world a better place to live. It's up to us to continue to carry that torch."

"Yes, and without guns and bombs." Mae added as she joined them.

They left the exhibit as a tight knit group and walked around the wooded area outside. At first, they talked about the exhibit and then Mae played the role of catalyst as the conversations shifted to shared stories from the past week on their trip. By the time they boarded the shuttle to return to the hotel, they were all laughing.

The next morning, as they packed up their belongings, the collectibles and tee shirts they had bought, Bev and Eddie sat down with their parents on the edge of the bed as Bev spoke.

"Eddie and I are so grateful for this amazing trip and the experiences we have had as a family we will always remember." They presented their parents with a gift that included a miniature space needle and a card filled with words of thanks and gratitude, hand written by Bev.

After the train ride back to Vancouver, the drive back home seemed exceedingly long, and it was if there was a collective yawn in the car as they passed the "Welcome to Ranvon sign".

As they pulled in the driveway, he was waiting for them to return.

"Hello neighbours, how was your trip to the emerald city?"

Everyone was tired and Larnie left it to Mae to chat with Henry while he retrieved the luggage.

Seeing Henry jarred him out of the movie of the trip's highlights that was playing in his head. Once the last piece of luggage was in the house, Larnie grabbed his and Mae's and made his way up the stairs to their bedroom.

After placing the luggage on the bed, he immediately moved to the closet and pulled out the box of "Dad's stuff box 2". He pulled back the time magazines and his heart briefly raced as he didn't see it right away, but then there it was. The velvet case just under one of the playboys. He glanced at the door and regulated his breathing as he listened intently for anyone coming up the stairs. Thinking he heard footsteps, he quickly closed the lid on the box, put it back in the closest and turned his attention back to the luggage.

The day Eddie returned from the trip, he was anxious to tell others about it and he phoned Gabe. Gabe told him that a group of them from the grad class were planning to get together. The group ended up congregating at Eddie's place, with his mom in the kitchen making them snacks as they all hung out in his bedroom. Teenager after teenager came through their doors and made their way up to his room. Gabe was there as was Nadia, Angelo, Pete, Raj, Connie, Mina and others. He made out with Mina the night of their grad and he hadn't been sure what to expect since. Mina made her intentions known as she immediately cuddled up to Eddie as if they were a couple. He didn't have any pictures developed yet, but he had the brochures from the Space Needle, the art museum, a brochure of the hotel they stayed at and some post cards showing the Mount St. Helen's volcano. He had everyone's attention in the room as he told them about the ash at the train station and the earthquakes. More people continued to arrive and his mom would direct them to go up stairs to the bedroom, "second door on the right", he'd hear her yell and his room was packed.

Eddie was telling the story about the killer wales they saw during the train ride, when Keith walked into the room and in tow behind him, holding his hand, was Cindy. Eddie suppressed his inner voice that sarcastically asked, "What happened to Mickey?"

"You mentioned killer wales?"

Eddie answered Keith, without looking at Cindy as he re-told an abbreviated version of the story.

"I used to see killer wales in Port McInerey when I was a kid. Any other wildlife you see?"

He stared at Cindy briefly and looked away before saying, "nothing like the wildlife I saw after our grad ceremony."

The laughter from his response allowed him to cast his eyes her way to show his displeasure without others picking it up. He wished he'd been more specific about who was invited and felt a sense of relief when she got up to use the bathroom. Gabe went over and whispered in Keith's ear, as she was gone. That was Gabe. Always astute to what was happening and looking after him. When Cindy returned, she and Keith left shortly afterwards.

CHAPTER 24
Larnie

Two years later, 1982.

They had just watched the Vancouver Canucks defeat the Chicago Blackhawks in their improbable playoff run as they advanced to the National Hockey League's Stanley cup final. It was May 1982 and a moment he would never forget.

When the playoffs started in April, Bev phoned home and announced that she was engaged to her British boyfriend Arthur. Eddie had made plans to move to Vancouver for a new job as a long shoreman. The winds of change were blowing through the family as Larnie reduced his schedule at Thetis to three days a week, as his new career as a journalist grew legs.

After the celebration of the Canucks win with his dad, Eddie bounced into the kitchen for more to drink. It was shaping up to be a great spring he thought, when he heard a thud.

"Dad?"

Eddie raced back into the living room where his dad laid unconscious on the floor beside the coffee table.

Mae, who was at the neighbours at the time, joined Larnie in the ambulance as they rushed him to the hospital. He had not regained consciousness when they arrived at Ranvon General where a doctor, who took him immediately into the operating room, greeted them.

Mae, gripped with worry, anxiously paced up and down the hospital hallway. Eddie implored her to sit with him while they waited. Each minute ticked by as if it wouldn't end and it was nearly and hour before the doctor reappeared. They both stood up, griping onto each other as they moved to hear what he had to say. The doctor looked directly at Mae and spoke in a low voice just above a whisper.

"Your husband is awake now."

Mae gasped and held her hand to her mouth as the tears descended into her fingers.

"He is quite groggy. He has a concussion from when he fell. He fell from a heart attack. His heart is weak and his kidney's are failing. We will be running more tests later and I can give you a more specific update then."

Eddie's grip tightened around his mom as his mind went into a fog trying to navigate what was happening.

The doctor looked at Eddie.

"You father shouldn't have too many visitors and perhaps he should just see your mom first."

Eddie was perplexed at this, as he didn't know at the time that his dad specifically requested to see just his mom. He nodded in response and watched the doctor lead her through the doors to his ailing father.

When they arrived at the hospital, Eddie had phoned Bev and she told him she would get a flight out as soon as possible. At the sight of his mom disappearing behind the doors he asked again to use the phone at the desk and he called Bev collect. Bev asked a bunch of questions he had no answers to and just told her that it didn't sound very good. She had arranged to fly out that night and would be arriving in the morning.

When his mom emerged about an hour later, the look on her face, jolted his fears to life.

"Your dad isn't well Eddie. They don't think...."

They stood clinging to each other for several minutes and a nurse came by and asked if she could help as she placed a box of tissues on the chair beside them.

Mae looked up into her son's soft blue eyes as she mustered her strength.

"Your dad wants me to get something from the house for him and he wants to see you. He can't speak too fast or very much Eddie, so take it easy."

Eddie nodded as his mom's emotions stole her voice.

As he walked into the room, he saw his dad's closed eyes amongst the tubes and machines. Eddie tried to walk like a cat towards the bed, but his dad opened his eyes at his presence, as a smile slid across his face at the sight of his son.

His dad's voice was soft, slow but deliberate. Eddie told him about Bev's plans and he said, "I'll hang on until she gets here." The response brought a flood of tears as his dad used up a limited reservoir of strength to pull Eddie in close. He then whispered into his ear.

"There is so much I want to say to you and tell you. How proud I am of you and how well I know you will do in life. Your mom is going back to the house to get a couple of things I want to give you."

Eddie stood up and reached for the tissue on the bedside table.

"They are diaries that your grandfather kept. Listen carefully Eddie. I want you to read those before sharing them with anyone and be careful with what you do with them. There are some revelations in them."

"I will. For sure I will, Dad."

"One of the things you'll read in there is of a necklace your grandfather took from a Japanese concentration camp during the war. I have that necklace and it's very valuable."

Eddie leaned in with intense focus.

"In the bottom of my tool box in the garage is an appraisal of the necklace. I would like you to make sure you get that and keep it to yourself. You can get the necklace later - it is in our bedroom."

"Dad, I..."

Larnie gripped his hand with a force and strength that startled him.

"Listen to me Eddie. Carefully, please. That necklace could be dangerous. It could change your life. It has a lot of history to it that I haven't pieced all together. Don't forget what I've told you. Sometimes there is nothing we pay more for than money. Don't let that necklace change who you are."

Eddie wanted to tell his dad that he knows about the necklace, though not its value, and that he has one of his grandpa's diaries. But as he looked at his fragile state, it all seemed moot and pointless. Instead, they spent the time reminiscing about the Seattle trip and their experiences together. Eddie was expressing the lessons in life he had learnt from him, when the nurse came in and said that they needed to run more test. Eddie left to wait in the lobby for his mom to return.

Mae drove home, as her heart raced and her face absorbed a flood of tears. The words from the doctor before she left rang in her ears - "You should plan to get his affairs in order." Her mind didn't register any more details after that statement.

She pulled into the driveway and rushed into the house before anyone would see her. Larnie sounded desperate when he gave her the instructions to find his dad's two diaries located in some box in the far right corner of the closest. As soon as the door opened, she raced into the house, up the stairs, and by the time she had pulled out the box from the closest, she was heaving, and out of breath. "Just calm down for a minute and think", she told herself.

She pulled out the Time and Playboy magazines without much thought and a velvet case and placed them all on the bed beside the box. She saw two books that fit what old diaries would look like. Frayed corners and worn covers. She opened both of them, saw the writing of her father-in law, and stuffed them into her purse without a thought of what they may say. She threw the magazines back into the box, put the lid on it, put it back in the closest and then went into the bathroom to wash her face and "take a minute to breath" she told herself.

When she came out of the bathroom, she went for her purse and saw the velvet case that she had forgotten to return to the box. Not wanting to take the box out again, she opened the case to see what was inside. It was empty, so she tossed it into the closet in the general direction of the corner.

Mae handed the diaries to Eddie when she arrived back at the hospital and they spent the rest of the night at Larnie's bedside. It was one thirty in the morning and Eddie had fallen asleep in the chair when a nurse came in and suggested they go home and get some sleep as she promised to call them if something changed. Mae nodded in agreement and said they would be back in a few hours when her daughter arrived from England.

When they got home, Eddie clutched the diaries and said he was going to the kitchen for a drink. He watched his mom head up the stairs for the few hours of sleep she hopefully get and once she had disappeared, he opened the door to the right of the kitchen and stepped into the garage. He stood still, as his eyes adjusted to the low light and reconnoitered the scene in the garage, which contained his dad's tools and had become a storage place for a variety of items. His eyes finally settled on the toolbox stuffed beside some rakes and shovels.

The appraisal from Danoon Jewelry was over three years old. The details and assessed value jolted him and cemented his feet to the floor as his mind raced. He pressed his fingers to his forehead, as his mind seemed to overheat with everything it was processing; he stuffed the appraisal in his pocket and finally sought relief inside on the couch.

~~~~~~
~~~~~~

Eddie stayed out of the fray as his mom and Bev argued over the funeral arrangements. Bev wanted his body cremated and his ashes spread at Hathaway where they shared many memories. His mom almost violently shook her head in response as she called cremation "of the devil". She wanted to purchase a burial plot. Bev called the cost of that "stupid and wasteful". The four days of emotions and sleepless nights, most of which was spent at the hospital, had taken its toll and was spilling out in their heated debate. When Bev finally relented, they both collapsed in the couch in a state of exhaustion and a tidal wave of tears.

He watched his mom as she tried to hold it together. Family members had arrived, including their Uncle Jim and Aunt Marg and Aunt Annabella and Uncle Chad as well as various cousins and friends. His mom appeared in a relentless state of exhaustion that kept her worry just below the surface. He could see it on her face in the mornings and just before bed. She kept it inside her, but Eddie knew his mom's worry was bringing her sleepless nights. She wasn't sure what her financial outlook would be now or what the future held. He wanted to tell her about the necklace, but he wanted to get it re-assessed and have a plan of who to sell it to first.

The presence, support and love he received from Bev, Mina and his mom was as oxygen for his body each day. That necklace gave him hope for the future. He knew from the appraisal that its value would provide his mom with a lot of comfort and give him and Bev other options in life they hadn't considered possible, but he still wanted to be cautious until he had it in his possession and properly assessed. He planned to retrieve it from his parent's bedroom after the funeral when they would be going through his dad's belongings and then he would seek out a buyer. It was thoughts about the future and those plans that would keep him out of a state of shock, sadness and hopelessness.

There were over four hundred people at the funeral and they all stayed for the reception at the church afterwards. The group included journalists and other staff from the paper that had gotten to know Larnie over the few years he'd worked there. They shared stories about his positive outlook and how he'd encourage them at the paper and in particular his dogged determination to research a story well. There were members from the church, Mae's quilting club, Larnie's fishing buddies and people from every house in the neighborhood. Almost everyone from the Thetis warehouse where his dad worked was there as well. Derek Thetis spoke as he remembered losing his own father. He turned to Mae as he said, "Your husband was an integral part of the Thetis family". Eddie wondered if that "family" would be there for his mom afterwards. The latest news was that Thetis was restructuring itself to survive and the workers may get a cash value on their pensions. How much was a subject of heated debates and rumours.

A table was set up with a book for guests to print their names and leave thoughts of condolences to the family. Eddie watched people line up to write in the book. He didn't recognize many faces. His dad's life had touched far more than he ever realized. He took a long pause when he first saw a young woman who looked like Cindy, but then realized the person was shorter and clearly someone else. It transported his mind briefly back to her as he wondered what she was up to. It would have been odd, he thought, to see her at the funeral. He didn't attend her mom's funeral three years previously. The thought softened his heart towards his first girlfriend. Three years since they broke up and they had since both lost a parent. Now at his dad's funeral, his heart felt for the suffering Cindy must have endured when she lost her mom. For a moment, he wondered if he should contact her. But they had not seen each other since they had that awkward and callous exchange when she was in his bedroom with the other friends he had over after the trip to Seattle. As far as he heard, she didn't live in town anymore anyway.

The reception was winding down and Eddie overheard several neighbours and friends promise his mom that they would help her out and support her over the coming weeks. Eddie took great comfort in this as he had still planned to proceed with his plans to move to Vancouver. Some of those stayed to help cleanup and his mom asked him to go back to their house for extra containers to take the leftovers home in.

~~~~~~

As soon as Eddie pulled into the driveway, he noticed the upstairs lights. His voice echoed in the car, "What the hell?!"

He took out his keys but as he got on the doorstep, it was obvious the door was unlocked.

"Hello?!" "Hellloo?!"

His voice filled the entryway as he turned on the light. The upstairs light appeared to be coming from his parent's bedroom and so he made his way up there, taking the stairs two at a time, oblivious to any risks to his own safety. As he got to the top of the steps, he saw the door that was always closed had been swung wide open. His eyes fixated on the entry to his parent's bedroom and he inched closer to the open door.

"Hello?! Anyone here?!" "Hello?!"

He stopped at the doorway with his mouth agape as his eyes scanned the scene. Strewn on the bed were various items including magazines, post cards, trinkets, medals, coins and papers. At the base of the bed were two empty boxes and their lids. One box was upside down and the other on its side had been stepped on. The writing on the box lid on the floor was unmistakable: "Dad's Stuff Box 2". The adrenaline hit his veins as he cried out,

"No! The necklace!"
~~~~~~

He was frantic in going through everything on the bed as he threw the items from one side to the other looking for the velvet case. He then turned around to the open doors in the closet. Clothes from hangers had been knocked to the ground and he picked up each piece and tossed it aside in a thorough search of the closest. He then repeated his search as he tossed the clothes to the opposite side. His chest was heaving and his shirt wet when he came out of the closest and went back to searching the contents on the bed again. Finally, he sat on the edge of the bed with his hands covering his face. The ring from the phone downstairs gonged in his ears and knocked energy into his state of distress.

"Hello?"

"Eddie? You sound out of breath?"

"Sorry Mom, I just ran to get the phone."

"Alright, but what's taking you so long?

As he held the phone to his ear, he could feel the heat being pulled from his body and he turned around as he felt the cool breeze and saw that the back door on the other side of the kitchen was wide open.

"Eddie? Did you hear me?"

"Yes. Yes. I was just busy getting the containers."

"Well, don't bother. We found some here. You stay there. Bev, Arthur and I are going to get a ride back to the house from Edith."

"Mom. You can't come back to the house right now."

Chapter 25
The Necklace in France

The pearly white satin hugged the upper part of her body and let loose below the waist where it fanned out into the shape of an upside down trumpet. Her face, covered by a lace veil couldn't contain her wide smile. Mae watched her daughter, wearing the same dress she wore on her big day twenty-eight years previously, with moist eyes and a beaming smile.

Eddie sat at the wedding reception watching his mom. He had not seen her happy for over a year, since his dad's passing.

"Come dance with your mom, Eddie. This place looks like a castle doesn't it?"

"It is a castle, Mom. This place used to be home to a Duke and Duchess in the 1800s. It probably has more stories to tell than our country does."

Bev had planned to get married in Ranvon, with her dad escorting her down the aisle. She struggled to create a different image of her wedding after her dad's passing and Arthur's parents stepped in, offering to pay for the rental of the Belvoir Castle in England. Bev protested at first as too costly and that it would delay the wedding, as they had to wait for an opening. But then when she took a tour of the place "it just seemed perfect" and "how can I say no", she said.

"Before you dance with him Mom, I want to have a dance with my little brother."

At first, he felt strange dancing so close to his sister, but she took the lead.

"You look stunning Bev as well as the setting."

"Ah thanks. So, how's my little brother enjoying Vancouver?"

"It's good. Gives a lot more options than Ranvon. I have a lot of friends there now."

"Mina's not one of them?"

"Mina and I are still friends. She's going to school at UBC and I don't see too much of her."

"Oh, I see, so how's the job? Mom's proud of you and says you are making good money?"

"It pays well for sure and is unionized with good benefits."

"That doesn't sound overly enthusiastic?"

"Well, I've learnt how to operate a crane."

"You make it sound so dull."

"When I left the mill in Ranvon, I wanted to do something more creative and I'm just not sure this fulfils that as I hoped. Mind you, the people I work with have strong backs and creative vocabularies", Eddie laughed as he thought of some of the characters at work.

It was easy for him to envision a long career as a long shoreman. He had learnt how to operate the various cranes and loading equipment and felt efficient and confident in the job that provided a pay rate higher than most. But something hung inside him, something unsettled that threatened to unhinge the connection between that easy life to one that fulfilled him. His dad's words to do something that "you enjoy and challenges you" still sang to his heart. Loading cargo on to ships for a living didn't feel like quite the right fit for him. He had started scanning the want ads in the newspapers, but hadn't seen anything that piqued his interest and certainly nothing that paid as well as he had become used to.

"I guess you and Arthur are going to live in England forever, now?"

"You make that sound like its some final, forever after thing. Life's not a fairy tale though and forever is a long time. Who knows? It's home now and I'm studying to be a marine biologist, as you know. Lots of opportunities around here for that and Art's job and family are here. Dad taught us to be adventurous and not to sell ourselves short. I live by those words, so who knows."

As he chewed on her words, his thoughts drifted to his dad and his last days. What did his dad intend him to do with the diaries that were such a priority near the end of his life for him to have? It was a question that rolled around in his thoughts over the past year.

He hadn't revealed any details he read in them to anyone including his mom, who didn't ask. Why his dad guarded them with intense diligence would be obvious to anyone who read them. They revealed family history he wanted to keep buttoned down. Was there a way he could release just fragments of the diaries? The life of a teenager and young adult in a single parent home in the 1920s. The conditions and challenges of living during the great depression and his grandpa's resourcefulness that got them through it. The stories about his grandpa's newspaper articles. The changes the world war brought to his grandpa's world and to their family. He pondered how those changes affected his dad and down to him and Bev.

The richness of the diaries and their writer's style of telling the stories was captivating, educational and inspiring, he thought. But then there were the things he felt were too explosive that could supersede all else that his grandpa wrote. The details about the necklace. The necklace that was stolen that only he had knowledge of. The disclosure of what his grandpa faced when he got home and the heartache, indignation and shame within the family. Was it necessary? Are some secrets from the past best left buried? Eddie had contemplated these things many times over the last year.

"So Mom says you are going to France after the wedding?"

"I am. I figure I came all this way "across the pond" that I should take advantage of it and see more."

Bev laughed at Eddie's feigned British accent when he said "across the pond".

That was not his reason for going to France.

After the robbery at the house the day of the funeral, he had spent a lot of energy on his own investigation of who the thief may have been. The police showed no inclination to investigate beyond what they concluded that day at the house. They took pictures and notes and concluded much the same that he had. A thief, perhaps someone who knew they were away at the funeral, had broken into the house and was looking for something. The person or persons then left by the back door in a hurry, likely as they heard the car coming into the driveway. Family members were queried as to their knowledge of anything the thief could have be looking for. When his mom said "No, I don't really know what was in those boxes", it confirmed to him that she had no knowledge of the necklace. Bev said the only thing she knew about was the two silver medals from world war two. The police retrieved the medals that they found on the bed and had bagged, "are these the medals you remember, Ma'am?" Eddie gave a similar response as she confirmed that they were. He made no mention of the necklace, the appraisal of which he kept in his wallet.

His investigation into the necklace had led from one dead end to a new lead to another dead end. Was it someone who left the funeral early or perhaps a person who didn't attend the service but would have known they were not home? He figured the former was more likely as the perpetrator could have been at the house much sooner otherwise. Then there was the matter of who would have known about the necklace to search for it? Eddie parked that question as he poured over the names of those that signed the memory book. It was a collection of family, friends, work colleagues of his dad, neighbours and acquaintances. There were many names on the list that he didn't recognize and others that he couldn't read from the poor handwriting. He made a list of potential suspects. There were two people at the newspaper that his dad often mentioned in his conversations. Could he have told one of them about the necklace?

Reid McDonald was the first one he put on the list. Reid left the service early and Eddie thought he was an overly quiet man for someone who was a journalist. Reid wrote about local sports and community events in the paper. Eddie checked out his house and vehicle and saw no pattern of change in his life, but he met a few times with another journalist, Pat Hallinger whose reputation for writing agitating articles about politicians and sports figures made him a controversial figure in the community. He saw McDonald pass something to Hallinger in a paper bag once, but he could not determine what it was. Hallinger was someone his dad mentioned a few times and he wasn't at the funeral, and so he was added to the list. A couple of months later Hallinger renovated his house and he had bought a new car. Eddie circled his name on the list.

Others that he made note of included two neighbours: Elsie Olson and Henry Harris. Elsie was a friend of his moms and over at the house on a regular basis. She would be very familiar with their house and Eddie noted that the two houses, built by the same developer, were close to identical. She had been over to their house on a more frequent basis since his dad's passing and his mom spoke of her fondly. Eddie viewed her with suspicion as someone who may have other motives. He knows she left the service early because he remembers seeing her car in her driveway when he pulled up that fateful day. If she was such a strong support to his mom, why did she leave early? Observing her for several days had produced nothing. When she invited his mom to go on a cruise ship to India with her and that she would pay, his suspicions spiked. The first cruise ships had just started to come into the port of Vancouver and they seemed impossibly expensive. How could she afford that and why wouldn't she go with her husband? He circled her name on the list as well. The other neighbour, Henry Harris, "Double H" as he would sometimes call himself, also left the service early. Eddie found Harris to be mostly annoying, as he would fill every empty space with nonsensical chatter. He was nosy enough to find out about the necklace and lived next door, so he was added to the list. When the fall hit and he bought a new ride on law mower for his small yard, Eddie almost circled his name too. Though he noted that Double H's personality fit with the expensive and seemingly unnecessary purchase a couple of months before winter.

Other names that stood out for him from the service were two from Thetis, John Cheo and Lance Limbcome, the Jeweller Graeme Montgomery and his Uncle Chad. Then another name that was recorded in the guest book at the funeral he couldn't ignore. While he was not sure if he'd have recognized him, he was certain he didn't see Jeff Blackstock at the service. Yet there was his name, written in the guest book.

The two from Thetis were known friends of his dad and with Thetis in financial uncertainty; he put them on the list. Cheo had stayed with his wife until the end and didn't leave early, so Eddie put a light cross through his name. Limbcome left early and Eddie watched him closely for any changes in his lifestyle. He always found the man to be grandiose in the stories he'd tell.

Montgomery had flown in from Australia for the service, which seemed extravagant and he left the service early. But the only information he could get on him was that he retired to Australia where he owned a farm. Eddie circled his name on the list too.

The other person on the list that he circled was his Uncle Chad. He loved his Uncle growing up and always called him Uncle, though he was actually his second cousin. He remembers fondly how his Uncle Chad would join in a game of street hockey with his friends, playing in his business shoes, shirt, and tie. His friends would marvel at how his uncle would switch hands throughout the game and he could shoot right or left. Now he viewed him with some suspicion. He certainly had the opportunity and knew their house well. Why did he leave the service early? Shouldn't he have stayed to help? Then when he bought a new convertible with loud whitewall tires, Eddie circled his name on the list.

Then there was Jeff Blackstock. Was he at the service because his dad wrote the article about his deceased wife? Cindy is one individual Eddie knows for certain had knowledge about the necklace. Could she have told her dad?

But each time Eddie would watch or come up with something on a person on the list, he'd find nothing else to help locate the necklace. He wanted to put it to rest. It caused him to suspect individuals, including those close to him, like his uncle and their former neighbours and he wondered if unfairly so.

He had concluded that his search for the necklace had consumed too many of his thoughts and dominated too much of his energy and time and it was time to drop the whole matter. He'd stew about any new discovery related to it. It crowded out other pursuits in his life. It was like a force that was always hungry that he would continue to feed with every small morsel of new information he'd unearth in the quest to find it and the thief.

But then one day as he was passing a newsstand in Vancouver, an article in an American newspaper caught his eye by its title: World War II artifact found? The article described a gold necklace that a museum in France had acquired. He studied the black and white picture of the necklace in the article and it certainly looked like it could be the necklace he remembered. Was it the same necklace? Had someone sold it to the museum and if so, who? He was determined to find out and had arranged his travel include the museum.

"I hope you are going to Paris when in France? Art and I have been there and the Eiffel Tower is a must see, Eddie. It is almost twice as tall as the space needle. And Paris is such a beautiful city."

"It's on my list, for sure Bev. Hey, how do you think Mom's doing?"

"She's having a good time here, but I worry about her. Do you think she got enough money from Dad's pension?"

"Bev, your wedding and the trip here has lifted her spirits a lot. I can't remember the last time I saw her so happy. I'm in Vancouver now and don't see her often, but we talk on the phone three or four evenings a week. She doesn't talk about the money situation and won't say much when I ask her - she just says she's okay and will manage. They had insurance on the house so at least she doesn't have a mortgage payment. I know she has good supports in the community and she has taken on a job at a sewing shop."

They talked about the troubles at Thetis and were at least thankful it was after their mom received the cash from their dad's pension. The news story was that the workers might get forty percent of their pension money if the company goes under. Their Uncle Chad advised their mom to take the cash out of the pension, rather than monthly sums.

"I plan to contact Mom more myself once we get settled after the wedding. She should be moving on with her life. I miss Dad so much as we all do, but she is too young to..."

"I know sis. You have a day after the wedding before you are heading out, right?"

Eddie could feel his sister nod as she rested her head on his shoulder. The discussion had lifted emotions within her that struck the same chord in him.

"How about we plan to take Mom out for tea before you and I leave here? Just the three of us?"

Eddie left for France the night after they had tea with their mom. She kept telling them she was fine financially and that they shouldn't worry and needed "to live your own lives". Her independent spirit lifted theirs. Bev and Eddie looked at each other with comfort in their eyes and laughter in their voices that their mom would be okay when she went out of her way to enunciate words that would have left them searching for a dictionary.

"You two should lose the mesmeric concern with my financial well being. I am not as desultory as you seem to think."

With his mom's voice ringing inside his head, Eddie headed to the airport and his flight to the south of France.

~~~~~~

Now Eddie stood at the entrance of the Museé Dauphinois. His attempts to pronounce the name or read the brochure he picked up was his own version of mission impossible. It was the first time he had been in a foreign country where he didn't speak the language and not everyone he talked to could understand him. He thought he could get by easily enough, but sadly he remembered little from the French class he took in grade eight and truly felt like he was an alien transported to another world. He didn't need an interpreter to realize that the buildings he saw had been built by a generation of people before Canada had become a country. He took in the museum, keeping to himself but in awe of the exhibits when he spotted the glass display with the necklace. He pulled the article out of his wallet and held it up, with its black and white picture to the necklace in front of him. The picture seemed dull compared to the splendour of the real thing in front of him. The centre of the necklace stood out with a large diamond, whose sparkle hit him in the eye like sunlight coming through a window. He could see why there had been news about such a stunning piece of jewelry as the diamond reflected lights of blue in its colour. That wasn't its only feature. Square little chunks of gold circled the out edge of the necklace. Eddie counted six of them as he tried to visualize the necklace he and Cindy had looked at in his parents' closet that day.

"Quite stunning, isn't it?"

Eddie hadn't seen the gentleman beside him and was startled to hear someone speak English, though in a heavy British accent.
~~~~~~

"Oh, sorry didn't mean to surprise you there, good chap. I see you holding that article and figured you speak English."

"I do and thank you."

He held out his hand and introduced himself as Nigel Nguyen, a professor of history at a University in England. He was there, having been drawn to the museum when he read about the necklace. Eddie asked him if he knew the origin of the necklace and Nigel told him that is a mixture of some facts and legend. The necklace was a relic that was commandeered during the Second World War and had resurfaced recently. The questions were who commandeered it and from whom. That is where the legend comes in, he said. Many believe pieces like these were taken out of Malaysia and other countries in the orient by the Japanese as the Japanese raided countries and accumulated wealth in gold and precious stones.

Eddie took down Nigel's contact information and asked him if he may contact him for more in the future for his expertise. Nigel laughed as he gave his information, "Not sure I am much of an expert, more of an enthusiastic amateur on these things, but sure." He saw Nigel as a potential resource who could help if the necklace in front of them was indeed his grandfathers.

"Thanks again, Nigel. Hey before you leave, can you read French?"

"Yes. A much helpful thing if you are going to spend any time in France."

"Yeah, so I have discovered. Can you tell me if it says anything about who the museum acquired the necklace from?"

"Of course."

Nigel pointing to writing beside the display.

"It's on loan to them from an Australian collector. You see here, it says his name, John B. Harris."

CHAPTER 26

A Life Turned Around

Water bottles, tires, rope, wood and random pieces of plastic made up the debris she collected, depositing what she could carry into the garbage bag with her. It's the evidence of shipwrecks and careless liter that the ocean brings to the shores of the rugged north coast of British Columbia.

As Meagan bent down to pick up a piece of plastic that a fish or bird might mistake as food, she heard the high pitch chirp of a bald eagle.

"Perhaps he sees the tattoo on your shoulder," her friend Nora remarked.

The tattoo shows a soaring eagle with the words: "Don't be afraid to spread your wings, you might be surprised at the heights you can reach."

An artist in Vancouver sketched and inked it on her right shoulder on the fifth anniversary of her mom's death. Nora had suggest the tattoo and emboldened her to do it. "In memory of your mom and as a slogan for a new beginning," she said. She certainly needed both at the time. After her mom's death, her initial determination was to use those words as a motto for her life. A series of impulsively bad decisions and an overall malaise of numbness derailed those aspirations and steered her life in a different direction.

After her mom's death, she instinctively knew that her emotional state was not in a good place to start any romantic relationship. That same vulnerability climbed into the arms of Peter, when he showed up. Somehow, the drunken Peter that she remembered at the campsite was forgotten as the gregarious, helpful guy she had first met, showed up. When she discovered that Peter liked his drugs with the alcohol sometimes, she should have ran for the hills. Nora told her to. Other friends too. But she yielded to the affection that came with the package and after nearly three years she had a drug habit herself and a sea of debt.

She had successfully pushed away any of her friends or family except those that simply refused to exit her life. She had a car accident when she was drunk one night that should have been a wakeup call, but instead just added to her woes and propelled her further into an abyss. To fix her financial troubles she made a series of poor decisions that took her years to recover from and some of her relationships remained shipwrecked as a result. One relationship she took advantage of was her Aunt Marg and Uncle Jim. She stole several items from them that she didn't think they'd miss, as she told herself that she'd "pay them back." But the fishing rod she sold had value "beyond dollars and cents" her Uncle Jim would tell her later. Her response that he was just being too sentimental would haunt her for the year that she avoided them entirely. She masked her shame with angry responses. But they kept calling. They hung in there with her. Nora did too.

Nora's "I believe in you" and "you'll get past this" mantras held strong. The outdoor hikes and adventures Nora dragged her on often provided the only reprieve from her "messed up" daily life and the torture it delivered to her thoughts every day. On one such trip, while they laid under darkness in a tent, her desperation erupted in tears she couldn't cover with other emotions or activity. To Nora, she opened the doors of her world that she had kept tightly closed. The financial hopelessness, the drug and alcohol use, the loneliness, the fearful anxiety about the future and the lack of desire to crawl out of bed some days. Nora started calling her every day after that to check in on her. She opened up about everything in her life to Nora and expected that she would eventually push her away too. But she didn't. Nora knows her so well she can tell her mood when they talk on the phone. Nora was one of only two people that she has ever told about the teeth. "Rock solid", she would describe her friendship and trust in Nora.

After the split with Peter, she took two years digging herself out debt and started the process of repairing relationships she had torched along the way. One of those was her father, whom she also stole from. Her relationships with her siblings had not be affected in the same way, but they were in a state of neglect.

When her dad remarried, the small wedding became the catalyst for a family reunion that they have continued every summer since. Before the wedding, her dad invited her out for coffee. She expected to see Cindy and Tommy there at the café, but it was just the two of them. He wanted a new start too. He apologized for not being there for her when she was growing up and for not being "more forthcoming" about the past with her mom. With her eyes swelling, she stopped him as he said that. She didn't want to revisit that past again. She had her own admissions to make and wanted to keep some details buried. They both should, she figured. She was unfair to him in the past and told him that. It started when they moved to Ranvon. In her head, she would accuse him of things that turned out to be false. The revelations of those untruths should have brought a renewal in their relationship, but her previous attitude towards him still influenced their relationship as she avoided him and often looked at him with scorn. It was feelings that had fostered inside her for so long that when her life started to spiral downhill, she blamed him for her mom's death. It was just easy and convenient to reach back to those feelings she held for so long than to deal with her own problems. She told him about her own healing and forward movement in her life and that she didn't fault him in anyway for her mom's passing.

When she saw Cindy at the wedding, it was first awkward and cold as her sister said,

"How are doing? You kind of fell off the earth there."

It was six months after their mom passed that she got wrapped into the life with Peter and that was the start of little to no contact with Cindy. Prior to that, they talked on the phone most nights. As the weeks went by without contact, they soon became months and then years. She knew Cindy had moved to a city in the interior. She felt shame for what her life had become and that she couldn't look after herself properly, let alone be the big sister she thought she should be. After the reception, they went for a long walk together. They laughed as they reminisced about their childhood and they held hands as they walked at times - just as they had when they were little girls and into their early teens. They caught up on each other's lives and made a commitment to be there for each other.

"I really need you in my life Cindy", she told her with an air of vulnerability. Cindy nodded as her cracking voice allowed a quiet, "Me too, sis." They called each other every week after that and made plans see each other several times a year.

They try to get together as a family at Christmas too, but sometimes life and work make it infeasible. Tommy moved to Alberta, works in the oil fields and is married with two small children and the drive in the winter to visit at Christmas was too much most years.

Two years after her split from Peter, Nora suggested the North Coast Trail hike. The first time, it took them five days as they experienced the rain and mist of the coast and camped on the beaches. Parts of the trail are defined by its mud and regardless of one's fancy footwork, succumbing to its ubiquitous presence is inevitable. In some sections, she wondered if full body suite would be required to navigate the swampy terrain. Then they would come to a section with wooden walkways. Like something out of The Hobbit, the walkways assimilated to the scene and are home to lichen, mushrooms and all kinds of forest fungi. They appear as part of the natural fabric of the forest around them rather than constructed by human hands. She would stop on the walkways and take several pictures in sequence to capture the size of the towering old growth sika spruce, hemlock and cedar trees that surrounded them. The views and wonder of it all nurtured her well-being.

They found the old Danish gravesites that spoke to the rich history in the area. The large tombstone deep into the woods of a twelve-year-old boy who stepped on a nail shocked and captivated her imagination of what it was like to live there a hundred years ago. Then there was the interaction with other hikers, many of them from other countries, which added culture to the adventure. When they finished that first hike, she told Nora the experience was "like food for my soul".

It was just before that hike that Nora took her into the tattoo shop. A multi day backcountry-hiking trip has been part of their time together every year since. Last year's West Coast Trail was an experience she talked about for months afterwards. Returning to the North Coast Trail every couple of years had become part of the tradition, along with the small empty bottle she would bring to collect sand from one of the beaches. Sand that she would add to the vase full of grains that her mom started collecting from beaches when she was young.

This year, they joined a team of hikers to assist in cleaning up the shores of the spectacularly long beaches they would cross on the hike. It was her second volunteer commitment. The other being a woman's centre, where she'd cook to help those who had no place to go and needed shelter from an abusive situation.

They had managed to hike close to fourteen kilometres, many of it over root balls and through muddy swamps, wooden walkways and old growth forest, before arriving at the beach. The grit from the sand cleaned off a lot of the dirt on their gators before they pitched their tent high on the beach and above the tide line. Nora pointed out the creek nearby that they could use for their water source as she pulled out the white gas powered stove and their freeze dried dinner. They watched the sandpipers on the beach and then the burnt orange sunset over the horizon, before crawling into the tent.

The crashing waves of the ocean provided a loud rhythmic sound that washed over her like a blanket of peace as she laid in her sleeping bag. She turned on her flashlight and reached for the note from her husband that she saved for this moment.

"Sweet and Salty: She is sweet and salty. She reminds me to tell her when I arrive somewhere because she cares about my wellbeing. She encourages me to do the things I love. Her touch gives a calm and sense of aliveness within my soul. She is gentle and caring and comfortable being vulnerable with me. Her heart is soft and sometimes it shows in her worry about the people she loves. She cares about her community and the world around her and makes a difference. She can be assertive and very pragmatic. She adds the salt and flavour to the lives of those around her. When we make love and she sweats, her salty taste is so sweet.

I know that you will be thinking about your mom this weekend and those salty tears will flow. Though I won't be there to absorb them for you, my heart is with you babe. I love you Meagan.

Xoxoxo

Mack"

Clutching the letter to her chest, she felt the sorrow rising in her throat as she breathed heavily and read it again.

Nora, asleep next to her, had stirred and reached over and touched her hand. Nora's silent comfort infused oxygen into her being.

It was nine years ago when she met Mack on the Juan De Fuca trail. His untamed curly brown hair and blue eyes and "tree trunk" legs captivated her as they interacted along the trail and during campfires at night. His voice would pitch with excitement when he showed off his knowledge of the woods, the wildlife and marine life they encountered along the way. He lived in a small town and she lived in the city, vowing, "to never live again" in a small town. She told him so. He bet her that he could convince her otherwise. "Really? So what do you offer in your bet?" she said in a flirtatious tone. He responded that if she didn't live in a small town sometime in the next three years, he'd buy her the best halibut dinner anywhere at a restaurant in Tofino, BC. "And what do you propose you get if you win?" The glint in his eyes as he responded told her that she was doomed to lose the bet. "A kiss."

Their first kiss happened at the end of the hike, with their packs on and overlooking the marine life in small ponds at Botanical beach. As they left, she told him he might need to come up with a different prize if he wins the bet. He said he already had something in mind, but would tell her when he was ready to collect.

Two years later, when they were on their honeymoon in Mexico, he presented her with a silk pink lingerie piece and said, "I'd like you to wear this for losing the bet." Six months after that, he'd tell her that maybe that wasn't fair after all as he asked her to make him breakfast topless. It was in their kitchen in the small coastal town that they would settle into.

The life they had fashioned together was unimaginable to her when she went on that first hike of the North Coast Trail with Nora. They now own a campground together that provides social interactions with tourists that include many Europeans and young adults seeking to catch the waves with their surfboards. She greets the visitors and cooks meals that they offer to the campers. Mack also pilots a floatplane occasionally and runs a fishing guide business.

One day, he left before the sun had arrived and when he returned he was sweaty and tasting like the salt of the sea. She looked at him and felt a hunger she couldn't contain as she kissed him the moment he stepped in the doorway. "Let me get washed up first babe, I smell like fish and sea," he told her. She reached down, pulled off his white tee shirt, grabbed his hand as she led him to the couch in their living room and then she pulled her own top off as she turned to face him. "I like your taste and smell, it makes me want you more." She thought back to that day and she read his letter again with a smile this time.

Before closing her eyes, she pulled out the picture she brought of their daughter Trudy, now five. Nora looked over.

"I'm sure her and Christine are having a great time together this weekend."

"I bet they are. Hopefully our husbands are not letting them just eat ice cream and cereal."

"Well, good night Nora."

Meagan turned on her side to go to sleep as she thought of their two daughters, growing up in a small town together. The wind blew at the tent as she listened to the ocean's sounds with the imbuement of serenity and the calming of her spirit it brought. The tide is going out she thought. With a warmth of contentment in her heart, she closed her eyes and let the orchestra of the ocean's crashing waves permeate her being as she drifted off to sleep.

CHAPTER 27

A Mysterious Life

There was surprising very little to go through after 91 years of life.

"So, this is it? This is what remains of a person's life after they leave this world?"

"Eddie, don't sound so dramatic. Your great aunt lived a full life. Most of us hope we get to live that long."

As he listened to his mom's words, it struck him the unfairness of it all. Why did she get to live to 91 and his grandfather, her brother, only 71? His dad only lived to age 49.

If his grandfather had lived that long and his dad was still alive, how different might his life be?

His Aunt Annabella was certainly no pack rat. Perhaps she had just culled out anything of no further value to her? Eddie, his mom and her husband of seven years, Greg, were the ones that stayed over after the funeral to go through her belongings. The caretaker at the home had asked if they could have everything removed within a week. He had retrieved the belongings she had in the storage area and deposited them in the middle of her 440 sq foot apartment in southern California. All that she had left behind was contained within that space.

As he looked around the room, his eyes could easily catch most of it. He made a mental note of what was there:

A twin bed, a TV that sat on top of a four drawer dresser, a TV stand beside the bed with a clock radio on top of it, a few pictures on the walls, a withering plant in the corner, a small kitchen table with two chairs and the half a dozen dishes his mom had taken out of the cupboards. Finally, placed in the middle of the room were the two boxes that came from the storage.

"Anything in the closets?" Eddie asked as he saw Greg open the bi-fold door.

"A few clothes, a housecoat, slippers and it looks like two pairs of shoes. She must have clothes in the dresser."

"I looked before I took the dishes out of the cupboards and it's not much. Mostly socks, underwear, and a couple pairs of pants. She has no pots in here, what did she cook with?"

"Mom, I think her meals were delivered. Remember we cancelled her meals on wheels service?"

"I guess, but all her meals? Anyway, most of this stuff can just go to the Salvation Army."

"Mae, perhaps we should call them now and arrange for pick up?"

As his mom nodded her agreement, Eddie started opening the boxes from the storage.

Old newspapers sat at the top of the first box, as if providing cover for anything below. Eddie lifted them out and put them on the floor next to him.

"Those look like stories from the war."

Her words signaled to him that she was watching even as she was cleaning.

"Just newspapers, no magazines?"

"So far, yeah."

"Your grandpa kept a lot of magazines I found when I went through his stuff from his boxes. Some of them were pretty disgusting. But I must say I sure got a pretty penny for the Marilyn Monroe playboy magazine. Apparently it was the first edition they came out with."

Eddie had never heard his mom talk about anything from his grandpa's stuff before, and it temporally froze his thoughts, as he looked over at her. Her mention of that magazine took him back to when he saw it in the closest as a teenager. He wanted to ask her what she got for it. As he was swallowing that question down his throat, she gave the answer.

"You see that new car I drove down here? Bought it with cash from that magazine. Should have sold it years ago when I really could have used the money."

Eddie turned his attention back to the open box as he wondered if his dad had known the value in that magazine. Below the newspapers were black & white photos, some grouped and bound together. These are true treasures, he thought. He noticed his dad's features in pictures of his grandfather. One was of his aunt, with youthful looks and long dark hair flowing down towards a summer skirt that she wore with a big captivating smile. The faint image of a sailboat in the background had him ponder where the picture might have been taken, as he flipped it over to read the handwritten words "Annabella, Aug 1922". Eddie put the picture aside as he made a mental note of the date. Sticking in the recesses of his memory was the year 1921. His great grandma moved that year from the States to Canada with her three children, except that Annabella disappeared on the way. She'd resurface years later as his grandpa tells in one of the diaries.

Flipping through the pics, he stopped at one of a young tall man with short hair and wearing what looked to be a white marine's shirt. Who is this, he wondered, as he flipped the picture over for the answer, "Marv, Aug 1922". He couldn't recall any conversations of a Marv, but clearly he was a friend of hers as she kept his picture all these years.

Then at the bottom of the box, wrapped in newsprint, were several cups, saucers and plates.

"Looks like someone's old china. Maybe your grandfather's mom passed it down to her."

Eddie realized his mom was likely watching him go through the pictures and he decided to ask her later if she knew any of the stories behind them.

At the bottom of the box were several tiny cups he could fit over his finger.

"What are these?"

He took pleasure in knowing it would elicit laughter from his mom, as she answered.

"You don't know what those are? Looks like your aunt had a thimble collection. They had a practical use for sewing, but for some people, they were something inexpensive to collect."

"What are we going to do with all this stuff?"

"Well, most of that looks like memories we should keep. I'll take pictures of everything and get a copy developed for your sister and you. Then the two of you can let me know if there is something you want. How does that sound?

"Sounds great, Mom. Bev might want that china."

"Then she can pay for me to ship it to Scotland."

Bev and Arthur had moved to Scotland a few years ago with their two daughters, now eight and five.

"Actually, now that I think about it, Greg and I are thinking of making a trip to Scotland next year to see them, maybe we can take these with us. Eddie, you and Vivienne and the kids should consider coming too."

"Well, let me know your plans and we'll talk about it. We just did the trip here to Disneyland."

He was being polite in his answer. He knew it was not something they'd be doing. Before the service for his aunt, he told his mom about his upcoming career change, but he didn't mention how unhappy Vivienne was about it. He felt it was his destiny of sorts and Vivienne saw it as a major disruption and unnecessary risk. The cost and time needed for a trip to Scotland in all that was prohibitive and unlikely. He wouldn't spend much energy thinking about it.

Eddie ripped the tape off the lid of the second box, and said out loud, "What treasures might be in this one?"

Sitting at the top, was a drawing, all in pencil, of a lobster surrounded by barnacles, driftwood, rocks, a few small crabs and ocean waves in the background. The drawing laid flat and spread across the entire width and length of the box. The level of detail engaged his senses as he took it in and pictured himself on the beach with the wind and ocean waves watching the crustaceans raise their claws towards him in a defensive posture. He used a small knife to lift the picture out of the box, which revealed several more hand drawn pictures. Pictures of forests, mountains, sea life and people.

"Where did these come from?"

Reaching for her reading glasses, Mae walked over to Eddie and bent down for a better look.

"Ah, yes. See that in small print in the corner? The initials, AT. Your aunt had a lot of artistic ability when she applied it."

As his mom turned back to her cleaning, he dug down to the last picture. The drawing highlighted the features of the young man, including his square jaw, long hair and chiseled biceps. He instantly looked familiar as he thought of the black of white photo of "Marv".

Under the pictures, he pulled out a large metal ladle with an exaggerated curved handle at the end. He looked for any markings on it as he held it up.

"Why keep this?"

"Looks like a big soup ladle. During the war, many folks had to ration their food and soup was easy to make as you could add almost anything to it. My guess is that ladle was something she used a lot. Maybe she kept it as a reminder of that time."

Eddie placed it beside the box as he reached in to retrieve several coins, both from the USA and Canada. Apparently, she had a coin collection. One set that stood out was a 1917 Canadian penny that was the size of a silver dollar and another 1917 penny that was the size of the pennies in his change. Must have been the year they changed the size of them, he figured as pulled out a binder that contained a stamp collection.

"Looks like a few stories behind these."

Eddie was thinking something similar as he chewed on his mom's thought and looked into the last item in the box that had rested under the stamp collection.

Before he lifted it out, he glanced back to see that his mom had moved into the kitchen area to clean. He suspected what it might be as he carefully handled the small notebook that had an elastic band around. The brittle elastic came off in his hands as he held it up. Doesn't appear anyone looked at this recently, he thought. The black cover was well creased with the edges fraying away. He opened the first page.

"Dairy and thoughts of Tony Teach. V. 1."

It had been several years since he last looked at any of the other diaries. After his search for the missing necklace came up dry time and time again, he eventually parked it out of his mind as the daily commitments of life took over. The diaries, his research notes from the hunt for the necklace and other material from his grandfather all sat in the locked cabinet at his house - over a thousand miles away. He hadn't opened it for several years, until just before this trip to California when he went to it in search of a phone number. It started with a phone call he got from England in the middle of the day.

"Hello?"

"Hi there chap?"

The voice, with the heavy British accent, was unmistakable.

"Well this is a pleasant surprise. What has Professor Nguyen calling me?"

"It's been a few years."

"Indeed it has."

"You still looking for information on that necklace of your grandfathers?"

"Oh you bet. Of course I am."

Eddie knew his excitement was emulating through the telephone line as he responded. He had all but abandoned hope of anything coming of this. He asked Nigel Nguyen so many questions the day they met he finally had to disclose the details that he knew about his grandpa's necklace.

He concluded that necklace in the Museé Dauphinois wasn't his grandfather's. He phoned the jeweller Graeme Montgomery who was in Australia and told him about the necklace in France. Montgomery said that he initially wondered the same thing when he saw the story, but the museum piece was not the same. While stunning and beautiful, it did not have the extremely rare blue diamond that was in the piece Eddie's father had brought into his jewelry store.

Nigel's voice matched his delight as he responded:

"Well, good chap, I may have uncovered a mystery that could solve the question of the origins of that necklace."

"Really? What are you waiting for Nigel, tell me!"

He could hear Nigel's joyful chuckle as he was about to answer.

"Well, a group of archeologist here have found Japanese molds used to melt gold into shapes. Shapes like the gold chunks you saw on that necklace."

"Uh huh."

"Those molds include Japanese symbols. The symbols, translated into English are: AK."

"Akitsugu Kishaimoto."

"Precisely what I was thinking. The mythical Kishaimoto treasure. Also, the brutal Japanese commander from World War Two who ran POW camps in the Pacific."

"This is quite the revelation professor. Are you sure?"

"Absolutely. Have you recovered the necklace yet?"

The "whoosh" of Eddie's sigh was loud and pronounced. He still had several potential suspects, but he had let it go years ago. It had taken up too much of his time, energy and mental capacity to continue to invest in it any further. This new revelation piqued his interest.

"I guess not then. Do you know anyone who saw the necklace that could verify if it has the Japanese symbols on it?"

"Yes, I have an idea. Nigel, does the necklace in the museum have the initials?"

"No. All signs point to it being created later as a replica of something."

They chatted a bit more about the mythical Kishaimoto treasure and how the recent discovery had breathed new life into the legend. "You know it also means any found pieces would be worth that much more now", the professor emphasized. Eddie was keen to know if it was indeed part of the Kishaimoto treasure; the monetary value of the necklace was secondary in his mind. The value and importance it added to the life story of his grandfather was what kept the story alive in his heart, even if buried at times. As soon as Eddie hung up, he made his way to the lock cabinet and the file he had created years previously. In a notebook where he recorded his findings, he found the phone number he was looking for. He hoped the number was still active as he reached for the phone.

"Hello I am phoning for Graeme Montgomery?"

"Oh hi there. Are you phoning about the will?"

"The will?"

"Yes. Sorry, perhaps you hadn't been informed, Mr. Montgomery has passed away. I am Robert Harris and I am the executor of his will. I have been receiving a number of calls about it and assumed that was why you are calling?"

"No, it's not actually. When did he die?"

"Let's see, it's June now, so that would be four months ago."

"Oh my condolences to the family."

"I will pass those on. Who am I speaking to?"

"Oh, just an old friend. Actually, it was my dad that was a friend of his."

"I see. I was going to say if you are listed in the will it may take several months yet to liquidate the assets, but it's certainly worth waiting for."

"I am not. Unfortunately. Thanks for your time."

Eddie hung up before Robert Harris got a chance to ask him anything else.

He was recalling those conversations when the weight of his mom's hand on his shoulder brought him back to the diary he held.

"Well, that looks like quite the find. You still have those other diaries of your grandfathers?"

"Yeah, I do. Haven't looked at them in some time though."

"Well, why don't you take that one and add to the collection. Maybe you could write a book on it sometime."

Eddie smiled, as he knew his mom's comment was her way of encouraging him in his decision to change careers and pursue one as a journalist.

He started to pack the stuff back into the box, when he spotted one last item at the bottom that had slipped underneath the box flap. He pulled it out. It was a black and white postcard with a lobster on the cover. He flipped it over.

"Ma, I am okay. I have a good life here. I am sorry for the worry I probably caused you and the missed birthdays. I love you. Annabella."

He looked at the post date and saw June 6, 1926. He slipped the postcard into the front flap of the diary.

After they packed up the final items and left, his mind would not rest without reading the details of the diary. Why hadn't Annabella passed on this diary when she gave his dad the one labeled V. 3? What does this diary reveal about his grandfather?

Eddie picked up speed on the I5 highway with these questions sending adrenaline through his veins. Vivienne and the kids flew down for the service so they could all go to Disneyland beforehand, but he insisted that he would take the long drive down to California so he could check out Standford University where he had applied for a journalism fellowship. Now the drive home seemed impossibly long. When he passed a state police patrol car, the instinctive easing on the gas peddle slowed down his thinking as well. He pulled off the highway and decided he didn't need to rush home, as he looked for a coffee shop.

He was oblivious to the other patrons in the café as he read his grandpa's words, written almost seventy years ago. A few of the pages were loose and flimsy and he was careful to limit his touch on each page, as if the words would lift off suddenly if he didn't treat them with respect.

Gaps in the story about his grandfather started to fill in. Like missing puzzle pieces tumbling into place. The diary detailed the move they made from "upstate New York to Canada". His great grandmother lost her husband to the First World War and would later take the three kids, including his grandfather to Canada, where she was from. His grandpa's words, written in reflection several years later gave him new insight on the war's impact on the family. As he looked at the date, it startled him to realize his grandpa would have only been fourteen when he penned these words.

"June 15, 1922

I watched Ma wait by the front window for days after the Great War had ended for word about Pa. My memories of him are fading and I wish I had written down the things I remember before they are erased from my memory forever. I was nine when he left. Pa and Ma argued for weeks prior to that date. I heard her tell him they could go to her home in Canada and he'd say "This is my country" and then "You don't think Canada won't be part of this war too?" My Ma didn't want him to go and she cried each night after they argued and Pa would comfort her as if something other than him caused her to be upset. I was confused by it all. I thought it meant Pa was going away for a while, maybe for more than two or three months and that Ma was scared. She would be left to look after us three kids while he was gone. I didn't understand that he may not come back and would be gone forever. My Pa was strong. He could pick all three of us up and twirl us in the air like riding a merry-go-round. I watched him carry chunks of wood that weighted so much I wondered if they were as heavy as our stove. Then he would split that wood with a big axe in smaller chunks. Some small enough for me to carry. He also played baseball with me. I couldn't hit the ball. I tried and tried. I cried when frustrated. He was patient. He wouldn't let us go back in for supper until I hit the ball.

Then when the man arrived and told my Ma that Pa was lost to the war, it changed everything. I miss my Pa."

Eddie always thought the basic story was that his great grandfather was killed in World War One and that after that, his great grandmother took the family to her home in Canada. But the diary tells how she struggled to make it work in New York State for a couple of years. She worked to support the family and they still relied on the neighbours and friends for help around the house and for food. Then when she decided they would move to Canada his grandfather and his Uncle Jake were excited about the move but his Aunt Annabella argued with her mom. "They argued ever night about it" his grandfather wrote as he remembered his Ma pleading with Annabella and telling her how much she would love Canada. Then he quoted Annabella in one argument where she said, "I am 16 now, can you even make me go?" It sent chills up his back reading it and thinking of his great grandma's heartache. She must have felt she was all alone in the big decisions for the family. Did that give her more reason to leave for Canada where she could live with her sister? What about all those other widows after the war?

He read his grandpa's stories about living as a teenager in Waterloo and the friendship he maintained with his childhood friend, Larnie. Larnie would come up to visit in the summer for "weeks at a time." They would play soccer, hockey, and baseball and water football in the lake nearby. When he came to the story about the move to Canada, he stopped and read it twice. "This!", his voice must have sounded like a shout as several patrons in the café turned to stare at him. Finishing the sentence in silence he figured this was why Aunt Annabella kept the diary.

"July 15, 1926

It happened five years ago and Ma decided to talk about it again. It was like fresh air had swooped into the house and while it caused Ma to cry, it relieved some of the unspoken tension this day brought each year. When we crossed the border into Canada and "our new life" as Ma said on July 15, 1921, we stopped for gas. That is when Annabella snuck out of the car and ran off. We couldn't find her. Ma wouldn't sleep or rest for the next month. She put up posters, she wrote letters to politicians and to the police. She said that Annabella "probably went back to the states to be with that boy." She talked to them at the border and they wouldn't help her. They said to her, "You have told us she is 16 and an American Citizen". Ma would go from fits of range to a cavernous sorrow where she would cry and moan. Then one day it suddenly stopped. She stopped searching or talking about it. I knew she was still in heartache. I could see it on her face everyday. One day I said, "I wonder how Annabella is doing". Ma responded, "Don't mention that name in this house again." That was it. We didn't talk about her again. Until this date. Ma came into the kitchen and simply said, "It was five years ago, you know. My sweet Annabella would be 21 now. I pray we see her again, soon." We could talk about it again. We could renew our search for her if we wanted."

Eddie figured his great grandma must have kept that postcard to herself.

As he got near the end of the diary, one of the last entries was a copy of a letter his grandpa wrote to his grandma:

"April 12, 1928

"Edith, my love, soon we will be together forever. When you said yes to marry me it was the happiest day of my life. That is in contrast to when I met with your father. I wasn't sure if he was going to give his consent. He asked me many questions about what my plans are to support you and why I wanted to marry you. He is very protective and wants you to be happy. I will make you happy, my sweetheart. I will win your father over, too. Just watch me. He will be proud to have me as a son-in-law.

You are the perfect fit for me and I feel I am living a fantasy to have the love that you have given me. I know I can be spontaneous and sometimes erratic. You conversely are so sensible and pragmatic but still support me. You believe in me in a way I have never felt from anyone before. You are gentle, which helps with my rough edges and so caring. You calm the storm that rages in me sometimes and are there to gently tell me when to apply the breaks to my sometimes "bull in a china shop" style. Your beauty catches my breath, my love. The first time I saw you, it was like all the light had left the room and the only light remaining shined on you. My body can hardly control the joy I feel inside to know this isn't a fantasy and soon we will be together.

Your love,

Tony."

Eddie read his grandpa's letter with a sense of sadness knowing what he would face when he would return from the war. Closing the diary, he thought of his mom's words to him when she saw it and it gave a spring to his step as an idea started to percolate in his mind.

CHAPTER 28

An Invitation to the Past

May 2000.

The 20th year high school reunion invite tickled Eddie's curiosity and sprinkled it with shots of excitement. Six months prior, his reaction to the invitation may have been to toss it in the recycle bin. The official finalization of his divorce the previous November provided some relief from the heartache of the previous eighteen months, but then the disputes with Vivienne over the custody of their two children had numbed his feelings as they welcomed in the New Year and the turn of a new century.

Like some of his colleagues and friends, the fever from the Y2K hype infected him. While some joined the conspiracy theorist that this was designed to bring an abrupt end to the computer age, he left the panic of such to others. His friend Rick cashed in all his savings and investments and stored it all in mostly small bills in his basement. "Small bills" he says to himself remembering Rick's words as he explained, in example-laden detail, how the society around them would crumble, rendering large bills as "uncashable" after the turn of the century and the crash of computers. He figured many would be in the same boat if that happened and at least the misery would have a lot of companionship. Rick's concerns and the hype gave him enough pause that he stocked up on canned goods, freeze dried food, matches, candles, flashlights, warm blankets and firewood. He would chuckle about it all later, especially the firewood, as he really had nowhere to burn it except maybe at the beach.

As he looked over the invitation again, he glanced at the draft of his book that sat on the kitchen table. A sudden urgent desire to blast through it and finish it swept through him. "Author" was a sweet sounding title to carry with him into the reunion. That would certainly startle some he thought as he slipped into the daydreams of his youth. Dreams where he was praised as a hero for some great accomplishment; except now it was as an author with a book that created a buzz and renewed interests in the plight of war veterans and those that survived the great depression of the 1930s. The title: How World War II Changed My Family's Future would provide the gateway to discussions about his grandfather and the diaries he kept.

Reality seeped in and pushed him back to the unfinished book that sat alone on the table. It had resided, in draft form, on that table for the past six months as discouragement intermingled with indifference would hit him each time he moved it to clean the table. At times, he would hear a voice inside that would haunt and taunt him about it as the ultimate unfinished project that would likely remain so. He'd promise himself to dive back into it, but then weeks would pass and he'd struggle with his inner voice chastising him for the failed promise and telling him it was hopeless.

"It is close" his editor and publisher had told him when he sent the draft to them six months previously, but it had several gaps in the timelines to fill in and parts where the story is just too "clunky". The gaps in the story weighed on him even as he submitted the draft. The largest obstacle remained that necklace his grandfather had taken from the concentration camp. He was fairly certain of details of the necklace, including the gold and the diamond in it, but without the actual necklace, he simply couldn't confirm anything with certainty. It had been over twenty years since he had laid eyes on it and he was a teenager at the time, who paid little attention to those kind of details. If the blue diamond was actually part of the piece and the markings on the necklace are what he suspects, then it could be from the Kishaimoto treasure. If he could just get his hands on it, even briefly, he'd have the answer to the questions that hovered over his book. Is the diamond an authentic blue diamond? Does it have the Japanese symbols for AK etched on the gold pieces? If he knew those, it would complete the puzzle; it would lift the mist off the details of the Japanese camp where his grandpa suffered. If not, it could be just a valuable piece of jewelry that may or may not have come from the war.

He even learnt how to verify a blue diamond and kept a magnifying glass with him for that purpose. But alas, though he kept details from the diaries and the appraisal of the necklace in his wallet, his search for it had gone stone cold years ago. All his efforts to find it were fruitless and just a major time drain. Then to add to the agitation, it became the obstacle that blocked his way to finishing his book. Maybe it was time to just move on and finish the book without the reference to the necklace? Without the reference to the Kishaimoto Treasure, he still had the trickle down effect the war had on the family.

Oddly, the invitation to the reunion had been the catalyst for renewed focus on his book as he picked it up from the table. Time to stop the empty promises to himself, he thought. He sat down and flipped to the chapter with details about the necklace, picked up a pen and started editing. His grandfather was a brave man, regardless of the history of the necklace and it was time he told that story with what he knew.

Four and half hours later, Eddie was satisfied with the edits he had made. He would make the changes on his computer later, but as he sat back with a sense of satisfaction, his eye caught the invitation on the table and he reached for his computer.

He emailed the organizer to confirm his attendance at the reunion, which was now just three weeks away. As soon as he hit send, he closed the computer, pushed the manuscript to its side and went on a hunt for his old high school yearbook from 1980.

Though Eddie hadn't looked at the yearbook in nearly twenty years, he easily spotted its cover amongst the tumult of books and magazines stacked in the closet. The "1980" in bold raised letters transported him back to a time when he would pour over the book, re-reading comments made by classmates and teachers.

He cracked open the cover and started on a journey back to his teen years as he flipped through the pages. Moving from one page to another at an even pace, he dog-eared those with scribbled words from old classmates to re-visit later. Several pages offered pictures of teachers and classrooms, whose importance was evaluated by the graffiti of drawings and notes from former classmates; he dog-eared some of those too. Mr.T, Michael Jackson, Madonna and David Bowie appear as drawings on one page with a picture of the words "Beat it!" scrawled on a well-worn locker.

Pictures from a school square dance and a talent show don a page and roller skating party pictures, with the mullet haircuts and four wheeled roller blades, another. Pages full of sports pictures are introduced with a cover drawing of Jimmy Connors, sweat dripping from his oily hair, mouth wide open as if frozen in a scream and his arms raised with his tennis racket hand. He scanned the pictures of young teens in motion playing rugby, soccer, hockey, volleyball, badminton, basketball and wrestling in search of his younger self and found none. Pictures from "the photo club" including drawings of various SLR cameras and rolls of 35-millimeter film had him regretting he didn't take up photography in high school as he would later discover it as an enjoyable part of his career as a journalist. When the next page completed its turn, he stopped frozen. The picture clearly had been lifted out of a magazine or maybe a newspaper and maybe photocopied. Perhaps the black and white imagine had been a late addition to the yearbook, given the timing. It was an event that will be forever remembered for their grad year - 1980.

The column of smoke billowing from the mountain that now had a concave top was unmistakeable. Vivid memories of the day come alive in his mind, including Cindy, who hadn't talked to him in months, running up to him with her arms wide open for an embrace as she screamed, "Oh my god, can you believe what happened?" He thought she was capitalizing on it as an excuse to approach him, but then she appeared genuinely shaken by the new of Mount Saint Helen's volcano. "Cindy" he whispered to himself. Cindy was just the first one he saw that day that express emotions from the event. Emotions that he remembers being an odd mixture of fear, excitement, anxiety, sadness and wonderment. Then the various stories of its impact, including the reported missing of that old guy who lived close to it, would dominate the local news. The event would be the topic in the hallways, the classrooms and playing fields for the remainder of the year, including at their graduation. Anyone with a personal story of someone who was impacted by it would be a sudden star amongst their friends. He remembers their valedictorian mentioning it in his speech as a metaphor for life and new birth as they were all about to complete high school and "explode" out into the world, like a flock of birds escaping a barn.

Looking back at that picture, shipped him back to the family holiday in Seattle that summer. Watching the orcas on the train ride, the ash falling on them when they arrived, the space needle, the laughter they shared and lasting images of his dad. There was the silly excitement he created when he discovered the coke machine would take Canadian quarters and then his dad dug into his pocket to find a handful of such. Seared in his memory was the emotion of his dad as they stood at the war exhibit and pondered what his grandfather endured in the war.

The drop splashed on the page as Eddie realized holding in the tears was puerile. He placed his thumb in the yearbook to keep his place and closed the rest over it as he let his emotions loose. Images of his dad flooded his mind. How many times has he asked himself "What would Dad think?" Things his dad said often lighted the way, but he wished he were present, with skin and bones intact and his calm voice, filled with lived wisdom, that would guide and help him sort through so much in his life.

As he gazed back at his manuscript, his emotions surged of the insight his dad could give to complete the book and how proud he would be of his son for writing it. The emotions became a mixture of sadness and anger - different sides of the same coin. How could he be robbed of a father for most of his adult life? How much more stable would be his mental and emotional state if his dad were alive? What experience would they have shared together? Could they have written the book about his grandfather together? It would be finished by now, published with the story about the necklace included.

He got up and paced around his place before retreating to the bathroom to wash his face and refocus his thoughts. He thought back to lessons he learnt from therapy when going through the divorce. Returning to the living room, he forced himself to the center of it, closed his eyes and attempted to park his mind into the meditative mode he had learnt to practice. The frustrations and impatience he felt when he first learnt to mediate had returned, as he could not get his "monkey mind" to be quiet and still. Then he started an internal lament that he couldn't push away. Basting in the self-depreciating thoughts finally became too much and he got up and made his way to the kitchen for a drink of water. Sipping the water, his dad's words came to him as if he was in the room with him. "It's about momentum, Eddie. All of life has a momentum to it and if your momentum is heading in the wrong direction, you need to turn it around. Stop it in its tracks if you can. Work on creating a new momentum in a positive way."

He put the glass down and with a new sense of determination, returned to the center of the floor, closed his eyes, took a deep breath and worked on bringing a stillness to his mind.

The thirty minutes of meditation was difficult and he had to work hard at quieting the voice inside him. As it had in the past, it calmed his spirit and he learnt again it was a better option than pacing around while he verbally spared with himself, as the internal storm would rage.

Taking a deep breath, Eddie returned to the couch and picked up the yearbook. He flipped to where he had left off and landed back on the picture of Mount Saint Helens with a water stain now in the center of the page. Quickly turning the pages, his focus was on the yearbook and his mind wandered back to his high school years.

The picture above the titles "Yoga Club", "Cheerleaders" , "Grey Cup Half-Time Dancers", "Aerobics" and "Girls Gymnastics" slowed his pace as he flipped through the yearbook to "The Golf Club", "Fishing Club", "Chess Club", "Library Club" and "Christian club". Teens in various outdoor activities and playing video games at stand up consoles triggered him to flip back between pages, before he finally landed on an image of his own profile in front of a video game console. The "McDonald yellow" block lettering of "Defender" were unmistakable as was his half-slouched figure with the baggy oversized jeans that had creeped just past his waist. He noted that he had his own mullet back then.

The next page brought the rows of pimpled teenage faces in their "judge looking" graduation gowns. Their hair done perfectly as the text below each picture gave a brief description of their lives and aspirations for the future. A future they had all now lived twenty years of.

The first to catch his attention was Charles Abrahamson. Chuck. The guy who bullied him and teased him about the missed shot in the hockey game all those years ago. The words below Chuck's picture reads as evidence of the bully: *"Chuck will never forget skipping out, the pretty girls, and hanging out with roller derby team of '78. He can usually be heard saying "Hey Stupid!" or "Hey bud, what is your problem" to those teammates who are too scared to go into the corners. Chuck plans to become a Bookie, living the good life, and meeting his vision of THE perfect girl. Last words: "Good-bye, good luck and good riddance!"* He shakes his head remembering how he'd cower and avoid Chuck anytime he saw him at a distance. The lens of twenty years adds to the immaturity of it. I wonder what bully Chuck has done with his life, he says to himself.

He then scanned the faces, looking for one of his old friends before his eyes set on the face of Gabe Chester. His best friend in high school. The young face of Gabe carries him to the times they spent together playing soccer, baseball, hockey, video games and watching the girls go by on the beach. Gabe stuck up for him, helped him with school, boosted his ego and was so naturally smart and caring. How did he lose contact with him? The last time he saw him was just after high school. Eddie found himself hoping Gabe would be at the reunion as he read the caption below Gabe's picture: "Dr. Bigbones" whose interests include soccer, basketball, hockey, swimming, video games and art, plans to attend university and work summers as a lifeguard, and, one day, to complete a Triathlon. His favourite memories include Bowron Lakes in '79, Mount St. Helens, Third Beach, the Montreal Canadians of '76-79 and the long midnight walks with ET, PJ & RD. Pet peeves are back-to-school commercials, sedentary lifestyles and smokers. Last words to everyone: "Become the best person you can possibly be – both in body and mind." "Dr. Bigbones," Eddie says to himself as he remembers the moniker that their Phys Ed teacher gave him when they were in grade 11. Gabe had accidently crushed Carl in soccer when they fought for the ball, leaving Carl with a bloody nose. Gabe felt so bad afterwards as his broad shoulders and bigger body swatted Carl off the ball as if he was an annoying bug. They would laugh about it later, as Carl, with pride, who would tell everyone that he was struck by "Dr. Bigbones". Oh and Gabe's love for the Montreal Canadians. He would tell him, "You should follow a team from Vancouver, in this province." He'd always shake his head and reply, "It's heartbreak man, pure heartbreak.

They are never going to win." Suddenly he missed his old high school friend.

He turned his eyes back to the faces that grabbed his vision and popped off the page. Raj, Pete, Keith, Nadia, Yvonne, Carl, Mina, Angelo and Cindy. Cindy. "Cindy Wade" he whispered to himself as he paused and studied her picture. Her deep brown eyes jumped out at him right away, even as they are set behind the wide, yet square like glasses she wore at the time. He laughed out loud thinking of some of the fashions back then with those Elton John inspired glasses. Looking at her picture, he remembers her full lips and that first kiss. Her curly brown hair that rested naturally at her shoulders and then those sleek cheekbones that gave her a sexy look others couldn't match in his grad class. Well, at least that was what he thought at the time. She ended high school with a reputation as a party person with a wild streak. What happened to her, he wondered. The death of her mom when they were in grade 12 and his dad's newspaper article about her mom strike him as images from the past. He feels a mixture of excitement and anxiety as he wonders if she will be at the reunion. They didn't end high school on good terms, that's for sure. But it was two decades ago. Curiosity on what she would have done with her life and what she looks like, put hope in his heart that she too would be at the reunion.

He turned back to the invitation as he began to think of who might come. It says to dress for a "Y2K theme" and to "bring your old high school year book", "maybe some of your old classmates will write in it again." Hmmmm, he wonders, how many will bring the yearbook. Some might find it embarrassing what their thoughts were back then. He turns to the write up below his own picture. "Eddie's favourite memories of high school, include: Hanging out with GC, RD and PJ and playing soccer and hockey, including those ruler hockey games and walking into short grade 8's. Monday mornings, tests and punk rockers are amongst his pet peeves. In the future he hopes to see the Canucks win the Stanley Cup (please!) and work at the mill while going to school for accounting. Last words: "Make your momentum work for you and thanks to all those who made it possible."

"Accounting and the mill?!" Gawd that sounds like such a boring thing to consider now. He also wonders how many of those grade 8's would be much taller than him now. Reading his own words from when he was eighteen brought back images of his dad. Those were his dad's words. Momentum and being thankful, two themes he drummed into him.

CHAPTER 29
Y2K

"Waking up early just to get to home room first, playing indoor soccer and on the hockey team together, that championship game (we were so close), pegging Brad in the nose with the hockey ball, Chuck's haircut, the square dance in 78, the luscious Bo Derek, video games and the defender competitions (okay, you rule on that one), marketing and geography and just checking out the girls. I guess I better stop writing because you want Mina and Cindy to fill up this book, Have a super super summer and see you at the beach. A wing rules! Your friend, Keith".

He was thankful for the time alone at his Uncle Chad's before heading to the hotel where the reunion awaited him. The spare room was certainly big enough after all the renovations on the house. Does a single guy really need this big of a house? He asked out loud, as if someone was there to answer.

He decided to read some of the comments from his high school yearbook, as he pondered the request to bring it to the reunion. How many would actually expose themselves by bringing the yearbook with them, so "old classmates could sign it again"? Twenty years had brought some embarrassing light to things they said when they were kings of their small world and feeling they needed to tell everyone what their plans were, even when they had no idea themselves. Keith revealed a few of those words. He remembered Keith and Cindy dating right after high school. Would Keith feel awkward about that comment now? Does he really want Mina or Cindy reading those twenty years later? What about Brad? Could the bloody nose he got from the ball that left Eddie's stick be a moment he wish was lost from the memories of high school? Eddie forgot about it until he had just read it.

As he mused about these things and the intriguing possibility of writing an article on it, his eyes moved further around the page he had turned to. They landed on the scribblings from a classmate he knew from kindergarten through high school.

"Eddie, we've know each other for so long I feel we grew up together. You are the defender champ! You've been a great friend so all the best for the future. Your friend always, Angelo."

"Your friend always." Ah, the promises they made to each other in high school. As Eddie wondered if Angelo would be at the reunion and what he was up to, the handwriting on the corner of the page was unmistakable, despite the years that had gone by.

"Eddie, I'm glad to know you – you are a very special person and I wish you the very best for the future. Your friend, Cindy. PS: Sorry for some heartache and drama and I'll never forget you reading those diaries to me."

With that, Eddie forcefully shut the yearbook and decided it was best to leave it at his uncle's place, as he got ready for the reunion. Memories of Cindy brought mixed emotions and he remained conflicted about the possibility of seeing her again. The chats they had about his grandpa's diary were vivid in his memory, refreshed recently when he started the edits on his book. His thoughts drifted to the opening paragraph about his grandpa, which he suddenly realized practically gave a shout out to Cindy. If she was at the reunion, should he tell her about the book? He escaped into thoughts of what she might look like after two decades had past, and found himself wishing she would be at the reunion after all. That is, *if* they dodge any chatter about their break up, and how she treated him the last year of high school.

He forced himself to stop overthinking everything. It had been twenty years, afterall. Does he even know who these people are anymore? Looking at his watch, he took a deep breath, and whispered to the room, "it's time to find out", as he reached for his chosen outfit.

Looking in the mirror one last time, produced a smirk and a wink to himself. His former classmates must see that he nailed the Y2K theme of the reunion with something that would catch just the right amount of attention, without becoming a main distraction. He wanted more of a formal look, while keeping with the theme. Blue dress shirt, with its theme-fitting streak of bright colours, dashing over the shoulder like a rainbow before dissipating into the corner. He hoped it wasn't so subtle nor too obvious the statement he intended. The idea of light coming through in the darkness of the shirt as a metaphoric response to those who believed the turn of the new century would usher in a post computer society that would leave humankind in perpetual darkness and living by candlelight. The tie he picked up complimented his outfit as a conversation piece. Lastly, there was his camera that swung from his shoulder.

He had planned, with the walk to the reunion, to be fifteen minutes late. Evading any potential awkwardness of being one of the first to arrive was on his mind as he looked at his watch and headed out the door.

Upon entering the hotel lobby, the sign was large that welcomed those to the reunion with an arrow pointing towards a ballroom around the corner. Eddie picked up his nametag at the table outside the room, thankful that no one seemed to be attending the table, at that moment at least.

He stopped at the door and took a deep breath as he expected a wide-open room and potential greetings from old friends he hadn't seen since he was a teenager. As the door swung open, he was transported into a tunnel covered in space blankets, yellow caution tape, glow sticks hanging from the ceiling and Y2K printed out in neon coloured signs. He walked gingerly through the short tunnel as the pin from his nametag dug into his palm as if to remind him of its presence. He exited the tunnel and stepped into the wide-open space that had a table of food on the far wall, a bar at the back and high round bar tables scattered in an irregular yet deliberate fashion. The air swarmed with voices as he looked down to attach his nametag. With the nametag in place, his chin lifted and his eyes adjusting to the light - he started to scan the room and consider his next move, when he heard her voice.

"Eddie! I was...well I was hoping I'd see you here. You didn't come to the ten year reunion so I wasn't sure. What've you been up to?"

Her deep brown eyes sparkled at him, just as he remembered in high school.

"Hi Cindy. Nice to see you. I must have missed the invite to the ten year. Say, you look terrific."

"Ah thanks. So what've you been doing with yourself for the last twenty years?"

"Well, I'm trying to save the world from living in darkness and making sure we all can share our music."

She let out that familiar giggle to his response.

"You can still make me smile, Eddie. Nice Napster tie. That shirt with the bright colours invading the darkness is unique and somehow looks...well, classy, I'd say. You should have some headphones to complete the look, don't you think?"

Eddie was surprised with the ease and casualness that Cindy reached over, clasped the tie, and let it slide through her fingers as they talked.

"Ah, you still have those suggestions for improvements."

Cindy's smile widened as she gave him a casual wink.

"What about you though? This elegant black dress you are wearing, even as it sparkles a bit, how exactly does it fit in with Y2K?"

"You don't like it?" she asked with a teasing flare.

Eddie smiled as his eyes scanned her body. She knew she had elicited the desired response and added for his pleasure a slightly bent knee as she tossed her weight on the stiletto heel of her shoe.

"Oh, I didn't say that."

"Well, I will take that as your style of a compliment then. You look truly great yourself, Eddie. Seriously though, I know you are not working for Napster, what are you up to?"

"Well that might be a popular question tonight. This might surprise you, but I work as a journalist for the Pender Voice. I also write articles for magazines occasionally."

"Wow, that's really something. So you work at The Voice, eh? I should have known that. Doesn't surprise me actually. Wasn't your grandfather a journalist before the war?"

"You remember? I'm surprised and...well impressed."

"Of course I remember. Reading those journals is one of the more memorable moments from my teens. Remember when you took me on "a date" to the library to research your grandpa's writings?"

Eddie's thoughts immediately went to his unfinished book and the open paragraph as he held back the voice inside to spill details to her.

"Of course I do. That was quite the time. So, what about you? What've you been up to?"

"I'm a paralegal secretary. Quite the journey to get there but I enjoy it. I live in the Okanagan, not like you in the big smoke of Vancouver."

"Yeah, but the Okanagan with the beaches in the summer time, pretty nice. Are you married? Any kids?"

"I'm divorced. Twice actually. I have a daughter. She is going to graduate from high school this year. How about you?"

"There you are my old friend!"

Eddie immediately recognized Gabe's voice and his pulse jumped with his feet as he quickly turned around.

"Gabe!" Eddie responded as the two men embraced. Gabe glanced over Eddie's shoulder.

"Sorry Cindy. I didn't intend to interrupt something."

"No, it's okay, you two catch up and I'll catch up with you later, Eddie."

"You look terrific old friend. That napster tie, don't know where you got it, but it is an eye catcher."

"Gabe. Wow, so good to see you. I was hoping you'd be here. I would use the cliché that you look the same, but I'm not sure either of us would have been able to grow the distinguished looking beard you have."

"Oh yeah, you got that right. Remember when we tried to grow facial hair for the hockey playoffs? I would check out my face in the mirror every morning for evidence of some peach fuzz and you had that pathetic thing you called a mustache, like someone drew a light pencil line under your nose."

The both laughed as they shared stories from their youth. Their conversation flowed easily with a flavour of urgency to it, like they had both been waiting to share so much with each other, and catching up was a race to finish.

"So how come you are a doctor in Ontario? Why not BC?"

"My friend, we are not going to cover twenty years over the next hour or two. That one is a long story, almost a book actually."

Gabe laughed as his look took on one of a reflective mood.

"Well, tell me the first couple of paragraphs of that book then."

"First couple of paragraphs, eh? Wait, you have to do the same. I've seen some of your work in The Voice. I want to hear how a small town scrawny anxious kid, who didn't realize how much the girls liked him, became this respected journalist."

Eddie smiled at the response as he gave him a friendly jab in the shoulder.

"Oh, I was scrawny alright but at least I wasn't the brainiac nerd, getting all those straight As. I don't think too many will be surprised that Dr. Big Bones is an actual doctor now."

"Touché my friend. Touché. Well, let's see I started my schooling at UBC but moved to Toronto when my sister moved there and...well got herself into a bit of mess. So I moved out there to be a support for her. Finished my PHD there and then...well I planned to move back to BC, but life...you know, kinda took over."

"Ah yeah life, I know what you mean." Eddie responded reflectively.

"So, bud, what about you? The hot shot journalist."

"Oh I don't know about that. Life took over. That's a good way of putting it. I worked in the mill in Ranvon, but then my dad...my dad had a heart attack and when he passed, I just didn't want to stay."

Gabe reach over and touched Eddie's arm.

"Sorry to hear that, how old were you when that happened?"

"I was twenty. Seems a long time ago but the memories are still fresh at times. Anyway, I moved to Vancouver in search of myself, I guess", Eddie let out a chuckle as if he just realized why he moved to Vancouver. "I managed to get a job as a longshoreman, then got off that ship and started working in the newsroom of the Pender Voice. Now I've managed to fashion a career and life as a journalist."

"So you write for a living, eh? Can't say I am surprised."

"Really? I wasn't much of a writer in school."

"Sure, but you always had the quizzical mind that wanted to investigate everything and I remember you kept a journal, right?"

"I did. Especially after I discovered my grandfather's journal."

"Hey, you two old friends, you going to stay off in a corner by yourself or join the party?"

His striking blond hair spiked in Billy Idol fashion, square jaw and lanky body splashed on the scene like a slightly more adult version of the eighteen year kid they remembered in high school.

"Anyway, let me introduce you to my girlfriend, Mimi. Mimi, these are two old classmates. Eddie Teach, played hockey and a better player than I was for sure and this is Gabe Chester who was like the smartest kid in class, next to me of course." The sarcasm in Chuck's voice came out forced and there was a moment of awkward silence hanging in the air.

Meanwhile, Mimi stood there, almost six inches shorter than Chuck with her shoulders straight and her posture, with one high-heeled foot forward, made a statement that she was not to be treated as merely a prop. Her straight shoulder length blond hair sheened to the reflections of the light, as it framed her green eyes inset above precisely chiseled Cleopatraik looking cheeks that cascaded up from full and puffy lips.

While Gabe was checking out Mimi, Eddie was watching Chuck. The thoughts bursting in his head of the high school bullying, provided a sting to the air hitting his nostrils.

Gabe was first to respond.

"Nice to meet you, Mimi. I see your boyfriend Chuck here has hung onto all that brashness he accumulated in high school."

"He was like that in high school, eh? Maybe there wasn't someone like me around to tame it."

Mimi's eyes flashed like light had hit them as she spoke and Chuck looked over at her as a hint of fear appeared in his pupils. Eddie caught the look and pounced as if he was back in high school, only now he possessed the courage he lacked as a teenager.

"So Mimi, Chuck didn't tell you about his escapades when he was in high school?"

"Well, that was a long time ago Eddie. Anyway, we just came over to say hi and to suggest you join the rest of us. Lots of old friends and...well, rivals in the crowd. I think we will go say hi to a few more ourselves and hopefully catch up later with you two."

"Sure, Chuck. Nice meeting you Mimi."

As they walked away, Gabe's gaze stayed paused on Mimi for several seconds before Eddie broke his trance.

"Well that was entertaining and not quite what I expected from him." Eddie put his hand on Gabe's shoulder as a warmth of friendship.

"I would like to spend more time catching up Gabe, maybe later? I think I'll join the larger group. You staying at the hotel?"

"For sure my friend, and yes I am. You?"

"No, I am at my uncle's place in town. But let's connect again before the nights over."

"Or tomorrow maybe, my flight is in the evening. Perhaps we can check out the old neighbourhood before I leave?"

"Great idea, Gabe, but let's catch more time tonight too?"

"Sounds like a plan."

"Shall we join the rest of this motley crowd?"

Gabe smiled in response as they both made there way to a group where Mina appeared in the center.

Ty, George, Carl and Dan were all there. Eddie was disappointed that Raj didn't make it to the reunion. Some friends he was hoping to see, catch up, find out what their lives had become and maybe renew a lost friendship that were built on shared experiences from growing up together. He asked several about Raj and no one had a clear answer.

George was as quiet and unassuming as he remembered from high school and had established himself in a career as a building contractor. Eddie imagined him as a hard working fellow that would get up early each day and be the last to leave the jobsite, just as he was when they played on the same hockey team. When he saw Carl, the scared look he often saw in his eyes as a kid had disappeared and he presented himself as an engaging person who was just glad to see everyone. When Eddie asked him what he does for a living, Carl produced a shining card that flashed with several images as he proclaimed "holograms". He said it with the enthusiasm of a new discovery as if no one else knew about holograms and he was introducing them for the first time. But as Eddie probed, Carl offered no concrete details on what he does with such holograms and the image of the elusive friend he knew in high school, whom he never really got to know, returned.

Ty had become an elementary teacher and moved to New Zealand. As soon as he saw Ty's name tag "Tyron "Ty" Montgomery", it was like something obvious that had been in front of him flicked on a light inside his brain. Thoughts of Ty's now deceased father, the jeweller, came to mind as he made a mental note to chat with him before the evening would expire.

"So what about you Mr. Teach, what have you been up to after all these years?"

Mina had not lost her charm, nor the flirtatious pitch she could throw in her voice.

Later Eddie sought out Cindy and spotted her in a hallway by herself. The "cluck" sound of a flip phone closing filled his ears as he approached. Their eyes met before he realized she was wiping tears from her eyes.

"Hi Cindy. Oh, sorry. We can chat later."

"No. No...it's okay Eddie. I was just on the phone with my daughter."

"Oh, is she okay?"

"Yeah, she's okay." Cindy glanced past Eddie as she confirmed no one was in listening range.

"She phoned after a fight with her dad about her grad. Doesn't sound like he is going to come for it and he sure doesn't want to pay for her dress."

Cindy rolled her eyes as she looked at Eddie as if he was the same boy from high school who would observe her facial and body language and patiently wait for her to finish.

"Oh Eddie. I shouldn't bore you with my problems. You just caught me in a moment."

He reached out to touch her shoulder, feeling the soft silk of her dress that glistened in response to his touch. Her shoulder dropped to the show of affection.

"You are not boring me Cindy, far from it. Life doesn't just come to halt because we are here at the reunion. You seem to be carrying a weight on your shoulders?"

"You are such a sweetheart. As observant and non-judgemental as you were in high school. The thing is, I'm struggling to handle everything going on in my life. Patty's father is being an asshole and he knows I am going through a bankruptcy right now, but refuses to step up and help with our daughter's graduation. He will just say she is being unrealistic in what she wants and "it's just a high school grad."

"Oh, I'm sorry. Patty is your daughter?"

"Oh yeah, I guess we loss touch and you didn't hear. She was born about a year and half after high school. Anyway, it's a tough time for her. She's about to graduate and now her mom - me - is struggling financially and just told her we may have to move. Poor kid. I wish Keith would just contribute towards her grad and get his ass there. Jesus, what is wrong with him! He and I may not get along, but Patty should have her dad at her high school grad."

The strong exterior she exhibited earlier in the evening disappeared and she gave into her emotions, muffling them when she collapsed into his arms.

As the tears stopped, she let go and he handed her tissue from his pocket.

"Look at you. What other guy carries tissue in his pocket? Thanks."

"Hey, I'm a journalist. It's good to be prepared for different situations."

Cindy apologized again for troubling him with her issues as she told him about her bankruptcy and legal battle with her ex-husband.

The bankruptcy is helping her get out from debts but is limiting her options as she tries to support her daughter in her graduation.

"Sounds like the bankruptcy is like scaffolding in your life right now."

"Scaffolding?"

"I'm sure it's just temporary to provide support to get you through the weeds of life. Not always comfortable, but necessary. I know a friend who got through it and I'm sure you will, too."

Cindy gave him a look of wonderment. "Scaffolding, eh?"

Eddie looked back into the room and saw many of their classmates mingling about.

"Yeah, we should get back in there, I guess. Eddie, I am staying at the hotel. Thanks to points I earn at work, I was able to use them for a room. I have something I want to show you, if we could take the time?"

CHAPTER 30

The Hotel Room

"Well this is my room. I can invite you in, if you promise to behave?" Cindy fluttered her eyes in an exaggerated fashion, as Eddie laughed.

"This was your idea, remember? Is that a promise *you* will keep?"

Cindy unlocked the door and opened it as she responded, "Well, I guess we'll just have to find out."

"So, it's your typical hotel room, not a lot of room. Make yourself at home. I'll just be a minute as I freshen up."

Cindy took leave into the bathroom and Eddie stood in the middle of the room, noting the bottle of wine on the table next to the TV and the suitcase on a stand in the corner. He loosened his tie and sat on the edge of the bed as Cindy came out of the washroom with newly brushed hair and an affectious smile.

"Well, I am glad you've made yourself comfortable. Would you like some wine?"

"Only if you're having some."

She had made her way to the wine at his response, and looked back at him with a slight shake of her head as she filled two glasses, walked over to the bed and handed him a glass.

"Always the courteous gentlemen, Eddie Teach. Shall we make a toast?"

"Sure. To renewed friendships."

"Hmmm, I like that", Cindy responded as the glass clinked. She took a small sip of her wine and then handed him her glass.

"Here, can you hold this for a sec? See, I'm glad you made yourself comfortable, but you really should just take the tie off, rather than leaving it hanging from your neck like that." With that she reached over and loosened the tie further, lifted it over his neck and placed it on the edge of the bed before sitting down next to him, as he handed her the glass back.

"Well, I see you have broken through all that shyness you had when we were teens."

Cindy held her mouth to swallow her wine before laughing in response.

"And you are still perfecting that sarcastic pitch of yours."

They sat on the edge of the bed and talked about their teenager years, teachers and classmates they adored and those they scorned. The conversation was lively and flowed easily with each taking turns to get up to refill their glasses. Any discussion about their break up in high school was avoided as an unstated agreement between them.

Cindy laughed as she recalled Eddie asking her out on a "date to the library" and Eddie responded saying he had to do something to tame her aggressive approach. She gave that same innocent look in her eyes, when she would mischievously enticed him into something.

"Oh there is that look. I see you still keep that in your repertoire", he joked as he reminisced about the time she marched him into his bedroom and onto his bed against the stated edicts of his parents.

"Marched you? Oh come on, you were a very willing participant."

"Participant or accomplice? You easily conscripted me into your endeavours. I was just along for the ride, I think."

Cindy gave him a playful push as he nearly fell back on the bed.

"Listen to you oh man of clever words, as you try to manipulate the memories of our youth."

Eddie laughed in response and he got up and used the bathroom. When he returned, Cindy had lost the playful look and though smiling, she had taken on a more serious expression.

"Hey, what's up? You seem serious suddenly."

"Still very perceptive, you are." Cindy patted the bed beside her. "How about you come and sit back down, I have something to give to you."

"Give to me?" Eddie quizzically responded as he sat beside her. Cindy put her hand on his thigh as she got up from the bed.

"Yes, it's in my suitcase."

As Cindy walked over to her suitcase and bent down to unzip it, Eddie took in the sight of her long legs, muscular calves and the high heeled shoes she had kept on the whole time, as if just for the sexiness they offered.

Cindy could sense his eyes on her and before turning around, she spoke in a deliberately casual voice, "Well, my dear friend, I have something that is a sticky wicket for me."

"Oh, what do you mean?"

Cindy reached under the clothes in her suitcase and Eddie watched her grab something that she then hid behind her, as she walked back towards the bed.

"Well, this is awkward and a bit delicate. I hope you will be patient and let me explain. I so respect you Eddie and don't want you to hate me the rest of my life for this."

Puzzled and curious, Eddie decided to grant the patience she asked for as he sat in silence while she made her way back to the edge of the bed.

She sat down beside him and looked at him with a softness in her eyes. She dropped her shoulders to relax the tension felt in her neck along with the echo of her heart in her ears.

"Eddie, I have thought about this moment for quite some time and I know I said this already, but please be patient and let me explain things without making any assumptions. Okay?"

Eddie reached over and touched Cindy on the shoulder, which felt stiff and he peered into her eyes that suddenly exhibited a look of anxiety.

"Of course, Cindy. You've nothing to worry about."

She slowly brought her arm around to her front and revealed the rectangular case with the well-worn velvet cover.

As soon as its burgundy velvet finish caught Eddie's eyes, he knew what it was and the joy of the discovery jumped up into his throat. His voice squeaked with a sense of excitement in response.

"You have it."

Cindy looked at him startled, yet relieved that he didn't say the "*you*" with any hint of accusation. Her lungs released the extra air they were holding as her shoulders sagged slightly and her voice lost its previous tension.

"So you know what this is then?"

"Oh yeah. Pretty sure anyway. It's my grandfather's old necklace." Eddie said with a certainty that surprised even himself, as Cindy held out the velvet case to him.

"Well, here you go, then. You should open it, to confirm."

As he opened the case, silence fell on the room and she hastily filled it. "When I was looking at this recently, well....you know...thinking I might see you here, I actually looked at it more closely. My adolescent mind didn't pick up that this may actually be quite valuable and important to your family. It looks very old and I wonder if that is a real diamond in the middle surrounded by actual gold? Eddie, is that the case'?"

"Oh yes, it is very valuable. You can't imagine actually." Cindy's tension returned, as she was startled and frightened at his response. She watched him for a few seconds as he slowly examined the details of the necklace as if looking for something. They sat in silence as he handled it delicately as if it might suddenly break and fall part.

"Cindy, how is it that you have this necklace? How did you get it?" Eddie's voice had a sudden edge to it, as his mind switched from the excitement of the discovery to how it was lost in the first place.

"Eddie, I....I was 18 at the time. We both were. You remember after high school you went on a trip that summer?"

"Of course. My family went to Seattle. I don't understand what that has..."

"Well, it doesn't matter really, except you invited a bunch of friends over to your place after the trip and Keith was one of those friends. Keith and I...." Cindy paused for a brief second at the words and the conflicting regret and joy they held. "Well, Keith and I were dating at the time and so I came along with him. I remember you talking about the trip and the ash in the sky."

Eddie placed the necklace back in its case and rested it on the bed as he turned his head and nodded in response. His eyes were now focused on her with a new intensity as he remembered when she showed up that day and the mixed emotions he had of seeing her but wishing it wasn't with Keith or in his house. She was brusque towards him after they broke up and her presence at his place brought an awkwardness and resentment he hadn't invited.

"I think that day was the last time I saw you until today, actually."

"Yes, I think you are right. I saw you from a distance in a café probably six months later, and I almost went in to say hi. I didn't because, honestly, I didn't know how you'd respond. I remember the way you looked at me that day at your place. You clearly wished I hadn't come along with Keith and I was...I was immature Eddie." Eddie tilted his head slightly in response as he looked in her eyes. Cindy looked down as she continued.

"Well, anyway, I was kind of mad at you and still bitter that you had dumped me."

"*I* dumped you?"

She reached out her hand and softly touched his shoulder as her voice took on urgency in response.

"Okay, okay....I know I was the one that broke it off. I just hoped you'd fight to get me back and I guess I didn't expect you to stop talking to me for the rest of the year."

"Wow, Cindy...that. Okay look...I want to respond to that but really...it was...it was a long time ago. We were different people. Can you just please tell me when you took the necklace?"

"Okay, well when we were all up in your bedroom that day, I slipped out to go to the bathroom and instead I went into your parent's bedroom and I found the necklace – it was exactly where we had discovered it that day....I didn't intend..."

"Impossible."

'Sorry, what?"

"That's not possible, Cindy. The necklace wasn't taken then. The necklace was taken by a thief almost two years after high school."

"I thought you might think that it was taken at your dad's funeral."

Eddie stood up from the bed and looked down at Cindy as if she was the thief that he had now found and caught.

"How do you know that? I didn't even know that you knew my dad died?"

Cindy picked up the accusation in his voice and felt her own fury of being wrongly accused, as her voice took on a bite in response.

"It wasn't me Eddie. It was my sister who was there. She was at the funeral, not me."

"Your sister? Why would she be at my dad's funeral?"

Cindy's throat constricted as she tried to push the words out.

"Cindy, can you please just tell me why your sister was at the funeral?"

"Just give me a sec, please," as she took a deep breath.

"She went because she knew him. They had spent time together. Your dad and her. Your dad uncovered truths about my mom that really helped her. Meagan spent time with him and he showed her some of your grandpa's war mementos. That is what she told me." Cindy looked up to Eddie disbelieving face. "You didn't know this?"

"What? No. How did he know her?"

"Meagan worked at the jewelry store where your dad took jewelry in to have it appraised. The necklace was one of those things."

"Meagan," Eddie whispered to himself as he glanced at the velvet case, now resting on the bed.

Eddie took a deep breath, taking in what he was hearing. The image of Meagan at the funeral snapped into his mind, like viewing a vivid picture he had long forgotten. How did he miss this in his search? He walked over and picked up the velvet case. Cindy stood and reached out to grab his free hand, which he allowed for a second before pulling away and walking to the centre of the room. He kept his back to her now as he sought to contain his emotions. The words came out of his mouth with a speed and sense of urgency he couldn't keep in check.

"Cindy, I'm confused. How does Meagan being at the funeral fit in with you having the necklace? When did she give it to you and why?"

Cindy sprung from the bed and moved towards him as his questions bounced off the walls, but Eddie moved further away as he sensed her close presence. Now Cindy's words were coming out in rapid fashion, as they consumed the air between them.

"Whoa, whoa, Eddie. You are letting your mind race to things that are not true. Don't assume things. Please, let me explain first what happened. I can fill in the gaps that have you upset. You need to know that I never intended to..."

He turned around to face her as she spoke and let his words cut into hers, enunciating each word with an angry edge.

"Cindy! Just. Tell. Me. What. Happened. Okay? I'll listen, I promise."

"Okay, Eddie you were always better at patiently listening than me. Please be that now."

"Cindy, I need to know."

"Okay, I know. I had rehearsed this in my mind about how to tell you this...so here goes. I took the necklace that day when I was at your house, but I took it out of the velvet case and I left the velvet case behind. I took it in spite, as some foolish way to have a memento from our relationship. I had no idea of its true value. I was wearing it that day I saw you in the café, I wish I had stopped for you to see me. Eddie, can we sit down again as I explain this?"

"I'm good standing." Eddie turned to face the wall.

Cindy bent her right knee, digging the heeled shoes into the carpet, as she remained standing, now facing his back. Her speech picked up the same rapid pace.

"Okay. I understand. So, I had the necklace and I just kept it in a jewelry box at home. Honestly, I had planned to return it at some point. But then my life got kind of crazy. I got pregnant and we were still sorting things out from my mom's death and my dad was drinking a lot. I just forgot about it Eddie. I did, honestly."

He resisted the urge to turn around or interrupt. He didn't want her reading any emotion on his face as he imagined her at 18 - young, scared and pregnant. He had seen how scared she could get when they were dating all those years ago. Though she always worked on masking it with talk and odd behaviour, the rush in her voice to push out the words gave away the anxiety they held.

"So..."

Cindy's breath filled the air and Eddie felt the residual wind from it on his back.

"The necklace just sat in my jewelry box and I had completely forgot about it until about two years later....I don't know, maybe less or more. Anyway, Meagan. Well, Eddie you have to give me some time to explain this or you won't understand it all. I need to go to the bathroom first though. Is that okay?"

"Of course."

"You won't leave?"

"Leave?! Of course not. I need to hear this Cindy."

Cindy quickly moved to the washroom and closed the door as she reached to turn the tap on. She washed her face with shaking hands as she worked to calm her nerves and emotions.

Eddie stood still at first. He turned around to confirm the washroom door was closed as he took a glance over at the bed. The mental energy of the emotions he felt and the physical standing was taking its toll. He felt tired and the bed drew him to its comfort.

He took the necklace out of its case as he sat on the bed. This was all that really mattered now, he thought. He had found the missing piece. How he found it was important, but not imperative or even necessary. He had found it and now he could properly finish his book as he reached into his pocket for his wallet and the small magnifying glass he carried. The details he saw on the necklace, including the glistening blue diamond, the gold pieces and the Japanese symbols on the gold, brought an excitement to his bones. The paper in his wallet confirmed they were the same symbols he recorded that are for the English initials AK. It only took a few seconds of viewing the diamond through the magnifying glass for him to confirm its authenticity. He grabbed his camera and took several pictures of it, to record what he already knew. The joy he felt seeing it, knowing this was the necklace and it indeed had Kishaimoto's initials, was percolating back into his being when he saw the door of the bathroom opening. While still on the bed, he quickly turned around so his back would be facing her again.

Cindy grabbed the tissue box as she exited the bathroom and moved to the bed to sit beside him.

"Okay, thanks for being patient, Eddie. So, where was I?"

Eddie left the necklace on the bed as he got up, moved back to the center of the room, and turned to look out the window.

A flock of pigeons exploded out of the roofs eaves and Eddie flinched as he would when watching a horror flick and was frightened by a scene that had build.

"Meagan."

"Yes, Meagan. So Meagan had a car accident that was her fault..."

"Her fault?"

Cindy's voice took on a more even pace now as she continued.

"Yes and that is important to know. No one was hurt...well, not badly anyway. But the car, which belonged to her friend's dad, was new and expensive and was totalled. Meagan was drinking, not a lot, but enough to blow over the limit. The insurance wouldn't pay for the car and she had to. She had no money though. She was also trying to climb out of other debt and so she became desperate about money. Eddie, it consumed her."

She looked towards him and he hardly moved. She filled her lungs with air as she thought back to her sister and the necklace. She told Meagan about the diary and the necklace Eddie had discovered. She was a teenager and her older sister was her confidante. The excitement of the discoveries were bottled up inside and releasing them to Meagan was natural. Meagan told her that the description sounded like a necklace Eddie's father had brought into the store she had worked and they used hard velvet covered cases in the store, like the one she described.

"Cindy, please go on."

"Of course. When Meagan was down about her situation and desperate, she mentioned the necklace, your dad had. I did wonder if it was the same necklace, but I didn't say anything. Your dad was still alive then, I think. Eddie, I am so sorry about your dad. I know that must have been a very hard time for you."

"Yes, it was. You went through that with your mom and so you probably understand better than most."

She watched him closely as he responded, there was emotion in his voice that had softened and was quieter. She hoped he would turn around and when he didn't, she continued.

"Yes it was. Thank you. I wanted to tell you what happened with Meagan so that maybe you'd understand. See later when your dad died she told me she was going to the funeral. At first, I thought it was a nice gesture on her part. Your dad had written the article about my mom and uncovered truths that changed our lives and had a huge impact on Meagan. I didn't realize she also went in hopes of getting the necklace, but I guess that was part of her plan. She was desperate at the time, Eddie."

The silence filled the room as Cindy paused.

"When Meagan went to the funeral, I guess she saw the velvet case, recognized it and took it. Later when she was telling me about the funeral, she told me she thought the family must have sold the necklace, as all she found was the empty velvet case. I asked her details about the velvet case, including its color and from that, I was fairly certain that I had the necklace she was looking for. So then..."

Eddie turned and faced her and Cindy stopped mid sentence as she looked at his face for signs of sympathy.

"Something isn't right there, Cindy. The velvet case wasn't at the funeral. It was in at our house."

Cindy studied his soft blue eyes through the stare he gave her. She was missing something from what happened and wanted to protect her sister but competing for her allegiance was the man in front of her. Meagan was hardly talking to her at the time but she phoned Cindy after the funeral in an emotional and frantic state. She said she found the velvet case in the box of World War Two memorabilia Cindy had told her about. She told Cindy she took it and put it in her purse, that it felt light but she couldn't check until she got to the car where she found it was empty. She asked Cindy if she knew where the necklace might be and Cindy just said no.

"Oh of course, right. I guess it was after the funeral and back at your house. When she talked about the necklace, she said it wasn't at the house.

"She said, "It wasn't at the house"? Was that her words?"

"I think so. It was a long time ago, but that's what I remember. Why is that important?"

"The funeral was not at the house and neither was the reception."

"Okay, maybe she was invited back to the house later?"

"Cindy, while we were at the funeral, someone broke into our house and my parents..."

Eddie paused as images of the scene in his parent's bedroom flashed before him.

"My mom's bedroom was ransacked."

"Eddie, I don't know anything about that, honest." Cindy held her hand to her heart in a show of sincerity. "You don't think Meagan broke into your house, do you?"

"Going by your story, yeah I'd say that's the case. I left the funeral reception early to get something from the house. When I got there, the door was unlocked and who ever was there had targeted the bedroom upstairs and left by the back door off the kitchen. There was a big mess left in the bedroom and all the contents of the two boxes in the closet were dumped on the bed and floor. I looked and realized that the necklace....well the velvet case at least I guess, had been taken."

"Seriously, I didn't know this. Meagan didn't tell me that." Cindy looked down as her own emotions started to spike and her low whisper died in the room. "Oh Meagan, what did you do?"

"Eddie, did she take anything else?"

"No, it doesn't seem so. Perhaps she just didn't have time. We called the police and they said it appeared to be someone looking for something specific the way things were rather frantically scattered everywhere in the room. They also believe the person left in a hurry."

Cindy picked up the velvet case on the bed and with it in her hand, she stretched out her arm - as if to offer it to him along with a plea to join her on the edge of the bed. Eddie took in her gesture but didn't move as he stood staring at it.

"Eddie, why don't you come sit with me. This has been a tiring discussion, you should sit."

He remained standing, as his stare became a glossy gaze that presented a mind that was elsewhere.

Cindy filled the gap of silence again as she placed the velvet case on the bed and dug her heels into the carpet as a sign of moving from the bed.

"Eddie, did you hear me? I am sure those wheels in your head are turning again. Come sit down with me."

Cindy got up, took the few steps towards him and reached for his hand, which he accepted with a look of appreciation. She led him to the edge of the bed where they both sat. As they sat on the bed, Cindy kept his hand in hers as a lifeline she was determined to hold on to as long as permitted. Eddie's memory was reworking itself as it replaced the many thoughts he had of who the thief was with this knowledge. Cindy watched him, as time seemed at a sudden sluggish pace. She looked into his eyes before breaking the silence again.

"So your family knows that the necklace was missing and assume the thief took it?"

"Oh, no. Not a chance of that. Well at least I don't think so."

Eddie's attention returned to the conversation as he picked up the confused look on her face.

"Well, of course you'd think that. I should have figured. You see, no one in the family knows about the necklace except for me and well...my dad did of course. As far as I know, anyway. I was planning to reveal it in the book. I couldn't do that with it missing."

Eddie looked over at the velvet case laying on the bed beside Cindy and his face broke into a slight grin.

"Now I can."

Seeing Eddie's spirit rise with his last statement, she picked up the velvet case and placed it his lap. Eddie picked it up with his free hand and placed it on the bed beside him.

"Eddie, why would you keep that from your family?"

The relaxing atmosphere seemed to soften the edges that had developed in the room as Cindy's thumbs moved gently over his fingers that sat in her palm.

"Oh sorry, I am still trying to figure out how some of this fits in. My dad kept the necklace a secret. He didn't want it to change our lives like it could. You know, because of its value. Of course, you and I discovered it that day in their bedroom but my dad didn't know that. Well, maybe he did, I don't know...Anyway, when he was dying he told me more about it."

Eddie's mind played the scene in his head like a movie he had watched many times over.

"Dad, that necklace could have made life so much easier for us. Why didn't you sell it?

"Eddie, I am not sure how much easier it would have made things. It would complicate life, that's for sure. I discovered it and its value when I was just trying to plan a nice holiday for us. I wasn't looking for something that would so change our lives like that would have. Sure I thought of selling it many times, but in the end I was content with my life and its direction and I didn't need the disturbance that thing could have brought. That necklace led me to discoveries about my dad, your grandpa. Discoveries that I may never have known otherwise. It changed my view of him and changed me for the better. That is far more valuable to me than any monetary value the necklace may hold."

He remembered his dad's reference to the necklace as "that thing" as if it was important to depersonalize it. As his mind drifted back to his dad's words, the pressure in Eddie's eyes started to let loose and Cindy reached over with her thumb to catch one of the drops on his cheek.

"You thinking about your dad?"

Eddie nodded.

"I sometimes think of my mom too and what might have been."

"Yeah, I know. He taught me lessons I hold with me today. I was just thinking of one of those."

"Oh Eddie. Your dad had a big impact on my family too. Do you remember the article he wrote about my mom after she died?

"It's funny you mention that because I don't know how I forgot about it. I remember him writing about your mom, but.... Sorry I don't recall any of the details, Cindy. I do remember wondering about how you were doing when he wrote it."

"Do you know why he wrote that article?"

Eddie looked at Cindy and sensed there was something he was missing, some truth he should know.

"Well...maybe I don't have the whole story on this. Dad was fashioning a part time job as a journalist and he wrote some human-interest stories. I think he told my mom that your family had asked him to write the story."

"Well, not really. Your dad wrote that article after he had spent time with my mom before she died and then after several discussions he had with Meagan. Eddie, I think there is lot more to this story than you know. What your dad discovered about my mom changed our lives, especially Meagan's. I wish I had brought my copy of that article with me, I would just read it to you. In it, your dad found out that my mom had been raped as a teenager and....oh I shouldn't say much more, I thought you would know all this."

This time it was Eddie's turn to catch a tear off her cheek.

"That article mentioned the injuries my mom overcame from the accident when she was young but your dad also stated that she survived hardships in high school. He didn't elaborate in the article, but what he discovered solved a mystery in the town she grew up in and part of that was what my mom endured. My mom kept that bottled up for many years inside her and we only learnt of it after her death and because of your dad."

Eddie turned his body as he reached out towards her and Cindy lunged into his arms as if grasping for a life preserver. Her sobs, muffled by his shoulder, transported him back to when they were teens and the comfort she sought in his arms when she mourned Meagan's move to the big city. The degree she absorbed his body into hers as she heaved from the sorrow was beyond what he experienced with her as an emotional teenager. He wondered if more than just thoughts of her mom and Meagan were caught into the storm of emotions. Perhaps, the struggles she had shared with him earlier was piling on too?

Eddie took in the comfort and pleasure in their embrace as he realized how much he had longed for it when they had reconnected earlier in the evening.

"It's going to be okay, Cindy. I understand. Well, obviously, I don't know everything that happened, but I believe you about the necklace. The important thing for me is that necklace has been found. This resolves several puzzles for me and that is of greater value than the thing itself."

Cindy broke away from his shoulder and looked up from her swollen mascara smudged eyes. Before she could respond beyond her look of wonderment, Eddie put a finger to his mouth.

"It's my turn to talk now. Thank you. Thank you for taking care of the necklace and bringing it back to me. Sure you shouldn't have taken it in the first place, but you were an emotional teenager. We all were. You have showed great honour bringing it back to me. I assume your sister was never told you have it then?"

Cindy gently nodded in response before whispering, "I got the velvet case from her later but she doesn't know about the necklace. No one knows, except you."

Eddie shook his head in a motion of respect and astonishment. "You kept that secret. Amazing. You are amazing."

Cindy shook her head in protest as Eddie cupped her chin in his hand to stop the motion.

"Thank you for sharing so much with me. I know many of those things are very personal. Things about your mom and Meagan. Thank you for coming tonight and for being you."

They embraced in an extended hug again as Eddie began to formulate in his head what to do next. As they slowly moved out of each other's arms, Cindy found her strength to speak again.

"I should fill in more of the gaps of the story for you. I am not sure what all you know."

She then explained how his dad had discovered the teeth that Meagan had planted in the jewelry box for him and that was why his dad sought Meagan out and how it led to the story about her mom's rape when she was teenager. She broke down as she told him about her mom's loss of her battle with Parkinson's that led to her suicide. She left out any details about his dad's visit to her mom before her suicide. She thought of Meagan's statement that, "Some secrets are best kept secret," as she did. As she spoke, Eddie picked up the necklace again and appeared to be studying its details as Cindy continued to explain herself. She told him about Meagan's new life and how well she was doing. She didn't want her sister's lasting image to be that of a thief.

She watched Eddie's determined focus on the necklace. "Hey, you said something about writing a book?"

"Yeah, it's still just a draft. It's about how the war changed my grandpa and consequently my whole family. The diaries and that necklace play a critical role in the book."

Eddie closed his eyes as he thought of the opening paragraph.

"I begin the book with a statement that is something like this: "The trajectory of our lives are impacted by individuals who we interact and become intimate with. A brief conversation or action can change our focus, our attitude and the momentum of our lives. This story was given life by an assertive, inquisitive, though sometimes reckless, seventeen year old girl who wouldn't let something go."

"That's an enticing opening. Who are you talking about?"

"You Cindy."

Eddie opened his eyes and refocused them on the velvet case in his hands.

“Wow, I don't know what say. Will you send me a copy of your book when it is done?"

"For sure. Hey, can I ask your thoughts on something?"

"Anything."

"You've shared personal matters about your mom and so now it's my turn. No one else knows this, I think. It's from one of my grandpa's diaries. When he came back from the war, he discovered that my grandma had an affair while he was fighting for our country. She may have thought he was lost to war, I don't know. Should I include that in the book?"

"I think some secrets...."

"Are best, kept secret. Yes, good advice and thanks."

"Eddie, I am sorry I took that necklace and kept it for so long. I hope it didn't cause your family any hardship?” Eddie responded in a reflective and deliberate tone, “It's okay. No, not any hardship. It fits even more with my opening anyway and completes a puzzle I have been working on.”

"A puzzle?"

Eddie moved his fingers over the diamond in the necklace as his eyes caught the purple and blue reflection it gave off. "Well, sort of. I have spent time going through my grandpa's diaries and wondered what happened to this. My book is incomplete in part because I didn't have the details of this necklace that I can now fill in. Just a sec, Cindy."

Eddie got up from the bed and went to the office desk in the room. He picked up a pad of the hotel paper and a pen before he returned to the bed. He laid out the necklace on his lap as he drew out a rough picture of it and wrote down details of the gold, the diamond and the markings on the necklace.

Cindy watched him with fascination and filled the silence as he drew.

"That necklace has features that, honestly, I didn't pay much attention to until recently. I kept it in a box with things from my youth and I only took it out recently as I was thinking about the possibility of seeing you here. It had me thinking about your grandpa and the things we discovered back then, like that diary and his life in the 1930s. I remember how captivated I was about the stories you'd read me from his diary."

"I want a drawing of its features to for my book. Hey, can you give me your address so I can send you a copy when I am finished it?"

Eddie flipped over the paper he was writing on and wrote down her address and e-mail.

"And my phone number is 604 867 5309."

Cindy watched to see if he would reciprocate with his phone number.

"Thanks, I'll send my contact information to the email address.'

Eddie flipped the paper back over and looked at the drawing he had completed of the necklace. Then seemingly satisfied, he folded the paper and put it into his pocket. He then placed the necklace back into the velvet case and looked at Cindy with a sense of fulfilment.

"So why draw out the necklace like that?"

Eddie got up from the bed as she was asking the question.

"Cindy, I want to get back down stairs to the reunion and catch a few people before they leave. I hope you don't mind."

She got up and kissed him as if it was the last time she might see him.

"I hope we can get together again?"

Eddie looked at her with pride in his eyes.

"You may have a lot going on in your life, but you are a fine and beautiful person, Cindy. I'll send you my contact information and let's see how it goes from there?"

Cindy pulled him into a hug as she whispered in his ear.

"For sure Eddie. I hope you don't forget me."

Eddie looked at her again.

"Oh, you don't need to ever worry about that. You know it's amazing how much time and the momentum of life changes so much. Yet somethings stay with you forever."

"Sounds like something your dad would say."

"Yes, it is. Indeed it is. Thank you for this night that you've made very special." With that, Eddie turned and headed towards the door. As he reached for the handle, he turned around and looked at Cindy who now had expectations and wonder in her eyes. Eddie moved back towards her as he held out the velvet case with the necklace to her.

"Cindy, thank you for returning this. It resolved the mysteries in my head." He took her willing hand in his and placed the necklace in it.

"Here, you take it. Just don't tell anyone where you got it from." He kissed her, lightly on the lips, as he turned and left the room.

As Eddie entered back into the hall, it was clear that many had left the reunion already as he scanned the crowd looking for Gabe.

Chuck made eye contact with him as he approached.

"Hey there big guy. Looks like wherever you disappeared to was more fun?"

"Yeah sure Chuck. Don't mean to be rude, but do you know if Gabe is still here?"

"It's okay I understand, not like we got along in high school. I might not be the only one though that notices your missing tie."

Eddie instinctively reached up to his neck to confirm the missing accessory.

"I haven't seen Gabe for a bit, but maybe ask Mina. I saw them chatting. She might know"

Chuck pointed to where Mina stood in the middle of the group that added laughter to the room.

"Thanks, Chuck. High school was a long time ago and you seem like a decent guy. I'd like to see if I can find Gabe if you don't mind".

"Of course. I understand. He was your best friend in high school."

Eddie approached Mina and her friends and he looked at Mina who was smiling in return.

"Sorry, I don't mean to interrupt, but do any of you know where Gabe is?"

Mina reached into her purse and pulled out a crumpled piece of paper that she reached out to hand him.

"He gave me this note to pass to you. It's his contact information, I think."

Connie, who was also in the group, spoke up.

"Before you seek out Gabe, looks like someone else is looking for you." As she nodded towards Cindy who was marching towards the group.

Eddie turned around as he heard one of them say, "perhaps she has your tie."

As Cindy approached the group, Eddie could see that she had re-done her makeup but her hair and clothes had lost the perfect picture look and smirks splashed on the faces of the women around him, in response.

“Hi everyone." Her eyes meet Eddie’s as she mouthed, "Can we talk?” to which Eddie nodded.

He turned to the group. "Excuse me," and he held up the note Mina had passed him as he nodded a thanks to her before turning towards Cindy.

He pointed to a private area away from the crowd and close to the doors of the room. They walked towards the spot as Cindy whispered.

“Do you mind if we step out of this room for a minute? I know people are watching, but still.”

“Oh, of course.”

The doors opened to a large open area just off the lobby and they walked over to a glass window giving a view outside. As they stood, Cindy reached into her purse.

“Your tie. It fell on the floor.”

“Thanks.” Eddie took the tie and stuffed it into his pocket. Cindy watched him with a renewed softness in her eyes and relaxed posture.

“Can I get a hug?”

He didn’t hesitate in embracing her in a warm and tight hug that lingered as he wondered what she might do next.

Cindy pulled out of the hug and looked at him from head to toe as if checking him out for the first time.

“You’ve really become quite the remarkable individual, Eddie. There is actually something else I wish I could get from you.”

“Oh?”

Cindy reached into her purse again and pulled out the velvet case.

“This is yours and you need to take it back.”

“That’s not necessary.”

“I insist Eddie. I can’t keep it.”

She handed him the necklace, which he took with a gracious look.

"The thing I want to ask you for is this. Whatever it is you have inside you that allowed you to give me that necklace, I wish I could have some of that."

ACKNOWLEDGEMENTS

"All of life has momentum to it. You can use it to your advantage, if you choose. You can passively allow whatever wave of momentum catches you to take hold, and hope for the best. A better life awaits for when you choose to watch for the waves that will fuel your passions, and give you energy and purpose. Watch for those waves to come in and catch them."

Larnie Teach

The momentum to write this, my first novel, has been kept in motion by many people that make a difference in my life. For the words of encouragements, advice, and reviewing of multiple drafts: Ron Sharp, Gabby Anderson, Randy Voth, Diane Anderson, Doug Dykens & Alison Anderson. For those that have inspired me in this writing: my late Uncle Earl Anderson, my late father Frank W. Anderson, many of those I know who've suffered from mental illness (and several that I respect greatly), and those that fought in the second world war.

I especially want to thank Raye Anderson for her support in steering me in the right direction when I got off track, the detailed counsel on several passages and for the many times she brought a wind to my momentum to complete this.

I thank FriesenPress for their guidance and words of encouragement in a their Editor's evaluation of my book. Thank you to MethodMike and Fiverr for the great book cover design.

I hope you have enjoyed following the lives and emotions of Larnie, Eddie, Cindy and Meagan, in settings that take place mostly in the early 1980s. A time before the internet, cell phones, a thousands song in your pocket, PVRs and apps. A time when the grocery stores were stocked with over 30,000 less different items than we have available today. A time when we shopped more "locally" and often knew the owners of the places we patronized. I mention all this, because what has happened – so very suddenly it seems – has made this a strange time for me to release my book.

I write this on April 5, 2020. On March 10, 2020, I attended an NHL hockey game, with an attendance of 18,871 people. The next day, the World Health Organization declared the COVID-19 virus a pandemic. As we all avoid any gatherings of more than a few people, I find I can't rewind in my mind the last few weeks and not get a sense of the enormity of the changes. Routines have been broken, businesses have closed at least temporarily and many of us are wondering what our lives, communities and world will look like after this. As we all reflect on such things, I leave you with this from Larnie Teach.

"Listen to me Eddie...Don't forget what I've told you. Sometimes there is nothing we pay more for than money."

Frank N. Anderson

Don't miss out!

Visit the website below and you can sign up to receive emails whenever Frank N. Anderson publishes a new book. There's no charge and no obligation.

https://books2read.com/r/B-A-BALJ-TXKEB

BOOKS 2 READ

Connecting independent readers to independent writers.

About the Author

FRANK ANDERSON lives in British Columbia and has five adult children. He enjoys hiking, running, kayaking, camping, reading and writing. Pursuits that all find their way into this first novel of his.